Last Chance
RANCH

CHRISTMAS WITH ANGEL
TRACE'S TROUBLE
FLETCHER'S FLAME

LEXI POST

Last Chance
RANCH

CHRISTMAS WITH ANGEL

TRACE'S TROUBLE

FLETCHER'S FLAME

Acknowledgments

For my own Chief Robert Fabich, Sr., who once again came through with his expertise. Thank you for all your patience as you taught me about fire and how it behaves.

And for my sister Paige Wood, whose advice is invaluable to me as well as her expert abilities. Her honesty is both rewarding and humbling.

For my critique partner, Marie Patrick, who was integral in getting these stories to publication, and for Grace Bradley, a wonderful editor and a great friend.

Thank you to all whose sharp eyes reviewed the final drafts of these books: Merritt Crowder, Eileen McCall, KC Crocker, Lisa Guertin, Marianne Hughes, Karen Roma and Pamela Todd.

A special thank you:

…to Teresa Fordice for giving me the name for Black Jack in *Trace's Trouble* and sharing her story about the horse she loved.

…to Bette Read for telling me all about Ruby Ranch in Phoenix. It was the inspiration for my Rainbow Acres Refuge.

If anyone is looking for a small dog that needs a forever home, please contact them. They have a great core of volunteers that will help get the animal to you http://www.rubyranchrescue.org/

 ...to Paige Tyler for granting permission for the use of the characters of Lexi Fletcher, Dane Chandler, Captain Earl Stewart, Tory Wilcox, Nate Boone and Jax Malloy from her Dallas Fire & Rescue Series world.

 Fletcher's Flame is dedicated to Digger, a very special bearded dragon, who crossed the rainbow bridge way before her momma was ready to lose her.

Christmas with Angel

BY

LEXI POST

Christmas with Angel
Last Chance Series, Book #1

By Lexi Post

Cowboy firefighter, Cole Hatcher, is determined to do what's right and take his fiancé with him to his mother's annual Christmas dinner party. After all, she *is* his mother and the rest of the family will be there.

Lacey Winters can't forgive her future mother-in-law for keeping her and Cole apart for eight years. While she loves Cole's family, including the five they are living with, she wants to spend Christmas alone with Cole on Last Chance Ranch.

But there are worse things brewing than family drama. This Christmas day, nothing goes as planned…for anyone.

Christmas with Angel: Last Chance Series Book #1 is a "bridge" book. It is the sequel to *Cowboy's Match: Poker Flat Series Book #2* and the prequel to *Trace's Trouble: Last Chance Series Book #2*. The Poker Flat Series was inspired by Bret Harte's short story, *The Outcasts of Poker Flat*, first published in 1869. In Harte's story, four members of Poker Flat society—a gambler, a prostitute, a madam, and a drunk--are banned from the western settlement when a sudden urge to be virtuous overtakes the citizens. On their way to the next settlement, the outcasts stop to rest at the base of some high mountains. An innocent couple, a young man and his fiancée (a tavern waitress), comes down from the mountains and rests with them. This cast of characters explores the relationship between the innocent and the tainted in Harte's story.

In *Cowboy's Match*, the story asks the question, what is tainted and what is innocent? In *Christmas with Angel* the question becomes, can some be less "tainted" than others, and when all is said and done, does perspective play a role in the determination?

Chapter One

Last Chance Ranch, Arizona

December 23rd

Cole Hatcher added two pillows to the makeshift bed of sleeping bags on the hay. He'd unzipped each and spread them out so he and Lacey could crawl in together. Maybe if they could have a little privacy, they could settle their Christmas issue.

He'd pilfered all the snowflake decorations from the tree inside and hung them from the beams. In his mind, he'd envisioned it to look like it was snowing, but in reality, it looked like plastic, glass and felt snowflakes hanging from beams. Lacey would get it though. She couldn't expect more than this from her cowboy.

Adjusting the garland around the stall walls, he pulled over the small table he used for grooming the horses and placed it next to the bed. With a rag he'd grabbed from the house, he wiped it off and placed a bottle of wine on it with two plastic cups. "That should do it." His Christmas Eve present was ready, though a few hours early.

Stuffing the rag in his back pocket, he turned the battery-operated lantern to low and set it next to the wine. "Perfect."

As he headed out of the barn, the six horses in residence

paid him no heed except for Angel. Her wary eyes watched him until he was out of sight.

Giving Angel to Lacey had been the best thing he'd done for that horse, besides take her from her owner. She was so fearful of men that her bond with Lacey had grown strong.

Now if he could just get his fiancé onto the same page with him, life would be great again.

Cole strode across the dirt yard, the only sound to break the crisp night air, the two note call of a whippoorwill. The quiet beckoned him, but he needed Lacey to truly enjoy it. The house lights should have been welcoming but with his two cousins in residence, one baby, Billy and his grandparents, the four bedroom house was packed.

He took the stairs to the porch two at a time. Pulling back the screen door, he opened the heavy, ironwood front door. As he stepped in, he had to stop himself from stepping back out.

The baby cried upstairs while his two cousins, Logan and Trace argued. A door slammed on the upper level then Trace stomped down the stairs, yelling back over his shoulder, "I'll be watching the game with Grandpa if you come to your senses!" He nodded to Cole as he passed by.

Old Billy, who used to work and live at Poker Flat and had just spent two months in rehab for alcoholism, ambled through the front hall from the kitchen, a bottle of water in his hand and a smile on his face. The television in the living room clicked on just as Billy entered and the volume increased substantially.

Cole winced, the noise level and activity in the house was almost painful. Like Lacey, he couldn't wait for their own home to be completed, but it barely had walls and was far too incomplete for them to have the privacy and quiet they needed.

Since Lacey had given up her casita at the Poker Flat Nudist Resort, they had nowhere to go…except the barn.

She was probably in their room where she always retreated right after dinner to crunch numbers, do research, or iron clothes for work. He ran up the stairs, excited to show her the present he'd arranged, and opened the door to the bedroom.

Lacey stood next to the bed, her deep pink sweater fitting her like a second-skin, wisps of blonde hair escaping her long braid. Her maroon skirt flowed about her, accentuating her delicate femininity. He still couldn't believe this hot woman was his. She had a basket of laundry dumped out on their bed, clean clothes strewn over the quilt and a small pile folded to her right. He walked straight to her and wrapped his arms around her waist from behind. "I have a surprise for you."

She stilled then sighed. "Is it ear plugs?"

He kissed her neck beneath her ear, loving how tiny she felt against him. "Even better."

She dropped his fire department t-shirt and turned in his arms. "Better is good." She lifted her arms around his neck. "Don't get me wrong. I love your family. There just seems to be so many of them in this particular house. And now that Billy's here, it makes it very cramped."

He looked into her light brown eyes that reminded him of amaretto. "You love my family? Even my parents?"

She lowered her lashes and stared at his chest.

Damn, he needed to wait to discuss that. Talking about his parents only brought up what his mother had done to break them apart. That didn't set the mood he wanted. He wouldn't press it now. "So aren't you a little bit curious about my surprise?"

She lifted her gaze to meet his. "Is this my Christmas Eve present?"

His family had always exchanged gifts on Christmas day, but maybe he and Lacey could start their own tradition. "Yes, just a few hours early."

She looked over her shoulder at the clock sitting on the nightstand. "Only three hours and seventeen minutes early. Should I wait?"

He started to grin but it turned to a grimace as his cousin's baby let out an ear-piercing wail. "You might be able to, but I can't."

At the sound of the baby's scream, Lacey buried her head against his chest. She lifted it to look up at him. "I could use a surprise right about now."

"Good." He kissed her on the forehead then let her go so he could take her hand. As he took a step toward the door, she resisted. "I thought you were going to give me a surprise."

"We have to go outside for this."

She pointed to the pile of clothes. "But I need to finish folding the laundry."

"Leave them. This is more important."

"Okay." She let him pull her down the hall.

When they got to the top of the stairs, he released her hand and stepped aside so she could descend first. Another screeching wail sounded from above, and they both picked up their pace. As he opened the front door, the television volume increased another decimal in the living room and from the corner of his eye he caught sight of Billy who had joined his grandfather and Trace.

Lacey stepped onto the porch and sighed.

No sooner had he closed the door than she placed her hand on his chest. "Do you hear that?"

He listened. The quiet was almost deafening until four hoots, sounding like a bouncing ball, broke the silence. "You mean the Screech Owl?"

She smiled slyly. "No, I mean the quiet."

He grinned. "Wait until you see my surprise." He took her hand and they walked down the steps toward the barn.

"I hope you didn't get me another horse. I'm very attached to Angel and I think she'd get jealous."

He shook his head. "No, it's not a horse. Luckily, I haven't had any calls this week. Maybe the Christmas spirit has people being kinder to their animals." He frowned at the thought of what else the Christmas season brought. "Now if we could just get Christmas tree fires under control, everyone could have a happy Christmas."

She squeezed his hand. "I've never understood the need for a live evergreen tree in the Arizona desert. It's so dry. If a person wants to smell evergreens, they can always go up to Prescott for the day or take a hike right here in our own mountains."

"You make the house smell great with those scented candles you use. I'm glad you found them in the glass jars."

She stopped at the entrance to the barn and looked at him. "Can you turn off the firefighter tonight and give me the cowboy who loves to save abused, hurt, and unwanted horses?"

He grinned sheepishly. "I'll try. Actually, your surprise is definitely from the cowboy." He winked.

Lacey's gaze roamed over him, and he couldn't help but count himself lucky all over again. To have found her a second time, at a fire no less, had been sheer luck. That she was just as dedicated to his horse rescue ranch as he was, was a bonus. Her wizardry with the finances had also improved their solvency. But to have captured her heart once more against all odds was the greatest luck of all. "If you keep looking at me like that, your surprise might have to wait."

She widened her eyes. "Like what?" She even batted her lashes.

He laughed and pulled her into his embrace. "I love you, soon-to-be Lacey Hatcher."

"I know." She stood on tiptoe to give him a kiss.

When she didn't deepen the kiss, he had to stop himself from lowering his lips to hers again. The open barn door was not the place to start making love to his woman. Reluctantly, he released her, but grasped her hand again.

After pulling the large door closed behind him, he led Lacey through the barn, passing the filled stalls until she slowed by Angel. He understood and let go, continuing toward the last stall, not wanting to disturb the bond between her and the rescued horse.

No sooner had Lacey turned toward the white Arabian, than Angel gave a soft nicker and walked to the stall door. Lacey pet the badly marred head, cooing to her like one would talk with a baby.

Cole never tired of watching their connection. He had almost given up hope that Angel would ever interact with humans again after the abuse she'd take from her former owner. That the horse came into his life shortly after he had found Lacey again made him think it was fate. Though the horse shied away from men, she completely trusted Lacey.

When Lacey finished, she walked slowly toward him, or was she sauntering toward him? Shit, his muscles tensed in anticipation.

She still wore her clothes from work, her long skirt swishing against her white cowboy boots. The sweater showed off her figure even if it didn't reveal even a hint of cleavage. It was hard to believe she worked at a nudist resort. He was thankful once again that the resort had a strict policy about employees keeping their clothes on during work. He would go insane if Lacey was supposed to work nude. On the other hand, because Kendra owned the nudist resort she was expected to be nude. He had no idea how Wade handled his fiancé being naked half the day. Cole couldn't do it.

But Lacey was sexy even with her clothes on, especially after a long day, when her braid had loosened and her messy wheat-colored hair made it look as if she'd just spent an hour in bed with him.

He watched her eyes closely as she approached. Her gaze was riveted to him and his chest puffed with pride. When she licked her lips, he had to force himself to stay still as every tendon pushed at him to move.

Finally, her gaze flitted to the stall behind him and her lips formed a pleased smile. "Oh Cole, it's the best present you could have given me."

He released the breath he'd been holding and opened his arms. "You like it?"

She walked straight into his embrace. "I love it."

"It might get a little chilly tonight."

She shrugged. "That's why I have you to keep me warm."

"Just to keep you warm?" He frowned. "I was hoping to start a fire inside you."

Lacey's short intake of breath had his cock taking notice.

She wrapped her arms around his neck. "You are as good at starting fires as putting them out."

"Only for you." He lowered his head and kissed her.

She pressed her body against him and pushed her tongue between his lips. He caught it with his own.

Every nook of her mouth was like new territory. He tasted the tartness of the wine she had with dinner and a flavor that was all Lacey. His hands roamed over her back, feeling her sweater slide against silk.

His cock hardened at the thought of what his Racy Lacey might be wearing underneath.

She pulled her lips away abruptly. "You have too many clothes on."

"I was thinking the same about you." He wiggled his brow. "I bet I can take my shirt off faster than you can." He let his arm go slack in anticipation of the race. They were always betting about sex.

She kept her arms around him. "And what does the winner get?"

"I'm thinking, choice of position." At his words, a shiver ran through her body, sending lightening straight to his balls.

"On the count of three. One. Two. Three."

No sooner had she dropped her arms than he reached back and pulled his flannel over his head. One button pinged across the stall, hitting the wood, as his face cleared the tail of the shirt.

Lacey had brought the sweater up over her head, but her face was still hidden.

Cole stared at the pale pink corset that cupped her breasts and accentuated her waist and hips. With her skirt still on, she looked like a saloon girl from the old west.

As she pulled the sweater free, she took a breath and her areolas peeked above their confines.

He swallowed hard.

"Are you admiring my new corset?" She smiled slyly, the vixen.

He shook his head as he traced a finger along the top edge of the satiny lingerie. "No, I'm admiring this." He pushed his finger inside the cup and flicked at the hard nipple beneath."

"But you like it, right?"

"I think it might require a closer inspection." He used his other hand to burrow beneath her other cup and lift the breast above the soft satin so the corset held it up for him to view her rosy tip. "Hmm, I'm liking it more and more." He performed the same readjustment on her other breast then stood back. "Now that's perfect." He stared at her hard nipples held aloft. "I really like it."

"I'm glad." Her lips formed a seductive pout. "But I lost the bet."

He reached out one hand and brushed his fingertips across her hard nipples. "Yes, you did."

Her chest rose as she sucked in a breath at his touch.

He loved how responsive she was. "I think it's time you took off your skirt so I can decide exactly what position I want you in."

She cocked her head. "And that must be determined by what I'm wearing underneath my skirt?"

He nodded. His soon-to-be wife never failed to surprise him when they crawled into bed at night. Her love of lingerie had him anticipating their alone time even during dinner. He was definitely the beneficiary of that little fetish. It didn't take much to get Lacey hot, but in the house, she had to keep quiet when they made love, and that took something away from the experience for her. Tonight, she could let go completely with no one the wiser.

Lacey untied the bow at her waist and pushed the skirt down to the barn floor before stepping out of it.

He was too distracted by the movement of her breasts at first, to understand her smile.

"So what position would you like?" Her voice was teasing, a sound he hadn't heard in over a month.

This had definitely been needed. He lowered his gaze and raised his brows. "I can't decide until you take off that damn slip too."

She giggled, another sound he hadn't heard in a while. He needed to do something about that. The stress of building a house, working, caring for the horses with so much family around was too stressful for the only-child Lacey.

As she shimmied out of her slip, his jaw dropped and his cock hardened.

Chapter Two

Cole's proper, no-swearing, always sweet Lacey stood before him in white cowboy boots, white lace stockings that rose to her thighs where they hooked to the corset. The satin of the lingerie came to the tip of her mons where a ribbon on each side of her folds snaked its way between her legs. He swallowed hard. "Turn around."

She did, slowly, stopping when her back was completely to him.

Shit, she could turn him on as easy as striking a match. The two ribbons had turned into one somewhere between her legs and that one hooked onto the back of the satin corset. Her round ass cheeks begged him to grab them and thrust inside her tight sheath, but he held himself back and simply enjoyed the view.

That's when he noticed something odd about her crease. "Lacey, what do you have between your legs?" His stomach dropped. If she had a bullet vibrator inside her then he'd know he had been seriously failing her.

She looked over her shoulder worriedly. "It was supposed to be a surprise."

He forced a smile. "So surprise me."

She bent forward and spread her legs.

He took a step closer as his heart started to race. There was something attached to the ribbon that lay along her crease. Unable to resist touching her, he spread her ass cheeks, his dark tanned hands a stark contrast against her paler skin, and his cock grew painfully hard. His voice was gruff when he spoke. "What is it?"

She looked back at him, her forehead creased in worry. "It's a small butt plug. Adriana said—"

"I bet she did."

"You don't like it?"

He forced his hands to let go of her ass while he tried to gain control of his raging need. "Not like it? Shit Lacey, it's so fucking hot, I'm going to come before I get inside you."

"Really?" Her smile was hopeful as she wiggled her butt before him.

He grabbed it to stop her. "Is that what you want? For me to come all over your ass instead of inside you?"

She straightened quickly. "No."

He let her break his hold as she turned around. Just knowing she had the butt plug inside her, that it would press against him as he entered her, had him fisting his hands, trying to control his need.

"Adriana said you would like it."

He rolled his eyes. Adriana Perez, former prostitute and current bartender at Poker Flat Nudist Resort where Lacey worked, had already educated his relatively innocent fiancée on a number of sex toys. Sometimes he didn't know whether to thank the woman or strangle her. His ardor cooled at the implications of Lacey's outfit and accoutrements.

"Did you wear that at work all day?"

Her smile faded. "Oh no. I wasn't sure if I would like it, so I slipped it in after dinner. I used the lubricant she told me to get. It was going to be my Christmas Eve present to you if I liked it."

"Do you like it?"

She twisted her hips about. "I think so. But Adriana said the best part was when you push inside me."

Cole closed his eyes and took a deep breath, counting to ten on the inhale and then exhale. When he opened his eyes, Lacey was clasping her hands in front of her, hiding her mons from his view, a sure indication she was unsure.

He grasped her shoulders. "Lacey, that is the hottest outfit and sexual toy you have worn to date, and I'm just trying not to come before I can give you the pleasure you deserve."

Her face relaxed and she wrapped her arms around him, resting her head on his chest, her breasts crushing against his skin. "I'm so glad. I really want to see what it's like."

He released her shoulders and hugged her to him, his cock anxious to be let loose to dive into his woman. From habit, he reached down with one hand and grasped her ass to pull her tighter against him and his thumb slipped under the ribbon.

"Oh." Lacey pulled her head away to look at him. "It tingles when you do that."

"Do what? This?" He purposefully pulled at the lifeline to the butt plug.

"Oh Gosh." Lacey's hands grasped his waist even as she arched her back.

If he didn't still have his jeans on, he would have come all over her by now and if that's what it took to give her pleasure then he'd keep them on. He gently tugged the pink ribbon again.

Lacey pushed her ass backward, begging for more.

He pulled away from her and sat on a hay bale he'd set up by the side of the makeshift bed. It had just been delivered that day and along with its mates gave the stall a sweet, earthy scent. "Come here." He patted one of his legs.

She didn't question him. Ever since the popsicle night at Poker Flat, she'd been more than willing to trust him with her sexual explorations. Lacey sat sideways on his leg.

He chuckled. "No, Racy Lacey. Straddle my leg and face away from me."

Despite her frown, she did as he requested. With an arm around her waist, he pulled her tight against him, knowing full well it would move that pink ribbon.

"Cole, if you keep doing that I'm going to come."

He grinned behind her head and breathed in her clean-linen scent, enjoying the softness of her hair on his face. "And what if I do this?"

Keeping her anchored to him, he brought one hand up and rolled her left nipple between his thumb and forefinger.

"Ah." Lacey let her head fall against him.

He moved his other hand up to give the right nipple equal attention. His gorgeous woman arched her back, pressing her breasts into his touch.

He chuckled silently, loving how much she enjoyed his hands on her. Gently, he clamped her nipples between his fingers. When she pulled back against him, he didn't let go, allowing her to determine the exact pressure she liked.

"Cole."

"Yes?" When she didn't say anything more, he let go of her tight nubs and anchored one arm around her again. With his other hand, he smoothed down the pink satin on her torso until he reached her mons, lightly covered with golden-blonde curls. He couldn't see where he was, but he could imagine, and like a blind person, let his hand explore her folds.

Wetness coated his fingers and he smiled into her hair. She was so ready, she made his cock painfully hard. As much as he wanted to release it from its confines, he refused to until he brought her to her first, of what he hoped would be, many orgasms of the night.

Lacey started to make short moaning sounds deep in her throat, causing his balls to tighten.

Shit. As much as he wanted to play with her more, he had to bring her to release.

Quickly, he moved his fingers from teasing her opening to her clit and rubbed it upward. She always enjoyed that stroke.

And he wasn't wrong. Her hips started to rock against his busy hand, which pulled on the pink ribbon strapped to the butt plug.

"Oh gosh, Cole."

He tried to ignore his urgent need and focused on his fingers working her hard nub while he loosened his hold to allow her to move against his thigh, his jeans catching the ribbon far better than his bare thigh would have.

Lacey started to pant and her movements against him grew frantic until she squealed out her release.

Cole's heart warmed to have his only love fall apart in his arms and he brought her slowly back to earth while he counted to a hundred, trying to ignore his demanding cock. When he reached that high number and could feel Lacey relax, he removed his hand and licked at the juices on his fingers.

Wrong thing to do.

~~*~~

Lacey wasn't exactly sure how she'd gone from sitting on Cole's lap, coming down from a very different orgasm than any she'd experienced, to kneeling before a hay bale.

"Bend over." Cole's voice was rough with need.

She loved that tone. The one that told her she could make him so hard he couldn't wait. It happened every time he brought her to orgasm first. Willingly, she bent over, but lifted up an inch as the scratchy hay brushed her sensitive nipples.

The sound of Cole's zipper opening behind her had her anticipation growing.

When his hands spread her ass cheeks, moving the butt plug just a hair, her body tightened all over again.

"Shit, Lacey. This looks amazing."

"It feels amazing too."

"Good. How does it feel with this?" Cole slid his large cock into her with one long thrust.

"Yesss." As her sheath expanded to accept him, he pushed against the plug in her ass and a wave of indescribable feeling flowed over her.

"Come with me." Cole's entreaty sent electricity flowing through her veins, but as he glided out of her and re-entered, everything started to spark.

His hands grasped her hips, keeping her cheeks spread. He had to be watching the butt plug and a thrill raced down her spine right to the center of her ass. Her sheath tightened around his cock as he exited her, his hands keeping her in place, only to pull her toward him as he pushed in again, his width stretching the ribbon on either side of her folds and pulling on the toy inside her.

Her muscles turned to mush as Cole's rhythm picked

up speed and she couldn't hold herself away from the hay anymore. The scratching of it against the tips of her nipples as Cole pushed and pulled her back and forth brought squeals of delight she couldn't contain.

The multiple levels of stimulation overflowed her senses. Her entire body tensed and she released a scream of pleasure.

"Lacey!" Cole's shout echoed through her as her orgasm crested and his come filled her. Every nerve jumped for joy at their mutual ecstasy.

Cole's hands held her tight to his pelvis as he bucked a couple times with residual pleasure.

She looked back to find his eyes closed, his head tilted back slightly and his massive chest muscles tense. Her firefighting cowboy wasn't just over the top muscular, he had a heart of gold to go with it. Happiness floated through her. She was so thankful they had found each other again.

Cole opened his green eyes and smiled at her. "I love that I never know what I'll find beneath your clothes."

She shrugged. "You'll always find me."

He chuckled, and she dropped her head at the vibrations that hit her sensitive spots.

Cole pulled out of her, and she sucked in her breath as his glide hit the toy in her butt. She had doubted Adriana, who told her how arousing it could be, but now she understood. She'd have to make the bartender a plate of her favorite cookies after this.

She knelt and quickly unhooked the corset, shivering as she removed the toy and set everything aside.

Cole took off his jeans and boots before pulling her back to lie against him on the soft sleeping bag. With one hand he covered them, and her quickly cooling body welcomed his warmth.

She laid her head on his shoulder and crossed one leg over his. "So I take it you liked that?"

His hand on her back held her against him. "I did. How about you?"

She nodded as she smiled up at him. "Definitely."

He squeezed her against him. "So should we keep this Christmas Eve gift-giving idea as our tradition?"

"I'd like to, but let's make it just one gift on Christmas Eve and the rest on Christmas day."

"That sounds good to me." He paused. "We won't have to spend every Christmas day at my parents. Maybe we could move around each Christmas, even having the family dinner in our new house when it's done."

Lacey stiffened. "As long as dinner at your parents' house is the last in the rotation."

"Lacey. We need to go to my parents' this year."

She leveraged herself up on her elbow to better look him in the eye. "No, we don't. I told you. I'm not spending Christmas dinner at your parents' ranch. They're the reason we lost eight years of being together…like this. I'm not ready to forgive them for that."

"They were just trying to do what was right for me."

"No, they weren't. They were doing what was best for them. They didn't care about you."

Cole tensed against her. "That's not true."

"Really?" Her stomach churned as it did every time she thought about what the Hatchers had done to their son. "Then why did they refuse to help you with your horse rescue ranch? Why did they tell Dillon he could have Sunrise Creek? Because they cared about you?"

"That's not fair, Lacey. They're my parents."

She couldn't contain her anger any longer. She sat up, pulling the sleeping bag with her. "Yes, they are and they should have put their child before their own selfish need to be important. Who's going to be at the party this year? The mayor? The governor? Or is it some millionaire who's looking for a horse?"

"I'm sure the town manager will be there, but that's not why we should go. It's the right thing to do. They're my parents."

She fisted her hands. Cole would always want to do what was right. "I think it's the wrong thing to do. I think they should suffer for a few years." She snorted. "That's assuming they would even notice you weren't there."

Cole sat up, too. "Thanks." His face was hard and her stomach clenched at the hurt in his eyes.

"That's not what I meant." She sighed and clasped her hands over the sleeping bag. "Why can't we stay here? Everyone will be gone to your mother's. We could actually have some time alone, enjoy each other, maybe go for a ride."

Cole shook his head. "What are you going to do at our wedding? Or are you planning to wait eight years for us to marry?"

"No." She reached for his hand and grasped it, but he didn't hold hers in return. "I want to marry you. The sooner, the better. I just can't spend Christmas day with them. That's supposed to be a day of happiness and I'm bitter and angry at them for making you dump me all those years ago and for turning their backs on you when you wanted to start the horse rescue. It's only been two months since we found each other again. I just need some time to come to terms with what they did."

Cole looked away. "Time away from them isn't going to help. Only if you are around them will you be able to see they aren't monsters."

"Or they may prove they're even worse than I thought."

His gaze came back to hers, his brows furrowed with hurt. "I'm their son. If they are such monsters then I guess I'm not nearly good enough for you." He stood, pulling his hand from hers to grasp his jeans. "I'm going back in the house with *my family*."

"Cole."

He ignored her, stuffing his legs into his pants. "When I get off my shift on Christmas morning, I'll come back here and see if you've changed your mind. If not, I'm going to my parents anyway." He grabbed up his boots and shirt and strode out of the barn.

Part of her wanted to go after him, but the other part was too angry to move. Couldn't he see that while he was raised to do what was right, his parents had no such compunction? They had treated him so poorly and yet he remained loyal, like an abused dog.

She didn't want to make it hard on him, but she just couldn't forgive them. Thanks to the rumors his mother spread, she and Cole lost eight years together. If she made him choose between them and her, he'd just shown her which way he would go. His parents would win again. Why couldn't he understand how she felt? Why did he have to push her so soon?

Shivering from both the cold temperature in the barn and her loss of Cole for the night, she snuggled between the sleeping bags. She wanted to go in, but if she did, he would see it as her agreeing to go, but if she went to his parents' house the chance that she'd make a terrible scene was very good and that would drive the wedge between them deeper. She hated that the Hatchers were once again tearing her and Cole apart.

She stared up at the snowflakes hanging from the rafters. Cole had given her such a thoughtful present and she'd ruined it. She looked around and noticed the bottle of wine for the first time. For some reason, that little gesture made her heart break. Tears filled her eyes, and she closed them against the ache in her chest.

Chapter Three

Cole woke at the sound of footsteps on the stairs. He glanced at the clock. It was three in the morning. Whoever climbed the stairs obviously didn't know where to step. He heard at least four of the stairs creak before his bedroom door opened.

He closed his eyes and waited. When the bed dipped, he silently sighed in relief. He had hoped she would come in before now, but at least she was inside. She pulled the covers over her, but didn't touch him.

He hated the hurt feeling in his stomach. Lacey was his world and usually they were on the same page about important stuff, but this thing with his parents was tearing him up.

The bed started to shimmy. What the…oh shit. She was shivering.

Anger resurfaced that the only reason she'd come in was to get warm, but he couldn't ignore his instinct to take care of her.

Rolling toward her, he threw his arm over her like he usually did in his sleep, pressing his chest against her chilled back and carefully keeping his hardening cock from touching her ass. When her cold hand grasped his forearm around her waist, relief that she still wanted his touch calmed him.

He didn't blame her for not wanting to spend Christmas day at his parents in Orson. Maybe he could keep the visit short, just a couple hours so they could start to see each other as relatives.

Then he and Lacey could stop by her parents, even though the Winters had told them they didn't have to, understanding Lacey's wish to spend her first Christmas with him. He admitted he wanted his parents to accept that as well, but since they hadn't, he was obligated to go.

He wasn't excited about visiting her parents either, but for a completely different reason. Guilt.

Lacey pressed her ass against his cock and his mind switched gears immediately, causing his cock to grow hard again. Her gift to him tonight had been very hot, her ass filled with the sex toy and pressing against him in her sheath. His cock hardened even more. Luckily, her even breathing made it clear she was asleep.

There was no way he would lose her. He had to find a way for her and his parents to at least get along. He could just imagine his wedding. His mom would whisper to her friends how disappointed she was that he had married "that little firebug" as she called Lacey, or she would predict the marriage wouldn't last. Lacey's fellow employees at Poker Flat Nudist Resort would close ranks around Lacey to defend her and would probably do everything in their power to shock his parents, friends, and relatives.

He had to figure out something. As he came up with one scenario after the other, discarding each in turn as unworkable, the minutes ticked by. In no time it was five in the morning and he had to get up and head over to the fire station. Reluctantly, he released Lacey and rose from the warm bed.

Though there was a chill in the air, he just threw on his sweatpants and headed for the bathroom. As he showered and shaved, his mind continued to focus on his problem. His father wasn't the issue. It was his mother. Dad just went along with what his mother wanted because it was easier that way.

He never understood his mother's drive to be important. His mom's sister, aunt Bonnie, was nothing like that. She was perfectly happy with her little shop in town, now that they had sold their ranch.

A knock on the door had Cole pausing as he dried off.

"Hey Cole, you almost done?"

"Yeah, Trace. I'll be right out." His cousin was another who had high hopes of acknowledgement and prosperity, only in his case they had crashed and burned with his divorce. Cole couldn't muster any resentment toward Trace. He'd learned the hard way.

Wrapping a towel about his waist, he grabbed up his sweatpants and opened the door. "All yours."

Trace stood there, his sun-streaked brown hair sticking up due to serious bedhead, in a white hotel bathrobe, probably from his days of homelessness until his wife froze his accounts and he was forced to move back in with aunt Bonnie. As far as Cole was concerned, his cousin was better off without the Ice Queen.

"Thanks." Trace closed the door and Cole moved down the hall to his room. Trace and Logan's predicaments made him even more appreciative of Lacey. He couldn't blame her for holding a grudge. After all, even he had thought her guilty of setting the fire. Now he just had to find a way to mend fences so he could keep both Lacey and his family.

Opening the door to his room, he was disappointed to

find her gone. He'd hoped they could talk more calmly before he went to work. He glanced at the clock. Shit, he had to go. Quickly, he threw on his department t-shirt which was wrinkled from him throwing the clean clothes on the chair last night when he'd stormed in. He switched into an equally wrinkled pair of jeans then donned his boots. Grabbing up his cowboy hat on the way out of the room, he flew down the stairs and strode into the kitchen.

Coffee was ready, but his grandparents' door was still closed. That meant either Trace or Lacey had made it. He filled a travel mug then walked behind the stairs where the half-bath was located, now designated as Lacey's bathroom by his grandmother. The door was closed.

He wanted to say something, but finally gave up. Nothing he could say would keep them from another argument. He'd wait until tomorrow morning when he came home. He walked through the living room, completing his circle of the downstairs and headed outside.

"Have fun at work." Trace sat on a porch chair, sipping coffee.

His cousin's shiny new boots made Cole smile. "I will. At least I won't be mucking out Samson's and Lightyear's stalls."

Trace lost his grin. "Great. I expect you'll sleep through the night without a screaming baby in the next room, too."

"Only if the sound of the fire bell doesn't wake me, but this time of year, the chances of having a quiet night are about nil." He frowned as he jogged down the steps.

"Yeah, there is that. Good luck."

Cole raised his hand without looking back as he walked toward his truck. Once inside, he glanced back at the house. Trace had gone in and there was no sign of Lacey. He'd see her tomorrow morning. Hopefully, she'd be a little more willing to compromise.

He turned on the engine and backed his truck toward the house before heading down the driveway to the dirt road that would take him to Route 93.

It didn't take long to drive through the just waking town to the station. As he got out of his truck, Mason, the usual fire engine driver, pulled up. Cole waited for him to exit his SUV. "Morning Mason."

"Hey, Lieutenant. Heard you're pulling an extra-long shift today."

Cole nodded as he fell into step with Mason. "Just a couple extra hours. Giving Clark a little morning time with his kids on Christmas day. Then I'm off for four days, so I figured I could give up a couple hours."

Mason shook his head. "If I had a girlfriend as sweet looking as yours, I'd be hightailing it home as soon as I could." He slapped Cole on the back. "You're a better man then I am."

Cole gave the man a wan smile. He didn't feel like he was a better man. His argument with Lacey sat like a wet firehose in his stomach. He had the next twenty-four hours to figure out what to do. Mason was right. He had something special and he needed to do whatever it took to hold on to it while still doing what was right.

~~*~~

Lacey held her cup of coffee as she stared out the large living room window framed by garland, the lights not twinkling as they were unplugged during the day. She hadn't said goodbye to Cole, too much of a coward to come out when she heard his distinctive stride descending the stairs.

Now she wished she had. What if he got hurt? Or worse? She always worried while he was at work, but today it was doubled.

"Hey, Blondie, why the sad face? He'll be home tomorrow."

She didn't even try to smile. "I know, Trace, but every shift means he's putting himself in danger. I can't help but worry he could get hurt. He even admitted that this time of year has an increase in house fires. I wish they would outlaw live Christmas trees. Then he'd be safer and less people would lose their homes."

Trace put his arm over her shoulders. "I agree with you, but I think trying to get that law passed here in Arizona would be as difficult as finding gold in the ranch's old copper mine. Just not going to happen."

She patted his hand. "I know. But a girl has to have a dream."

He chuckled at that. "I thought that monstrous ranch house you're building on Fire Hill was your dream."

She smiled. "First of all, it's not that big and second of all, who said I was limited to one dream?"

Trace stepped away and held up his hands. "No one. Last I heard there's no limit on dreams. I certainly hope not. Just when all mine came true, I lost them." He headed for the front door. "Now I get to muck out Samson's and Lightyear's stalls. Hope I remember how. Last time I did this I was sixteen years old."

This time she smiled and winked. "It's like riding a bike, you never forget how. You don't forget the smell either."

"Thanks." He gave her a pained look before he opened the front door and headed for the barn.

She didn't envy him his task. As the latest family member

to arrive at Last Chance Ranch, Trace was assigned the worst chores, but it was expected. Cowboys accepted that they had to pay their dues. Trace would do a great job. He always made sure every corner of the barn was—oh no!

She set her coffee cup down on the coffee table and ran out the door after Cole's cousin. When she got to the barn, Trace was standing at the entrance to the last stall where she and Cole had started their Christmas Eve tradition.

He turned as she ran up, frantically trying to remember if the corset could be seen from where he was standing. When she reached him, he turned toward her, his eyebrow raised. "I take it this is yours and Cole's doing?"

Her cheeks heated. "We just wanted a little alone time last night."

"Smart idea. I might just try it myself. Your friend Billy tends to snore. He's not that loud, but sometimes he sounds like a burro."

She moved slowly into the stall. "Just think when our house is finished, you can have our room."

"Yeah. That's one thing I can look forward to." Something in his voice had her stopping.

"You okay?"

He shrugged. "Sure. Do you want me to pick this up for you?"

He was definitely not happy, a regular state for him after losing the woman he loved, his ranch and his substantial bank account all at once. There wasn't anything she could do to help him with that. Cole said Trace needed time. "No, I'll clean it up. Then I'll take Angel out into the corral so she will be more comfortable while you work in here."

Trace shook his head. "The man that abused her should

get the electric chair. To mar such a beauty should be punishable by death."

Lacey silently agreed. "He's awaiting trial, but don't worry. Cole will be testifying along with the vet who treated her when she first came here. I'm counting on him going to jail."

Trace turned and headed for the tack room. "I hope they throw the book at him."

As soon as he was out of sight, she searched behind the hay bale and found the corset and sex toy. She quickly wrapped them in one of the sleeping bags. Then she zipped up the other sleeping bag and rolled it up. Two trips to the house later, she had put everything away, setting the bottle of wine in their room. She was more determined than ever for her and Cole to stay on the ranch tomorrow. They needed some serious time alone and not just for sex.

Missing the rest of her caffeine for the morning, she headed downstairs and picked up her coffee cup. When she entered the large eat-in kitchen, she found Logan half asleep in a chair and Cole's grandmother, Annette, cooing to the baby as she fed her. For such a tiny girl, six-month-old Charlotte had the whole house jumping to her tune. "Good morning. Is there any coffee left?"

Annette nodded without taking her eyes off Charlotte. "There sure is. I just made a new pot for sleepyhead over here."

Logan scowled at his grandmother. "I'd like to see how chipper you'd be if I put Charlotte in your room for a night."

Lacey couldn't help her lip quirking upward. Cole's oldest cousin and most confirmed bachelor was not taking to fatherhood very well. It didn't help that there was no mother in sight. "I'm sure she'll start sleeping the night soon, won't she, Annette?"

Annette wiped a bit of baby food off Charlotte's lips before replying. "Of course she will, right, sweetie? You'll sleep through the night eventually, when you're good and ready."

Logan's scowl darkened and Lacey's heart went out to him. She wanted children, but not for years yet. She couldn't imagine having one now, never mind being a single parent. Then again he should have expected it to happen eventually. He had the striking features of his mother's side of the family, a sharp jaw and dark eyes with wrinkle lines in the corners from squinting in the Arizona sun. Add to that his short ponytail of sun-streaked brown hair and lack of inclination to smile just made him that much more of a challenge to the cowgirls.

"There's some homemade cinnamon buns I made last night in the refrigerator, Lacey." Annette spoke, but didn't take her eyes off the baby. "If you're looking for breakfast, they warm up in the microwave pretty well."

"They're very good." Logan's comment surprised her. He wasn't one to offer praise often.

She'd had Annette's cinnamon buns before and she didn't need any extra encouragement. "That sounds perfect. Anyone else want one warmed up while I'm at it?"

"I ate, honey, didn't I, Charlotte?" Annette didn't let the baby answer. Instead she got another spoonful of food into Charlotte's mouth. She was totally enraptured with her great-granddaughter, which was one of the reasons Logan had come to Last Chance Ranch. The man clearly needed help raising his child.

"I'll take one, if you don't mind." He looked longingly at the pan she pulled from the fridge.

"Logan Williams, you already had two." Annette's voice was stern, even if she didn't spare a glance for her grandson.

Lacey looked over her shoulder at him and saw his hopeful

expression dissolve into a frown. Poor man. Taking out a bun, she put it on a plate and set it in the microwave. He needed all the food he could get in order to handle his work on the ranch *and* taking care of Charlotte when his grandmother tired.

When the microwave dinged, she took out a second bun and put it in the microwave. She really did like Cole's family. In a way, she wished his mother had been adopted, but since she had the exact same chestnut colored hair Annette used to have and most of her facial features, there was little chance of that. Where had her future mother-in-law picked up her high-end ambitious streak?

The microwave dinged again and she took the two plates to the table and set one down in front of Logan before grabbing her coffee and sitting down with her own.

"You're an angel, you know that?" He took a bite of the warm, sugary bun.

She chuckled. "Can't say anyone has ever called me that. If you want a real Angel, there's one in the corral right now."

Logan looked at her strangely before understanding dawned. "I'm glad that horse will let you near her. She looks at me like I'm the devil or something."

She couldn't respond because her tongue was enraptured by the heavy cinnamon treat in her mouth. After swallowing, she sighed. "It's not you. It's just men in general and I think the bigger you are, the more afraid she is. Cole had to drug her just to treat her. I'm so glad he uses a female vet or I think Angel would have died."

Annette stood to put the spoon and bowl she'd used for the baby into the sink. "Cole's a good man. Every horse he's brought here has needed this place. Now with more help," she paused to look at Logan, "we can take more horses."

"Thanks to you and Ed." Lacey smiled at Cole's grandmother, but the woman waved it off.

"We just had a place that wasn't being used anyway. He's done the bulk of the work." She unstrapped Charlotte from the highchair and picked her up. "Now I'm going to go play with my beautiful great-grandbaby because her daddy needs to fix the arm of the porch chair in the far corner like he's been promising Cole for the last two months."

"Grandma, it's Christmas Eve."

"That's right and it would make a nice present for your cousin when he gets home from the fire station tomorrow morning. Now go. You have plenty of time before we have to leave for your mother's house."

Logan unfolded his tall body from the chair and shuffled out of the room. It wasn't that he was lazy, he was just in a perpetually bad mood. Then again, no sleep would do that to a person.

Annette turned toward Lacey. "Are you sure you're okay being alone here overnight? We won't see you until the big dinner party tomorrow evening. Are you sure you don't want to come with us today?"

Lacey didn't want to insult Annette by telling her how much she was looking forward to the peace and quiet. "I'll be fine. I have a few projects I plan to work on and I want to be here when Cole comes home tomorrow."

"Okay, honey. Would you mind throwing the rest of the dishes in the dishwasher for me?"

She smiled. "I'd be happy to." When Annette asked someone to do something, there was only one answer. Yes.

"Thank you." She nuzzled Charlotte as she walked from the room. "Are you ready to play dress up with granny?"

Lacey popped the last bite of cinnamon bun into her mouth and chewed slowly. She'd been an only child and the busyness of Last Chance was sometimes overwhelming, but now, when it suddenly went quiet, it made her wonder what it would be like for her and Cole in their new house.

Standing, she picked up her plate. The privacy would definitely be welcome as would the quiet. But maybe they could start another tradition, one where his family came over for Sunday dinner.

She rinsed her plate and added it to the dishwasher along with the few dishes and cups in the sink. As soon as she finished her chore, she would wrap the last presents she had bought for Cole.

An uneasy feeling crawled up her spine. She hated not kissing him goodbye and telling him she loved him. Crossing her fingers, she pushed the button on the dishwasher and it whirred to life. *Please, let there be no fires today.*

Chapter Four

Tired, Cole dropped into his bunk at the firehouse. Two fires in one day and it was only nine o'clock. That had to be some kind of record. The last house had tugged hard on his heart. The little blonde girl with her braid over one shoulder and a stuffed bunny in her arms reminded him too much of Lacey. His fiancée may have been a teenager when her parents' carriage house caught fire, but like the little girl, she'd been inside and had to escape through flames.

The little girl at the fire was heartbroken because Santa wouldn't know where to find her tonight. Lacey had been heartbroken because he broke up with her. That guilt just piled on top of the guilt he already had. Lacey said it was his mother's fault he dumped her, but if he had really loved her, he would have rebelled. He hadn't been smart enough to know what he had back then. He was smart enough now.

So why wasn't he telling his mother to take her Christmas party and shove it?

Because she was his mother.

He couldn't get around that fact. He'd been brought up to respect his parents and be loyal to family. That meant when his mother asked him specifically to be at Sunrise Creek Ranch for Christmas dinner, he needed to go, especially after he and Lacey had spent Thanksgiving at Last Chance.

The sound of the alert tone had Cole throwing off the blankets and running to the pole. Once down in the locker room, he stuffed his legs into his turnout pants as he listened to the particulars coming in from dispatch.

"Fuck! What a Christmas season this is turning out to be." Mason grabbed his coat and ran for the truck.

Cole was right behind him. "It's another house fire. Shit, I hope they all got out." As the fourth man jumped on the engine, Mason pulled the truck out of the garage and onto Copper Win Road.

Less than four minutes later they pulled into the neighborhood and could see flames licking up the side of an old house. This area of town was referred to as the "old" section even though homes didn't date back more than fifty years. Still, that meant none probably met present day fire codes. Mason stopped the engine and one man jumped out and secured the hose to a hydrant. Cole waited for the signal then turned to Mason. "Go."

The truck rolled to a stop, three houses up the street. A woman with two children stood at the end of the driveway. He strode toward her. "Is anyone still inside?"

"No. It's just me and my two children. I just ran to the store for milk. I wasn't gone more than thirty minutes."

Cole's heart slowed now that he had confirmation no one's life was in danger. He spoke into his radio. "No one's inside. Let's knock this baby down and see if we can't save Christmas." After ordering another man to use the two and a half inch hose, Cole strode to the police unit that pulled up.

"Better evacuate the nearby houses in case the wind shifts. Just a precautionary measure. These houses are old." The officer nodded and he and his partner took over crowd control.

Cole moved back to the woman with the two children.

The little girl in her mother's arms was clearly scared. The poor kid.

"Mr. Fireman, can I get in the firetruck?"

He turned his attention to the boy whose eyes were filled with excitement. He probably would have reacted the same way at his age. "Not tonight, son. But your mom can bring you over to the station any time after Christmas and we'll be glad to give you a tour."

The boy frowned before leaning into his mom's hip.

"Ma'am, do you have any idea how this fire started?"

She shook her head.

"Do you happen to have a live Christmas tree?"

"No. I can't afford that. I couldn't even afford to buy more propane when we ran out last week. I was waiting until I got paid on Thursday."

Standing in the street in a pair of jeans and a sweatshirt, her children in their pajamas and winter coats, she looked like any other family in the neighborhood who stood gawking as his men worked to put out the fire.

A growing concern for his men forced him to delve deeper. The reason for the fire was Detective Anderson's job, but Cole's men could be walking into a potentially hazardous situation. "Ma'am, what kind of heat do you have?"

"Propane." She scowled. "It's also what I cook with. I've been using the propane in the grill to heat water."

Cole's gut tightened at the thought of what she may have done. "What did you do to stay warm?"

"I used an old electric heater I have. It only warmed the living room, but that's where we've been having a camp out." She looked down at her son before raising her brows, signaling the need to put a positive spin on it.

Cole couldn't stop his groan, but thanks to the noise of the fire and water, she didn't appear to hear. "So you all had sleeping bags on the floor?"

She brushed the hair away from her daughter's face. "Yes. It was a tight fit, but that's what it would be like in a tent. I used my father's old sleeping bag from when he used to go fishing and my kids had the ones their grandmother bought them a couple years ago."

He'd bet his next paycheck the mother's sleeping bag, the oldest and least flame retardant, had been pushed against the heater which started the fire. In a way he was relieved. At least they had a chance of saving the building and didn't have to worry about propane fuel or a kerosene heater, which had been his concern.

One of his men called over the radio. "We have it under control."

Cole took a breath. "Good. It appears it may have been caused by an electric heater."

"Seriously?"

He grimaced as the firefighter's voice game over the radio loud enough for the woman to hear.

He directed his man. "Soak it down good. We don't want any embers floating to the houses next door."

"Got it, Lieutenant."

The young mother looked embarrassed as he turned back to her.

"I was just trying to keep my kids warm. No one here

knows I'm out of propane." She grabbed his arm. "You won't tell them, will you? I mean, I don't want them to know how tight money has been for me."

Though many emotions barreled through him at the mother's plea, disbelief overrode them all and he had no idea why. It was completely irrational. Pushing aside his strange irritation, he tapped into his sympathy for her plight. "Ma'am, don't worry. I won't be talking to your neighbors. We all experience financial difficulties at one time or another." He certainly had before Lacey took over his finances. "I'm sure, like me, your neighbors will be happy that you and your children are alive and unharmed."

The woman glanced at the crowd being kept away for safety's sake before meeting his gaze, her own uncertain.

"Why don't you take your children back there where you all will be safe, and I will see what I can do to get this fire out completely."

She nodded and turned, but then looked back at him. "Thank you." He nodded once, and she walked into the crowd of neighbors, all anxious to hear from her what happened.

Once she'd left, his irritation returned. He shouldn't be so bothered by the woman's concern about what her neighbors thought, but it was like a blister that had finally started bleeding. He strode back to the engine and Mason. "How's the pressure?"

The man gave him a searching look. "Fine, why wouldn't it be?"

He shrugged carelessly as he looked at the small house, not really seeing it. "Just tired of tragedies at Christmas."

"I don't think this one will be a tragedy. Everyone is alive and at least half the building will be saved. We do have a pretty good reputation around here for putting out fires."

Cole snapped his head around to look at Mason and found the man smiling.

"Yeah, you're right. We do good work." He walked away to look at the scene from the side, away from everyone. His irritation at the single mother still bothered him. The poor woman just lost part of her home and was barely making ends meet with two kids. Who was he to judge her? Gossip running rampant in a neighborhood could ruin it for a person living there. He of all people knew that. It's what originally drove Lacey from Orson.

So why did he take the woman's comment to heart?

He started back toward the engine. It was probably just all the calls in one shift. They usually got about two a week. He was spoiled.

The fire took little time to extinguish. He handed the woman the paperwork and asked her to bring it down to the station in the next couple days. It was Christmas Eve and she had more pressing problems than finding her insurance company name and number, if she even had insurance. Still, it was almost midnight before they rolled into the station again.

Some of the men headed straight for the kitchen. No surprise as once the adrenaline rush had worn off, they were starving, but he just wanted to get some sleep. Hanging up his gear, he trudged upstairs to his bunk and lay down.

Relaxing into the bed, he focused on Lacey, her bright smile, golden hair, mahogany-colored eyes. His heart swelled that this woman was his and he finally drifted off to sleep.

The sound of the alert tone woke him again. He glanced at the clock. 3:00 a.m. What the fuck?

~~*~~

The sound of a quail near the house woke Lacey. She glanced at the clock. It was already after seven. Cole would be home at noon. Her heartbeat sped at the thought, but her stomach tensed.

It was Christmas day.

She wanted to believe they would have a wonderful day alone, unwrapping the presents downstairs and eating the dinner she'd had Selma, the cook at Poker Flat, make for her as a surprise for Cole. It was in the refrigerator waiting for his decision. She'd even bought peppermint stick ice cream for dessert. It actually had pieces of candy cane in it, Cole's favorite Christmas candy.

She threw the covers off and sat up. If only she could be sure she could convince him to stay. If not, she might very well be spending the day alone.

She stood then headed for the bathroom. No way. If he had to go to his parents because it was "the right thing to do," then she'd drive over to Poker Flat and hang out with Adriana and Billy and anyone else who was there. But in the meantime, she would hope for the best and prepare to welcome Cole home for Christmas.

After showering, she pulled out the special lingerie she'd bought just for Christmas Day. It was a red body stocking with a few delicate green bows that hid nothing. It wasn't the typical mesh that Cole had seen her wear in a bra on occasion. This body stocking had spaghetti straps so the neckline revealed her cleavage, but then there was a strip of see-through red nylon over her nipples. Below that, large holes between three and five inches in diameter were cut out so a lot of her skin showed, including the bottom of her breasts, but all her critical areas were covered, except that pulling a cut-out to a strategic place was very easy with the stretchy nylon.

What she liked most about it was it was comfortable, yet it gave her a soft stimulation when she had no clothes on. She loved wearing sexy lingerie under her clothes on a daily basis. She was always excited to see what Cole thought of it at night, plus during the day, she smiled often as she thought about what she had on, which no one guessed at.

Throwing on a pair of jeans, a red sweater since it was Christmas and her brown cowboy boots, she jogged down the stairs to find breakfast. As she ate a leftover cinnamon bun and drank her coffee, the lack of noise started to bother her. How odd? She always wished for a quiet morning like this and now that she had one, it felt strange.

She shrugged. She'd just become use to all the activity since Billy and the cousins had joined them. She looked forward to sitting at the breakfast table with just Cole, chatting about what they would do for the day.

And if Cole was at work? She could always come back to the Williams house and have coffee with Annette…except Annette would be totally involved with little Charlotte. Hmmm. She could go into work early on the days Cole worked then she wouldn't notice being alone.

Standing, she picked up her plate and after rinsing it, put it in the dishwasher. Feeding the horses wasn't her usual chore, but since no one else was home, she was more than happy to do so. Grabbing her jean jacket off the hook by the door, she stuffed her arms into the sleeves and stepped outside.

She breathed deeply before walking down the steps to the porch toward the barn. The sun was shining and she left her jacket unbuttoned, the day already warming up. Once inside, she grabbed the pitchfork and dug into the loose hay Logan had piled up for her the day before.

She could certainly lift a bale of hay, even if she was small, but Cole and his cousins were quick to help her. Still, it caught her off guard when surly Logan would go the extra mile for her, or Trace, who had no use for women after the fiasco with his wife, actually gave her a reassuring squeeze like he had the day before. She could only chalk it up to being part of the family. A warmth filled her chest at the thought. She liked being part of the mish-mash family on Last Chance. As an only child, she just wasn't use to all the activity.

After pitching hay into Lightyear's stall, she moved on to the next one where Tiny Dancer awkwardly stood at her approach. Each horse had its own unique personality and she loved them all, but hopefully they would all find forever families.

After feeding the rest of the horses, she moved to Angel's stall. "Hey, sweetie. Ready for breakfast?" She pitched in the hay.

The scarred white Arabian walked toward her, ignoring the food and instead stuck her head over the stall door.

"Good morning to you too, Angel." Lacey looped her arm around the mare's neck and pressed her cheek to the horse's cheek. "Would you like to go for a ride a little later? Maybe check on the new house?" She moved her head away and stroked the horse before giving her a couple pats and stepping back.

Angel stepped back and finally lowered her head to eat.

Lacey returned the pitchfork to its hook on the wall and headed back to the house. A ride out to the construction site would make her feel a lot better about her future and would waste some time until Cole got home.

The sun had increased the temperature already, so she

left her coat on the peg by the front door and went into the kitchen to grab a few jelly beans, Angel's favorite treat, and a granola bar for herself in case she got hungry. Pulling a water bottle from the fridge, she had her hand on the door when she remembered Cole's rule. If she ever went riding by herself, she had to bring a gun with her. He said there were too many dangers in the desert and most of the acres of Last Chance Ranch had no cell service, an issue they would have to tackle at their new house.

She stepped around the corner to the gun case. All the men had their own guns, but Cole had shown her how to use his 12-gauge shotgun. She liked it because her aim didn't have to be perfect, and it wasn't.

After taking it out and pocketing a few shells, she closed the case and headed outside to the barn.

The last thing she needed to do before taking Angel out was to move Samson and Lightyear into the corral. She set her water, snack and the gun in the empty stall she and Cole had made love in, then strode to the tack room and pulled a halter off the wall. Luckily, Samson had learned to tolerate her over the last couple months since she started coming to Last Chance, and he didn't give her any trouble as she looped the halter over his head and led him to the corral. Once he was safely closed in, she moved to Lightyear's stall, but she couldn't open the stall door. "Really?"

She stared at the 4-wheeler blocking the door. If Billy were the one who left it parked there, he would be mucking out Angel's stall when he got back from Poker Flat. The keys were still in it, but she didn't want to startle Angel, so she disengaged the brake and pushed the machine a couple feet until it was out of the way.

Rolling her shoulders and taking a few deep breaths, she opened the stall door. Trace had already put the halter on Lightyear since the horse hated anyone touching his face. Luckily, he tolerated a halter or bridle well and she led Lightyear out into the corral. Gingerly, she released him from the halter and he shook his head as if the one minute walk from barn to corral had been an eternity.

Striding back into the barn, she found Angel waiting for her. She chuckled. "Hmm, I guess someone is anxious to go for a run."

The horse eyed her, watching her every move as she went into the tack room and brought out a bridle. She wasn't the best horsewoman, but Angel was a good girl for her when they rode.

She struggled with the weight of the saddle as usual, but the wood steps Cole set up for her to help her throw it onto the horse's back worked perfectly. Maybe she should think about exercising with weights.

Once she had the saddle secured and double checked, she stuffed her snack and Angel's treat into the saddlebag and secured the gun. She brought Angel out of her stall and using one of the steps again, she mounted, walking them outside into the bright day.

Lacey kicked Angel into a canter down the long road to the construction that would soon be her new house. There wasn't a cloud in the sky and the cool temperature had disappeared. She'd bet it was already over sixty degrees. The land was still and quiet with no breezes blowing and just a couple large birds catching the thermals far overhead.

She loved the varied browns of the desert dotted with the green of the saguaro cacti and the scrawny mesquite trees.

They'd had to clear most of the mesquite from the top of the Fire Hill where the house was being built, but there had been no saguaros up there so they hadn't needed to relocate them.

Within fifteen minutes, she slowed Angel and they walked up the hill to the construction site. Cole was right. They did need a barn here. At least for horses that needed his care around the clock. Then she could keep Angel nearby. Everyone living on the ranch understood Angel's fear, but the men often forgot that just being in the barn working caused her a lot of stress.

Lacey leaned down and patted Angel. "I'm going to take care of you, sweetie. You're just plain stuck with me." She sat up again and guided her horse around the construction site. There were some walls up, and pipes sticking up from the poured slab, but there was still so much to do. She looked forward to the day when she and Cole could make love in their own house…anywhere in the house.

She smiled. She'd have to insist on a sturdy kitchen table.

As she and Angel came around the end of the house, she heard a hum in the distance. Shading her eyes against the morning sun, she could see dust billowing along the road. It was the ATV.

Chapter Five

Her heart jumped at the sight. It had to be Cole. She looked at her watch, but it was only quarter after nine. Maybe the man he was covering for this morning finished opening presents with his children early. She nudged Angel into a walk down the hill. She'd like to gallop up and meet him, but that would put added stress on Angel. She didn't like the ATV and she only tolerated Cole.

As the vehicle approached, she squinted to see her fiancé, but it wasn't him. Of course it wasn't. Cole would ride Samson.

Dread formed in the pit of her stomach. Was it another firefighter come to tell her Cole had been injured? She gripped the reigns at the thought. Angel stood completely still waiting with her.

Finally, she was able to make out the face of the man driving the ATV and she didn't recognize him from the fire station. Nor was he one of the family she'd met. He had dark, bushy eyebrows and a white, unkempt beard. His shoulders looked to be in a permanent hunch, but she couldn't be sure because his shirt and vest hung off him like they were far too big.

The man pointed at her and yelled across the distance still between them. "Give me that horse!"

No sooner did she understand his words than Angel bolted. Lacey grasped the pommel to stay on as the horse raced away farther from the main house and the man determined to catch them.

Lacey's heart beat as fast as a rattlesnake's rattle as the implications of her predicament became clear. The man had to be Angel's former owner, Ray Norton, the one that had beat her within inches of her life.

Fear and anger tore through Lacey. He'd obviously expected everyone to be gone for Christmas and planned to steal Angel back. She wouldn't let that happen.

She let Angel go where she felt safest. That was northwest of the house and into an area Lacey had never been. She glanced back to see Ray still after them.

The horse turned and started up an incline of a canyon. The shale slipped out from beneath Angel's hooves and Lacey held tight, her breathing now as erratic as her horse's.

"Come on girl, you can do it."

Angel seemed to take heart at her words and battled through the loose rock until they made surer ground. As they rose, smaller rocks gave way to large boulders and stone formations carved by the wind. Finally, Angel slowed near the top of the canyon wall and Lacey guided her behind a long row of tall boulders, where she halted.

Once she was behind the natural monoliths, she checked to be sure she was hidden from Ray's view. From Angel's back, she could see over a five foot incline where there was a plateau of nothing but sagebrush and Joshua trees. If she headed up, maneuvering around the trees would make slow going and the man would easily see her and Angel unless they had a larger head start.

Lacey slid off her horse and pulled the gun from the saddle. She hugged Angel and pet her, pretending a calmness she didn't feel. "Stay right here, girl," she whispered. More than a little nervous, she crept up to a spot between two large boulders to look through a crack between them.

The sight was a little reassuring. The ATV spun out on the shale at the bottom of the hill, making no headway at all. She could hear the man swearing even over the sound of the engine.

Her body lost some of its tenseness. If the ATV couldn't make it up the canyon wall, then they were safe. She could take Angel onto the plateau and try to find a way home. Moving back to the horse, she gave her another hug. "It's okay, girl. We'll be safe soon."

Her last word sounded loud and she listened to the suddenly quiet canyon. Had he turned around and left? Creeping back to the crack, she peered down below. What was he doing?

The man had turned the ATV back down to solid ground and turned off the engine. He jumped off and reached behind his back. When his hand came out from behind him, the sun glinted off the metal of a handgun.

"Oh crap."

Angel huffed behind her.

"It's okay, girl." She reached into her pocket and grabbed a shotgun shell. As much as she'd like to kill the man, she wasn't sure she had it in her. She hadn't even shot a snake yet.

Loading the gun with the shell, she had just reached into her pocket for another when his voice travelled up the canyon.

"Get your prissy ass out here, you worthless nag!" A shot rang out and Lacey dropped to the ground.

Angel reared, tearing the reins from the rock they'd been looped around.

"Angel, no!" Lacey scrambled up to grab at the reins, but her horse was too fast. Within seconds, Angel had raced up the last five feet of hill and disappeared over the rim, just as another shot rang out, hitting the dirt above Lacey's head, which sent tiny pebbles ricocheting everywhere. "Ow!"

Despite her dive for the ground, a pebble hit her arm, digging in so hard, it took her sweater with it.

"Fuckin' horse!" Ray's anger was bone chilling.

She ignored the pain in her arm, the need to see compelling her forward as she crawled to the crack again only to see Angels' former owner trying to hike up the shale base of the incline.

He slipped and fell at least three times before he finally found a handhold that brought his feet to more solid ground.

Sugar, in minutes, he would be up the canyon wall and after Angel. Despite the hammering of her heart, she steadied her shaking hands and lifted the shotgun just above the crack in the rock and aimed for a spot over the head of the ascending man. Squeezing her eyes shut, she pulled the trigger.

~~*~~

Whisper Adams rubbed her eyes, certain she hadn't seen what she thought she saw. Nope, she was still seeing a white horse with an empty saddle walking among the Joshua trees. This required investigating immediately.

After wiping her Uncle's mouth with a Christmas napkin, she set the bowl of oatmeal down. "I'll be right back, Joey."

The man's eyes implored her to be careful. He'd heard the muffled gunshots as well.

"Don't worry. I'll take Sal with me."

Grabbing her Glock 42, she stuck Sal into the waistband of her jeans and opened the trailer door.

"Well, strip me naked and throw me in a lava pit." The white horse was still there, pawing at the dirt and walking in circles like it was lost. But horses didn't get lost. They always knew their way home, their way back for food. Something was seriously wrong.

Whisper walked slowly toward the agitated animal who meandered among the Joshua trees just outside the circle of her front yard. When its gaze rested on her, she stopped and held out her hand as if she would shake hands. Keeping her gaze on the horse's eye, she slowly turned her palm toward the desert floor and lowered her hand forty-five degrees.

The horse's nostrils flared but it didn't move away. That was something.

Without taking her eyes from the horse, she bent her knees and knelt on the ground.

The horse's head lowered, but it still didn't move.

Okay, she could be patient. She lowered her hand until her palm was flat on the desert floor in front of her.

Finally, the horse walked toward her.

She remained still as it sniffed her hair and clothes. When it stopped, she carefully stood up and lifted her palm to the horse's neck, never once breaking eye contact. But when her hand rubbed over rippled skin, she moved her gaze and froze.

This horse had been abused. Rage burned in her stomach and she removed her hand to avoid communicating her emotion to the horse. Bile rose in her throat and she turned away as her body trembled. She clenched her hands in an attempt to keep from vomiting, but it was no use.

She leaned over as her breakfast came up, spilling to the

hard packed earth. It didn't take long to empty her pissed-off stomach. When there was nothing left, she wiped her mouth with her sleeve and turned to find the horse watching her. She grinned sheepishly. "Just a little weakness of mine."

Now that she'd gotten that out of the way, she ran her hand over the horse, not hesitating as it passed over brutal scars that conjured up beatings with chains and nasty whips. As she walked on the other side, she found the marks to be less. For the scars to have healed meant the horse was no longer around the person who had abused it. For that she was thankful.

"I'm going to call you Sacnite. That means white flower in one of the Native American languages. Don't ask me which one. I think maybe Mayan. I get them mixed up. Never was good at quizzes. They're a waste of time if you ask me."

She finished her inspection. "I don't know who would abuse such a beautiful mare. You're safe now, but you're awfully sweaty. I bet you're thirsty, too."

She picked up the reins and led the horse toward the trailer then dropped them. "Wait here and I'll get you some water."

Turning her back on Sacnite, she unburied an empty plaster bucket from the shed she'd built and brought it to the side of the trailer. She had to go into town tomorrow anyway to refill their water, so she wasn't worried about giving the horse what was left. Even if that weren't the case, she'd rather go without water than make an animal give it up.

After filling the bucket full from the spigot on the trailer, she brought it to Sacnite.

The horse lowered its head and drank.

Now she'd have to see what she could find for food. She had some hay leftover from last week when Motley left. Damn burro didn't even say thank you.

Moving around the trailer to where a palo verde tree leaned against a boulder that provided some protection from the sun at certain times of the day, she picked up an armful of the hay Motley left and brought it to where Sacnite drank.

The horse lifted its head from the water and shuffled the hay around a bit before deciding it was good enough to eat.

Seriously? This horse must be used to fresher hay. Reluctantly, her gaze shifted to the well-worn, but obviously expensive saddle. Ignoring the implications, she walked into the trailer to report to her uncle. He may not be able to move or talk beyond a grunt or groan, but his hearing was still good.

When she entered the cool interior, his gaze swung to her.

"It's a white mare that has been abused. She must have run for a while. I gave her some of the hay from last week's visitor."

Uncle Joey nodded jerkily to show he understood, but then he raised his right eyebrow, the one that didn't sag.

She plopped down in the chair opposite him, careful not to hit the three foot Christmas tree with her elbow. "You want to know about the gunshots."

He nodded again.

She looked away. "Probably just some hunters out looking for quail or deer. It's snowbird season. All kinds of tourists come to Arizona to do crazy stuff."

A grunt issued from Joey's slack mouth.

She refused to look at him, well aware he didn't buy her explanation for a minute. He wanted her to investigate further. For an eighty-three-year-old man who'd had three strokes, he could be downright pushy. Of course if she were in his position, she'd be worried about what someone might do to her as well.

She finally looked at him. "Alright already. I'll go find out what happened. Happy?"

Joey's mouth opened, the closest he could get to a smile.

She stood, throwing her hand to the side in dismissal. "You're a taskmaster Uncle Joey. I should call Social Services on you."

She grabbed her brown cowboy hat that had seen better days and plopped it on her head. About to open the trailer door, she stilled. If someone was hurt or dying out there, she may need more than her gun.

Pushing aside the silver and gold garland, she pulled her canvass shoulder bag from the hook near the door, she stuck her arm through it and on further thought, grabbed up her rifle as well.

"I'll be back in a couple hours at most. You eat enough for me to be gone that long?"

Joey nodded again, his eyes watching her every move.

"Okay." She pointed to the clock across from him. "Noontime at the latest." After getting a look of understanding in the man's eyes, she opened the door and headed out.

~~*~~

"Fucking bitch!" The sound of sliding rock accompanied the swearing.

Lacey released a relieved sigh before opening her eyes to see what happened. There was a big hole not three feet away from where the man had been standing. Her hands started to shake again at how close she'd come to killing him. He was nowhere to be seen, but she'd bet a carton of Cole's favorite orange popsicles he had scurried behind the large red boulder not far from the hole she'd made. And she'd bet a plate of Selma's churros that the man was hurting too, if not from shotgun shot then from the rocks she'd hit.

At the thought of rocks, her arm drew her attention. It still stung, but it would probably bleed profusely if she pulled her sweater and dislodged the stone. The idea had her brow sweating. Maybe if she was careful with her movements, she could just leave it alone until she got home.

Tears sprang to her eyes. How the heck was she supposed to get home with Ray shooting below her and no horse to ride on? She was miles from the main house now. She looked up to the rim, but didn't see any sign of Angel. If she crawled high enough to see, she'd be an easy target, especially for a madman who tried to get back a horse he'd beaten by shooting at it.

Determination rose. There was no way she'd let that man anywhere near Angel again. If she had to shoot him, so be it. Reaching into her pocket, she brought out the shells she had left. Only two. She wasn't exactly a good shot as proven by the hole three feet away from where Ray had stood when she'd actually been aiming for over his head.

"God damn, mother fucking, cock sucking stinking bitch." The grumbling coming from below had her blushing. Even Cole and his cousins didn't swear that much. Then again, they knew she'd been raised not to swear at all.

"Ow! Fuck. Fucking cunt! If I wanted to bleed to death, I would have got me a bronco." A stone flew out from behind the boulder.

At least she had confirmation of where he hid. She looked down at her watch. It was almost ten. What if she couldn't get back before noon, when Cole was supposed to come home? Would he think she hid from him on purpose because she didn't want to go to his parents' house? Right now she wished she was at his parents'. It would be a crap load safer.

More grumbling came from behind the rock, none of it reassuring. The man was pissed.

She glanced up at the rim, hoping Angel didn't come back to find her. She had no doubt the man below would kill her horse the second he saw it.

"Hey gal." The voice from behind the rock was sickly sweet. "I just want my horse back. What do you say you let me get up this canyon wall and find it? No reason for either of us to get hurt over a horse."

She clasped the shotgun closer to her chest. She was out of her element here. Give her a spreadsheet of income and expenses with capital expenditures and depreciation figures thrown in and she was happy as a miser in a gold vault. Facing a man with a gun determined to get back the horse he abused was more Cole's area of expertise.

What would Cole do? Would he rush the man? Shoot at him with only two shotgun shells left? Engage in conversation, trying to convince the man to leave?

"Hey chickey, what do you say? Do we have a deal? I walk up this fucking mountain and you just let me pass. All right?"

Oh gosh. What should she do?

Wait it out.

Of course. She relaxed as her confidence grew. Cole would remain silent. The man was incredibly patient.

She watched the boulder so hard it started to look like it moved. Then something did.

The man took a cautious step out, keeping his hand on the rock. She had an excellent view of him and she didn't like what she saw. His whole demeanor screamed selfishness and carelessness. As she stared, she could see that what she thought was a dirty appearance was actually a hundred tiny holes in his clothing and skin. He had definitely been hit by rocks and possibly by some of the shot. Blood marked his bare arms and face. Part of her shuddered that she'd done that, but half of her rejoiced. She was shocked to find herself so blood-thirsty.

He looked up the canyon wall, past where she hid, toward the rim. He studied the top, obviously hoping Angel would show herself.

Idiot. Angel was smarter than that. Hopefully, she'd kept on running. The jerk below didn't deserve her. What he deserved was life in prison, but Lacey doubted he'd get that.

Reaching into his vest pocket, he took out a flask. His head moved slightly as he scanned the entire wall, probably wondering if she was still there. Then he opened the flask and took a swig.

Only a coward finds courage in a bottle. Adriana's words to her one afternoon came back to her. If that was true, she might be able to play on that cowardice. She didn't want that man taking even one step closer to her position. Looking around, she scrambled back and picked up a hand-sized rock.

She brought it to her spy hole. She'd have to make sure he was looking down when she threw it.

He took another swig then capped the flask and returned it to his vest.

"Okay, gal, I'm coming up." He waited another minute before he took his hand off the boulder he'd hidden behind. He stepped forward. The shale slipped out from under his foot and he tottered as he tried to stay upright, losing more ground.

She couldn't have asked for a better position.

Minutes went by as the man struggled to make some headway. Giving up, he rested against his boulder and took out his flask again, before wiping the sweat from his brow with his vest.

Lacey let her hand on the rock relax. Maybe he would give up and go away. But her gut said he would come back if he did.

When he put the flask away, he studied the canyon wall again.

She watched, afraid to make a sound.

His lips moved up into a grin and her stomach dropped. Oh sugar. Now what?

He walked back behind his boulder.

Lacey held tighter to the rock in her hand and focused on where the man had disappeared. She listened intently, but couldn't hear anything past the pounding of her heart.

She caught movement out of the corner of her eye. A few rocks tumbled down the canyon about a quarter way up at the very end on the concave wall. She opened her mouth to breathe, her lungs too tight for her to take anything but shallow breaths as she stared at the place where the rocks fell. It was probably just a jackrabbit or even a desert mouse.

But even as she assured herself of that, her gut twisted. There was plenty of cover on that side of the canyon for him to hide behind. Unable to keep still another moment, she pulled her arm back and let the rock fly in that general direction.

The rock hit the ground ten yards below her and started numerous stones cascading down the slope. Some hit the area where she thought Ray was climbing, but not strong enough to cause an issue for him if he was there.

She could try to go down the other side, but she would

be in the open while he had cover, and it would leave Angel vulnerable. Ray could continue over the rim and find her horse.

No, this was her best stance against him for herself and Angel. If he couldn't make the rim, he couldn't get to her horse.

Holy sugar, she hadn't loaded another shell yet. Reaching into her pocket, she pulled out the two remaining shells. Loading both into the shotgun, she wiped her sweaty hand on her jeans before closing the chamber. If she had to shoot twice, the second would have to be to kill.

Turning back to her view, she scanned the rocky side of the canyon wall, all the way up to the ledge she was hiding behind. No sound could be heard and no movement seen.

Keeping her finger away from the trigger, she grasped the gun tightly. She scanned the entire side, focusing more closely on the area above where the loose stones had fallen. For all she knew, he was still behind the boulder at the bottom.

Then a noise to the right caught her attention and she held her breath to listen. She didn't hear anything else, but when she glimpsed brown leather moving between two boulders half way up the mountain, she released her breath and shivered. Fear fueled her movement as she took aim, closed her eyes and pulled the trigger.

Chapter Six

Lacey stumbled back a step with the recoil as it hit her shoulder awkwardly.

"Holy fucking Christ!"

At the sound of rocks falling, she opened her eyes to find Ray sliding down the side, the boulders he'd been sneaking behind having moved, leaving an opening she could see clearly through.

Once he'd found more cover, he yelled out. "Listen, girl, I just want the horse. I don't give a fuck about you!"

No kidding. All he cared about was himself. She didn't answer. Instead, she sat on the ground and forced herself to let go of the shotgun. How much longer were they going to play this game. She only had one more shell. What if she shot to kill him and missed? What if she didn't?

She licked her dry lips, wishing she had the bottle of water she'd stashed in Angel's saddlebags. Some Christmas Day this was turning out to be. She clasped her hands together, her nerves stretched as far as they could go. Why couldn't Cole come home early? She looked at her watch. It wasn't even ten-thirty yet. Once he got home, how long would it take him to find her?

She couldn't wait for Cole. She had to do something. Her choices were simple, hightail it up to the rim and try to outrun the man or kill him.

Unclasping her hands, she worked the soreness out of her fingers from holding the gun so tight. Some rancher's wife *she* would make. Her fingers were used to working a computer keyboard, not the trigger of a gun.

She rubbed her shoulder, only to find she had blood soaking through her sleeve. The recoil must have dislodged the stone. Cole had taught her how to hold the gun, but in her panic mode, she'd forgotten. There wasn't much she could do about the blood. Besides, it was already slowing.

She stood up, bringing the gun to her shoulder in the right position as she remembered her shooting lessons.

Line up the sight with the target. Take a breath, squeeze the trigger, and this time keep your eyes open. Lacey could hear Cole chuckle as he instructed her. She'd hit everything but the old trash can he'd set up as her target.

Keep her eyes open. Of course. She could do this. She froze. If she kept her eyes open, she would see the shell kill the man. She really didn't want to do that, but if he forced the issue, she had no choice. Finding her resolve cowering behind her appendix, she forced it out of hiding.

She could do this. She could do this. She could—what was that?

A single stone rolled down from the rim. "Angel?"

"I've been called many things, but never an angel."

Lacey swung the gun toward the husky voice, her finger found the trigger and she took a breath.

"Hey Cole, wake up."

Cole opened his eyes to find Clark standing above him. "What time is it?"

"It's a little after ten. How was the shift?"

Cole sat up and threw his legs over the side of the bed, but kept the blanket over his naked package. He looked past Clark. "It sucked. We had four fires."

The firefighter whistled. "Wow, that's got to be a record. When did you get in from the last one."

"About seven. Hey wait a minute, I thought you weren't coming in until noon."

Clark smiled. "That was the plan, but my kids were up before dawn too anxious to see what Santa brought them. Those little buggers went through their presents in record time and when they were done, it was more like 'daddy who?' So I figured since they were so into their new toys, I might as well come down and take my shift. I really appreciate you staying the extra hours."

Cole grabbed up his t-shirt. "I was happy to help."

"Well, I really appreciate it. If you ever need a favor, just let me know." Clark headed for the kitchen where the scent of bacon and sounds of the new shift talking filtered in.

Cole's stomach growled. Yeah, he better grab breakfast before heading home. It would be a long time until his mother's big dinner. Lacey didn't expect him until noontime anyway.

He'd showered after the last fire, too gritty to wait, so he threw on a clean pair of underwear and his jeans and strolled into the kitchen.

He waved off a few "good mornings" and "Merry Christmases" and went straight to the counter where scrambled eggs, bacon, home fries and three open boxes of donuts sat lined up, mostly pillaged already. Filling his plate, he sat at the table where the men asked about the fires, having heard tidbits from the last shift as they left for home.

After satisfying their curiosity and finishing his breakfast, he filled a travel mug with coffee and headed out to his truck.

He'd just turned the engine over when his cell phone rang. The number was too familiar. He glanced at the clock. It was only eleven, so he turned off the truck and answered his phone.

"Merry Christmas, mother."

"Merry Christmas, Cole. Are you on your way yet?" She sounded excited. No surprise there. His mother loved her parties.

"I'm still at work, but about to head home. I thought dinner isn't until three."

"Oh it is, but I was hoping you could come a bit early. The Kahnes are going to be here and their daughter Hailey. You remember her, right?"

Vaguely. He'd barely spoken three dozen words to the woman in the last three years, but she was rich, and therefore, at the forefront of his mother's mind. "Yes, I remember her."

"Oh good. She is looking forward to talking to you again."

Really? His mother knew he was engaged. She just preferred to forget. Another reason he needed Lacey to come. "I'm sure she and Lacey will have a lot in common." He had no idea if they would, but it was one way to stop his mother's machinations.

"Lacey? Oh right. Anyway, I just wanted to make sure you were still coming. Your aunt Bonnie said that Trace said that you might be staying at your grandparents, but I knew that couldn't be true because your grandparents are coming here and everyone is so looking forward to seeing you."

Since when? His mother was up to something. "And I'm looking forward to seeing 'everyone'. Is there anyone special you have coming this year, I mean besides the Town Manager and Hailey?"

"Oh yes, of course Rafael is coming, but also the Brittons, and Mr. Greyson, and Senator Rodriguez and just maybe the CEO of Hanson Enterprises. When I told her you are a fire fighter, I swear she almost fainted. She so wants to meet you."

Ah, now the pieces were clicking into place. He was her show-and-tell this year. That's why all the pressure. "It sounds like a great dinner party. I take it I can't wear jeans then."

"Oh honey, you can wear whatever you like. Do you think you could bring your helmet? I'm just betting there's a lady or two who would love to have her picture taken with you."

"Sorry Mother. I'm not allowed to bring that with me." He'd just have to remember to take it out of his back seat before heading down to Orson. There was no way he was posing for pictures. Show-and-tell was one thing. Pictures brought it to a level he refused to go.

"Oh, I see." From the sound of his mother's voice, she was not happy with him. "But you are coming. You wouldn't disappoint me again, right?"

He barely kept himself from crushing his phone in his hand. "No, I wouldn't. I'll see you this afternoon."

"That's my boy. Kisses." The line went silent.

Cole threw the phone on the seat and stared at the firehouse. As much as he wanted to tell his mother what she could do with her party, she was his mother and he would do what she asked. But he wouldn't like it. His idea of leaving after an hour was becoming much more enticing.

If only they could have a simple Christmas dinner, just him and Lacey, his brother and his parents. But his mother's Christmas dinner, which she had catered, had become known far and wide, at least in Pinal county. She was queen bee of her little hive and she needed to stay on her throne. He just didn't understand why. Why was it so important for her friends and neighbors—

Cole stilled. Just like the woman at the third fire last night. His mother was like her. Now he understood why he'd lost patience with the single mom with two kids. Like her, his mother had her priorities messed up. That's what Lacey had been trying to tell him, but he refused to listen. It didn't change the fact that his mother was his mother and he had to do what was right, even if she didn't, but he could definitely see why Lacey was so upset.

Turning over the engine, he put the truck into gear and headed onto Copper Win Road. Relief permeated his gut now that he understood why he and Lacey could not agree. He'd just been too close to the problem to see it through her eyes. Now that he did, he was sure they could come to some kind of agreement.

Shit, when did Christmas become such a problem?

~~*~~

Lacey gripped the shotgun, focusing her attention on keeping herself from pulling the trigger before it was time. She told herself it wasn't Angel's former owner, but the scared part of her refused to listen. That a voice came from a boulder on the same section of the wall as herself had her in a panic.

She could barely handle one man out to get her, she couldn't handle two. The husky voice hadn't sworn, so it wasn't him, but it could be someone working with him.

Yeah, right, Lacey. He just called on his cell phone in a place with no cell phone service whatsoever and asked one of his buddies to drop down from the rim without making any noise.

She licked her dry lips. Maybe her lack of water was causing her to hallucinate. Could a person hallucinate a sound?

"Are you going to put that thing down so I can come out, or are we going stay in this position all day?"

Her finger on the trigger tightened, but she caught herself just in time. "Who are you?"

"I'm Whisper."

Huh? Fighting her panic, Lacey stood straighter. She needed whoever it was to think she was confident. "Step forward, slowly."

She kept the gun level, her finger on the trigger, but when a tall woman with long, straight black hair dressed in a flannel shirt and jeans unfolded herself from behind a short rock, Lacey lowered the gun.

"You shouldn't lower your gun until you're sure I'm not a threat."

Lacey raised it again, her gaze drawn to the woman's high cheekbones and steel gray eyes. "Why are you here?"

The woman pointed toward the rim. "I heard the shots from my trailer. Figured I probably should find out if it was tourists hunting or something else. From the way you shot at that man trying to crawl up this canyon, my guess is you're not hunting."

Lacey shook her head. "You live up there? I didn't think there were houses for miles around."

"There aren't." The woman stepped forward and placed her hand on the barrel of the gun and lowered it. "I don't like neighbors, so I set my trailer up there. So what's going on here?"

Lacey studied the woman who had to hunch over a bit to keep from being seen over the boulder cover Lacey could walk behind. She had a tan woven shoulder bag that didn't close and she wore a very worn brown leather cowboy hat. There really was nothing to lose by telling her. Lacey felt better just having the strange woman show up.

"Wait." She moved to her crack and looked below. "Crap, I don't know where he went."

The woman moved to another spot and peered down the canyon. "He's behind the boulder about a quarter way up on this side."

Lacey looked at the boulder but couldn't see anything. "Are you sure?"

The woman looked irritated. "Yes, I'm sure."

Something about her demeanor gave Lacey confidence in her. "My name is Lacey Winters." She held out her hand.

The woman shook. "I'm Whisper Adams." Her eyes narrowed. "So now that we got that out of the way, want to tell me what's going on?"

Okay, so being nice wasn't one of the woman's strong points. "The man down there is trying to steal back his horse. It was taken from him after he beat it within inches of her life. My fiancé nursed her back to health and this lowlife came here on Christmas day expecting no one to be here and instead found me on Angel."

She paused and looked up at the rim. "Have you seen a white horse with scars and a trail saddle?"

Whisper hesitated, but then she nodded.

Lacey's heart beat easier. "Oh, good. She's afraid of people, especially men. I hope I can find her when this is over."

The sound of rock falling caused them both to look out at the hillside. Ray scrambled behind another boulder, much closer than before. Lacey leaned toward Whisper. "You don't happen to have a gun, do you? I only have one shell left."

Whisper reached into her waistband and pulled out a handgun. "I don't go anywhere without Sal. My rifle is up there though. I couldn't climb down here with it and remain unnoticed."

Before Lacey, could move, the woman stood, aimed and shot.

"Fucking bitch! I'm bleeding!" More grumbling came from below, but Lacey was too stunned to pay attention to it.

Whisper sat down. "I couldn't get much of him. The bastard is well hidden." She shrugged. "At least he'll be limping around the canyon. That will make his movements awkward and give me another opportunity to kill him."

Lacey grabbed Whisper's arm. "We can't kill him."

The strange woman stared at her as if she was some Native American ghost risen from the ground. "Why not?"

"It's wrong."

Whisper's grey eyes turned to ice. "No, what he did to that horse is wrong. That's torture. I'm offering him a quick death."

Lacey let go, not a little nervous now. "I completely agree with you, but we can't take the law into our own hands."

"Yeah, I guess you right." Whisper sighed. "If I killed him I'd have to move again and I like where we are now. Too bad.

The earth is better off without his kind around." She studied Lacey. "So what's the plan? Injure him so he can't shoot, then get you back home. I'm assuming you live somewhere out here."

Lacey relaxed a little, glad Whisper had relented, but the idea of shooting Ray until he couldn't return fire had her stomach feeling queasy. Based on Whisper's facial expression, she looked forward to torturing him.

"I do live here. Actually, I think I'm still on our property."

Whisper raised her eyebrow. "I don't see any house. You must own a lot of land."

"It's not mine. It's Cole's and his grandparents. They operate a horse rescue ranch. That's why we have Angel. So far though, I've been the only one she would let ride her. I'm glad I went for a ride while waiting for Cole to get home or that man below us might have stolen her." She glanced down at her watch. It was only quarter after eleven. "My finance won't be home until noon. Even then, he won't know where to look for me."

"Then I guess I'll have to stay with you until he gets here. Unless our piece of trash decides to show a bit more of himself and I can take his gun from him. Since you only have one shell left, that won't do enough damage to make it safe to leave here." Whisper looked skeptically at her. "Or I could just leave if you don't like my company."

Something flashed in Whisper's eyes before she looked down, her hand gripping her gun tighter. Lacey's heart reacted. This woman had more to her than met the eye, and after a year of working at Poker Flat Nudist Resort where her boss hired only those who needed a second chance, Lacey recognized a damaged person hiding a good heart.

She smiled at the woman for the first time and laid her

hand on hers. "I'm thrilled to have your company. I don't know what I would have done without you. Please stay."

Whisper didn't look up, but the tension in her shoulders eased a bit. "I guess I can wait with you a little longer. If worse comes to worse and your man comes back in an hour, my guess is he'll be hightailing it out here looking for you." Whisper snorted. "After all, it *is* Christmas."

Oh boy, she wanted to know a lot more about Whisper. There was so much in her attitude that screamed she'd been hurt.

Rocks sliding down the hill caught their attention and they both moved to their view holes. Whisper raised her gun and shot.

"Ow! You fucking cunt! That's it!"

"Get down." Whisper threw herself at her.

<h1 style="text-align:center">Chapter Seven</h1>

Cole turned down the dirt road that led to the Last Chance Ranch. He hoped that he and Lacey could talk about the Christmas dinner issue calmly now. He didn't like that they'd gone more than a day without speaking. It was like wearing jeans that didn't fit right. It was bearable, but downright uncomfortable.

He glanced at the dashboard on the truck. It was only eleven. Maybe they could take a ride out to their partial house. That always put them in a good mood. Dreaming of their life together as man and wife would definitely help. That's what he would do. Suggest a ride to the house.

As Cole turned off the dirt road and under the ranch sign, he took in the truck and horse trailer parked on the ranch and his pulse rate increased. Either it was a horse in need or someone had come to buy one of his horses. Stopping his truck next to the trailer, he turned it off and jumped out. He was down to only six horses, two of which couldn't be sold, so if there was another horse, he had room. The question would be, how bad was it?

There was no horse inside the trailer, so he strode to the barn. Relief that there was no new horse stabled there had him turning and striding to the house. They must have a buyer then.

Excitement coursed through him. It happened every time one of his horses went to a new home. He wouldn't let just anyone take a horse, and trailer or no trailer, he wasn't letting any of them go today until he inspected where they were headed. He always made sure the new home was well equipped to handle one of his damaged beauties.

He took the steps two at a time and threw open the front door. After walking into the living room, he strode through the kitchen, but no one was there. "Lacey!" He yelled as he walked upstairs. Where was she? Where was the buyer?

Not finding her there, he came downstairs and strode back outside to check the corral. Only Sampson and Lightyear should be there. Sampson couldn't be sold and they were still working with Lightyear. He couldn't be touched around his face which made putting the bridle on tricky. He'd been stung over a hundred times by bees and his face was very sensitive, either that or he imagined it was. As Cole came within sight of the corral, it was clear no one was there.

What the hell? "Lacey!"

Still no answer. He swung back to the area of the dirt yard where they all parked. Lacey's crossover vehicle sat there. Where was she and the owner of the trailer? His muscles tensed as his mind skittered toward crime scene-like possibilities.

Sprinting to the truck with the trailer, he threw open the unlocked door and rifled through the glove compartment for a registration.

Ray Norton.

Cole's blood ran cold. "Lacey!" He jumped up into the bed of his truck to get a better look around, but couldn't see anyone. His heart beat erratically as a hundred scenarios played out in his mind. Ray kidnapping her and taking her into the desert to have his revenge was front and center.

Cole whipped out his cell phone. He didn't give a rat's ass if he was panicking or if it was Christmas. Nothing was more important than Lacey. He dialed Detective Sean Anderson. "I just got home. Ray Norton is at my ranch and I can't find him or Lacey."

"Whoa, hold on, Cole. Remind me who Ray is?"

"The bastard I'm testifying against in an animal abuse case."

"Shit. Okay, don't do anything until I get there."

Cole froze at the sound of a distant gunshot, his heart squeezing his chest so tight he couldn't breathe.

"Cole, did you hear me? Cole?"

Finally, he forced air through his lungs." I just heard shots. I'm heading out."

"I'll call for back-up. I'm on my way."

Cole stuffed his phone in his back pocket and ran into the house. Going to the gun case, he grabbed a rifle.

The shotgun was missing.

Did that mean Lacey had it or had Ray taken it? Lacey always used the shotgun because her aim wasn't good. He had to hope she had the gun with her. He took a box of twenty bullets and stopped by the front door to get the ATV key.

Shit, it was gone. Billy better have left it in the vehicle. Throwing the front door open, he ran for the barn.

"Fuck." There was no ATV. Did Lacey use it to get away from Ray? He had to get to her.

He pulled a bridle from the tack room and looked around the stalls before remembering Sampson was outside. "Cole, you need to keep your head on straight." As he started out, he glanced back at Angel's stall. Empty. Pieces fell into place.

He ran for the corral. Ray had planned to steal Angel back, but Lacey took her first. That meant Ray had the ATV and was hot on her trail.

"Come on, buddy. I know you're not used to bareback, but every second counts." Once he had the bridal on, he vaulted onto Sampson's back and raced them through the open gate. He hoped Lightyear stayed nearby, but he refused to lose the seconds that it would take to close the gate. He had to get to Lacey fast.

As he and Sampson approached his partially built house, he slowed to study the tracks. Sampson pranced, anxious to keep running. Luckily, it wasn't hard to pick up the trail. Ray didn't even attempt to hide where he was going, barreling through plant life like he mauled horses.

Another gunshot echoed off the walls of the valley. If he had to go by sound alone, he'd never find her in time, but the tire tracks were clear. Kicking the more than willing Sampson into a gallop, he focused on the trail, not willing to lose one precious second.

His and Lacey's last argument came unbidden to his mind. All over his mother's stupid party. And like an idiot, he'd taken insult, storming off and leaving her alone in the barn. She was the most precious thing in his life. He should have stayed and talked it out, even argued some more. Instead, it hung between them for more than a day and now… Cole swallowed hard, trying to keep the images at bay of Lacey lying on the desert floor, blood seeping from a wound, slowly feeding the dry earth.

He pushed Sampson, the underbrush passing by in a blur. At one point he had to stop and backtrack to catch the trail again. He kept Sampson at a lope after that so he could follow the tracks. If they went too fast, he'd lose them again. He couldn't afford another delay.

The tracks veered off and he knew where they led. "Hold on, Lacey. I'm coming."

Three successive gunshots rang out, chilling Cole to the bone. His panic exploded inside him at the sound.

~~*~~

Lacey hadn't even hit the ground before three shots were fired at the boulders they hid behind. Stones flew, one catching her in the leg, another hitting her in the forehead. She bit her lip to keep from crying out.

Whisper rolled off her and crouched, facing the sculpted monoliths that served as their cover. "That bastard."

A large chunk had been blown away where they'd been standing. The two of them were forced behind one section of rock now.

At the look on Whisper's face, Lacey's blood ran cold. "Whisper, what are you thinking?"

"Hey, an eye for an eye." She got down on her stomach and moved to the hole. Lifting her gun above the edge, she shot.

Lacey heard stone falling and Whisper looked over the break in their cover and aimed this time.

"Jesus fucking Christ." The rock cascade grew louder and Lacey moved next to Whisper to see that she'd shot Ray in his leg. He slid down the sidewall, only stopping when he hit a cactus.

Whisper lowered her head to aim and shoot again.

Lacey pulled her arm. "No. Stop."

The woman's irritated glare didn't intimidate Lacey in the least. She'd faced worse from the people in her own town when they thought she was an arsonist.

The woman scowled. "He's still moving. I thought you wanted me to wound him until he couldn't hurt you."

"No, that was your idea."

Whisper's eyebrows rose before she looked away. "Whatever."

Lacey dared a quick peek through the hole. Ray dragged his leg as he awkwardly scrambled to find cover. Movement beyond him caught her eye. "Cole." He was on Sampson and galloping toward her faster than a dust devil spun.

She looked at Whisper who was busy reloading her gun. "Cole's here. He's found us." Tears gathered in her eyes as relief washed through her.

Whisper took a look through the opening. "So he is. I guess you'll be okay now. Just as well, I need to get back to my uncle."

Lacey grabbed Whisper's arm as she started to crawl away. "Wait. Thank you."

The woman looked back at her. "Just make sure that worthless piece of shit gets put behind bars for a long time."

She nodded and let go. Whisper crawled beneath the opening, and then disappeared among some boulders.

Lacey carefully sidled up to the new break in the wall and looked to find Cole. Her heart pounded the breath from her at the sight. Cole galloped furiously toward the canyon wall, but Ray leaned against a boulder, his arm crossed in front of him as he aimed his gun at Cole.

Rage like she'd never experienced filled her body. In one quick motion, she grabbed the shotgun and aimed at the man's back. Taking the breath Cole told her to, she pulled the trigger, keeping her eyes open.

"Argh!" The man went down as if someone had pushed him from behind and stone flew everywhere.

Cole pulled up and jumped from his horse, a rifle in his hand as he ran to crouch behind some sagebrush. "Lacey!"

She stood in front of the hole and waved. "Up here!"

"Stay there."

She nodded and sagged to the ground with relief. She dropped the useless gun on the ground then started to shake. Had she killed him? He may deserve to die, but she didn't want to be the one who did it.

As her eyes filled with tears, she brought her knees to her chest and rested her face on her jeans. She didn't want to be a killer. It was bad enough being accused of arson, but what if she was accused of murder?

He started it. She wiped her eyes at the childish thought. The fact was, he started shooting at her. She was only protecting herself and Angel. She fisted her hands as she looked above her. Where was her horse?

"Lacey?"

She looked to her side to find Cole standing there. "Oh Cole." She threw herself into the comfort of his large arms.

"God Lacey, I thought I'd lost you." He crushed her to him, making it difficult to breathe, but she didn't care. His quick heartbeat beneath her cheek made her shallow pants worth it. He was warm, alive and…shaking? She squeezed him as tight as she could, his hard body making her feel safe again.

He leaned her back and stared at her face. "You're bleeding." He lightly ran his finger across her forehead.

She'd completely forgotten about the stone hitting her there. "It was just a rock that ricocheted. I think I got one in my leg too. Oh sugar, I hope it didn't tear my lingerie."

Cole's mouth quirked up. "You have lingerie on your leg."

She gave him a devious smile. "As a matter of fact, I do. It's part of your Christmas present."

"Shit woman, you being alive is Christmas present enough for me." He pulled her close again as if he couldn't quite believe she was still breathing. "Christ Lacey." His voice sounded gravelly. "When I discovered that bastard was here and you and Angel missing, my heart froze and then the gunshots…fuck, I couldn't lose you again, ever." He rubbed her back as if reassuring himself she was still alive.

"Wait." His arms stilled and he peered at her left arm. "God woman, you've got blood all over you."

She twisted to look at her injury. "That's what happens when you trade gunfire on a stone hillside."

The sound of sirens echoed against the canyon walls.

She stiffened. Would they take her away? On Christmas? She didn't want to know, but she had to. She didn't dare look at Cole, but her voice shook "D-D-id I kill him?"

Cole's chuckle vibrated his body and she looked up. "What?" Irritation burned through her that he could find her funny. "It's a legitimate question."

"Ah Lacey. You did quite a bit of damage, but no, you didn't kill him. Your shot sprayed and got some in his ass along with a few stones, but it wasn't a direct hit, at least, not that shot."

"Oh. I did everything you taught me." She let her shoulders

sag. "Just as well. I really was trying to shoot him. He was about to shoot you."

"I noticed." He placed his hands on her shoulders. "I was so hell bent to get to you, I forgot about Ray. When he stood up with that gun, I was just about to jump off Sampson's back, but you took care of that threat for me." He studied her. "When I tied the man up, I noticed he was winged by one shot and I think his shin bone may have been shattered by another. Did you bring a handgun too?"

She shook her head. "No. I had help."

"From who?"

Her gut said Whisper wouldn't want to get involved. She certainly didn't seem excited about helping and didn't leave any warm fuzzies behind when she left.

"Lacey. What is it?"

"I don't think she would want to talk to the police."

"She?" Cole looked off into the distance. "I don't think she'll have much choice. Where is she?"

She shrugged. "I don't know. When you arrived, she left."

Cole studied her. "Left where?"

She pointed up. "The same way Angel went. Can we go find her now?"

"Absolutely not. I'm taking you home and getting you bandaged up. Angel will find her way. She knows where her food is."

"Hey, Cole!" Detective Anderson looked up at them. "Is this your animal abuser?"

"Yes. He probably needs an ambulance."

Sean nodded. "Is this your handy work?"

He looked at her and smiled. "Nope. I have one tough lady."

The detective whistled. "That's one way of looking at it. I'll take care of this trash, but I'll need to talk to you two."

"Is tomorrow soon enough?"

"Afraid not. This guy has really made a mess of my Christmas."

Cole turned back to her and squeezed her tight again. "You ready to head down? It's pretty slippery. How'd you get up here in the first place?"

Her heart constricted. "Angel."

He cupped her face in his hands. "We may have to start calling her Guardian Angel after this."

"We need to climb up there and check to see if we can see her." She started to shake as the adrenaline she'd been functioning on the last couple hours slipped away, leaving her exhausted and worried. "I need to know she's okay as much as you needed to know I was okay." Tears started down her face as what little control she had disintegrated. "I have to know."

She stared into his green gaze, willing him to agree.

Cole's indecision flashed across his face as his gaze flickered over her. She jumped on it. "Please, Cole."

"Ah Lacey. I'm so damn happy you're alive. I can't stand to see you so upset." He gently brushed away her tears. "All I want to do is get you home where it's safe, but I can see that will have to wait. But if we can't find her or her tracks right away, you agree to go home and let me take care of you and send Trace out here to find Angel when he gets home. Okay?"

She smiled and wiped away the rest of her tears. "Okay."

Hope rose strong, and she headed up the few feet of gravel as fast as she could. When her head cleared the rim, she halted. "Angel!" Her heart filled with joy. She scrambled up the rest of the way, happy when Cole put his hand on her butt and boosted her up over the top.

She ran to Angel and hugged her. "Oh sweetie, I'm so glad you stayed nearby." Her tears started again, but this time they were happy tears.

"I'm not so sure she did."

Lacey looked back at Cole. "What do you mean?"

He walked slowly toward her and leaned over to untie the reins from the Joshua tree next to the horse. "Someone tied the horse here."

"Whisper."

"Why do I need to whisper?"

Lacey giggled. "No, Whisper is the name of the woman who stayed with me and shot at Ray. She's not going to get in trouble, is she? I only had one shotgun shell left to keep him away."

Cole moved toward her and grabbed her to him again. "Shit, Lacey, now your repeating yourself. You should have never been in such a position." He held her tight, his eyes tearing up as he gazed at her. "You mean more to me than anything."

She wrapped her arms around his neck. "And you mean more to me than anything. That's why I shot at Ray. If he'd hurt you, I would have made him regret it for the rest of his life. Let's go home."

He nodded just before his lips claimed hers in a possessive kiss that had her knees weakening. When he finally broke away, she held on to him. "Okay, now you need to give me a minute."

Pride infused his voice. "Take all the time you need."

She grimaced at him, her nerves completely frazzled and tired.

He studied the landscape riddled with Joshua trees. "Where did this woman named Whisper come from?"

The change in topic took her a moment. "I don't know. She said she lived up here somewhere and heard the first two shots."

Cole pulled her against him again. "Can you stop talking about gunshots until we get home? My stomach is still a mess from finding you gone and Ray Norton's truck and trailer parked in our yard."

Her throat closed at the thought of what Cole must have envisioned. She would have gone into major panic. She nodded.

"Good. Then let's go home."

Chapter Eight

Cole stood on the front porch and watched as Detective Sean Anderson started his car and headed down the dirt driveway. Sean was a good man even if he did make Cole leave the house when he became upset while Lacey explained what happened.

At first he just paced across the dusty yard, visions of killing Ray Norton with his bare hands sustaining his anger. It was only when one of the horses neighed that he was able to break away from his one-track daydream and do something more productive.

The warmed up meal from Selma that featured tamales, had not only tasted delicious but also served as a release after the morning's events. The peppermint stick ice cream finished everything off in a festive way. He was glad he'd invited Sean to stay.

The mystery woman, Whisper, made the event a whole lot more complicated, but Cole wasn't about to complain about that. According to Lacey, the woman saved her life. He didn't envy Sean his task of getting the woman's side of the story. First, he'd have to discover where she lived.

That was his biggest concern about Whisper. Where she lived. That was Williams/Hatcher property over the canyon rim and if she was on it, he could have a squatter issue on his hands.

The best result of Lacey's harrowing experience was that Ray's charges had increased to shooting with the intent to kill. Even if a good prosecutor couldn't get that to stick, there were plenty of other charges that would keep him behind bars for a long time to come.

As Sean's taillights faded, Cole turned and headed back into the house. The sun was already past its zenith on Christmas and he hadn't spent much time with Lacey all day.

His phone, hooked to his jeans, vibrated again. He pulled it off and looked at the number. Same one as the last eight calls. He dropped it on the love seat where it wouldn't disturb him. His mother could wait. He grinned. That was the right thing to do.

He strode into the kitchen where he found Lacey loading the dishes into the bottom tray of the dishwasher. Her enticingly rounded ass in a clean pair of faded blue jeans had his body taking notice.

Cole silently moved up behind her and pulled her hips against his growing erection.

"Oh my." Lacey wiggled her ass against him, making him harder.

He reached down and cupped her breasts in his hands, pulling her upright against him, the need to have her close too much to resist, even if her red button-down shirt and his denim one was still between them. He lowered his head and licked the edge of her ear. "I want you."

Her body shivered against him, exactly the response he'd hoped for.

Licking down along her neck, he found the spot where her pulse beat hard and latched onto it with his mouth, sucking hard. A hickey may be very high school, but he wanted to mark her, brand her as his. Somehow it seemed like the way to stave off the panic of almost losing her.

She leaned her head away, allowing him full access as her heartbeat sped up beneath his tongue.

He released her skin for an instant and licked the spot before sucking again, instinct driving him on.

Suddenly, Lacey leaned forward and brought her shoulder toward her head. "Cole, wait."

He reluctantly released his mouth, but he continued to hold her tight. "What is it?"

"Look. It's three o'clock. We were supposed to be at your mother's by now. What will she say when we arrive two hours late?"

He loosened his arms but didn't release her. "We?"

She turned in his embrace, but didn't actually look at him. Instead, she smoothed her hand over the fire department insignia on his t-shirt. "Yes, well, I did a lot of thinking on that canyon wall."

He swallowed his rage as the band-aid on her forehead reminded him of her danger. "You mean while being shot at, you had time to think?"

She nodded but still didn't look at him. "I did. I realized your parents may not be as bad as I had made them out to be in my own mind."

"You mean they aren't monsters?"

Her gaze snapped to his. "I never said that. You did."

She was right. He grimaced. "Maybe because deep down that's what I believed. I didn't realize it until I was on my way home, but my mother really does have her priorities screwed up. It took you, plus a misguided woman whose house was on fire, and my slow brain, to finally figure it out."

Lacey rested her hands on his shoulders. "But she's not a monster. Ray Norton is a monster."

Cole's heart constricted with anger and fear all over again. He squeezed Lacey to him. "You're right. And I almost lost you to him which is why I'm spending the rest of Christmas day alone with you…preferably naked."

She moved her hands to around his neck and pressed her breasts against his chest. "Maybe not completely naked." The sultry gleam in her eyes had his cock getting hard again.

"Am I to understand that my Racy Lacey may have a Christmas surprise for me?"

She wiggled her eyebrows. "I guess you'll have to discover that for yourself."

"That's exactly what I plan to do." Without another word, he scooped her into his arms and strode out of the house.

"Cole, what are you doing?"

He grinned. "I'm taking you out to the barn. I figure since you started Christmas with Angel, we should continue it there."

She kissed his cheek. "I think that's a wonderful idea."

With Lacey still in his arms he stopped in front of Angel's stall.

Lacey called the horse, but it just stood and looked at them as if they were crazy. "I think she is happy to have fresh food and water."

He remained there, watching the rescue horse as she lowered her head and took some hay into her mouth. His heart filled with contentment. He had a challenging career, a mission that fulfilled him, and the love of his life. He couldn't ask for anything more.

Lacey's featherlight kiss on his neck sent a perfect peace flooding through his body. He stepped back and strode to their special Christmas stall. Letting Lacey's feet touch the ground, he held her, looking into her eyes. "I love you."

She smiled. "I love you too."

A need to make her his forever filled him. "Let's get married."

She laughed. "I think this ring on my finger means you already asked me that and I said yes."

He grinned, unable to help it at the sight of her laughter. "No, I mean now. Well, not today, but right away. Nothing big. Just here with our family. Hell, even at our unfinished house with just a minister and two witnesses. I don't care, just soon. I want to call you my wife. How about New Year's?"

She stilled. He could see her brain thinking of details, maybe even calculating the expense. He didn't want her to think with her head but with her heart.

Quickly, he lowered his head and kissed her lips, nudging his way between them to possess her mouth. His tongue entwined with hers, tasting the lingering flavor of peppermint from the ice cream. She moaned and her body melted against him. His cock grew hard and he broke the kiss.

"What do you say? Will you marry me on New Year's?"

Lacey opened her eyes and the love in her gaze fed his need. She smiled wide, her eyes sparkling. "Yes. I'd love to start off next year as your wife."

He whipped his hat into the air. "Yeehaw!"

She laughed. "Oh, I have an idea."

Cole's stomach tightened with anticipation at the gleam

in Lacey's eye. "About the honeymoon?" He winked, even as his mind raced to figure out how many vacation days he could wiggle out of his captain on such short notice.

Lacey's grin was pure mischief. "We can definitely discuss that, but I was thinking about the actual wedding."

"Yes." He raised an eyebrow and pulled his head back slightly. This was a new side of his wife-to-be that he'd never seen.

"Let's invite our parents to the ranch for a New Year's Eve party. Then after the clock strikes twelve, surprise everyone by getting married."

Cole felt his jaw drop open. His mother would be furious with them for not coming to her Christmas party. She probably wouldn't even come if they invited her to a party they held. She was like that. If she heard they had married without her present, she would…

Lacey's smile faltered. "You don't like it?"

The possible scenarios started to converge. His mother does come and brings the Hailey woman only to be surprised by the wedding. Or his mother sends his father and is in tears when she finds out they married but dad tells her it's her own fault. He grinned. "Are you kidding? I love it! A surprise wedding. Lacey you are a genius." He lowered his head and treated himself to another taste of her lips.

She ended the kiss quickly. "So now that we've settled that, are you ready to unwrap your Christmas present?"

His disappointment over the short kiss was forgotten as his whole body tensed. "More than ready."

She pulled out of his embrace. "Good, because I have a Christmas stocking just for you."

He cooled, unable to hide his disappointment. "A Christmas stocking?'

Lacey laughed again. "Yes. It's a Christmas *body* stocking." She unbuttoned her top button and licked her lips.

He swallowed as his mind conjured sexy images of Lacey, but as she slowly undressed for him, they were all replaced by the sexual reality of his soon-to-be wife. With his cock rigid and his heart full, he watched, his gaze never leaving each piece of red covered or uncovered flesh she revealed.

Yup, he was the luckiest man in the world.

"You know, I just sat down."

Faust's ear twitched, but otherwise he didn't move.

"Okay, already." She really didn't mind getting up, but she didn't want him to know that. She was actually pleased to see he was still alive. He hadn't been around for a few days. Moving slowly, she stood then walked back to the trailer to open a side compartment that housed a mini-refrigerator. She imagined it was originally designed for tailgating or partying, but she used it for much more important reasons. She pulled out the meat scraps she'd been saving.

Returning to Faust, she held the plate out. "You want to check and make sure it's good?"

He stood, afraid to move forward but in need of food. Finally, he sniffed the air about a foot from the plate. When he reached his paw to topple it, she threw the scraps a few feet away. Faust bounded onto the pile and started wolfing it down.

Hmm, could a coyote "wolf" or did he "coyote" it down? She grinned and resumed her seat, setting the empty dish on the ground and lifting her beer to rest it on the arm of the chair.

She watched the coyote eat until every tiny scrap was gone before it trotted back toward her and sat.

"Sorry, Faust. That's all I have."

The coyote stared at her a minute then lay down on his haunches with his paws in front and lowered his head.

That was what she should do soon as well. She took a swig of beer, her mind drifting back to Lacey. Was she cuddled up with her cowboy all safe and snug now? Probably. Whisper didn't need a man. When she was young, she'd had Uncle Joey to keep the vultures at bay, but she soon helped with the chore of evasion and survival. Now she protected him.

The question that had bothered her all afternoon came to the fore. How far had Lacey ridden from her home to end up so close to their camp? Whisper really didn't want to move again, not when she had everyone in town trained. But if Lacey and her man were close by, that would be a problem.

Whisper tipped her head back as she swallowed the last of the beer. It would behoove her to take a walk tomorrow morning and discover exactly how close her nearest neighbor was. Despite what she wanted, it may just be time to move again.

"Faust, I'm heading to bed." She rose slowly, her empty bottle in hand.

The coyote opened its eyes and lifted its head.

"Be a good coyote and keep an eye on the place, will ya?"

Faust laid his head back down and watched her.

"Good boy. Have a good night." With that, she turned toward the trailer and quietly entered.

The End

Trace's Trouble

BY

LEXI POST

Trace's Trouble
Last Chance Series, Book 2

By Lexi Post

Cowboy Trace Williams thought he had trouble when his wife served him with divorce papers, forcing him to move to his cousin's horse rescue ranch. But that was nothing compared to handling the female squatter he's supposed to evict from Last Chance Ranch. Though she's a crack shot and has no use for politeness or subtlety, her ability to communicate with animals has him seeking her out on behalf of the ranch…and himself.

Whisper Adams lives off the grid. She cares for her invalid uncle and watches over the wildlife that finds her. The animals are more trustworthy than the people she's encountered. So when a hard-bodied, easy going cowboy arrives at her trailer and causes her heart to race, she's anxious for him to leave, until he asks for her help at the ranch.

Since they end up together more often than she prefers, Whisper doesn't deny her attraction to Trace, who introduces her to new experiences, from riding horses to an erotic night in bed. But mixing with people, any people, opens her to new threats. This relationship might cost Trace his heart, but it could very well cost Whisper her life.

Trace's Trouble was inspired by Bret Harte's short story, "Miggles," first published sometime between 1868 and 1872. In Harte's story, the stagecoach can't cross the swollen river because the bridge is out. Therefore, the passengers seek shelter at Miggles' house.

Miggles is a former prostitute who sold her saloon and bought a place where she could take care of Jim, one of her dying clients, who sits unresponsive in the living room. The six men from the coach find Miggles incredibly attractive and rush to help her whenever she asks. During dinner, her watch dog makes himself known outside so she offers to introduce him to everyone, but when she opens the door, they discover her watch dog is a half-grown bear. The two ladies in the party decide by then that Miggles is beneath them.

Miggles provides dinner for everyone, but when it's time for bed and she shows the women to her room, they make Miggles feel unwelcome, so she sleeps at the foot of her patient in the living room where the men have bedded down. The following morning, she is gone and the men say goodbye to Jim, but linger in the hopes of seeing Miggles one more time. Finally, they board the stagecoach and leave.

On their way down the road, the coachman pulls up on the horses suddenly because on the crest of a nearby hill, is Miggles, her hair blowing in the wind and smiling as she waves a white handkerchief goodbye. When the stage stops at the next town, the men file into the local saloon, get a drink and the judge among them makes a toast to Miggles.

But what if Miggles was an outsider for a different reason, yet she still cared for an older invalid man and got along well with nature's creatures? Could she find acceptance in today's society if she found the right man? Would he delve beneath appearances or would he make an erroneous judgement about such a unique woman?

Chapter One

"**S**top right there unless you'd like your head blown off."

At the husky voice, Trace froze, bringing Lightyear to a halt as his gaze swung to the barrel of a rifle barely visible behind the single boulder amidst the Joshua trees and sagebrush. There wasn't supposed to be anyone out here except a woman with a trailer, and so far he'd seen neither. Drug dealers? Coyotes? His right hand itched to grasp his rifle from its scabbard attached to Lightyear's saddle.

He studied the area past the rock. Were there more? There was no other place to hide so completely. He didn't see anyone else. One delinquent he could handle. "Just out for a ride." He smiled crookedly. "Enjoying the day."

"Then turn around and enjoy the day somewhere else." The voice came again, but the rifle barrel remained steady. Whoever held that gun was in his element.

Shit. First he's tasked with doing Cole's dirty work, and then he has to come across some territorial drifter. He frowned at his remembered conversation with Cole.

"You want me to do what?" He tipped his cowboy hat up to stare

at his cousin as if he'd just sprouted six legs and a long, poisonous tail.

Cole had the decency to look uncomfortable and lowered his leg from the rail of the training corral. "I don't have a choice. If she's been up there too long she could claim the land as hers under Arizona squatter laws. This Whisper woman needs to move her trailer off our land. You know the boundaries. She probably won't have to move very far. She's up over the rim of the north canyon."

Trace had little sympathy for the opposite sex at the moment, including his soon-to-be ex-wife, but he couldn't see kicking the woman off their land when she'd just saved Lacey's life. Didn't really speak of gratefulness to him. "Does Lacey agree with you?"

Cole started to turn. "It doesn't matter. It's what needs to be done."

Trace stepped in front of his cousin, not the least bit intimidated by Cole's scowl. "You can at least wait until after New Year's. Shit, with this kind of 'thank you,' you'll be lucky if the woman doesn't seek us out and kill us all in our beds."

"Just do it." His cousin stepped around him and strode toward the house.

There was no way this scenario was going to go well for Cole and possibly for the rest of them. To hear Lacey talk about Whisper, the woman walked on water, able to shoot a flower bud on a saguaro cactus from a half mile away.

Trace pulled off his hat and wiped the sweat from his forehead with his bandana then stuffed it back in his pocket and lowered his Stetson. He liked Lacey. She seemed to be a decent woman, one of the few left. She was going to be fit to be tied.

He grinned. Now that was something he'd like to see. It would serve Cole right for being so ungrateful and sending him to do the dirty work. Trace turned back toward the corral to find Lightyear, the mahogany-colored bay with black points that he liked to ride, standing near him.

Ignoring the horse's face, he patted its withers. "I guess you and I are going to cause some trouble, boy."

The horse shook its head to dislodge a fly, but Trace chuckled. "No, not for us, but for your righteous owner." He entered the corral and carefully bridled Lightyear with a unique technique he'd developed. The horse was far too sensitive around his face, thanks to an encounter with a traveling swarm of bees.

Lightyear's face had swelled so much he could barely breathe. His owner had left him for dead, but a caring neighbor had called animal welfare. Cole and his vet had nursed the poor horse back to health over a year ago, but it still couldn't stand having its face touched.

Once Trace had the bridle in place, he added the saddle blanket, saddle and cinched the strap. Patting the horse on his side one more time, he mounted.

"Let's get this over with, buddy." Trace kicked Lightyear into a trot and they headed out to the canyon. His cousin had a big heart for horses, but when it came to people who didn't toe the line, he had no give at all.

Too bad Trace hadn't had the same strict rules for right and wrong as Cole had. Instead, he'd been blinded by a love that wasn't reciprocated and would soon lose everything he'd worked so hard for. He should have known. He would never get involved with a down-on-her-luck woman again.

In the meantime, he had a roof over his head and a job he enjoyed. Most of the time.

Now wasn't one of those times.

"Today would be nice. I got better things to do than shoot and bury trespassers. Turn your fancy ass around and get out of here." Though the voice definitely sounded irritated now, he smiled inside at the man's confidence.

Careful to keep his hands still, Trace cocked his head.

"Then we have a problem. You see, this is my cousin's land and I'm not the one trespassing."

After a minute or two of no response, but with the rifle barrel still steady, Trace slowly moved his right hand down by his leg. The problem was, even if he did get to the rifle, he was a sitting duck up on Lightyear.

"Who's this supposed cousin?"

At the question, he stilled. Maybe he wasn't talking to a criminal. This could well be the husband of Lacey's Whisper. Preferring to settle the issue peaceably with no one getting hurt, most especially himself, he leaned forward in the saddle, hiding his right hand completely from view. "Cole Hatcher. His fiancée Lacey was up here recently."

"No, she wasn't."

Ah, the man knew who Lacey was. Trace listened intently as a muted swearing and grumbling came from behind the rock. He couldn't quite make out any particular words except "hell."

Grasping the rifle in his hand, he gave Lightyear a tap with his right foot. The horse started to move forward.

"I said turn around!"

Trace moved his left hand toward Lightyear's face. "Whoa, it's okay, buddy." He scratched beneath the horse's ear and Lightyear reared. Gripping the horse with his knees, he swung the rifle around and shot the rock where the barrel was visible.

"Dammit." The barrel moved then. "Freaking-a, what the hell are you doing? I could have shot you."

He still felt like a sitting duck, but since the man hadn't shot him yet, it meant he wasn't trigger-happy. "Show yourself."

A laugh sounded from behind the boulder. A very husky, feminine laugh and Trace's pulse accelerated.

"Now why would I do that?"

The voice was no different, but as Trace imagined a woman instead of a man, it no longer felt threatening. Instead, it had his imagination running wild without any clothes. Intrigued, his curiosity got the best of him. "Are you Whisper?"

The silence was deafening and he brought the rifle up again. He may have imagined that feminine tone. He hadn't been with a woman since he was served the papers for the divorce. He should probably find himself a one-night stand soon or he'd be thinking the fence post was a woman.

"Who wants to know?"

"I'm Trace, Cole's cousin. He sent me up here to talk to you."

Again silence. There was no way the rifle-bearer was a woman. Women weren't that patient, or that quiet, at least not in his experience.

A figure unfolded itself from behind the rock and Trace's breath got stuck in his lungs. Startling silver eyes peered at him from beneath a worn, brown-leather cowboy hat. Beneath those eyes was a straight, elegant nose, high cheekbones and full lips that remained closed. A stubborn jaw anchored the lower face while small wisps of black hair framed the sides, the rest tied back somehow.

"So talk."

Trace blinked, letting the rifle go slack. As he took in the rest of the image, his interest cooled. The woman wore a loose red-and-black flannel shirt, a brown leather vest, a handgun stuffed into the waist of her baggy jeans and square-toed cowboy boots that had seen better days. Alarm bells went off in his head. A down-on-her-luck woman. Shit. "Are you Whisper?"

Her nod was barely discernable.

"Hello, miss. I understand you have a trailer up here."

Again, a slight nod.

He wasn't used to silent women. His wife talked nonstop, mostly about what she needed. Lacey, who he actually thought was a decent woman, also needed to fill in the silence as well, but at least with important stuff.

His task was important, at least to Cole. "Can I see it?"

"Why?"

So I can tell you it's on Hatcher-Williams land and you need to move it. He glanced down at the rifle held loosely in her hand. Lacey's comments on what a great shot Whisper was had him rethinking his plan. Maybe the straightforward approach wasn't the best. "Lacey said you lived up here with someone."

"Yeah, my uncle." She still didn't move, but her gaze flicked between him and Lightyear.

Interesting. "Can I talk to him?" Maybe a man-to-man conversation would be easier.

Her lips quirked up on one side just slightly, just enough to rivet his gaze. "Sure. This way."

Trace took a moment to get Lightyear moving, his mind still stuck on the image of her full, feminine lips, but once he set the horse to a walk in between the Joshua trees, it became apparent that riding wasn't the easiest way to move forward.

Quickly, he jumped down and carefully pulled the reins over Lightyear's head so they wouldn't brush along the horse's face. He grasped them low and guided the horse between trees, keeping the blue jeans and brown vest in sight.

Whisper's long, straight black ponytail swished back-and-forth with her stride, catching his attention and holding it to the point he almost walked into a prickly pear cactus. Shit, as if the Joshua trees didn't make this area of the high desert a challenge enough to navigate. No wonder he and his cousin had rarely ventured up here as kids. How the hell did they get a trailer in here?

Finally, they emerged into what looked like a natural clearing of hard-packed earth and there sat a large trailer covered in the dust of the environment. In front of it sat a single Adirondack chair and a chiminea. With a quick scan, he could see a shed to the left and slightly behind it, a cord running to the trailer. A generator? To the right of the home sat an ATV under the shade of a wooden carport-type structure.

"He's in there." Whisper grabbed his attention once again and he raised an eyebrow. "You're not coming in?"

"It's too close in there with more than two people." She waved her hand toward the trailer even as she sat in the chair, the rifle on her lap. "Go ahead. You can introduce yourself."

Trace released Lightyear's reins. "Stay there, buddy. I'll be right back." Anxious to talk to a man instead of Lacey's odd friend, Trace strode quickly to the trailer and knocked.

"Oh, go ahead in. Uncle Joey won't bite."

Then why did he suddenly have the feeling she wasn't giving him the whole story. Opening the trailer door, he stepped inside and took off his hat. His first impression was Christmas from a cheap department store had dumped into the large space. The second was that it was a lot roomier than he expected and a lot nicer. His third impression was that the man with his back to him might be hard of hearing because he didn't turn at his entrance.

Trace cleared his throat loudly, so as not to startle the white-haired gentleman as he walked to the chair directly across from him. He turned, extending his hand. "Howdy, sir, I'm Trace Williams."

When the man looked at him but didn't move, Trace noticed more. The pale-blue eyes staring back at him were sharp, but the rest of the face sagged on the left side. The hair was neatly trimmed, but thin, and the entire visage was marked by sunspots and wrinkles, common among the elderly in Arizona. Both arms lay in the man's lap, relaxed.

Something was seriously wrong here. "I understand you're Whisper's uncle, Joey." He raised his voice.

The man squinted a tiny bit before he gave a small jerk of his head, which was obviously a nod.

So the man was not deaf at all. "May I?" He pointed to the chair.

Uncle Joey gave another jerk of his head.

Clearly the man had suffered a stroke, but was still all there. A strong sympathy for Joey's plight had Trace searching for alternatives to his mandated task. He couldn't imagine what it must be like to be in Joey's shoes. He looked the man in the eyes. "I wanted to meet you. Did you know your niece saved my cousin's fiancée?"

Joey gave a jerk of his head again, but his gaze made it clear he was pretty proud of Whisper.

An unforeseen curiosity got the better of Trace. "Did you raise Whisper?"

The man's mouth opened on one side then he rolled his eyes.

Trace grinned. "So she was a handful, huh?"

Joey jerked his head again.

"I have to tell you, that doesn't surprise me. What happened to her parents?"

Joey looked down then returned his gaze to Trace's.

"Okay, I'm guessing they died. Was it an accident?"

Again the older man's head jerked.

He could tell Joey was enjoying their "conversation" so he kept at it. "And she was pretty young?"

The man jerked again and gave a short grunt.

"Hmm, so young. So not a teenager yet?"

Joey's eyes lit with pleasure and he jerked his head again, his mouth partially open.

Trace was thoroughly enjoying himself as he learned Uncle Joey's mannerisms. It was similar to understanding a horse. Cole could go to hell. There was no way *he* was kicking these people off the land.

"So how long have you two been up here? A long time?"

Joey didn't move at all.

Trace relaxed. Maybe there was no need for them to move. "So somewhat recently. Hmm." The shed and ATV cover said it had at least been months. "Would you say less than a year?"

Joey didn't move.

Damn. "Would you say under two years?"

Joey jerked his head.

He was no expert on squatter rights, but for some reason the two-year mark made him uncomfortable, like he'd heard that timeframe before.

Joey's eyes flitted to his right and Trace turned his head to look out the large window facing the "front yard" of the home. His jaw dropped.

Whisper was with Lightyear, stroking his nose and cheek, talking to him. He looked back at Joey. "That horse can't stand anything touching his face. How is she doing that?"

Joey's eyes lit with pride once more, but the only sound he made was a short grunt. Trace got the feeling Whisper's uncle wasn't surprised in the least.

Maybe he should be bringing Lightyear up here for his training. He turned back to watch Whisper. Her connection with his horse reminded him of Lacey's connection to Angel, but she'd formed that over months.

"She's good with horses, isn't she?"

He glanced back to Joey to see him jerk his head. Then he moved his eyes up and down.

What could that mean? "She's had many horses?"

Joey didn't move.

"She likes to ride horses?"

Joey rolled his eyes.

Trace laughed. "I'm not very good at this, am I?"

The older man jerked his head and his mouth opened, which Trace was pretty sure was the closest he could get to a smile.

The door opened. "What's going on in here?"

The cowboy, Trace, looked at her as if he'd been caught doing something he shouldn't. Then he moved his gaze to Joey and chuckled.

Whisper's stomach tightened. *Uncle Joey was hers.* Even at the thought, she recognized it for being silly, childish and selfish, but he was and always had been. She didn't want some drop-dead gorgeous, hunky cowboy with short sun-streaked brown hair and warm reddish-brown eyes muscling in on her territory. "You can leave now." Damn. Even to her that sounded rude. "Uncle Joey isn't used to so much stimulation."

Trace returned his copper gaze to her and her heart hiccupped. It'd been doing that ever since she stood up from behind the boulder and met him face-to-face. She didn't like the feeling at all.

Joey grunted.

She looked at Joey. "Don't you go giving me any lip now, old man."

Trace stood and bowed toward her uncle. "It's been a pleasure chatting with you. Hope we can do it again sometime."

Her traitorous uncle jerked his head before the tall cowboy walked toward her. Though the trailer was spacious for her and Joey, Trace took up too much space. He was taller and broader than she was and solid muscle, at least that's how it appeared from the outline of his clothes.

She backed up into the kitchen to let him proceed outside. But instead, he donned his cowboy hat and waved her toward the door.

She gave an exaggerated sigh and opened the latch, stepping down onto the hard-packed earth.

When the cowboy closed the door, she turned on him, a smirk curling her lip. "So, did you find out everything you came up here for?"

The man studied her, his eyes hidden by the shadow of his hat. "Yes I did, thank you."

Huh? "Good. Now you can go."

He cocked his head. "I would think with no one around for miles you wouldn't mind a little company for a change."

"Nope." At least not his. He had her stomach in knots and she didn't like it. "Not real partial to people. Animals are much better company."

Trace laughed at her statement, sending a pleasant sensation over her body, like the sprinkle of a light rain.

"I have to admit to having that thought a time or two, especially in the ranch house. But the barn can be peaceful, even soothing. I like listening to the sound of a horse munching on dinner while another chuffs and moves around in the shavings." He looked off in the distance as if seeing every detail. "As dusk comes on, you can hear the crickets, and the desert mice scampering back into their nests." His gaze locked with hers. "Nature is more straightforward than man."

Feeling a sense of kinship with him at his description, it took her a moment to catch the undertone of bitterness in his final statement. Her mind eased as she sensed he might understand. "Yeah, I get that. A horse lets you know exactly how she feels. You also know how a coyote or mountain lion feels the second you find yourself in their company."

He grinned. "You in the company of those animals often up here?"

She shrugged. "Faust comes by when he's hungry and—" At his intent stare, she halted. "Anyway, you were leaving, right?"

"Yes, but not right away. I find the company up here far too fascinating."

She glanced back at the trailer for a moment before nodding. "Yeah, Uncle Joey's a hoot."

"I enjoyed chatting with him. He said you two have been up here almost two years."

He got that from Joey? Her defenses went up as fast as a rat trap. "Maybe."

He pointed at the shed. "I figured it was a decent amount of time from the looks of that shed. That would have taken time to build and it's a bit weathered."

This cowboy was a little too observant for her comfort.

"How'd you get all the wood here? Do you have something you hitch to your ATV?"

She shrugged, not in a hurry to reveal any more than he'd

already guessed. She didn't need him to be poking around in her background. Last time someone did that, her two deadbeat cousins had come after her within hours. According to her parents' will, if she was incapacitated, Timmy and Keith would inherit all the money except what was needed to care for her, so she and Joey had had to move again. She didn't want that happening again. She really liked this area of the state.

When she didn't answer, Trace strode toward the front of the trailer where she had the ATV parked.

"What are you looking for?"

This time *he* didn't answer. Instead, he ducked under the ATV shelter and examined the trailer hitch.

It was definitely time for him to leave. "Hey, I got some chores to do. If you're done visiting, I'm fine with you leaving." She got his attention with that.

His head snapped up. "You really don't like people, do you?"

It was more that she didn't like what people wanted from her or how he—they—made her feel. "No, I don't."

He backed up. "I apologize. I was just curious. Your lifestyle is, well, admirable. I think I'm a bit jealous. I forgot about how rewarding a simple life could be. Having your own place and the open desert all to yourself is a bit of heaven."

Heaven? Yeah, it was kind of like that. She'd never met anyone else who understood.

Trace took a bandana from his back pocket and lifted his hat to wipe his forehead, then returned the cloth to where it belonged. "How did you get the trailer out here?"

She shrugged. He may appreciate her lifestyle, but he asked too many questions. She left her truck in town with the vet. Dr. Jenna used it when she needed to transport larger animals in return for keeping it safe and out of the dry desert environment.

The arrangement had the additional benefit of keeping Whisper's cousins off her trail. They'd come through town shortly after she arrived, asking about her. Jenna told them she'd seen Whisper head west, mainly because Whisper was in the office with a sick gray fox at the time and Jenna didn't like the look of them.

All Whisper needed was the ATV most of the time anyway.

Trace studied her, his eyes visible now that he stood on the shady side of her home. His face was too damn handsome. Far more rugged and mature than the boyfriend she'd had when she was a teenager.

"Whisper, you can trust me. You don't need to hide from me."

She'd learned from her two cousins not to trust men, except for Joey, who had looked out for her, kept her safe. Uncle Joey was different. "I'm not hiding. I'm just living. Me and Joey are good. Why did you come here?"

Trace looked away. "My cousin asked me to. He was curious about the woman who saved Lacey. You made quite an impression on her. She admires you a lot."

Why did he keep saying nice things? "Lacey's a good person."

He grinned. "That she is." His tone turned bitter and he shifted his weight, scraping the heel of his boot in the dirt. "One of the few women I can say that about."

She wanted to know what a woman had done to him because it was obvious he'd been on the short end of that stick. Her curiosity caught her off guard. Why should she want to know anything? He was just a nosey cowboy.

"Don't you want to know what happened after Cole brought her home?" Trace was back to studying her.

"What do you mean?" Obviously, they got home safe.

"I mean Ray Norton, the bastard who beat Angel within inches of her life. The man you shot up."

Anger surged through her as she grasped who he meant. "I hope he died."

"I wish." Trace shook his head. "He's still alive, but you'll be happy to know he'll never walk again without a limp."

"Not good enough." She clamped her mouth shut before she said any more.

Trace's lips lifted up into a sympathetic smile. "My feelings exactly."

She started to smile, but caught herself. He agreed with too much. She glanced down at his dirty boots. They were in excellent shape beneath the dust. His boots were too nice. Nope, she didn't trust him as far as she could throw him.

She turned away, not willing to let him see her face. Maybe if she—

A screech, followed by a scuffle sounded near the shed. "God damn eagle!" She raced toward the creosote bush and quickly spotted the dust and flapping feathers. "Go pick on someone your own size!" Her heart beat hard as she swatted at the golden eagle trying to grab the baby jackrabbit.

Trace's cowboy hat hit the eagle in its chest and it finally backed off. She crouched to pick up the baby, careful to avoid touching the long cut along the side of her large ear.

"Shoo." Trace walked by her, but she ignored him as she checked Viola for other injuries. It looked like the scratch was the only wound. She could save her. She looked over the ground for Sebastian. He was gone, probably scared off. Shit.

"That eagle is going to be pretty hungry."

She stared at the black boots in front of her but refused to be drawn in. Instead, she rose with the baby rabbit and headed for the trailer.

"Whisper, you know it's nature's way." His voice saying her name buried itself in her brain. Something she could think about later.

"Go away. I'm busy." She needed to get Viola's scratch cleaned, keep her warm and watch for shock. Jackrabbits depended on their ears and this one was barely a few days old. She also needed to find Sebastian. He would be lonely without Viola. She opened the door to the trailer, trying to remember where she'd stored the empty box from the coffeemaker she bought last month.

"You're welcome." Trace's hard voice made her hesitate.

She looked back over her shoulder. Trace had re-donned his hat, his body stiff. The life of an animal was far more important than a man's feelings. But despite her best intentions, she nodded. "Thank you." She let the door slam behind her.

Chapter Two

Trace stared at the closed door. That had to be oddest conversation he'd ever had with a woman, with anyone. He'd prided himself on his charm when he was younger. So much so he'd been blindsided by Yvonne. So engrossed in charming her from her shyness, he'd failed to see it was all an act. He'd thought of himself as her knight in shining armor.

Trace grunted as he carefully looped the reins over the pommel and mounted Lightyear. His armor was pretty tarnished now, not to mention bent in too many places to be repaired. It was time to dump it.

Clicking Lightyear into a walk, he headed back to the rim. Despite his mixed feelings about asking Whisper to leave Cole's land, once he'd met Joey, he refused to say anything. He may be a fallen knight, but he wasn't heartless. Neither was his cousin. He was confident he could get Cole to let them stay.

As he crested the rim, he allowed Lightyear to pick his own way down the canyon wall. He had complete faith in the animal even though he had to lean far back in the saddle in a couple places that were seriously steep. He still couldn't believe Whisper had touched Lightyear's face. When he got back to the barn, he'd try it to see if she'd worked some kind of magic.

As they reached the bottom of the wall, he gave Lightyear his head. The quarter horse was named after the speed of light for a reason. According to Cole, he was bred from two racers. Trace just couldn't imagine anyone giving up on such an amazing animal. A tinge of guilt kicked his conscience. He'd had a couple dozen horses, but even now he couldn't remember their names. The cowboys who worked for him had taken care of them. He'd lost touch with his roots, trying to achieve what he thought was success. He'd become a rancher and left his real cowboy boots to gather dust.

As he passed Cole and Lacey's new construction, he couldn't help but think of the sprawling ranch house he used to own. When he'd built the giant stone fireplace, he had envisioned nights cuddled up with his wife before a roaring fire, but that never happened. There was never time.

His mother said his rising star had risen too fast. Maybe she was right, but he sure as hell would have liked to at least be able to afford an apartment now. Maybe once the final papers were signed, he'd have something left after the lawyer took his percentage.

As he rode up to the barn, his brother, Logan, walked Tiny Dancer toward the corral. The young paint stepped gingerly and seemed to breathe a sigh of relief once she was left to her own devices.

Logan had let his hair grow longer, but he still looked hard and grumpy. He held Tiny Dancer's halter in his hand as he stepped up to meet him. "Were you successful in ousting the squatters?"

Trace halted Lightyear. "I'm not sure they're squatters. I think Cole needs to hear the whole story."

Logan shook his head. "Don't know why he sent you to play the bully. If he'd sent me, they'd be long gone by now."

"No, they wouldn't." Trace's gut tensed with growing anger. "You would have been back here in fifteen minutes with a bullet wound. That woman greeted me with the barrel of a rifle."

Logan laughed. "I guess you still have the Williams' charm then because I don't see any bullet holes in you."

His anger eased. "Nope, and I found out a lot about our outlying tenants that Cole will find very interesting."

"Whoa, if your goal is to let them stay, good luck with that." Logan patted Lightyear on his side and turned toward the house.

Trace urged the horse toward the barn. He had no doubt he could help Whisper and Joey. All he needed to do was talk to Lacey. Between the two of them, Cole didn't stand a chance.

After jumping down from Lightyear, he led him into his stall and carefully removed the bridle before unsaddling him. He pulled a pitchfork from the wall and gave the horse a healthy lunch. "There you go, buddy."

He hung up the pitchfork and headed toward the barn door then halted. He was far too curious about Whisper to let go of the fact that she patted Lightyear on the face. Letting himself into the stall, he barely laid his hand on Lightyear's nose as he ate. The horse threw its head up and neighed.

"Sorry, buddy, I just had to check." With a secret smile on his face, Trace let himself out of the barn and headed for the main house. Now he had more ammunition against Cole.

As he stepped inside, his grandmother's voice from the kitchen greeted him.

"I think that's a wonderful idea, but how many were you hoping to invite? I'm not sure we can fit many more."

He walked in, nodded to his grandfather and gave his grandmother a kiss on the cheek. "Many more what?"

Lacey and Cole stood near the fridge. Cole wasn't in his fire department shirt for a change, but he still looked huge next to his delicate wife. It was all that gym equipment at the station. Lacey wore a button-down blouse and long skirt, probably because she had to work later today. Her blonde hair was neatly braided on one side and the two lovebirds held hands as usual. He couldn't remember his wife holding his hand. Did they even do that while dating?

Lacey beamed at him. "We're throwing a New Year's Eve party." She switched her gaze to his grandmother. "I was actually thinking we could have it in our partially finished house. Cole said we could get one of those heaters they use with tents when it's too cold outside, and we can rent tables and chairs. I was thinking of having it catered."

His grandmother set down her ice tea in surprise. "That's actually not a bad idea. You have no walls dividing the rooms yet so we could even dance."

Lacey looked at Cole. "Do you think we could have a DJ? The plywood floors would be perfect for dancing."

Cole kissed Lacey on the forehead. "Of course, what would a New Year's Eve party be without dancing?" His brow furrowed. "I'm just not sure who we can get for the catering or the DJ on such late notice. It's only three days away."

Trace listened for a few minutes as the four discussed possibilities then quietly backed out of the room. He'd probably be asked to help with setup and maybe a few errands, but as far as planning, they didn't need him. Just like his wife's parties. She hadn't wanted his input in the planning, though he did make sure he was there. He'd been so concerned about someone else catching her eye that he failed to realize her eye was on his bank account, not his guests.

As he stepped out onto the porch, a truck pulled into the ranch with a trailer hitched to it. He'd learned from Cole shortly after moving to Last Chance that a truck and trailer was cause for excitement. Either a horse was being brought for rehabilitation or it was a potential buyer who didn't know Cole insisted on checking out the future homes of his horses.

Trace jumped down the stairs and met the driver. An older cowboy stepped out. "Howdy, I'm Don. Animal Welfare sent me to drop off these two horses."

Trace looked back toward the trailer. "Two?"

Don started to walk to the back. "Yeah. There's actually three in total, but one wasn't ready to travel yet. The vet's watching her overnight."

Trace helped Don lower the ramp. "Why have they come here?"

Don halted. "Starvation. The family of five came upon hard times and instead of selling their 'beloved' horses, they just stopped feeding them. They said they thought the grass would be enough." He spat on the ground. "You should have seen the place. There wasn't a blade of green left."

Trace braced himself as Don backed a gray Palomino out of the trailer. The horse's ribs were so well defined that Trace had to swallow to keep his anger from boiling out. It was important to stay calm around the new horses. Glancing over at the closest corral, he was glad to find it empty. "Let's bring him over here."

Don looked at him. "You don't want him in the barn?"

"Not yet." Trace walked with the man. "We need to evaluate him first."

Don shrugged and handed the reins to Trace. "Then you take him and I'll get the other."

Trace entered the corral with the gray. The horse's eyes looked dull, as if he'd given up hope of ever having a decent meal, and he had a minimal hair coat despite the cooler temperatures this time of year.

Trace looked up from his examination to see Don leading what would have been a handsome Missouri Fox Trotter if the horse had any energy at all. Instead, the horse's head hung low, its blond mane filled with brambles and its café au lait coat dirty.

Don handed the reins over to Trace, and he brought the animal in. Taking off the halter, he climbed over the fence to face Don. "What are their names?"

"I have the paperwork in the truck."

As they headed for the man's vehicle, Logan strode out of the house. "More horses?"

Trace motioned toward the corral. "Take a look."

Don pulled the paperwork from the front seat and sifted through it. "Storm is the gray Palomino. The Missouri Fox Trotter is Rogue and the mare that is still to come is…" The man shuffled through the papers. "Ah, here it is. Mystique." The cowboy frowned. "Strange name for a horse if you ask me."

Trace grinned. Not so strange if the family of five had three children into comics.

"Are you Cole Hatcher?"

Trace glanced toward the house to see Cole and Lacey coming outside. "No, but this man is. I'll let him take it from here."

Trace passed by Cole on his way to catch Lacey. "You still have another coming."

Cole nodded as he passed.

Lacey stood at the edge of the porch, watching his cousin. Trace bounded up the steps and stood next to her. "How's it going, Blondie?"

She didn't look at him. "It was going great until these poor horses arrived. How could anyone do this to such magnificent creatures?"

Trace agreed with her, but then again, he'd never had to choose between giving up his horses and feeding his kids. His horses had been taken from him, he had no children, and he was homeless, so it was a moot point. "Not everyone was meant to own them."

Lacey looked at him. "That's an understatement."

"Now, your friend Whisper would never let a horse starve. I bet she'd give a horse her last meal if that's what it took."

"Whisper?" Lacey was staring at him now. "What about her?"

He shrugged. "Nothing. By the way, she says hello."

"Trace Williams, what did you do to her?" Lacey leaned toward him, her brows furrowed.

He kept his grin to himself and held up his hands, backing up a step in mock fright. "Whoa, settle down there, I was just passing on a message."

Lacey advanced. "But you saw her. Did you find where she lives?"

He nodded. "Yes, ma'am. I found her just like Cole wanted me to."

Lacey halted her progress. "Cole?"

At the look on Lacey's face, Trace felt a twinge of guilt,

but at his remembered conversation with Joey, and Whisper's affection for Lightyear, he pushed his advantage. "Yes. He sent me up over the rim to find her. She takes care of her uncle who appears to have had a stroke. He is completely dependent on her."

Lacey's gaze softened. "I knew it."

"Knew what?"

She smiled. "I knew she had a good heart, but she's been hurt. Did she say anything about her family?"

Family? Trace hadn't even considered there might be someone else living there. Whisper could have a husband for all he knew and that was why there was no truck there because the man of the house was at work. Actually, that made a lot of sense since the trailer couldn't have been pulled in there with the ATV.

He didn't like that her husband would leave her out in the desert alone with her uncle like that.

"Trace? Did you hear me?"

He refocused his attention on Lacey. "I don't know if she has a husband. She didn't mention one."

Lacey gave him an odd look. "You have to show me where she lives. I need to talk to her."

He'd like nothing more but didn't want to press his luck with his cousin. After all, it was only because of Cole and his grandparents that he had a roof over his head. "I'd be happy to, but you should probably talk to your fiancé first. He's not too happy about her living up there."

"Why not?"

"You'll have to ask him."

"What aren't you telling me, Trace?" Lacey took a step closer.

"No way, Blondie. That's a conversation between you and Cole. I was just delivering a message." He backed up another step and opened the door to the house. If he didn't miss his guess, he and Lacey would be riding up to Whisper's trailer by tomorrow afternoon.

He wasn't sure why he looked forward to that visit, but he did.

~~*~~

Whisper closed the book of Shakespeare comedies. She'd read from *Twelfth Night* in honor of her two guest rabbits. She'd named them after the comedy about twins, since they were almost impossible to tell apart, until Viola got scratched.

After setting the book on the side table next to Joey's bed, she pressed the button that elevated his head six inches higher. He slept much better that way.

Satisfied with the height, she stepped over to the small box on the kitchen floor and checked on Viola and Sebastian. When she'd finished getting Viola settled earlier, she'd gone back to the scene of the trauma and found Sebastian cowering under the shed. Now the two babies slept on top of each other, finding comfort in their companionship.

Pulling her coat off the hook by the door, she put it on before sticking Sal into the waistband of her jeans. The Glock came in handy if a rattler got too close. Stepping to the fridge, she pulled out a beer, popped the cap and took a swig. Hmm, the perfect ending to an interesting day. Walking to the door, she quietly let herself out.

Once outside, she settled herself in her chair and buttoned her coat. The temperatures were dropping lower at night, leaving a frost on the desert floor in the morning. She looked at the chiminea, the ash from her last fire still inside. She didn't feel like making a fire. It wasn't cold enough to expend that kind of effort.

Taking another swallow of beer, she leaned her head back and stared at the sky. She watched and waited for the first shooting star of the night. Minutes went by before one finally streaked across the heavens and burned up on the horizon.

Some people believed the stars were good omens and others thought them bad. With the number of shooting stars out in the desert in Arizona, she thought it safe to bet they meant nothing in the grand scheme of tiny men's lives.

Not that she'd had many men in her life. Her dad, her Uncle Joey, and her teenage boyfriend were pretty much it. She saw nothing wrong with that until this morning when Trace decided to mosey on into her life.

She allowed herself a slow smile. The man was sexy, not that she'd ever let him know that. He made her insides all squishy and caused her to have a hard time focusing.

Whisper let her eyes close as she pictured Trace when he grinned, his white teeth gleaming against his tan face. The dark stubble around his lips and his chin just made him appear more rugged. Despite his new clothes and boots, she sensed a strength of purpose in him. That and just brute animal strength.

She opened her eyes. Is that why she felt comfortable around him? Because she could relate to the animal side of him? Hmm. She closed her eyes again. That was an interesting observation. The fact was, his animal side was pure male. Large forearms visible below his rolled-up sleeves attested to that. She'd love to see him without a shirt on.

He'd have a stomach like an old washboard and chest

muscles that rivaled a martial arts expert. His jeans had been tight and she hadn't missed what a great ass he had as he leaned over to check out the trailer hitch.

She wouldn't mind hitching her wagon to him any day…in her dreams. They were almost the same height with him maybe a couple inches taller. She liked that. At six feet, she was taller than some men.

They could throw a blanket down under the stars and take off their clothes. She flushed. Would he find her enticing? She would love to just look at him in the moonlight. His body would be hard, strong, making her tingle with the thought of pressing herself against him, flesh to flesh. He would be gentle at first, the part she liked. He could cup her breasts in his large hands and his thumbs could stroke across her nipples. Sharp pings of pleasure would flow from there straight to her vagina.

She loved the tightness she would feel as her nipples were fondled. He could lower his mouth, still holding her breasts aloft, and lick each nipple before biting lightly, making her knees weak. Then he could suck, his mouth encapsulating her whole nipple, tugging at her. She would grasp his shoulders to keep herself upright.

While his mouth continued its homage to her breast, his hand would sneak down to find the black curls that hid her sex. His finger would spread her nether lips and seek out her opening. Her knees would give way and he'd gently lower her to the blanket, his strong arms cradling her descent.

Once she was laid out before him, he would first spread her hair about her and admire its texture. Her last boyfriend found her long hair mesmerizing. But then Trace would spread her legs as well, wanting to prepare her as much as possible for the inevitable.

Kneeling between her thighs, he would spread her folds and his finger would seek her entrance, slowly gliding inside and then out, mimicking what he would do. But unlike her one other lover, he wouldn't stop there. Having seen how much she enjoyed his attentions to her breasts, he would lean over her and nip at each one.

She'd very much like it if he stayed kneeling and played her nipples between his thumbs and forefingers to distract her with pleasure even as his penis nudged her opening.

The pleasure of her nipples would build the tightness in her womb, making her limbs feel like licorice in the hot sun. She'd float in the pleasure of weightlessness.

Then Trace would plunge himself into her and reality would return. She'd be patient while he rutted and as with an animal, she'd praise him for his performance. Because he was a cowboy, after he pulled out, he might hold her close as if it all meant something special.

Something cold and wet touched her hand and she jerked her eyes open. "Faust."

The coyote sat back on his haunches and stared at her.

"Holy moly, you scared the shit out of me. You shouldn't sneak up on a person when they're daydreaming." She looked the coyote over. He never came so close. He must be seriously hungry.

"Okay, okay, let me see what I have saved up." She stood and the animal backed off. Taking a sip of her beer, she set it on the wide arm of the chair then strolled to the outside compartment that housed a mini-fridge. She took out a plate of scraps she'd saved. "I'll warn you now, there's not much. You've only been gone three days this time."

She walked past her chair and set the plate down, not in

the mood to make him beg. That he'd actually touched her bothered her. His cold nose reminded her of the cold feeling she experienced after sex. Walking back to her chair, she sat and watched Faust eat.

Despite the lackluster ending to sex, she could still dream and enjoy the best part. It had been so long, over twelve years. It might be worth the risk to try it again. But first she needed to find out why Trace had been up to visit her in the first place. Her gut told her he hadn't lied, but he also hadn't told the entire truth.

Faust held the plate with his paw as he licked every grease particle from it. She grinned. It was so easy to please animals, give them food, water, shelter if they needed it and a little affection in some cases and they were as happy as a black bear with a salmon.

But people complicated things. They needed money, lots of it and would do anything to get their hands on it, including taking it from a child and lying to their own kin. Most of her greedy relatives finally got on with their lives by time she was ten, but two on her mother's side, Keith and Timmy, did nothing but try to get at her money, legally or illegally.

She thanked her parents every day for leaving her in Uncle Joey's custody. Joey hadn't known anything about raising a child, but as an accountant, he'd known how to protect her inheritance.

Now it was her turn to protect him. She really didn't want to move and Joey liked it here better than any other spot they'd been. She loved it here, too, but if her good deed of helping Lacey on Christmas day brought Trace snooping around one more time, she would probably have to get out the map… again.

A sigh from the coyote caught her attention as he lay down facing her, just a couple yards away. "What would you do if I left?"

Faust's ears turned toward her, but otherwise he didn't move.

"And there's Viola and Sebastian to think about now, plus who knows when Motley is going to return, the ungrateful burro. Nope, I can't leave this spot quite yet. Too many depend on me right now. I'll just have to lay low and avoid Trace as much as possible."

Yup, that's what she'd do. If he showed up again, she'd hide. There was only so much he could get out of Joey and she was pretty sure he had little patience. Men generally didn't have any, so he would eventually go home.

Having settled another weighty life question to her satisfaction, Whisper finished off her beer. "I'm heading to bed, Faust. Keep an eye on the place, will ya?"

The coyote opened one eye as she stood then closed it again.

She smiled. Was there such a thing as a watchcoyote as opposed to a watchdog?

~~*~~

Trace leaned back against Lightyear's stall as the short veterinarian tried to coax Mystique to eat. The chocolate-brown quarter horse hadn't eaten anything by mouth in the last forty-eight hours and they were all concerned. The vet who had kept her overnight had fed her intravenously and while that was still an option, it wasn't the long-term solution they needed.

Cole's vet, Dr. Jenna, was stumped. "There's no medical reason I can find for her not eating."

Logan scowled. "Fine. Then feed her like the last vet did until we can find the solution."

Jenna threw her hands up. "And what's wrong with figuring that out now?"

"Because she's starving now."

Lacey placed her hand on Logan's forearm. "Maybe you could go outside and call Cole to give him an update?"

Trace could see what Lacey was doing, diffusing the conflict, and he held his breath until Logan finally nodded. "Fine." He stalked out of the barn, disappearing from view.

Jenna sighed. "Thank you. It's hard to think when every word you say is being challenged."

Lacey smiled. "I figured as much. So what options do we have?"

"That's just it. I've tried everything I know. Maybe we need a horse whisperer." She rolled her eyes and Lacey smirked.

Trace froze as the image of Whisper petting Lightyear streaked across his mind. "It can't hurt to try, right?"

The women turned as one to stare at him. Lacey shrugged. "No, but I'm not sure there is such a person in all of Arizona."

Jenna shook her head. "There are a few who claim to be, but who knows."

Trace pushed off the wall and stood straight, his gut telling him he was right. "I know someone who can help. Whisper."

"Whisper? Why do you say that? I know she's good with a gun…" She looked at Jenna. "Don't ask. Why do you think she could help with Mystique?"

He grinned as his confidence in the woman's ability rose. "Because I saw her pet Lightyear on his face and he didn't move a muscle."

"What? No way." Lacey's eyes widened.

He nodded. "Yup. And I watched her with my own eyes as she fought off a golden eagle to save two baby jackrabbits. She even told me she's better with animals than with people."

Lacey smiled. "Do you think she'd come? You didn't tell her about Cole's stubborn need to have her move off the land, did you?"

Trace shook his head. "I was hoping you could bring him around."

"And I will. Just give me time."

"We don't have much time with Mystique." Jenna laid her hand on the matted coat of the mare. "I'll have to feed her intravenously like Logan suggested just to keep her alive if she doesn't start eating in the next couple hours. I know Whisper. She brought a couple wild animals into my clinic, but I have no way of getting in contact with her."

Trace stared at the vet. "You know Whisper?"

The woman looked away. "Not well."

She clearly hid something about Whisper and he wanted to know what it was, but the mare's welfare had to take priority. "I can go get her, but if she comes here, I'm sure she's going to want someone to stay with her Uncle Joey."

Lacey clasped her hands again, a nervous habit she had when she was concerned. "That's right, she said she had an uncle. Grandpa's off golfing and he took Billy for his caddy again. What about your grandmother? If Annette goes, do you think Whisper will come?"

He grinned. "If she knows it's to help an animal, I'm ninety percent sure she will."

Logan strode in. "Cole said to do whatever it takes to keep the mare alive."

Trace clapped his brother on the back, his good mood incongruent with the serious circumstances, but he had to admit he was pleased he would be seeing Whisper and Joey again. "So what do you think of watching your baby daughter for a few hours? I want to take grandma to visit someone."

Logan looked wary. "And this helps the horse how?"

"Come back to the house with me and I'll explain."

~~*~~

Though Logan had been doubtful, Trace had complete confidence that Whisper could help. His grandmother rode with him. She had her white-and-gray hair pulled back into a tight bun and she wore a blue sweater and jeans with brown cowboy boots. Though one of those slender older people, she had a spirit that was made of steel and she ruled the roost at Last Chance. It might be why grandpa was forever off golfing, fishing or hunting. Despite grandma's years, she was still an excellent horsewoman and Sadie, her horse, was strong and steady.

He pulled up a hundred yards from the canyon wall and waited for his grandmother to halt next to him.

"The wall is not too difficult for the horses once you get past the shale."

She waved off his words. "I've been up here many times, Trace. Just lead the way."

Of course, he should have known. Kicking Lightyear into a gallop, he headed for the canyon wall. Halfway up, he looked back to see his grandmother had made it past the shale and was close on his heels. It puzzled him his own mother had given up riding so early. Then again, it may have been her financial circumstances. Without dad to run the ranch, and himself too busy with his own spread, her move into town had become a necessity. He'd thought Logan had it all under control. Another misjudgment on his part.

Once he reached the top, he waited for his grandmother then led the way through the Joshua trees. Now that he knew the way, it was just as easy to stay on his horse. He had to grin when he recognized the boulder that Whisper had hidden behind. There was no rifle barrel there now, nor any command to halt.

When they broke into the dry clearing, his grandmother sighed. "I remember this spot. Your grandfather and I camped out here a couple times. How nice that someone else has found it."

"Whisper lives here with her Uncle Joey. I don't know if there is anyone else though." He didn't want there to be anyone else, but that was stupid if he'd thrown out his armor. Quickly, he dismounted then helped his grandmother down.

"I'm looking forward to meeting both of them."

Trace strode to the door and knocked. Not hearing anyone, he knocked again. This time he distinctly heard a grunt. He opened the door and let his grandmother proceed him.

"You must be Uncle Joey." She took the man's hand and patted it before sitting down in the chair opposite him. His grandmother was an angel in his book.

He clapped his hand on Joey's shoulder as he came around to his front. "It's me, Trace. I brought you a little company. I hope you don't mind."

Joey rolled his eyes and opened his mouth.

"Is Whisper here?"

Joey jerked his head.

Trace looked at his grandma. "That means yes." He

turned back to Joey. "We need Whisper's help with a horse. If she agrees to come with me, my grandmother, her name is Annette, will stay here so you won't be alone."

Joey rolled his eyes again.

Trace chuckled. "I know what you mean. Everyone babies you. But if I were you, I'd milk it for all it's worth."

Joey's mouth opened again.

"We'll be fine, Trace. Go find Whisper and get back to that horse."

He nodded before turning to Joey. "See you later when I bring Whisper back. Cross your fingers she's willing to go, or you'll be seeing me a lot earlier."

Joey jerked his head and Trace left the trailer.

Now to find Whisper. The ATV was still under its cover so she had to be on foot. They had a rare rain last night, so he might have a chance of tracking her. Walking the perimeter, he found where she'd gone into the desert. Following her footprints, he kept an eye out for rattlers. This time of day they were generally sleeping and he wanted to keep it that way.

The area behind the trailer was less populated with Joshua trees. Instead, it had the typical prickly pear, saguaro, and jumping cholla cacti. But there were a lot of palo verde trees as well as large boulders. He saw the ATV path and as much as he wanted to discover where she went on the machine, it was more important that he find her.

He stopped on top of a boulder at the edge of a particularly rocky area, trying to find her tracks again. This could take all day. She could be miles from the trailer for all he knew. Then again, he couldn't see her leaving her uncle for too long. Climbing onto a very large boulder, he yelled, "Whisper!"

Shit, her name made yelling a contradiction. His voice didn't carry the consonants. He could fire off his gun, but he'd left it attached to Lightyear's saddle. He tried again, cupping his hands around his mouth. "Whisper!"

He listened, but his only response was silence. Damn, he needed to get her to Last Chance. His gut told him she could help and Mystique didn't have much time. He kept walking, trying to find any sign she might have stepped back down onto the desert floor.

Frustrated, he finally turned back the way he'd come to double-check the tracks he'd found. He halted. Now there were more tracks leading away from the boulder field. What the fuck? He would have seen them. She was out here and she was evading him.

He didn't have time for playing cat and mouse. Jumping down onto the desert floor, he stalked along the trail she left, a slow knot tightening in his belly at the time they were wasting. Growing more angry by the minute, he started to run, following the trail between trees and rocks, weaving in and out. Finally, he caught sight of her black ponytail as it disappeared down a small hill.

Gritting his jaw tight to keep from yelling, he ran full out, determination fueling his body. At the pounding of his boots on the hard ground, she finally turned and saw him.

"Whisper, stop."

She started to run.

He wasn't letting her get away. He kept after her, gaining until she was barely an arm's length away. He could have waited the two seconds it would take to grab her arm, but he was tired of wasting time. He threw his body toward her and toppled her to the ground, being careful to take the brunt of their fall.

"Let me go."

He rolled her beneath him. "I don't think so."

Chapter Three

Whisper's hat had come off and the sun glittered in her silver eyes. Her cheeks were flushed from her run, and he could feel her heart racing. He could also feel every womanly curve and that startled him. Some of those curves were bigger than he expected. "Why were you hiding from me?"

"Get off me."

"No, we need your help."

"I said get off me." She squirmed beneath him, her strength surprising.

"Whisper, listen to me. We have a horse that needs your help."

She stilled. "Why me? You have a vet."

Now how did she know that? Unless Dr. Jenna had talked about Last Chance. Is that how she found the spot for her trailer?

He shook his head. None of that mattered now. "Jenna doesn't know what to do. She says she can't find any reason why Mystique won't eat. I suggested you."

Her eyes widened. "Me? Why me?"

As his anger dissipated, his body started to react to the warm female beneath him. Not a good thing. He doubted Whisper would appreciate his interest in her body, so he moved off her and stood, offering his hand to help her up. "Because you said you liked animals better than people. Animals sense that."

She looked doubtful, but placed her hand in his. He held on as she gained her feet then reluctantly let her pull her hand away. That was strange in itself. She was not his type at all, especially since he'd sworn off down-on-their-luck women. She was tall and dark. His wife had been short and platinum blonde, though not a natural platinum.

Whisper brushed off her jeans, not saying a word. Then she bent over and picked up her hat. When she'd batted it a few times against her thigh, she placed it on her head. "I just want to be left alone."

The sincerity of her voice caused a tumult of reactions inside him. Understanding, disbelief, hurt. The last surprised him. "You mean you haven't become addicted to my charming smile and magnetic personality?" He couldn't help the touch of bitterness that crept into his question.

Her hat shaded her eyes as she contemplated him, probably wondering if he was serious or not.

"Listen, Whisper. You're this horse's only chance. We're desperate."

"You must be if you came for me. But I can't leave Joey for that long."

He could see she would throw out every possible excuse not to go. Time to rope her in. "I've brought my grandmother. She's already with him. Mystique has been starving for days. The only way they could get any nutrients into her was with a needle. If she doesn't eat on her own soon, we'll have to put her down."

"No." Whisper's quick denial seemed to startle her as well as him. She looked away, one hand burrowing into her front pocket. "Okay. But don't blame me if I can't help."

Relief and anticipation spread through him. "Thank you."

She nodded, but didn't say anything until they reached the trailer. "You brought a horse to get me?"

"What else would I bring?"

"An ATV, a truck."

He bent low and cupped his hands to help her mount. "Those wouldn't make it up the canyon wall."

She looked toward her ATV then back at him. "I've never ridden a horse."

He stood straight, staring at her. What the hell? Whisper was a study in contradictions. It would take a person a lifetime to figure her out. The challenge of that had his blood racing before he squashed his enthusiasm. The last woman he tried to "figure out" had cost him everything he had.

"It's not so important to have my help now, is it?" The bitterness in her voice had him softening.

"Your experience on a horse has nothing to do with saving Mystique. I was just surprised because most people out here know how to ride, but it's not a problem. All you have to do is place your foot into my hands and when I boost you up, throw your right leg over the saddle and sit. Do you think you can do that?"

"Oh, I can do that, but can you boost me? I'm pretty heavy." That she didn't say she was fat or put herself down, and instead just stated the facts, had him grinning.

"I think I can handle it. Ready?"

She ignored him and walked to Sadie's head. "If I'm too heavy for you, you just let us know, okay?"

The mare's ear twitched as she butted her nose against Whisper's shoulder. She walked back to him. "Okay, let's do this."

She made it sound like a major chore. He couldn't wait to see what she thought once they headed out.

With little effort, he helped her up into the saddle. "Nice view from up here."

He chuckled. Now why didn't it surprise him she wasn't scared? Mounting Lightyear, he walked him next to Sadie. "You will want to hold on to the saddle horn, especially as we descend. Sadie will follow Lightyear. Once we get to the bottom, I'll have you hold the reins and we can move a bit faster. Mystique needs you as fast as possible."

Never one for too many words, Whisper simply nodded and wrapped her hand around the saddle horn.

It made him want to know what she thought. That in itself was an oddity because most of the women he'd known always told him what they thought or felt unless they were just being stubborn, but Whisper simply preferred to keep to herself. As he started them toward the canyon wall, he grinned at the thought of the impression she would make on the rest of the family.

Whisper used one hand to pat the horse now and then as they approached the rim. The views from horseback were breathtaking. She'd never seen her little slice of heaven from this height and it reinforced for her that she'd picked the right spot.

The problem was Trace and his family. It had been just over twenty-four hours since she'd seen him last and he was already back. Despite her attempt to elude him, the damn desert floor had given her away. On the other hand, if they were going to put down a horse, she was glad he caught up with her.

Her body flushed as she remembered his weight on top of hers. She'd melted on contact, not something she was happy about, but she was a female and she wasn't immune to the hardness of his chest and the strength of his thighs. On one hand, she wanted what she dreamed about. On the other hand, the reality of the culmination was so disappointing.

Maybe she should try it. If she was able to help the horse Mystique, she could ask for sex in return. She was pleasing to look at and Uncle Joey had told her a long time ago that it was a rare man that didn't want sex with a pretty lady. Her uncle had never married nor had he brought home any of the women in his life. He always told her, she came first.

Her heart swelled with love. Uncle Joey was first in her life, too. Instead of being selfish, she'd ask for gingerbread ice cream for her uncle as payment. It was his favorite, and they only made it in Canterbury and only at this time of year.

As Sadie started to descend, she could tell the horse knew where to walk and Whisper placed her trust in the animal. At the bottom, after a few sliding steps on the treacherous shale, Sadie halted next to Trace.

"How are you doing?" He looked at her with concern.

"Fine."

His lips quirked up on one side as he shook his head. "I should have known you'd be comfortable on a horse. Take those reins in your hands so we can pick up the pace."

After a brief instruction, Whisper kicked Sadie into a lope. The movement of the horse at first felt strange, but after a few minutes she caught the rhythm. The urge to go faster rifled through her and she signaled Sadie to run.

"Whoohooo!" She loved the rush of the breeze against her face, and the fast gait of the horse beneath her made her feel like the god Apollo riding his chariot across the sky. Or at least what she figured he felt.

"Whisper!" Trace rode up beside her, a scowl on his face.

She smiled at him even as the wind took her hat and whisked it away. He looked stunned and fell back a bit, but she didn't care. She'd never felt so alive.

Looking back, she watched him spin Lightyear around, jump from the horse, grab her hat and jump back on. Now she understood the phrase "poetry in motion." Trace's movements were fluid, making everything look easy when she knew they required a lot of strength and skill.

He caught up to her within seconds and nudged Lightyear toward her, forcing Sadie to correct her direction a bit. She looked forward again. They were almost to a partially constructed building on a hill. "What's that?" She had to yell over the sound of the galloping horses.

Trace leaned over and pulled the reins from her hands, signaling the horse to slow, probably because they were getting close to people.

"That was amazing. Can we do it again on the way back?" She looked at him, the half-smile on his face too endearing. What would his lips feel like on her own?

"You really liked that, didn't you?" He handed her hat to her and she smacked it against her thigh to loosen the dirt, careful not to hit Sadie.

"That was the best experience I've ever had in my life. Thank you." She plopped her hat on her head.

He raised his brow. "Even better than sex?"

"Oh, by far." She reached down and patted Sadie on the

side of her neck. "What a good girl you are. You are my new favorite animal."

"I thought I was." Trace's words caught her attention and she looked at him.

There was something behind the teasing words. His mouth said one thing but his eyes said another. He almost looked hurt or insulted. She couldn't decide. "You're a human. That's a whole different category."

She returned her gaze to the roughed-out road they traveled. "What was that big building being built on the hill?"

"That will be Lacey and Cole's house when it's done. I think they're just waiting for it to be finished so they can get married. That will be an interesting ceremony. My aunt Beverly never approved of Lacey."

Whisper had never seen anyone get married before. It would be nice to see Lacey get married. Lacey was a good person. If her husband-to-be's mother didn't like her, they shouldn't invite her. That would ruin what could be a wonderful day for Lacey. She hadn't missed how Lacey's eyes had lit up when she mentioned her fiancé, even while they were pinned down by the gunfire of the animal abuser.

She found herself getting anxious to see Lacey again, and Sacnite. Shit, what was the name Lacey called the horse? Something white. Snow? Ghost? Angel? Angel. That was it.

"You seem awfully deep in thought. Are you trying to figure out how to get the mare to eat?"

She snapped her head to the right, having completely forgotten Trace. Strange. People usually made her very uncomfortable. She never "forgot" they were around. "No. I won't know that until I sense her feelings."

Trace raised an eyebrow, but he didn't laugh or look

doubtful. She let out her breath. Maybe he really did believe she could help. That encouraged her. She was used to people doubting her on every level.

"Here we are." Trace jumped down from his horse in one smooth movement, reminding her of a mountain lion who came by once in a while. Maybe that's why she was more comfortable around Trace. She could relate him to an animal.

He stood next to her horse and raised his hands. "Ready to come down?"

"Not really, but I guess I have to if I want to help." She took her feet out of the stirrups and leaned forward so she could swing her leg over the horse's rump.

"Whoa there." Trace's hand on her leg startled her. "Leave this foot in the stirrup then swing one leg over and I'll help you down. Don't hit Sadie's rump."

She could do that. Putting her left foot back in the stirrup, she swung her leg extra high to avoid hitting Sadie but as she came around, she lost her balance and started to fall backward.

"Don't worry. I've got you."

She landed in Trace's arms, her left foot still attached to the horse. Shocked he could hold most of her weight, she quickly dislodged her foot.

She looked up at him. "Sorry."

He stared down at her, still holding her. His eyes turned dark and her heart started to tap hard like a woodpecker at a tree. He was so close she could see the long, dark lashes that outlined his eyes.

"Is that Whisper?" Lacey's voice came from the barn as she strode toward them.

Trace gently propped her up straight and she adjusted her hat, just to have something to do.

"It's so good to see you again." Lacey enveloped her in a big hug, despite the fact she was a good half foot shorter.

Whisper looked at Trace, but he just grinned. Hesitantly, she wrapped her arms around the woman and tapped her on the back. "Good to see you're still alive."

Lacey pulled back. "Only thanks to you."

"I don't know. You were doing pretty well on your own."

Lacey hooked her arm and started walking her toward the barn. "No way. I was a goner if you hadn't shown up. I actually aimed to kill that bastard and hit the ground three feet in front of him."

Whisper halted. "You tried to kill him?" A new respect for Lacey built.

Lacey scowled, a look Whisper hadn't seen before. "Dang right I did. He was going to shoot Cole."

Understanding dawned. Lacey was a sweetheart, but threaten those she loved, like her horse or her fiancé, and watch out. She let Lacey move her toward the barn.

When they stepped inside, she halted again. Jenna, the vet, stood next to a stall and a man leaned against the opposite one. From the scowl on his face, he wasn't happy. A hand on her shoulder had her turning her head.

"I understand you know Dr. Jenna. The brooding man over there with the baby in his arms is my brother, Logan. Don't mind him. He's in a perpetual bad mood. He doesn't get much sleep because his daughter is only six months old and likes to get up at all hours of the night."

She could feel Logan's anger simmering beneath the surface, but when he looked back down at his daughter, his whole demeanor changed for the better. She took in that observation and stored it for contemplation later. "Where's the horse?"

Lacey let go of her, walking to the vet and finally pointing to a stall. "This is Mystique. She and her two companions, Rogue and Storm were all starving. Rogue and Storm came first and they are eating, but the mare won't."

Whisper ignored the vet and Logan and moved to the stall where the horse stood facing the far wall. Opening the door, she went inside. She swallowed hard to keep the tears at bay as she got a close-up view of Mystique's ribs. Careful not to touch her, she moved to the mare's head.

Oh God. There was no spirit left in the body. Whisper straightened her shoulders, determined to find a way to understand the horse. She knelt on the ground before Mystique. She focused on the horse's eyes. Mystique's gaze remained down.

Whisper lay down, where the horse couldn't avoid seeing her. The deep-brown eyes were scared and something else. Whisper didn't breathe, holding the horse's gaze, and then a feeling of stark loneliness settled in her bones. Her eyes watered, the feeling too close to her heart for comfort.

She reached her hand up and touched the horse's nose. "I can help."

Slowly, she sat again, still watching Mystique. The horse's head remained down, but her gaze followed her. Just the tiniest show of curiosity, but it was a spark of life.

Hope built in her heart. "I'm going to stay with you until we get things right." She looked toward the stall door where Lacey waited patiently. "Where are Rogue and Storm?"

"We have them in the corral, outside."

Whispered nodded to show she understood. "I need to take her out there."

Lacey's brow furrowed. "Are you sure?"

"Yes." Ignoring Lacey, Whisper let her gaze return to Mystique. The horse continued to watch her. "We're going to see Storm and Rogue now."

The horse's ears twitched.

Whisper's confidence grew. "Storm and Rogue will be happy to see you again."

This time the horse's ears perked up.

She stood slowly. "You want to see Storm and Rogue?"

The horse continued to watch her, so she moved to the stall door. "Are you coming to see Storm and Rogue?"

Mystique turned around and Whisper opened the stall door.

Trace stepped forward with a halter. "I can put this on her."

She nodded but continued to talk to the horse. "Put this on so you can see Storm and Rogue."

Trace worked quickly then handed her the reins.

She never stopped talking to Mystique as she led the horse toward the corral, constantly mentioning Storm and Rogue. As they drew closer, Mystique's nostrils flared. When a weak whinny from the corral drifted to them, the mare lifted her head to look.

Whisper sensed the second Mystique recognized her friends. There was no pulling on the reins or answering sound, but there was a calmness in her walk, like someone coming home.

Trace met her at the gate and opened it to let them in and closed it behind them.

Immediately, Storm and Rogue walked over to greet Mystique. The mare trembled as she was welcomed.

Whisper turned to Trace. "Feed them all, now."

Jenna leaned on the corral fence. "The other two have eaten, they need to wait."

"No." Whisper looked at the vet. "Feed them all now. It doesn't have to be a lot."

Trace headed toward the barn. "I've got this."

Jenna ran after him, but Whisper returned her attention to the horses. Storm scratched Mystique's back with his teeth and the mare's head rose higher to return the favor. Rogue moved himself to be side by side with her.

Whisper's tension eased. Now that the mare was reunited with her friends, maybe she would eat.

Trace strode toward her carrying a bucket of grain. Again she was reminded of an animal, but not a mountain lion this time. Instead, his broadness reminded her of a black bear she'd once seen up north standing on his hind legs scratching his back against a tree trunk. Yet Trace's stride was all his, confident, strong, sexy.

She snapped her gaze back to the horses and her idea of asking him to have sex with her resurfaced. No, gingerbread ice cream. Remember?

Trace climbed the fence and dropped down inside the corral. He softened his landing by bending his knees, obviously not wanting to startle the horses. He moved to the tray that had been put out for them and emptied his bucket. "Come and get it." He grinned at her as he stepped aside.

Storm immediately moved, jostling Mystique. Rogue followed and Mystique, not wanting to be left alone, joined them. As soon as she saw the food, she lowered her head and ate with her friends, sandwiched between them.

Whisper sighed with relief even as Trace walked toward her. "You did it."

His look was full of pride and she felt her cheeks flush. She shrugged. "I guessed."

He shook his head. "No, I saw you in there. You understood her. Is that why your name is Whisper? Because you are a horse whisperer?"

She chuckled. "Not even close."

Trace stared at her a moment before his face softened. "I like the sound of your laugh."

She didn't know what she was supposed to say to that, so she kept her mouth closed.

His grin reappeared. "You have my curiosity piqued now. You must tell me how you got your name."

She leaned back against the fence, pleased by his attention. "It's not that exciting. I guess I was a loud child. My mom used to tell me to whisper to help me control the volume of my voice both inside and out. She said it so many times around my little friends that they started calling me Whisper. After my parents died, I begged Uncle Joey to let me change it. After many years, because he is one stubborn cuss, he finally gave in and at the age of thirteen I officially became Whisper Adams."

There was no reason to tell Trace that Joey allowed her to change it in the hope that it would throw her relatives off her trail, but they eventually caught up to them…again.

"Joey told me your parents were gone. How old were you when they passed?"

"I was eight." That had been the worst day of her life. The day her life had changed forever. In a way, she was thankful because she'd learned how people really are.

"Shit. That's tough." He looked away, watching the horses. "I lost my dad when I was thirty and I thought that was hard."

He looked back at her. "I can see now why you and your uncle have such a close bond."

She gazed into his eyes. They were the color of perfectly brewed tea. They definitely had her waking up. What would he do if she asked him for sex? Suddenly, the idea of rejection loomed large and she looked away. "I should get back to him."

"Right." He turned and opened the gate.

Lacey and Jenna were just leaving the barn. Lacey came up and gave her another hug. "You did it! I'm so glad you came. You have to stay for dinner."

Whisper warmed at Lacey's honest enthusiasm. "I can't. I need to feed my uncle."

"Oh right."

Jenna held out her hand. "Thank you. Now I know who to turn to when I get stumped. I always said there was more to an animal than just the mechanics. You proved me right."

"I hope she gets better." Whisper glanced over at the horses before turning to Trace. "Don't separate her from them until she's back to the weight she's supposed to be. Feed them as Dr. Jenna told you but feed them together. If you put them in the barn at night, be sure to have the other two across from her so she can see them."

Traced grinned. "Yes, ma'am."

At movement behind him, she looked past Trace to see his brother carrying his baby to the house. Though he cradled his child with care, she sensed a lot of anger and hurt in that man. She didn't like being near him and was glad he stayed away. She refocused on Trace. "Can we go?"

"Of course."

~~*~~

Trace smiled as he mounted Lightyear. He'd only been awake half an hour after a long night of thinking about Whisper when Lacey decided she had to invite her new best friend to the New Year's Eve party tomorrow night. Since he was the only one, besides his grandmother now, who knew where Whisper was camped, he was asked to play escort.

He had absolutely no problem with that. Whisper was a puzzle he just couldn't let remain unsolved. She acted like no other woman he'd ever met. Her lack of ambition alone was odd not to mention her preference for silence instead of talking. He wanted her to talk more, which had never been the case for him when it came to a woman.

It was curiosity that spurred him on. Though he no longer trusted his gut, it kept telling him she was exactly as she appeared, no hidden agenda. Also, it appeared she had no interest in him, which was good. They could be friends.

"Is it much farther?" Lacey crested the canyon rim and brought Angel up beside him.

He grinned. "Tired already, Blondie?"

She rolled her eyes at him. "Hardly. I still have a hundred items on my to-do list for tomorrow's party and I plan to complete every one before Cole gets home tomorrow morning."

"Have you two talked any more about Whisper staying here?"

Lacey shook her head. "No. Between the party, the new horses and his schedule at the fire station, we haven't had a minute together. But don't worry, I told Annette what Cole wanted to do and after her visit with Whisper's uncle, she's on our side."

"Wow, I never pegged you for the devious type."

She swatted him on the arm. "I'm not. I just know we owe a lot to Whisper and though Cole thinks it's the right thing to do to make her move, I know it's wrong. I just need to make him see that. You know how stubborn he can be about walking the straight and narrow. I need all the help I can get to make him see, in this case, the path to what's right is different than what he thought."

"I hope you can make him see the light because if he doesn't, he and I are going to have more than words."

Lacey stared at him. "Why would you care if she has to move?"

Good question. "Just wait and you'll see. You'd have to have a heart of stone to meet Joey and see what she's built and still force them to move."

"And we all know your heart is mush." She winked.

He shook his head and kicked Lightyear into a walk. He hated that she was right. He did have a soft spot that was as big and as weak as a newborn calf, especially with women. Family was one thing, but he needed to be a lot more distant with other women. More like Logan, but without the angry cloud.

By the time they arrived at Whisper's trailer, he'd convinced himself Whisper didn't need his help and could hold her own against Cole, especially with a gun. So he needed to keep his distance. Now that Lacey knew where Whisper lived, she could play guide to whoever else needed to come up here.

"Wow, this is a lot nicer than I expected." Lacey jumped down from Angel and wrapped the reins around a mesquite branch. "What a great spot." She turned around and took in the view.

Trace grudgingly agreed. Whisper and Joey had spectacular desert scenery. There were rock mountains on opposite sides with unique shapes carved upon them. On the south side was the Joshua tree forest they'd come through, a fascinating sight in itself and the west side was full of scrub brush and cacti with palo verde and mesquite trees thrown in for good measure for as far as the eye could see.

Swearing coming from inside the shed caught their attention just before a shapely butt covered in tight jeans appeared, backing out of the shed. From instinct, he ran over to help. "Here, I can do that for you."

Whisper dropped what she'd been pulling and snapped upright. "Where the hell did you come from?"

He smirked. "Last Chance Ranch, where else?"

She stepped back, shaking her head. "Why has my secluded spot suddenly become the trough at feeding time?"

He kicked himself for rushing to help. He'd startled her and now she was pissed and he couldn't blame her. And what happened to keeping his distance?

Lacey came to his rescue. "Whisper." She stepped right up to Whisper and gave her a hug.

Whisper scowled at him, and he shrugged. He was just the guide. Not his fault.

When Lacey was done, Whisper managed not to scowl, but he could tell she was still unhappy about their visit.

"So what are you doing here?" She addressed her question to Lacey.

Lacey smiled. "I asked Trace to show me where you lived, so I could invite you to my New Year's Eve party tomorrow night."

Chapter Four

Whisper coughed. "You're kidding, right?"

Lacey shook her head. "It's a very special party and I wouldn't even be alive to host it if you hadn't helped me on Christmas day."

Trace's already high opinion of Lacey rose another notch. The woman really knew how to get to people. If she couldn't get Cole to change his mind about Whisper living here, no one would. He might not have to bloody his cousin's pretty face after all.

"You don't know that." Oh, Whisper was pretty tough too. "You could very well have kept that piece of trash at bay long enough for your fiancé to rescue you."

Trace moved his gaze to Lacey, thoroughly enjoying the debate.

"Oh no, I would have run out of shot long before Cole showed up."

"But you could have started an avalanche of stone or something."

Lacey shook her head. "It really doesn't matter if you

saved my life or not. The fact is, I met you and I like you and I really want my friends to be at this party."

"Friends?" That one-word question from Whisper had Trace sucking in his breath.

Why did he get the feeling the woman had never had a friend? He tried to steel himself against the sympathy that rushed through him, but it was hopeless.

Lacey pretended Whisper hadn't just revealed a heart-wrenching fact about herself. "Yes, friends. I really need my friends at this party because Cole's mother might show up and, well…" Lacey looked down as she paused.

Holy shit was Lacey good at this. He almost felt sorry for Whisper. She had no clue she was going to this party.

Lacey continued. "She doesn't like me. She thinks Cole can do better. That's why I need my friends there, you there. Basically, I need people who will keep me from telling the woman off."

Whisper's lips quirked upward just a bit and Trace felt a sudden yearning to see the woman actually smile or laugh fully or somehow show joy beyond a quirk of her lips or a small chuckle. She wasn't angry like Logan, just reserved and always wary. He wanted to know why.

"If you're looking for someone to hold you back, I'm not the one. I'm more likely to tell her off myself." It was clear Whisper thought she'd just won the debate.

Trace held his breath for Lacey's comeback.

Lacey's shoulders slumped. "But that's the other reason I need you there. I'm afraid that when she says something snide or nasty to me I'll be so hurt I'll run from the room crying."

Trace stood frozen. Sweet, innocent, honest Lacey was a master manipulator! He would never have believed it if he hadn't heard it with his own ears. He grinned. Cole had no idea what he was in for. At least Lacey loved his cousin, so the man was safe.

He glanced at Whisper and could see her wavering. He would be so proud of her if she didn't cave in, but then it meant she wouldn't be at the party and he was absolutely sure the party would be much more interesting with her there.

He watched as she studied Lacey then she sighed. "No. I don't do parties."

Trace had to swallow his laughter at Lacey's shocked face. He wanted to cheer for Whisper, but that wouldn't go over well with either woman.

"Why not?"

Whisper shook her head. "I don't like people."

"But you like me, don't you?" Lacey was honestly hurt.

Whisper nodded.

Lacey pointed. "And you like Trace, right?"

He held his breath as Whisper's gaze moved to him. Her eyes revealed nothing and for a few moments she just stared at him. Finally, she nodded.

Shit, her answer was far more important to him than it should have been.

Lacey continued. "And you know Dr. Jenna. She'll be there."

Whisper caught on quickly. "Doesn't matter. I have to stay with Uncle Joey. You can't tell me you have someone in your family who would rather stay here with him than be at the party."

Lacey grinned. "Already thought of that. We'll bring Uncle Joey to stay the night at Last Chance. Logan hired a babysitter so she and Uncle Joey can watch over baby Charlotte."

Trace liked the way she'd phrased that. Uncle Joey may be an invalid, but his brain was far from a child.

Whisper's eyes widened before she glanced at the trailer.

Lacey pressed her advantage. "I'm sure your uncle would enjoy meeting more people. Please, Whisper. I really want you to come. It won't be the same if you're not there."

He couldn't keep quiet any longer. "I promise if at any time you feel uncomfortable and want to leave, I'll bring you back here."

Her gaze snapped to his again. "Okay, I'll go." She gave him her answer, but Lacey threw herself at Whisper, enveloping her in a hug. Trace raised his eyebrow and shrugged, but he was jealous of Lacey's freedom of expression. Why the hell couldn't he hug Whisper, too? And kiss her? And—shit.

Lacey broke away. "Thank you so much."

"I get to leave when I want." Whisper's voice was hard.

Lacey nodded enthusiastically. "Absolutely. Trace or Logan or—"

"Trace." Whisper was adamant. "Only Trace."

His chest swelled even as Lacey looked at him. "Of course. You know Trace the best. He can take you home whenever you're ready." She turned back to Whisper. "Now I'd like to meet Uncle Joey."

Whisper shrugged. She'd obviously decided there was no stopping Lacey once her mind was made up. "Sure. Go ahead." She held her arm out toward the trailer and Lacey strode toward it.

He fell into step next to Whisper. "She's a tough one to stand against."

Whisper looked at him. "But she has a good heart."

"What about me?" He had no idea why he'd asked, but he was curious what her answer might be.

"Jury's still out."

He stopped and laughed. The absolute blunt honesty of the woman enthralled him. "Fair enough." He waited where he was as Whisper spoke to Lacey before Lacey entered the trailer.

Whisper turned back to him. "You wanted to help. Come on."

He'd already forgotten he'd made the offer, but Whisper seemed to want to take advantage of him being there. Too bad she didn't want to take advantage of his body too.

His cock hardened at the thought. Was she as busty as he'd felt beneath her clothes? Her jeans today showed she had full hips and ass. The kind a man could hold on to when pumping in from behind.

"Are you gonna help or not?" Whisper stood by the shed door, frowning at him.

"Yes." He strode toward her, hoping the heat he felt in his body wasn't obvious. "What do you need?"

She pointed at a big-ass generator. "I need to get this out so I can see to fix the wheel."

"Wouldn't a flashlight or lantern inside the shed be easier?"

"If you don't want to help just say so."

"No, I do. It was a legitimate question."

She sighed heavily, and he could have sworn she muttered the word "people" under her breath. "There is no room in the shed to work on the generator. I'd rather pull this out than empty the shed."

Okay, she had a point. "No problem. Let me drag it out for you."

Whisper finally stepped back and allowed him access to the machine. She'd already moved it a couple feet to the edge of the doorway. Luckily, there was no lip on the floor. She'd obviously built the shed by hand and the concrete slab rose about an inch from the ground.

Grasping the handle of the generator, he pulled, succeeding in getting a quarter of the machine outside, but of course the axel for the broken wheel was at the back. Now he would have to lift it as well as pull.

The lack of a breeze had him heating up quickly. Taking his bandana from his back pocket, he wiped the sweat from his brow before resettling his hat, then he anchored his feet and pulled again. Halfway there.

Again he took out his bandana and reapplied it. Shit, he'd be soaked in another thirty seconds. Without hesitation, he unbuttoned his shirt and whipped it off, throwing it on a bucket in the shed. He gripped the handles again, lifted and heaved.

His muscles strained as he determinedly dragged the generator the rest of the way out of the shed, even hauling it another foot across the desert floor. Taking his bandana from his pocket once again, he wiped his face then looked at Whisper in triumph.

Her eyes were wide as she stared at him. No, not at him, at his chest, and she licked her lips. The vision of her licking at his cock rose up before him and took his breath away.

Her cheeks were flushed, communicating her attraction.

He simply couldn't resist the pull she had on him and strode toward her. Her gaze didn't lift from his chest even as he halted less than a foot away. He took her hand and laid it on his pectoral. At her touch, his hot body shivered for an instant.

With his other hand he lifted her chin, forcing her gaze to

connect with his. His breath caught at the raw, unadulterated desire in her gray eyes. His cock grew hard with need even as his gaze dropped to her full lips. He had to have her.

He lowered his head and pressed his lips against hers. Her mouth opened and his tongue slipped inside. Hers met his and they tangled, sending desire coursing through his blood. He moved his hand to the back of her head, coaxing her head to the side so he could deepen the kiss, explore every nuance of her taste.

At her moan, he released her hand and pulled her tight against him, pushing his hardened cock against her mons. Her arms wrapped around his neck and she pressed her breasts against his bare chest. His cock jerked at the pressure of her hardened nipples through her shirt.

The woman wore no bra.

His need burned hotter than he'd ever known. He wanted to take her now, on the ground if need be. He moved his hand from her head to between them, easing away an inch to touch the hard nipple against him.

Her moan was loud and uninhibited as her tongue released his and her head fell back. He kissed her jaw while his fingers played.

He had to touch her. Quickly, he left her nipple and unbuttoned one button, just enough so he could slide his hand inside and feel the hard nub of her other breast.

"Yes. More." Whisper's husky voice spurred him on.

He pinched the tightened nipple before rolling it between his thumb and fingers.

Her hand moved from around his neck and she unbuttoned three more buttons in quick succession. "Taste." She held her other breast up in offering to him.

Shit, there was no way he would pass that up. He lowered his head, still holding her at the waist as she arched back. He closed him mouth over her areola and nipple, inhaling her intoxicating scent. Sage and mint filled his nostrils as he sucked.

"Yes. More."

He sucked harder, eliciting a moan from the woman in his arms. He let up and encircled her hard nub with his tongue before taking the nipple between his teeth and moving his jaw back and forth.

Whisper's pelvis pressed determinedly against his cock and he used his free hand to pull the gun from her waistband. He stuck it in the back of his pants then filled the void in her jeans with his hand. He burrowed down to feel soft panties keeping him from his goal.

Slipping his fingers beneath the light material, he found what he sought and his balls tightened at how wet her folds were. He slipped a finger inside her slick opening.

"Oh shit." Whisper sank to the ground and he knelt with her, pushing his finger deeper.

Her hips pushed up to meet him, her sheath grasping his single digit. He pulled it out and began to push two inside her, but her channel was tight. His cock throbbed at the thought of how it would feel, but his brain resumed control. She was too tight. He stilled, not wanting to hurt her, yet not wanting to stop. He gave the nipple in his mouth one more lick and pulled his head up to look her in the face. Her eyes were closed, her cheeks flushed and her mouth slightly open.

Her nipples peeked between her open shirt and her full breasts beckoned him to continue. He stared at the hard nipples awaiting his attention.

"You want to plunge inside me now, right? You can."

His gaze snapped up to meet her open eyes and resigned face. Cold water wouldn't have worked better to cool his raging cock. Something was seriously wrong with this picture. "Do you want me to?"

She shrugged. "If you want."

Her answer was the complete antithesis of what her body had been telling him just moments before. "When was the last time you had sex?"

She lowered her brows. "A long time. Maybe a dozen years or so."

Shock and relief barreled through him, sending mixed signals to his heart. That was a hell of a long time and could explain her narrow passage, but that meant she wasn't a virgin, which relieved his conscience considerably.

Still, her reaction to his potential penetration was strange. She was no wimpy miss and she was always honest and blunt. Maybe he needed to be as well. "Do you like sex?"

Her lips formed a real smirk that caught him so off guard, he almost missed her answer.

"Most of it." She lifted his hand that had been down her pants and pressed it against her breast. "I love this and what you did with your fingers."

His mind raced. Twelve years ago she would have been maybe eighteen? Younger? She liked being felt up but it was clear penetration was something to be endured. Holy shit, she'd probably had sex with some pimple-faced boy who was like a rutting horse. It was just a guess, but if he was even half right, he couldn't take her like this.

His fingers froze where they had been stroking the side of her breast. *I have to make this right for her.*

Her hand encouraged him to continue stroking but the

reality of where they were intruded. This was not the time or place to show her the wonders of sex. He smoothed his hand over her breast then clasped hers. "I want you, like this, but not here and not now. Not when Lacey can come out the door and find us like this."

"But you do want me?" Whisper didn't look him in the eye when she asked and his heart lurched.

He lifted her chin and forced her to look at him. "I do. I won't be happy until I have you completely." As the words left his mouth, their truth shook him, but he didn't break eye contact.

Whisper studied him, looking for sincerity, then she gave a quick nod and unwrapped herself from his arms. "Good."

He helped her to stand and turned away as she buttoned her shirt. He strode back to get his own when a hand on his waistband caught him by surprise. He spun, ripping his jeans from the grasp.

Whisper frowned at him. "You have Sal." She wrapped her arms around him and pulled the Glock from the back of his pants.

Shit, even that slight touch had his disappointed cock reacting.

She stuck the gun into the front of her jeans and then stared at his chest. "You better put your shirt back on."

"Right." He turned around again and somehow got his arms through the sleeves. He buttoned his shirt up slowly, needing a moment to let his body cool down again. Taking a deep breath and letting it out, he tucked in the ends of his shirt. Finally in control of his racing libido, he turned around to face her, but she wasn't there.

Noises coming from inside the shed as items were moved

around made it plain where she was. Shit, how could the woman go from being sexually aroused to working on a generator that quickly?

He started to step around the open door when he heard the door to the trailer close.

"Trace?"

"Over here."

He stepped to the shed opening and found Whisper's ass, once more in the air as she bent over a bench to pull out the drawer on a tool chest. He whipped himself back around and strode toward Lacey. Whisper had him in more knots than a cowboy had boots.

"I'm ready to go. I just have to say goodbye to Whisper." Lacey breezed by him, heading for the shed.

Good. He was ready to go too. Too ready. He walked over to their horses and unlooped the reins. He waited, his stomach rolling like a tumbleweed across the desert. He wanted Whisper. The revelation was a little too unsettling.

He'd sworn off women, especially those not in the best financial circumstances, yet she never talked about needing money or wanting something she couldn't afford, like Yvonne used to. Then again, Whisper didn't talk at all. Maybe her parents had gone overboard with telling her to be quiet.

At that thought, anger tightened his gut. Shit, here he was getting angry on her behalf when he didn't even know if her parents had said anything of the sort. What the hell? "Lacey. Let's go."

The two women looked at him before Lacey gave Whisper another hug and walked toward him. "Okay, okay. Hold your horses. I was just giving her some last-minute instructions about the party."

He cupped his hands and helped her to mount then stuck his foot in Lightyear's stirrup. "What possible instructions could the woman need for a party?" He swung his leg over and settled in his saddle.

Lacey looked at him and winked. "I had to tell her what time you'd be picking her up for your date, of course."

Trace stared as Lacey urged Angel into a walk between the Joshua trees.

"Date?" He glanced over at Whisper to find her watching him. She was one fine-looking woman. The idea found a warm place in his chest. He'd be proud to have her on his arm for Blondie's party. Grinning, he winked at his "date" then urged Lightyear to follow Lacey.

~~*~~

Whisper pulled her good pair of black cowboy boots out from the back of her closet and sat on the bed. She hadn't worn them since the last time she and Joey were at the lawyer's office, before his first stroke. It had literally been years.

She moved her arm to wipe the dust off them with her sleeve, but stopped herself just in time. Her shiny off-white blouse wouldn't look so good with dirt all over it.

She must have told Joey she wasn't going a dozen times during the day and at least that many times told him she couldn't wait. She was well aware of why she couldn't wait.

Trace.

She didn't want to go because she would have to act like people expected her to act. She didn't do that well, but Lacey had promised she could leave whenever she wanted. Whether she left early or late, she'd be coming home alone. She hadn't been alone at home since Joey had his first stroke three years ago.

Her uncle looked forward to staying overnight on Last Chance Ranch. Before his strokes, he'd been social. Not a lot, but he had a handful of friends he'd do stuff with, like play chess, go to a movie, check out a new art exhibit.

She'd seen the change in him over the last few days. Between Trace, his grandmother, Annette, and Lacey, she could see Joey's mind racing and his energy level was way up. Last night he'd let his gingerbread ice cream half melt before she could get him to focus on it. That never happened. He didn't go to bed until almost ten o'clock and he was just going to the ranch to babysit.

She picked up her boots and brought them to the kitchen. She used a paper towel to dust them off then she sat in the chair opposite Uncle Joey as she tugged them on. "What do you know, they still fit."

He opened his mouth.

She returned the smile as she stood. "Okay, final inspection. How do I look?"

Joey scrutinized her outfit from her long jean skirt to her high neck, long-sleeve button-down silk blouse. She turned around so he could inspect her tight bun, though she'd pulled a few strands out near her ears so she didn't look like a strict school teacher or something.

When she turned back, the extra material at the bottom of the skirt swirled a bit. It was kind of fun. "So? What's the verdict?"

Her uncle closed his eyes and took a deep breath before he grunted.

"That good?" Her feminine side trilled at his compliment. Because the blouse was off white, she'd worn a chemise underneath. By rights she should wear a bra, but she hadn't owned one since she was sixteen.

Joey jerked his head.

She sat down. "Thank you." She gazed at him, loving him for all he had done for her. It just wasn't fair he'd been dealt so many strokes. "You know you mean more to me than anyone."

Her uncle rolled his eyes and grunted. "Okay, so that's not saying much. How about this? I love you and I will never, ever leave you."

Joey closed his eyes and opened them.

She clasped his hand in hers and squeezed. "You know, you look pretty good yourself tonight. I hope you're not planning to pick up the other babysitter."

Joey grunted and she let go of his hand. "I'm just saying."

She looked at the clock in the kitchen. Trace would arrive any minute if Lacey had given him the right directions to the dirt road her ATV had created. At the possibility that he couldn't find her trailer via his truck, she looked out the window, suddenly wanting desperately to go to the party.

"I'm going to take a quick walk around the trailer just to make sure everything's okay."

Joey grunted.

"I know, I know. I'll be careful of my clothes." She grabbed up the blue wool cape she'd bought from a Native American woman at a craft fair that had come through town a couple years ago. It had designs on it she liked, but this would be the first time she wore it. Desert dust wasn't kind to good clothes.

Throwing the cape on, she attached the hook and eye clasps and grabbed up her flashlight before heading outside. The sky was almost dark, but on this last day of the year, night always came early.

She walked around the trailer, not really looking for anything in particular. It wasn't as if she needed to lock things up when the only people who knew she lived out here were Trace and his relatives.

The air was crisp already. She was pretty sure they'd have a frost tonight. At least she'd repaired the wheel on the generator yesterday. That particular machine would be keeping the trailer warm tonight for when she returned home.

Finishing her stroll, she meandered out toward her ATV road. Looking down it, a flash of light caught her attention as it bounced off a saguaro cactus in the distance. Her heartbeat doubled. Trace was coming. Turning, she strode back to the trailer.

She needed to get Joey's coat on before Trace arrived. She'd pulled the wheelchair out of the shed earlier, and it waited near the door outside. Would Trace carry Joey out or should she get him out? She always did it by herself when he had a doctor's appointment.

As she reached for the door, headlights blinded her and she covered her eyes. The truck stopped and the lights were turned off. Suddenly, she felt like a rabbit caught in a snare. What if it wasn't Trace? What if it was one of her relatives? Shit. She was so anxious about tonight, she hadn't even taken Sal outside with her for protection.

"Whisper?" At the sound of Trace's voice, she relaxed, but then a buzzing in her stomach started as he came into the meager light of the trailer's windows.

Her heart skipped a beat at the sight of him.

Chapter Five

Trace strode toward her in a white button-down collared shirt and silver eagle bolo tie. His broad shoulders were accented by the black sport coat he wore with swirling blue embroidery that was thin at the button and wide at each shoulder. New blue jeans, shiny black cowboy boots and a black hat that almost covered his short brown hair completed his ensemble.

She expected him to stop and say howdy or something, but he didn't. He stepped right up to her, took her in his arms and kissed her.

Whisper grasped his waist as his tongue dove between her lips and blazed a trail of desire from her mouth all the way down to between her thighs, leaving her breathless.

When he finally pulled his lips from hers, he kept his arms about her and just stared, his face unreadable, but his breathing as rapid as hers.

"Good evening, Miss Adams."

She smirked. "A very good evening it is, Mr. Williams."

He grinned, his white teeth flashing in the trailer's lights. He stepped back. "Let me see."

She put her arms out. "See."

He chuckled. "No. You must do the obligatory turn around. All I saw in the headlights was a sophisticated woman. I need to see if my eyes are playing tricks on me."

"Really?" She waited for him to say no, but he just stood there with his eyebrows raised in expectation. "Well, strip me naked and throw me in a lava pit."

He chuckled but twirled his finger at her.

She turned her back on him and looked over her shoulder. "Happy?"

He shook his head, stepped up behind her and encircled her waist with his arms. He inhaled slowly, his nose against her neck. "Hmm, you smell good."

She did take a shower. It was a party after all. She didn't smell the scent of her soap. She could only smell the spicy musk from his aftershave and feel how smooth his chin was against hers.

He squeezed her waist. "You feel good too."

He felt good to her, especially with his body flush against her back.

His lips found her neck beneath her hairline and he kissed her. After nibbling his way up to her ear, he pulled back. "You taste good too."

The lines from Little Red Riding Hood flitted through her mind and she laughed. "The better to eat you, my dear."

Trace's hold went slack, so she stepped away and faced him. He had a strange gleam in his eye and his smile wasn't quite full. "Trace?"

He shook his head as if to clear it. "Sorry, got a little sidetracked there. Is Uncle Joey ready?"

"Yes." She picked up her skirts and strode toward the door. "Let me just bring him out."

His hand on her shoulder, held her back. "Whoa there, cowgirl. That's a man's job."

She raised one eyebrow. "And who do you think carries him out here every time he needs to go to an appointment?"

Trace's smile faltered for a moment before he ushered her aside. "That may be, but you are not dressed for carting a grown man around."

She was about to point out that he wasn't dressed for it either, but it wouldn't do any good, so she waved him inside.

As she held the door open, she listened to him talk to her uncle. If there was one thing she'd have to admit, it was that every one of Trace's relatives had treated Joey with respect. She appreciated that. Others in the past didn't, which was one of the reasons she'd left the last mobile park down in Tucson. Uncle Joey missed the company, but too many of their neighbors made fun of him. Even those who were kind treated him like he was a baby. They just didn't get it.

"Here we are." Trace came out of the trailer holding Joey.

She let the door close and held on to the wheelchair so he could put Joey down.

Trace turned away from her. "It's not that far. Just open the passenger door."

She walked over to the truck and did as he asked. After settling Joey in the middle of the front seat and buckling him in, Trace held the door for her.

Taking her hand, he helped her up and waited for her to pull in the excess jean material of her skirt before he closed the door. She had to admit, he was quite the gentleman. Too bad she wasn't a lady.

She watched in the side-view mirror as Trace strode to the wheelchair and rolled it to the back of the truck before lifting it into the bed. The man moved with ease, much like his personality. After securing the wheelchair, he closed the tailgate then jumped into his seat behind the wheel. "Everyone ready?"

Joey jerked his head and she nodded.

Trace turned the truck around and followed the well-worn path back to town. It was definitely the long way around to Last Chance Ranch and she preferred riding over the canyon rim and through the valley on Sadie, but that could get treacherous at night between holes in the ground and snakes.

She liked the name of the ranch. In a way it fit her and Joey. It was their last chance for peace and tranquility. She'd tried living under the radar, but it appeared that "off the grid" was the only way to stay hidden and still have a life. "Why is it called Last Chance Ranch?"

"Oh, I thought you'd fallen asleep on me over there, you were so quiet." Trace elbowed Joey and he grunted, his mouth open.

She didn't mind. She was pleased that Joey was so excited. "That doesn't answer my question." She frowned at him, but he kept his eyes on the highway.

"Originally, it was because at a young age, my grandparents thought themselves getting up in their years."

"How old?"

He glanced at her and Joey. "Thirty."

Joey grunted.

She stared at him in surprise. "I agree with Joey. That's not old. Hell, that's my age now."

"I was wondering about that." Trace didn't look at her but didn't say anything else either.

"How old are you?"

"I'm thirty-two." His tone was bitter as if being that age was worthless.

"Why is that bad?"

"Because just a year ago I had accomplished so much. I owned a horse breeding ranch, my clients were happy, I could afford anything I wanted…except as it turned out, my wife."

Whisper's heart froze in her chest. She could barely get the words past her lips. "You're married?"

His laugh was more like a bark. "Not for long. Yvonne filed for divorce once she figured out how she could get everything I'd worked so hard for. I'm expecting the final court hearing any day. So far, it looks like I'm the big loser in this deal."

Ah, so that was why he was bitter. It made sense now. "So you came to Last Chance because it was your last resort?"

He chuckled, his good humor restored. "Something like that, though I use to spend half my summers out here as a child with my brother, Logan, and my cousins Cole and Dillion. So moving here was almost like coming home."

He held one arm in front of Joey as he made the sharp left turn onto a dirt road. It was so natural, he probably didn't realize he did it.

"So why is it called Last Chance if your grandparents were so young?"

"You're like a squirrel on a bird feeder, persistent. Like I said, they thought they were on the verge of being too old to start a cattle ranch, so they figured it was their 'last chance' to put down roots. Of course, back then, people didn't move around as much as they do now."

That was true. "I think the name fits well now because of the horses you take in."

"In many cases, we are their last chance, but luckily we are able to place a lot of them either with families or at trail riding ranches. We even have four we placed at Poker Flat nudist resort." He winked at her. "Can you imagine riding a horse naked?"

"That sounds like heaven. Is this resort nearby?"

He lowered his brows before holding his arm out in front of her uncle as he turned into the drive and under the sign of the ranch. "That's where Lacey works. Didn't she tell you that?"

"When I met Lacey we were being shot at by Sca—Angel's former owner, so no, it didn't come up."

He parked the truck next to a dozen other vehicles. "Many people coming tonight work at Poker Flat. Lacey also arranged with her boss to have rooms there for the people who came up from her hometown of Orson. No one will want to make the two-hour drive back there. Lacey has one of the security guards running a shuttle to the resort to keep everyone safe."

"So the resort is close?"

Trace stared at her. "Why? Do you want to go there?"

"If I can ride a horse like Sadie naked, then yes."

He shook his head. "I'm pretty sure the best you're allowed to do there is walk the horse." He grinned. "But I'd be happy to take you there sometime if you want to try it."

She liked the idea of the two of them riding naked. Trace was so in tune with his mount, she could almost see him naked on Lightyear, his solid thighs gripping the horse's sides as his abdominals worked like waves while he moved with his horse. Yes, she wanted to do that.

She turned to tell him so, but Trace jumped out of the truck and came to her door. She could get down just fine by herself, but she kept her mouth shut and allowed him to help her out. He was a gentleman, so she had to let him do what he needed to do.

He moved to the back of the truck and she leaned in to unbuckle Joey's seatbelt. "You're going to stay here in the big house, but don't be getting any ideas about fancy living or nothing."

Joey rolled his eyes and grunted.

"Yeah, you say that now, but just wait until you get into that cushy bed."

Trace rolled the wheelchair to where she stood.

"He needs his shoulders and head lifted about four inches higher than the rest of him at night. It helps him sleep better."

Trace leaned in and lifted Uncle Joey out of the front seat and set him in the chair. "Lacey already made arrangements for him to sleep in our grandparents bed because it's adjustable. They are going to take my room and use my bed and old Billy's bed for tonight. Billy is staying at Poker Flat. It's a big bed shuffle game."

"Where will you sleep?"

He shrugged. "I get the downstairs couch, but don't worry, it's plenty big. I've slept on it before."

She made sure Joey's feet were up on the foot rest and started to wheel him toward the house.

"Here, let me." Trace took the handles of the wheelchair from her.

She walked with him, unused to doing nothing. Joey was her responsibility. At the three steps to the porch, Trace turned the wheelchair around and pulled Joey up backward like a pro. It was another piece of information about Trace that she stored in the back of her mind for further contemplation at a later time.

Once they had Joey settled with the babysitter and baby Charlotte, they walked back to the truck. Just as Trace opened the door to the cab, a car drove into the ranch and stopped next to them.

"Hey good-lookin', is this the way to the party?"

Trace tipped his hat. "Yes it is, miss."

The sexy Hispanic woman looked Trace up and down. "I certainly hope you're coming too."

He chuckled, the damn flirt. "Yes, I am."

"Save a dance for me, cowboy." The woman waved and continued down the road toward Lacey and Cole's construction site.

Whisper didn't like anything about the woman. Couldn't she see Trace was with her? Hell, she'd learn to dance every song just to keep that lady away from Trace.

Trace caught her attention. "Up you go." After she was seated, he closed the door.

She waited for him to get in. "Who was that?"

"I'm not one hundred percent sure, but from her looks and the way she talked, I'm guessing that's Lacey's good friend Adriana, the bartender from Poker Flat."

"She's a friend of Lacey's?"

Trace chuckled even as he started the engine. "Yes. Hard to believe, isn't it?"

"I don't like the way she talked to you."

Trace leaned toward her. "Why? Are you jealous?"

Whisper thought about it a moment. "Yes."

His eyes widened. Then a seductive grin lifted the corners of his mouth. "I like that."

"You like that I'm mad that this Adriana flirted with you?"

"Yes."

She stared at him. "You're not making sense."

He snaked one hand behind her neck and pulled her closer, their noses almost touching. "Yes, I am. I like that you're mad at Adriana because that means you think of me as yours just like I think of you as mine."

He didn't let her respond. Instead he brought his lips to hers and kissed her, his tongue searching her mouth even as his other hand came up to cup her breast, his thumb rubbing back and forth across her nipple.

She grasped his shoulder and moaned at the pleasure coursing through her body and down to her vagina. She tried to end the kiss, but his hand on her neck refused to allow her to back away and she found his tongue pumping into her mouth as she melted against him.

Finally, he released her and sat up behind the steering wheel again.

She lay against the seat a moment while he lowered the windows.

"It's suddenly a little hot in here." He glanced back at her and smirked. "Ready to meet the family?"

She shook her head even as she raised herself to a sitting position. The thought of all the people who would be at this party had her blood cooling quickly. "I get to leave when I want. Remember that."

His face lost its grin as he pulled the truck onto the dirt road that led to Lacey and Cole's partially constructed house. "You can count on me."

She had to admit, she felt better knowing Trace would take her home as soon as she wanted to go. She planned to watch the party from a quiet corner, unless of course that Adriana woman decided to dance with Trace. Shit, she'd have to go everywhere with him. On one hand, that made her nervous, but on the other hand, she certainly wouldn't mind being next to him all night.

He smelled good and looked better than handsome. She was damn proud to be walking into this party with him.

Within a couple minutes, they were parked, out of the vehicle, and headed toward the bright light seeping through the plastic-covered holes that would someday be filled with windows. The subtle sound of a base beat broke the quiet night and the murmur of voices grew louder as they approached.

She found herself hesitating and Trace halted only three yards from the door. He grasped her hand and stepped in front of her. "Have I told you how beautiful you look tonight?"

She flushed with pleasure. "No."

He smiled and his free hand came up to stroke her cheek. "That's terrible because I think you look stunning tonight. I'm very happy you accepted Lacey's invitation to be my date."

Date? She hadn't had a date in forever. She was sixteen when she'd gone to a pizza place and had pizza with her first boyfriend. She barely finished her dinner before he was dragging her out behind the building to kiss her and suck on her tits. He didn't do nearly as good a job as Trace.

She pressed his hand against her cheek, the feeling new and strange but very enjoyable, then she turned her face and kissed his palm. It was rough against her lips. She liked that he was rough and hard.

Trace lost his smile. "If you keep doing that we'll never make it to this party."

Shit, he didn't like it. She dropped his hand. "I'm sorry."

He grasped her hand in his again. "Don't be sorry. I loved it."

She couldn't tell if he was simply humoring her. It was too dark. "Really?"

He licked her palm then trailed his tongue between two fingers.

A shiver raced from her hand to her heart. "Okay, okay. I believe you."

He laughed, his white teeth gleaming. "I can't wait to introduce you to everyone."

She stiffened as panic swept through her. If you can't say anything nice, don't say anything at all. Her mother's words from so long ago raced through her mind and she latched on to them as they flew by. She could do this. She wasn't afraid of these people. It's not like they were her relatives.

"Your face is wonderful to watch, Whisper. Are you ready?" Trace gave her hand a reassuring squeeze.

She nodded and he hooked her arm in his.

"Then let's go party this year away."

~~*~~

Trace couldn't believe how much he was enjoying Lacey's party. A party was a party, but to experience it with Whisper was proving to be a joy in and of itself. After introducing her to someone, he took time for them to find a quiet corner and let her digest what she'd learned. Her questions were fascinating and her observations spot-on.

He led her once again to a less-populated area of the giant room. He had to admit Lacey, his grandmother and Cole had worked magic. The entire construction site now looked like a wedding bower or even heaven. He wasn't sure which. There was plenty of room for dancing and eating, and the food and alcohol flowed, literally. There was a chocolate fountain and a gingerbread village with a marshmallow river running through it.

Whisper took another sip of champagne; a choice of drink he hadn't expected from her. She was beyond intriguing. "Don't drink too much of that. We still have the champagne toast at midnight."

She looked at him as if he'd just told her the world was flat. He chuckled. He'd never had this much fun at his own parties. Maybe it was the company.

"I like Kendra." He could listen to Whisper's low, husky voice all night and not grow tired of it.

He glanced at the couple he'd just introduced her to, the owners of Poker Flat Nudist Resort. "Hmm, I found Kendra difficult to read. Then again, this is the first time I've met her. Her boyfriend, Wade, I know because he's been here to look at horses. He's thinking about buying a couple more."

"That's why you told him about Storm, Rogue and Mystique?"

He nodded. Whisper would never refer to horses as just horses. To her, each was worthy of their own individuality. "Yes. My guess is, based on what you figured out, those three can never be separated or Mystique will suffer. Wade understands. Two of his horses, Sage and Daisy, are like that in a way. Sage won't budge without Daisy."

Whisper gave a small smile proving she had finally begun to relax a bit. "I'm glad your cousin is careful about who he gives his horses to." She pointed to his aunt. "I would never let her have a horse. She would ride it into the ground if it suited her. She is all about herself. See?"

He grasped her hand in an effort to avoid her drawing attention and watched as his aunt Beverly pulled a young, obviously wealthy, young woman over to talk to Cole, who was dressed in a formal western tux much like one Trace used to own. His curiosity was piqued by Whisper's observation. "How do you know that?"

She shrugged. "By watching her. When she gets into a conversation, she dominates it, demanding everyone's attention. After she leaves, you can see the people sigh in relief. It's like a twister came by and they are happy to have made it through without damage."

Trace laughed, drawing a bit more attention toward them than Whisper was comfortable with. At least that was his assumption based on the frown she gave him. "You are a genius."

"No, I'm not. My IQ isn't that high."

This time he stifled his laugh before it came out, but he couldn't help his wide smile. "As a matter of fact, that woman you described so well is Cole's mother."

Whisper's gaze left him and went back to his aunt. "Why is she forcing Cole to talk to that woman when Lacey is his fiancée, or does she think Cole would leave Lacey that easily?"

Trace nodded. "That's what she thinks."

Whisper shook her head. "Cole would never leave Lacey. If he did, he wouldn't last long."

Trace's blood chilled at her statement. "What do you mean?"

"She's his whole world. He'd give up everything for her, not that Lacey would ask him to. It's so obvious."

He frowned. He would have done the same for Yvonne and apparently he had given up everything, but he was still alive. In fact, he never felt more alive than when he was with

Whisper. Still, it rankled to be fleeced when his own motives had been honorable.

Maybe, as Cole once said, he was lucky to be free of the Ice Queen.

He studied Whisper as she watched the crowd. Her expressions were open and honest and nothing got past her.

She made to point again, but he still had her hand so she gestured with her glass. "Who's that over there getting a drink at the bar? The one with the black hair and brown cowboy hat?"

He looked to where she indicated. "That's my cousin Dillion. He's Cole's younger brother. He helps run Morning Creek Ranch, his parents' place. Cole doesn't mind that he handles the homestead. Cole is very happy here."

She looked back to his aunt Beverley. "That woman is barking up the wrong tree."

"Excuse me?"

Whisper shrugged and took another sip of champagne.

He couldn't help watching her lips on the rim of the glass. He loved the taste of her lips and her tongue. She wasn't shy at all, despite her lack of extensive experience. Maybe her observations of animals had her accepting how sex worked.

He froze in mid-swallow of his beer. Is that why she looked at penetration as something to be accepted? Had she ever had an orgasm?

His blood raced at the thought that he could be her first in all ways that counted. Shit, was it midnight yet? He'd half hoped Whisper would want to go home early, but he couldn't deny her this opportunity. It was good for her to socialize with people a little.

When he finally took his eyes from Whisper's lips, he

silently groaned. "Uh-oh. Here comes Cole's mom and that poor woman she is dragging about with her. Aunt Beverly was probably rejected by Cole and is looking for someone else to match her up with. Take my arm. Please."

Whisper widened her eyes before she gave him that half smile that started his heart racing before she took his arm. "Do you want me to bat my eyelashes, too?"

He chuckled. "No, but if it looks bad, a kiss couldn't hurt." Actually, a kiss on his cheek might just do the trick.

His aunt stopped in front of him. "Trace, we haven't had a chance to meet your friend here." Beverly gave a short nod to Whisper before focusing on him.

He hated that she called Whisper a friend. He wanted her to be more than that. "Aunt Beverly, this is my date, Whisper Adams."

Beverly spared Whisper a brief nod before presenting Hailey. "Trace, I'd like you to meet Hailey Kahnes. You remember the Kahnes family, don't you? They lived in the next town over from your parents' ranch."

He smiled politely. "Nice to meet you, Hailey. This is Whisper, my girlfriend."

Hailey looked relieved at his pronouncement and turned toward Whisper. "Lacey told us how you saved her life. She was very lucky to find you."

Trace watched Whisper shrug. "Fate."

"What high school did you attend?"

"I didn't. I was home schooled." Whisper appeared proud of that fact. It fit a couple of her puzzle pieces together for him. She had an unusual repertoire of knowledge, which was probably due to Uncle Joey's interests.

But his aunt sniffed, clearly unimpressed. His body

tensed. He'd never had the urge to smack a woman, but at that moment he had to clench his fist to keep from knocking some sense into his aunt.

Hailey shook her head. "That's not it then. Have we met before? You look familiar for some reason."

Whisper's face drained of color and Trace wrapped his arm around her waist to steady her. "I doubt it. She's local."

Hailey nodded, but wasn't convinced.

Beverly gave a tiny laugh, the fake high-society kind. "Oh, I doubt you know her, Hailey. Lacey tells me she lives in a trailer in the desert near this ranch. Hardly the same social circles."

Trace felt Whisper stiffen, but before he could defend her, Hailey nodded, leaned in and whispered, "She has no clue what circles I can ride in." She winked at Whisper and looped her arm in his aunt's. "So tell me, Beverley, who is that dashing looking man conferring with your mother? Perhaps you could introduce us."

Beverly quickly forgot about them and ushered Hailey off to meet Logan. Trace grinned. Good luck with that.

Hailey glanced back at Whisper once his aunt took over the conversation. She really thought she knew Whisper and Whisper was as stiff as a board. What was she afraid of?

"Hey, if you can't relax, I may just have to take you out on the dance floor to loosen you up."

Whisper's gaze shifted to the dancers who were two-stepping around the floor and her arm tightened on his. "Shit. Here comes that Adriana woman."

He caught sight of the bartender from Poker Flat and grinned at Whisper's reaction. There was something about a jealous woman that set a man's pride up another notch.

Adriana sauntered toward them, her curvy body not

hidden at all in the tight red minidress with spaghetti straps. He'd heard from Cole that the woman had a lot of sexual experience. It didn't surprise him, considering how hot she was.

When she was less than twelve feet away, his vision was suddenly blocked by Whisper's face. "Time for that kiss."

The second her lips touched his and her arms wrapped around his neck, he was lost. Her tongue dove into his mouth and he pulled her close, loving how free she was with her desire.

"Ahem. I don't mean to interrupt, but you're drawing an audience. Midnight is still thirty minutes away." The sultry voice took him off guard until he registered the meaning of the words.

Trace lifted his head and flushed at the dozen or so people who had turned around to watch him and Whisper. He kept his voice low. "Whisper, you need to let go. People are watching."

She released him and turned to meet everyone's stare then shrugged. "So?"

Adriana's laugh finally drew their attention. "Oh, I like you. Hi, my name is Adriana. I'm a good friend of Lacey's. She told me you're Whisper, another good friend of hers." Adriana held out her hand.

Whisper shook, but didn't say anything.

Adriana glanced from Whisper to him. "Well howdy, cowboy. I didn't realize you were taken." She sighed heavily. "Seems all the good ones are." She winked at Whisper, who continued in her silence.

Adriana swept her gaze over his girlfriend. "You look beautiful. I envy you your class."

Whisper's eyes widened then turned to slits. "What do you want?"

Adriana laughed again. "Oh, I do like you. A woman after

my own heart. Tell it like you see it. To set your mind at rest, I'm not interested in your cowboy and—"

"His name is Trace."

Adriana nodded. "I'm sorry. We haven't been introduced. Hello, Trace."

He nodded once, not willing to delay the woman's explanation.

"I'm more interested in you, Whisper. I don't like people threatening my friends and Lacey told me what you did for her when she was pinned down by that piece of trash, Norton. I also like a woman who can hold her own. I've had to myself a time or two."

Whisper's tension eased a bit. "You say you like people to tell it like it is. Tell me then, when is the wedding going to start?"

Chapter Six

Trace's heart lurched in confusion. "Wedding?"

Adriana's eyes rounded before she adjusted her countenance. "Why do you ask about a wedding?"

Whisper appeared insulted. "Really? Let's see, the room is decorated in white, complete with white balloons and doves. Lacey is wearing a long white gown and both Cole and his brother Dillion are wearing tuxes. They each have a boutonniere and you have a corsage. Both families are represented as well as close friends, and I heard that person over there say he was a justice of the peace."

Trace looked at every person she mentioned then stared at her.

Adriana also looked at her, eyes wide. She leaned in. "Shh, it's going to be a surprise. Right after the New Year. No one knows but the specific people you mentioned."

Trace grinned. He had to hand it to Lacey. She hadn't said a word about it and she talked a lot. Not like Whisper, whose longest discourse all night had been her analysis of the surprise wedding.

"I won't say anything." She gave him a stern look as if he would. "At least I know how long I have to stay here."

"Aren't you having fun?" Adriana cocked her head in his direction.

Whisper gave her signature smirk. "I think I'll have more fun after the party."

Adriana laughed and Trace's balls reacted. Whisper just told him she wanted sex. Shit, he'd leave now, but she was right. Now that they knew there would be a wedding, they had to stay. Of course, everyone else would stay until the midnight countdown. Even his grandparents were still up and it was getting close to the end of the year.

"Trace, it was nice to meet you. I just hope you have the stamina for this one." Adriana winked and sauntered off, flirting herself into a dance with Dillion.

He turned toward Whisper, loosely wrapping his arms around her waist, not caring what anyone thought. "I think we need to have your IQ checked. I'm more convinced now than before that you're a genius."

She looped her hands around his neck. "Nope, I'm short one point."

Holy hell, he couldn't catch his balance with this woman. Maybe he could even the playing field. "Want to dance?"

She stiffened in his arms. "I don't know how."

"The only thing different from dancing and what we're doing is shifting your weight from one leg to the other."

She looked askance at him. "That's not what I see other people doing."

"Just wait. If I don't miss my guess, the next song will be a slow song."

They stood still, listening to the country song end. Another song started. It was slow as he predicted. "Okay, now I want you to watch my cousin, Dillion. See how he's moving with Adriana?"

She nodded.

"Think you can do that?"

She hesitated, but finally nodded again.

Whisper closed her eyes as she leaned her face against Trace's shoulder like she'd seen other women do with their partners. Back when she and Uncle Joey were still on the grid, she'd watched television shows and movies where people danced. It always fascinated her how everyone could move the same, but here that wasn't the case. Some people weren't even moving to the beat.

She let her body meld to Trace's, catching his rhythm and following him, much like she caught Sadie's rhythm and adjusted her movement to the horse's stride. He slowly rocked her into the crowd, but no one else existed in their world.

She saw a hand touch Trace's other shoulder and he turned them toward it.

"May I cut in?" Logan stood there, his body radiating irritation.

Trace squeezed her tighter. "No."

"Excuse me, little brother, but that's not polite."

Trace sighed and loosened his hold. "Just for a few minutes. Understand?"

Logan nodded. "Sure."

Whisper was wrapped in Logan's arms within seconds before she even had a chance to voice her opinion. "What do you want?"

"I just wanted to talk to you." Logan was as stiff as she was.

"Then talk."

He opened his mouth then closed it.

"Just spit it out. No need to be polite around me."

One of his eyebrows rose in response. "Okay. How much has Trace told you about his wife?"

She shrugged. "Not much. From what he said, I understand the divorce is not final yet. From what he hasn't said, I've figured out she is taking his ranch, his horses and his bank accounts. I'm not sure he's decided yet if she took his heart as well. I think his pride is hurt that a woman stole everything he worked for right out from under his nose, but I'd bet his heart is bruised, not broken."

Logan stopped dancing and stared at her. "Damn, you're scary."

An old feeling of inadequacy started to rise, but she stomped it down. "I've heard that before. Is that it?"

Logan started the rhythmic rocking again. "Not yet. I just want you to know that just because Trace doesn't have any money left to his name, doesn't mean he can't make some. He's done it once and he can do it again."

"Why would I care if he had money?"

Logan looked uncomfortable for the first time. "I'm just saying if you decided to have a long-term relationship with him, he would find a way to take care of you."

"Listen, Jack. I don't need anyone to take care of me. Uncle Joey did it until I was eighteen and I've been taking care of myself and him since I turned twenty-two."

"Fine. Just don't go breaking my brother's heart or I'll find you."

Whisper couldn't help smirking. "I've had people more determined than you give up trying to find me. If I don't want to be found, I won't be." She also knew of at least two who would never give up, but Trace's older brother didn't need to know that.

Logan's lips quirked just a tad. "You may be just what Trace needs."

"Excuse me." Trace clapped his hand on Logan's shoulder. "It's getting a little too close to midnight for my girlfriend to be in your arms."

Logan let go of her, raising his hands like a gun had been pointed at him. "I was just leaving."

Trace pulled her against him, nice and close, and her body relaxed into his rhythm.

"What did he want?"

She gazed into Trace's warm brown eyes. "He was worried I would break your heart. Isn't that funny?"

He didn't smile. "That's not—"

The music stopped and the DJ drowned out everything with a ten-second countdown. Trace grinned and counted aloud.

The whole scene reminded her of the days when she and Uncle Joey sat in front of the television and watched the ball drop in New York. She hoped he was seeing it now.

A second after "one" was announced, everyone broke into cheers, except she and Trace. His gaze had softened and he lowered his head to kiss her.

She felt the difference at once. It wasn't a sexual kiss like the others. It was gentle and sweet, like she was precious to him, a feeling she hadn't had since she was five and her parents kissed her goodnight together, yet it was different, a grown-up precious. She liked it.

Trace pulled away and stared at her until Lacey pulled him around and gave him a New Year's kiss on the cheek.

Whisper stood and watched everyone hugging and kissing while Auld Lang Syne played loudly from the speakers. As she scanned the room, she noticed the woman, Hailey, staring at her. She shivered. Why did that woman think she knew her? She'd never seen her before.

She lost sight of her when Lacey pulled her into a hug. "Happy New Year."

She returned the greeting until Lacey pulled away.

"Come with me." Lacey hooked her arm and proceeded to the back of the house.

"Where's Cole?"

Lacey glanced back. "I think he's up there by the DJ."

Ah, it was the wedding. "Is your dad making his way back here too?"

Lacey stared at her a moment then laughed, a beautiful, joyous laugh. "Yes, he is. I should have known you would figure it out."

When they reached the east end of the space, Lacey pulled a flower arrangement off the wall. It looked similar to the others hanging in the area, but this one had a handle, long white ribbons and two tiny white doves nestled in it. Lacey moved to another one with shorter ribbons and one dove in it and handed it to her. "Here, you'll need this."

Lacey's dad had Kendra on his arm. Kendra looked expectantly at Lacey. "Okay, I'm here. What do you need to talk to me about?"

Lacey walked to another wall decoration that looked just like Whisper's and handed it to Kendra. "I want you two to be my bridesmaids."

Whisper nodded.

"I'd be happy to." Kendra smiled. "When are you getting—oh." Her smile turned into a smirk.

"We start in about one minute. Where is Adriana?"

Lacey was far too short to see over the crowd, so Whisper sought out the red-dressed woman. "She's coming."

Lacey heaved a sigh. "Oh, good."

Whisper was very impressed with Lacey's planning. She helped Kendra add a train to Lacey's dress that had been hidden on a chair in the back. When she looked up again, she tried to find Trace but didn't see him.

She was excited. She'd never been in a wedding and though they looked boring, she liked what they symbolized. Luckily, television had given her all she needed to know.

"Ready, Dad?" Lacey looked up at her father, though he wasn't even as tall as Whisper.

Lacey's father smiled down at her, a glowing smile as wide as the Grand Canyon. "Whenever you are, sweet pea."

The phrase whisked Whisper back to her childhood when her father said the same words to her before he took her up in his plane. Her heart contracted again with her loss and she clamped her jaw hard to keep her eyes from watering.

Just then Adriana appeared. "Made it."

The last strains of Auld Ang Syne finished and everyone cheered, but when the traditional wedding march began, the room went silent. The partygoers looked around. Kendra took the lead, parting the crowd.

Lacey signaled her to follow and Whisper went in step behind Kendra, the honor Lacey had bestowed on her finally sinking in. A warmth settled in her heart. She'd made a friend. She hadn't had one of those since she was eleven, back before

Joey decided they had to move more in order to stay ahead of her relatives.

She caught sight of Trace's aunt. The woman stood open-mouthed. She eventually snapped her mouth shut and turned toward her husband with a scowl. He promptly held up his hand and gave her a furious look. Beverly Hatcher swallowed hard and turned back to watch the progress down the opening in the crowd, her lips pursed together in disapproval.

Whisper had to smile slightly at that. It served the woman right. She should respect her son's decision in a wife, and Lacey was everything he needed. As she continued to walk by the surprised but smiling faces, she searched for Trace. She was almost to the DJ when she found him standing next to Logan, who stood next to Dillion. She glanced at the groom, who'd she'd met earlier in the evening. He'd said all the right words, thanking her for helping Lacey against the animal abuser, but she sensed a reserve.

Her gaze swung back to Trace. He looked more like a bridegroom than Cole in her opinion. If they were to marry, she'd want him to wear— She caught herself at the thought even as she turned and followed Kendra to the side. Married? Her heart beat erratically as the idea blossomed. She'd never considered she would. She'd never thought beyond taking care of Uncle Joey. Maybe subconsciously she figured she'd be too old to marry after he passed because she expected him to live a very long time.

But what if she found someone like Trace, who understood and cared about Joey? She started to smile when another thought hit her. The money. What would her husband think about the money? He'd probably love it. She scowled. Once again the damn money would rule her life. If it wasn't for Joey's medical bills, she'd give the whole inheritance away to charity. It was nothing but a pain in her ass.

"Whisper?" Kendra leaned toward her. "It's a wedding. There's no need to scowl."

She snapped her head to the side to meet Kendra's gaze. The woman had a smile on her own face. "Sorry. I was thinking of something else." She looked at Lacey's ecstatic face and gave it her full effort. She was happy for Lacey.

She glanced beyond the bride to look at Trace. His gaze was already on her, his look telling her far more than she could understand from so far away. Damn, he was a good-looking cowboy and he had a good heart. She could do worse. What would he think about the money? He didn't have any, so he'd either be thrilled or… What if he wanted to spend it all?

Whisper shook her head to stop her thoughts. She liked the man, but that didn't mean they would get married. Besides, he'd probably get tired of her strangeness and settle down again, this time with some cowgirl who really knew how to ride a horse.

An elbow to her ribs caught her unawares. "Oh."

Kendra whispered, "Stop frowning."

Shit. She put a half smile on her face and watched the bridal couple for the rest of the ceremony. It was the only way to show she was happy for them, which she was. It was her own situation that pissed her off.

Trace couldn't wait for the ceremony to be over. He was happy for Cole and Lacey, but their wedding made him want to whisk Whisper away and make love to her. He didn't even question his need to be her first as an adult. He wanted to explore her body as much as he loved exploring her mind.

Once Lacey and Cole shared their first kiss as a married couple, his palms started to sweat. The bridal couple could stay all night for all he cared.

Maybe there would be cake leftovers because he was leaving…with Whisper. When Whisper had agreed to come to the party as long as she be allowed to leave when she wanted, he'd expected her to want to go long before he was ready. He was ready now.

His brother started to move toward the center of their line and hooked arms with Kendra before following Adriana and Dillion. Trace grinned at Whisper, happy to see her half smile and gray eyes lighting up as he approached. He linked his arm with hers and led her down the impromptu aisle. "Did you like the ceremony?"

She looked at him. "It was boring in parts, but I'm happy for Lacey."

He chuckled, loving her honesty. "Would you be interested in leaving soon, or did you want to stay for the cake and the throwing of the bouquet?"

"I'm ready to leave." She looked at the crowd and frowned.

He glanced in the direction she looked, his protective instincts kicking in, but he didn't see anyone threatening. The only person looking in their direction was the woman named Hailey. Ah, it finally clicked. Whisper didn't want to be recognized.

An unbidden thought rose in his head. He didn't need Whisper's intuitive genius to put the pieces together. She lived in a trailer completely off the grid and said she preferred animals over people. Was she wanted by the law? Shit.

He continued to smile as they brought up the rear of the procession, his emotions spinning like a desert dust devil.

Could she have shot someone? She'd certainly shot up Ray Norton. If she did, his gut told him it would be because she protected herself, or someone else, like she had with Lacey. Maybe someone had threatened uncle Joey. He breathed easier at his conclusions.

They finally made it to the end just as Lacey and Cole took the floor for their first dance. He didn't let Whisper disengage from his arm, but continued to walk around the room, grabbing his hat and her cape from the table where they had sat for the dinner. When they reached the door, he stepped aside and let her exit. Settling his hat on his head, he quickly closed the door behind them.

He took a deep breath of the cool night air. If he didn't know better, he'd swear there was a touch of moisture in it.

The door opened behind him. "Whisper Adams."

Trace spun around to find Detective Sean Anderson standing there in a shirt and tie, his sport coat long gone, and a small pad and pen in his hand.

"Is there a problem, Sean?"

"Yes. This woman has eluded us for almost a week. I need to talk to her about the shoot-out in the canyon."

Trace kept his back to Whisper, determined to make the man go through him to get to her. "It's not even one in the morning. Don't you think this could wait until tomorrow? We can come down to the station if you like."

The detective raised a brow at his use of the word "we" but he didn't care.

"That's a nice offer, but I'm determined to take one day off this season. I was here on Christmas and Lacey told me what happened. But right now, it's her word against Ray Norton's and a second witness would help."

"Now is fine." Whisper stepped up next to him. "I'd rather do it here."

He looked at her. "Are you sure?"

She nodded, so he took her hand. "Then let's go over to my truck."

Sean nodded and followed them.

The truck was parked far enough away that they could hear each other. The other advantage in Trace's mind was it wasn't well lit. If Whisper had something to hide, he knew it would show on her face and he was determined to keep Ray Norton in jail and Whisper out of it. He'd heard the whole story from Cole and Lacey, and it could reflect badly on Whisper if viewed differently.

Whisper let go of his hand and faced the detective straight on. He was both proud of her and scared for her at the same time.

Sean started to ask questions and Trace gritted his teeth to keep from interrupting. But when Whisper said Ray Norton was only alive because Lacey wouldn't let her kill him, he had to step in. "I'm sure she would have held back on her own at the last second. She was teaching him a lesson, an eye for an eye. He abused Angel and she let him know what it felt like."

Sean raised his brow at him again, but didn't buy it.

At least she hadn't killed the man and she admitted she wouldn't have because of Lacey, so there was no "intent" to kill, but he could see the fine line she was balanced on.

"I think I have everything I need. Don't leave town in case I need more specifics. Your story corroborates Lacey's exactly, so Norton should go away for a long time, but we may need you on the witness stand."

Sean was too busy putting away his notepad to notice

Whisper's tension. She didn't like the idea of testifying, but kept silent. Shit, when had he become so adept at reading her?

Sean held out his hand to Whisper. "Thank you for being honest and talking to me here." The man smiled. "I'm looking forward to a day off tomorrow with my family. Usually this town is quiet and I hope it stays that way."

Trace wrapped his arm around Whisper as they watched the detective go inside. Whisper's preference to talk to Sean out here instead of in the police station sent more smoke signals that not all was as it appeared with her. But he didn't want to think about that tonight, or rather this morning.

When the door closed, Whisper stepped away and reached for the door handle of his truck, but he grabbed her hand. "Hey, where're you going?"

"You said you would take me home." There was anxiousness in her voice.

He pulled her toward him, wanting to reassure her, but his mind slowed as his body reacted to hers when she came against him. "I thought we could have our second kiss of this year under the moonlight."

He released her hand and she wrapped her arms around his neck. "There is no moonlight tonight."

Glancing at the sky, he chuckled. "I should have known you would have noticed that. How about our second kiss of the year beneath the stars?"

"Okay." Whisper lifted her mouth to his and kissed his lips chastely before pulling back.

"Hey, what was that?"

She tilted her head to the side. "That was the preamble. If you want the full experience, you need to bring me home, now."

He grinned. "Fine, I'll drive you home because I definitely want the whole experience."

She nodded as if they'd settled something important then stepped away. "Come on. I can't wait much longer."

Holy shit. Was she just anxious to get away from the party or was she ready to jump into bed with him? He took his handkerchief from his coat pocket and wiped his brow. The woman could rev up his libido in two seconds. He grabbed the keys out of his jeans pocket and clicked the button that opened the doors.

Whisper climbed in immediately, and he closed the door for her. As he walked around the truck, his mind took over and his concerns about her past floated to the surface again. Jumping in, he forcefully quelled them. There was always tomorrow for that. Tonight was the start of a brand new year, and he planned to start it off in the arms of the woman he lov—

His hand stilled as he reached for the ignition. Shit, he couldn't. He wasn't ready. He just liked her a bunch.

"What's wrong?" Whisper looked at him, the muted light from the building reflected in her eyes, making them appear silver, like the stars themselves.

Shit. He needed to stop thinking or he'd ruin everything. "Nothing."

"You're lying. What is it?"

He shook his head and started the engine. "Yes, it was something, but not something I'm going to share right now."

She frowned, but sat back and looked out the front window.

"Hey, you're too far away. Scoot over here where Joey sat, so I can be close to you."

She made a show of unbuckling her seatbelt and moving over, belting the middle one over her lap. "Happy now?"

She sounded irritated, but as he started the drive back to her trailer, she relaxed. By the time he'd parked the car, her hand was on his leg, her head rested on his shoulder and his cock was harder than ironwood.

She lifted her head and unbuckled, removing her hand from its teasing position.

Trace reminded himself that he had to take it slow with her. Hell, he might not even be able to push inside her, so he needed to cool down. He jumped out of the truck, but by the time he reached her door, she'd already climbed out.

He walked her to the trailer, hoping for that invitation inside. She opened the door and held it for him. Guess that was his invitation.

He grinned as he took off his hat and stepped inside. No "Would you like a cup of coffee?" or "Would you like to come in for a nightcap?" Nope, Whisper just held the door open.

Inside, she took off her cape and threw it on Joey's bed in the living room. "The bedroom's back here." She walked through a narrow hallway with two doors opposite each other. He assumed one would be the bathroom.

Her bedroom was the complete width of the trailer plus a slide out and it was long. Not cramped at all. It wasn't cheap either. Plush carpet lay beneath his boots and a state-of-the-art television was mounted in the wall opposite the bed. Of course, she had no satellite dish so that was worthless, but it did indicate to him that she was on the grid at some point.

The shelves around the television were jam-packed with books. They were piled on top of each other, taking up every tiny space possible. He looked at the titles to see if he'd recognize any. There was a volume of Shakespeare's complete works, a history of the world, beginner carpentry, A Christmas Carol, and a whole set of encyclopedias on animals. Each book focused on a group. He had to ask her if she'd found any useful information on horses. Turning to face her, his question died on his lips.

Chapter Seven

Whisper had taken off her blouse and camisole and was working on the buttons on the side of her skirt. His gaze focused on her breasts as they moved with her actions. When she undid the last button, the skirt fell to the floor and she was naked to her boots.

Holy shit! If he'd known she'd gone commando, he would have left the party before dinner.

She bent over, picked up the skirt and turned to a hidden closet behind the bed. After opening a panel, she pushed a button and he heard the hum of a motor. She hung the skirt on a hanger and closed the panel.

When she turned around his breath caught. She was so much woman. Full breasts were held above a four-pack stomach, wide hips and shapely thighs that cradled a neat bush of black pubic hair. He remembered how soft it felt against his hand.

She sat on the bed and tugged off her boots as if he weren't even in the room. He'd never been with a woman who was so comfortable in her own skin. It was incredibly attractive.

She stood. "Aren't you getting undressed?" She looked at him expectantly.

He'd never had a woman ask him that. "Yes."

He dropped his hat on a side table and hung his sport jacket on a wall hook that was empty. He started to unbutton his shirt, keeping an eye on her.

She reached up and pulled hair pins from her head until her long hair flowed down her back.

Trace stilled. Just when he thought she couldn't be more beautiful, more fascinating, more alive, she moved to another level.

She massaged her head then fluffed out the silky mass. "Now I remember why I don't put my hair up. It's too heavy."

He swallowed. How the hell was he supposed to take it slow when she looked good enough to eat?

"Do you need help?" Her question caught him off guard, but as she walked toward him, it registered.

"I think I do."

He watched her as she focused on the rest of his shirt buttons. Wasn't he supposed to undress her?

She tugged his shirt out from his jeans and finished her task. Then she put her hands under the shirt and pulled it down his arms, her breasts pressing against his bare chest as she worked it all the way to his wrists where the cuffs were still buttoned.

He took a deep breath, loving the feel of her hardening nipples. "You need to unbutton the sleeves."

She didn't say anything, just moved to do what was needed to get his shirt off. Once his wrists were free, she stepped around him and hung it on the hook.

She came back and went for the zipper on his jeans. He caught her hands. "Whoa, wait. I need to take off my boots."

She looked down. "Oh, yeah. Sit."

He did as she commanded, curious as to how she would help when there wasn't much space between the end of the bed and the television wall. It was a nice, big bed.

She turned her back on him and spread her legs. "Lift your leg."

He lifted his new black cowboy boot between her legs and she bent over to pull it off. His pulse raced at the view of her rounded ass and he swallowed hard.

"Lift the other one."

He did as instructed, but couldn't allow her to get away without touching her. With any other woman, her position would have been an invitation to another kind of sex, but this was Whisper, so he simply squeezed her butt. It was soft, womanly and enticing.

She pulled away. "What was that for?"

He grinned. "Just a thank you."

She looked at him as if he was the one who was odd, again reminding him that her sexual experiences had to be limited. Obviously, she hadn't even been touched on her ass. That thought sobered him and gave him the control he needed to keep from jumping her right there.

He stood and before she could touch him, he undid his belt and unzipped his jeans to let his cock breathe. He didn't look at her as he stepped out of his pants and turned to hang them by the belt loop. He'd love it if she pressed herself against his back, but she probably wouldn't know how exciting that could be.

When he turned back, he expected her to still be standing there, but she'd moved to the side of the bed and pulled the covers down. Despite her comfort with her body, he sensed a stiffness in her movements.

He strode around to where she held the cover and took it from her. Lifting her hand, he kissed her palm. Of course, he couldn't let it go at that and he licked her life line.

She pulled her hand away. "That tickles."

"What about this?" He took her other hand and brought her index finger into his mouth and sucked.

When he released her finger, he looked at her. "Well?"

"I like that."

The memory of their time by the shed flitted through his mind and he brought his hands up to cup her breasts. She liked her breasts played with the most, probably because she didn't know any other touch could be as stimulating.

He watched her expression as he brought his thumbs up to stroke back and forth across her hard nipples. What he wanted to do was bring her body flush with his, but the second his cock touched her, she might go into "acceptance" mode and when he penetrated her, if he could, he wanted her to crave it as much as he did.

She watched his fingers even as her breathing accelerated, but she made no move to touch him.

He lowered his head and heard the smallest intake of breath from her. Cupping one breast while his hand played with the other, he flicked the nipple with his tongue.

"More." Whisper's demand fueled his hunger for her and he pulled the nipple and areola into his mouth. While he sucked, he flicked the hard nub.

"Trace." Her breathy word sent sparks racing through his veins.

His name on her lips was like a match thrown onto a scrub brush during a drought. To know she enjoyed his touch started a fire low in his belly. He switched to the other nipple and sucked that one as well, but when he released it, he nibbled it with his teeth.

Her hands grasped his shoulders, revealing her pleasure.

He continued his attention to her nipple, tugging at it with his teeth and circling it with his tongue. Her hands dug into his shoulders, making it clear she was ready to lie down.

Lifting his head, he met her dark, stormy gray gaze. Desire was written all over her face from her eyes to her open mouth, where tiny quick breaths escaped. He couldn't resist her lips and pulled her upper body close.

An inch from the kiss, he whispered, "I want the full experience this time."

Her lips met his and she opened for him, letting him sweep inside her mouth like his cock wanted to plunge inside her sheath. Tasting champagne mixed with the minty flavor of Whisper, he stroked her tongue. Hers met his and he allowed her to explore his mouth. She moaned deep in her throat as he caught her tongue and sucked. It wasn't a shy moan, as if she tried to hide how much he pleased her. It was a deep-throated, husky moan that sent need straight to his cock.

Her pelvis pressed against him, but his mind signaled him to go slow, even though her mons pushed against his cock, the soft hair tantalizing him. He'd lose control if she continued that. Reluctantly, he ended the kiss, easing out of it with nibbles on her lips and chaste kisses to the corners of her mouth, wanting to show her exactly how important she was to him.

Her dazed look cleared and she gave him a half smile, the one that sent his heart into overdrive. "You're a good kisser."

He grinned, despite knowing she didn't have much to compare him to. Hell, it still felt good.

"Can we get on the bed now?"

His grin widened. "Of course."

He loosened his hold and she dropped onto the bed. "Good, my knees weren't going to hold me much longer."

He chuckled. He'd had no idea how rewarding it could be to make love with such unadulterated honesty. Thank God he had no doubts about his prowess in bed. His wife may have wanted his money more than him, but she never complained about their bedroom activities.

Shit, why did he have to think about her now? His body cooled instantly.

"Why are you frowning?" Whisper lay on her back, her hip-length hair thrown to one side and her curvy body just waiting to be pleasured.

He lowered his brows more. "There so much I want to do to you to make you enjoy this, I'm having a hard time deciding what to do first."

She shrugged. "That's easy. Suck on my nipples."

His cock returned to its hard state quickly. "Thank you, that helps." It took a lot of effort to avoid smiling.

"And then when I'm wetter, you can slide your finger inside me like you did yesterday."

He fisted his hands at her words and his cock jumped, something he couldn't control.

She noticed. "Is something wrong?"

He took a calming breath. "No." At her look of disbelief, it was apparent he'd have to be as honest as she was. "Your words get me excited, which makes it harder to hold back until I can give you an orgasm."

"But I'm already wet."

Count to ten. One. Two. Three. Four... By time he reached

ten, he had some semblance of control. Luckily, she didn't say anything else and just stared at his chest.

As much as he wanted to crawl between her legs immediately, his concern over her automatic response toward acceptance instead of enjoyment helped him to walk to the other side of the bed and lie down next to her. He propped himself up on his side so he could view her. "Your body is beautiful."

She looked at him but didn't say anything. He loved that she didn't deny his words. "Do you like the way I look?"

She nodded. "Especially your chest…a lot."

"So touch it."

She glanced warily at him before hesitantly placing her hand on him. "I like that you're warm." Her hand moved to his abdominal muscles. "And hard."

He wanted her to move that hand down farther, but she reversed her direction and brushed over his right pectoral.

"Your nipple is hard like mine get."

Shit, that boy who introduced her to sex had left out a lot. "Yes, and they feel to me like yours feel to you."

"Really?" She looked unconvinced. "So if I suck on them, they will get harder and you'll feel that pressure between your legs?"

His cock jumped again. Shit, this would be the toughest lovemaking he'd ever done, no doubt about it. "Yup." He tried to be nonchalant about it, but the idea that she might make her own move had his stomach tensing with anticipation.

Luckily, her attention was on his chest so she didn't see his cock's reaction to her words. He'd noticed she avoided looking below his waist, more confirmation she had no idea what pleasure his erection could give her.

She turned on her side to face him. He held his breath as she stared at his pectoral. Yes, do it.

No sooner did he have the thought then she leaned forward and took his nipple into her mouth, copying what he'd done to her exactly.

Fire-like pleasure shot straight to his cock, and he held himself back from grabbing her by the barest control.

She let go and inspected his nipple. "I like that."

He grimaced. "So do I." Luckily, her gaze was fixed on his very hard nub.

"Do you like this?" She reached toward his other nipple, her intent clear.

Quickly, he rolled her over onto her back. "I like it too much."

She gave him her smirk.

He shook his head. "I need more of you first. That's all."

Whisper glanced downward but she couldn't see his throbbing cock pressed into the sheets. "You want to—"

"No, I want to give you pleasure and hopefully an orgasm."

She lowered her brows. "But I told you I'm already wet. You can check."

He couldn't smile to reassure her because his cock was determined to see exactly how wet she was. Wet? Orgasm? Hell, she thought being wet meant she had an orgasm. "Whisper. Exactly how old were you the last time you had sex?"

"Sixteen."

She said she was thirty. Damn, he hadn't realized how close to the truth he'd been. She was practically a virgin. Unless she'd watched porn, which he highly doubted. She probably thought she knew everything from watching animals mate.

"You're frowning again. If you don't want to have sex, that's okay."

He closed his eyes. The emotions running through him too mixed up to let her see. Excitement, nervousness, need, caring—all caused his gut to tense. He wanted to make this special for her.

He opened his eyes and stared into her gray gaze, so puzzled by his actions. "I want to make love to you very much." He felt her tension ease. "I'm struggling with how much I want to make love to you and how much I want you to enjoy it."

"Oh, I will."

He shook his head. "No, not like you did when you were a teenager. You are an adult now, with an adult body and an adult man here to show you how much enjoyment you really can get from this experience."

She looked doubtful. "Are you saying there is more to it than what I've had and that I will like this other part?"

He loved that she was so quick. "Exactly."

She looked away as she contemplated that for a moment. Finally, her gaze returned to his. "I always wondered what all the excitement was about. You're saying I can feel like you feel when you come?"

He nodded.

Whisper's eyes grew dark. "Please. Show me."

His heart melted and a new confidence filled him. "You said you were wet. That is your body preparing for my cock to enter your opening."

She nodded, her eyes alight with interest.

"That's just the beginning. An orgasm will take over your whole body in exquisite pleasure. It is impossible to put into words and the only way to understand it is to have one."

"And you need to be inside me so I can have one?"

He shook his head. "No, I want to give you your first orgasm without having one of my own. Then we can do it together. How's that sound?"

Her lips twitched up at the corners just a bit. "It sounds interesting. What do I do?"

He grinned. "Just lie there and relax."

"I can do that." She gave him her half smile, her excitement at learning more communicating itself to his body.

She would definitely have the easy part of this if he did it right. He wished he had an ice cube right now to rub along his cock. The damn thing was far too excited. Then a thought occurred. "Stay right here."

He rose from the bed and rifled through his sport jacket. His fingers grasped the condoms he put in there and he brought them back to the bed.

"What are you doing?"

He threw the condoms on the sheet to be within easy reach. "I'm getting us protection."

"Oh, I totally forgot. I'm not ready to be a mother yet."

He stilled as a vision of Whisper showing her daughter how to shoot flitted across his mind. It was far too distracting to hold on to, and he let it go as he resumed his spot next to her, his cock behaving a bit better while he focused on his responsibility.

Whisper lay on her back, watching his every move. He leaned forward and gave her a gentle kiss, keeping his erection from touching her. When he finished letting her know exactly how much she meant to him, he ran his fingers through the mound of black hair at the juncture of her legs.

"I'd like to feel your wetness. Can you spread your legs for me?"

She did, immediately.

He smiled inside at her eagerness to learn. Careful to keep his hips from her body, so she wouldn't switch gears, he spread her folds with his fingers. Her juices coated her opening and his cock hardened more. "Did you like my finger inside you last time we were together?"

"Yes. It feels good when you suck my nipples."

His balls tightened at her words. Shit, she was so blunt, making this "lesson" extra hard for him. He leaned over and nipped at her nipple before sucking it in while he slid his finger inside her moist sheath.

"Yes, I like that." She lifted her hips toward his hand.

He slowly moved his finger in and out while he paid attention to her breasts.

She moaned, her hips pressing upward against his hand.

After releasing her nipple, he leaned back, his finger still buried inside her.

She opened her eyes. "I liked that."

He smiled seductively and her eyes widened. There was so much he wanted to teach her, but this first time he needed to keep it simple.

This time when he slid his finger out of her opening, he coated her clit with her wetness.

"Oh! What was that?"

"That's your clit. It's going to bring you to orgasm."

She didn't respond. Instead, she closed her eyes.

He sank his finger back inside her and rubbed his thumb across her clit.

Her breathing grew more rapid as he swirled her nub, watching her reactions with a keen eye. He wanted to build it slowly for her.

He increased the speed and pressure of his thumb, back and forth over her hard clit. Her sheath squeezed his finger in response.

"What…" A groan followed her question. "Oh, yes." The wonder in her voice helped him keep his control.

She deserved this and he would make it perfect for her. The honor of bringing her to her first orgasm helped him keep his focus. He increased the speed of his movement more, rubbing her clit, keeping the pressure where it should feel the best. Her moans became continuous.

Carefully, he pulled his index finger from her and added another finger, sliding both inside her pussy. Her sheath stretched to accommodate them this time.

Whisper's breaths came faster and her pelvis tilted to keep her clit in contact with his thumb. God, he wanted to kiss her right now, but he had to be happy with watching her have her first orgasm, a vision he ached to see.

Her voice grew louder, her hips more insistent as she instinctually pushed to the pressure she craved. She was so close.

He lowered his head and pulled her rosy nipple into his mouth, sucking.

"Ahhh!" Whisper's yell as she hit her climax rocked his heart. Her legs crossed as she pushed her clit against his thumb, her hips rising from the bed as her body vibrated with pleasure.

He kept the pressure on her nub, releasing her nipple to watch her. Her stomach rose and fell with her breaths and he could see the rhythm of her heart ripple her belly. Her lips were slightly parted, her cheeks flushed and her head turned slightly to the side.

He waited in anticipation of seeing her eyes.

When her legs relaxed, he withdrew his fingers and pressed his whole body against her side, unable to resist the draw of her any longer.

He'd never had the opportunity to bring a woman her first orgasm. This was important…for both of them.

Whisper finally opened her eyes and stared at the ceiling a moment, then turned her head and looked at him. Her gaze was almost black, but even as she focused on him it slowly turned to the gray he loved. "That was an orgasm?"

He nodded, unable to keep the smile from his face.

She returned his smile, not with her signature smirk or half smile, but with a full face, eyes crinkling, blow-him-away smile.

His life seemed to finally fall into focus in that one beautiful vision. He pulled her head toward him and gave her a gentle kiss.

Her hand locked on to his neck and she pulled her body flush against him even as her tongue breached his lips, but neither of them deepened the kiss. It was a kiss of completion, satisfaction and connection.

She pressed her pelvis against his cock and wrapped her leg over his, a good sign she might be ready for him. He held her tight, loving the feel of her along his length. They were almost the same height and every curve of hers melded into him.

She pulled her head back and gazed into his eyes. "That was…indescribable."

He grinned. "That's good." He ran his hand down her back and through her silky hair. She smelled good, felt good, and tasted good.

She looked away for a moment and then returned her gaze

to him. "Thank you. I didn't know. I feel like… It's as if you gave me a new life."

His heart lurched at her comment and he gathered her tight against him. He wanted to know so much about her, teach her about making love, riding horses and—His hand stilled even as his heart swelled. He wanted to love her.

He stroked her back again, well aware of how quick she was to pick up on a person's vibes.

She pulled her head from his shoulder. "So do you want to go in me now?"

He shook his head. "Not quite yet."

Her brow furrowed. "But I thought that was the point of sex."

"Not exactly. Well, yes, that is what it is with animals, but us humans make everything complicated, including sex."

She pulled back some more. "I don't think so. You know, I've had sex before even if I didn't have an orgasm."

"I stand corrected." He used his finger to trace a lazy circle over her areola. "Sex is like you expect, but making love means pleasure like you just experienced, only together."

Whisper swallowed. "Love?"

"You've heard that term, right? Making love?"

She'd thought she was in love with her first boyfriend but over the years she realized it was just infatuation. Did Trace love her? He'd just given her the best experience of her life. She was grateful. She cared about him, but love?

"Whisper?"

She snapped her gaze back to him. "Yes."

"So you have heard the term 'making love'?"

"Of course." It was a term, that's all. She heard it used in movies and on television shows. "I just thought it meant sex. It does, doesn't it?"

"Yes, but it's more than that. It's sex with a connection." He looked away. "It means something. Sex is just sex."

She didn't say anything. Trace seemed to be working out something for himself. She couldn't imagine having sex just for sex. Even her old boyfriend was someone she liked when they weren't having sex. Maybe Trace wondered if his wife used him for that too.

Whisper's heart hurt at that thought. He was a good man. What his wife did was wrong. She should go to jail, not make off with his money.

It was just like her own relatives, trying to snatch her to be her guardian and then later wanting to drug her to sign everything over. The last attempts were to commit her because she was "psychologically unstable." They told others it was for her own good, but they didn't make it a secret from her that they wanted her inheritance.

She understood how Trace must feel and she pressed her hand to his cheek. "Do you still want to make love?"

His gaze returned to her, and she sucked in her breath. His copper eyes looked at her as if he needed her just to breathe. She didn't know why, but she wrapped her hand around his neck and brought his lips to hers. She gave him the kind of kiss he'd given her at midnight, happy he'd come into her life.

When she pulled away, he stared at her a moment before his lips quirked upward in a crooked smile. "I like that, and you just gave me an idea."

She watched him, waiting to see what his next idea was. She definitely liked his ideas, but when he pulled away from her and lay on his back, she wasn't so sure anymore.

"I'm all yours. You can make love to me. Do what you want, what makes you feel good."

A thrill raced up her back and her vagina tightened. "And I can tell you what I want?"

He nodded.

She smirked and straddled him across his waist. "I think I'm going to like this." She leaned over and lowered her breast to his mouth.

He didn't hesitate. He licked around her areola and flicked at her hardening nipple. Then, as if he anticipated her wish, he took the hard nub in his teeth and pulled. Need shot from her breast to her pussy and her thighs contracted against him. She started to lift herself up to give him her other breast, but he held on to her nipple, flooding her with a strange sensation that had her juices flowing.

He clamped his mouth onto that breast and sucked gently. "More."

He increased the suction and her folds filled with her juices. She arched her back, pushing her breast toward him while pressing her pelvis against him.

Her thighs moved back and the hair above his cock brushed against her clit. The spike of exhilaration that went through her body came out her mouth. "Ow."

Trace immediately released her nipple. "Did I hurt you?"

"No. I…I brushed against your hair." She sat up on him, scooting back more. She felt his cock laying between her legs, but it didn't bother her. It was all in her hands when she'd take him inside.

She pointed to his hair. "That rubbed against my clit and it felt good."

"Let me see." Before she knew what he was about, he'd

used his fingers to separate her folds and then brushed them across her clit.

The movement sang through her sheath and it contracted with wanting. As he continued to play with her, she found her hips moving forward and back as she glided over his cock. "That feels good."

He continued his play with one hand and his other came up to tweak her nipples, back and forth from one to the other, even as his fingers went back and forth across her clit.

Her need built for that orgasm she knew was possible, but it was just beyond her reach. She arched her back, presenting him with her breasts, hoping the pinches and twirls would get her there, but they didn't. She pulled her whole body back in frustration. "It's not happening."

Trace lowered his hands to his hard stomach. "Why not?"

"I need your fingers inside me."

He shook his head. "What you need inside you is my cock."

She looked at his hard erection now sticking up in front of her. A penis had never brought her to fulfillment before, but she trusted him to show her that nirvana again. The memory of her first orgasm had her willing to try anything.

Lifting herself up, she positioned herself over him. "You're sure?"

"Yes, but come down slowly. You're very tight."

"And you're very big." But there was only one way to see if he would fit.

Chapter Eight

Slowly, Whisper lowered herself until his head touched her opening. Still doubtful, she let herself move down an inch.

Her sheath stretched at the intrusion, but it didn't hurt, so she went a little farther. "Oh, it feels full." As she lowered herself a little more, she felt that same flood of sensation that she had when he didn't release her nipple. It was a strange mix of helplessness and anticipation, and her juices flowed, making the last few inches an easy glide.

She sat still, fully impaled by Trace's cock and took stock of every feeling coursing through her. Her nipples were harder and ached, her clit pulsed as if waiting and her stomach was rolling around like a coyote scratching his back in the desert.

"How's it feel?" Trace's face looked tense, though his voice was calm.

"Different. Exciting."

He let out a breath. "Good, because you need to do it again."

"What?"

He threw his arm out and grabbed a condom. "You don't want to get pregnant, right?"

"No." She pulled herself off him fast and was immediately unhappy with the loss of the added pressure within her.

"Ugh." Trace closed his eyes as if he were in pain.

Shit, what did she do? Tired of showing how ignorant she was, she waited.

Finally, he opened his eyes. "Warn me next time you're going to get off. I almost came and that would have spoiled it for you."

"Already?" Even her old boyfriend didn't come that fast, though not much longer.

"Whisper, you haven't had sex in fourteen years, which is why your sheath is so tight. It's also why it feels so good and makes it hard for me to stay in control. After we have made love a number of times, it should loosen a bit, which will greatly help me."

A number of times? He wanted to do this again? Her heart warmed at the prospect. She liked how he made her feel.

In no time, Trace had the condom on and she was straddled over him again. This time she knew what to expect, but it was still tight, especially with the extra layer. When she had completely impaled herself again, she sighed. It did feel good.

Trace grasped her waist. "Don't move."

She hadn't planned on moving. She wasn't even sure how to, but sitting with him inside her was good enough for her.

After a minute, Trace's hands moved up her torso to cup her breasts. Just like he had before, he stroked his thumbs across her nipples. This time when the thrill from his touch went down between her legs, it was intensified, moving around her sheath and the cock inside. Her juices flowed at this new feeling.

He changed his movement and took both nipples between his thumb and fingers and pinched lightly. The feelings that coursed from her breasts to her pussy zinged through her, making her hips move involuntarily as she arched into his touch.

Her clit brushed against his pelvis, adding another layer of excitement streaming throughout her body. "Oh. I love that."

Trace continued to play with her nipples, alternately pinching and twirling, and the ache between her legs grew even as she rocked against him, her clit sending more pleasure to her core. It was too much.

She tried to pull back her chest but Trace latched on. Heat spread through her at the helpless feeling that swept her up, forcing her to rub her clit against him. She grasped his arms, unable to stop pushing against him.

Her orgasm was coming. It was just around the corner. She could feel it.

Trace's hands left her nipples and grabbed her waist, holding her against him as his pelvis pushed upward. "Whisper!"

Her orgasm exploded through her. Every nerve ending came alive as the cascade of ecstasy lifted her beyond herself, yet kept her hips grinding against the warmth filling her as Trace came. She was alive, free, filled with joy.

Finally, she wrangled control of her body and slowed her movements, still feeling spurts of sensation until her breathing calmed and she was able to stop reaching for every last spark of thrill.

She opened her eyes to find Trace watching her. She smiled. How could she not? He gave her so much and was so kind. That orgasm was even better than the last.

He grinned, completely proud of himself. "So what do you think?"

"I think that was awesome." She ran her hand over his chest, loving the way his hard stomach muscles contracted as she went. "I also think that I need to read more about sex. Uncle Joey's birds-and-bees talk was lacking a few details."

Trace chuckled, his body moving under her, causing sweet aftershocks to ping between her legs.

"That's usually a talk the mom gives. I don't imagine Uncle Joey knew exactly what to say to you."

She sobered, the mention of the word "mom" bringing the usual ache to her heart. She started to lift and halted. "I'm getting off now. Are you ready?"

"Wait." He moved his hand between her legs, making her think of having sex all over again. "Okay, you can rise now, but do it slowly, please."

She did as he requested and was glad she hadn't rushed it. It was an adjustment not having him inside her. When she crawled off and sat beside him, she saw that he had held the condom on so she wouldn't take it with her.

Trace got up and walked into the bathroom.

She took the opportunity to slide under the blanket and sheet, her body oddly cold without him nearby. She flicked the switch that turned off the main lights and left the low-level floor lighting on, so Trace could find his way back.

He returned in a few minutes and got in beside her. "Come here." He held his arm up.

Guessing he wanted her to lie next to him, she scooted over and put her head on his shoulder. She liked his warmth and threw her leg over his and her arm around his waist. "Hmm, I like this. Is this another part of making love?"

He chuckled, a sound she really enjoyed. "Yes, it is."

The position was comforting, like someone cared about her. She sensed Trace did, which made the feeling even better.

"I want you to tell me about your childhood."

She lifted her head to look at him. "Why?"

"Because I want to know."

She lay her head back down. "Okay, what do you want to know?"

His arm wrapped around her, holding her close against him, completing that feeling of being cared for.

"Tell me how your parents died and how you ended up with Joey."

She was glad she was crushed up against him because she hadn't talked about any of that…ever. She hadn't had to. Joey was there and no one else cared. She hesitated at that. Trace cared.

"My father was a mechanical engineer and he owned his own plane. He used to take me up in it for rides. We lived in Tucson then. Mom and Dad decided to go to Flagstaff for the weekend. I was to stay home with Joey. He is my father's brother. My parents' plane crashed between Phoenix and Prescott. They were both killed on impact."

Trace's arm squeezed her tight as she paused to swallow the lump in her throat. Talking about it was tough. "That's it."

"So you went to live with Uncle Joey?"

She nodded. Though there had been a three-year custody battle between her uncle and her mother's sister, her parents' will had held. She was always thankful for that. She loved her uncle.

She doubted she would have made it past ten growing up with her cousins Keith and Timmy. Their mother had run through her parents' inheritance in a few years, while her own parents had kept the money safe and growing. She found out later from Joey that her dad had insisted on working and providing for them, despite her mom's wealth.

Trace rubbed her arm, a comforting movement that she appreciated. Even thinking about her parents made her yearn for them, so she rarely did, never mind talk about them.

"You told Hailey you were homeschooled. Was that Joey?"

"Yes. He got me tutors in the subjects he didn't feel qualified to teach. He was an accountant so he taught me math and science and anything analytical."

"What about friends and doing kid stuff?"

She shrugged. "Some of the places we lived I had some kids my age I played with after they came home from school, but by the time I reached high school age, I didn't have much in common with most teenagers. No loss as far as I could see. That part of human development is strange."

It was more than strange, and by that time, she and Uncle Joey were moving every year and she found her peers boring. Everything was traumatic to them. Luckily, living in trailer parks had exposed her to so much Arizona wildlife and desert that she didn't miss having friends. Besides, now she had Lacey.

"I like Lacey but Cole seems reserved. Do you two get along?" She looked up at him.

His eyes widened. "That was quite the change in subject."

"Do you?"

"Yes, we get along fine…most of the time. Cole is a very by-the-book person, always focused on what's right. He just needs Lacey to straighten him out on what that is once in a while." He grinned.

"And what about you? What do you plan to do when your

divorce is final? Do you plan to find another cowgirl to settle down with and build up another ranch?" Her stomach flipped over as she said aloud what she'd been thinking and held her breath, not even sure why it mattered.

Trace's bark of laughter was not what she expected.

"First of all, I didn't marry a cowgirl the first time. I probably should have. And second of all, I haven't even begun to think about life after the divorce. It's hard when I don't know if she's going to get everything including my truck, or if the courts will see the light and give me at least half. That's the way it's supposed to be here in this state. Any martial property, which is all we had, is supposed to be split half and half."

He paused and she felt the anger churning inside him.

"I can't make plans until I know what I have and don't have. Besides, I'm perfectly happy at Last Chance, helping the horses who need it and pitching in so Cole and Lacey can have a good homestead. I'd lost touch with the beauty and satisfaction of working on the land instead of overseeing others. Believe it or not, I'm pretty good at mending fences, training horses, and roping cattle. I'm just a bit rusty."

So he was a cowboy after all. "Why are you rusty?"

"I guess you could say my focus changed to being a rancher. There's a difference."

She didn't know that and she stored the information away. But while they were questioning each other, she had something else she wanted to know. "How come you know how to bring a wheelchair upstairs?"

His face softened. "My dad. He had two strokes six months apart. He wasn't as lucky as Joey after the second. Logan and Mom were still at the ranch and cared for him, but I came over at least twice a week to give them a break and to spend time with my dad. He was more verbal than Joey, but physically, he was pretty bad off."

She sensed the grief of his loss, but he seemed to have come to terms with it. A lot better than she had when she lost her parents. "How long ago did he die?"

Trace's lips quirked up at one corner. "Most people say passed away, but it really is the same thing. It was about two years. Logan took it the hardest. He and my dad were very close. I guess you could say I was a mama's boy."

A noise outside the window caught her attention.

It caught Trace's too. He whispered, "Did you hear that?"

She nodded, her body tense. She never knew when Keith and Timmy would find her and noises outside were not a good sign. Luckily, it was usually an animal. She listened carefully.

Trace kept his voice low. "It sounds like someone is trying to get in your shed."

It did sound like that.

"Stay here." Trace rose from the bed and moved to his sport coat. He took what looked like a forty-four magnum from an inside pocket and stood next to the window where he opened the slats in the blinds. After a few minutes he let them drop. "I can't tell. It's too dark outside to see anything."

Whisper rose and walked by him into the kitchen.

"Wait, Whisper."

She threw on her coat and grabbed up Sal. If it was one of her cousins, she didn't want Trace to get hurt.

He grabbed her arm as she reached for the door. "Stop. You need to stay inside."

"Why?"

"Because I need to protect you."

Huh, since when? "I need to protect you."

Trace shook his head, but stopped when a loud noise came from the shed. He looked at her.

"It sounds like scraping." She listened some more but the noise stopped.

Trace held his finger in front of his mouth as he moved to the door. He had his hand on the knob when a loud bray broke the silence.

Whisper laughed with relief. "Damn burrow. Almost gave me a heart attack."

Trace stood rooted to the floor staring at her.

"What?"

He blinked. "I've never heard you laugh."

Really? She laughed a lot. Well, maybe more around Joey. Guess she was feeling more comfortable being around him. She liked that. "I'm sure I'll do it again." She winked. "Now move aside. I need to see what Motley wants."

"Motley?"

She brushed by him, grabbing her flashlight on the way out and strode to the shed. Motley stood there, staring at the building. "What is it now? Are you hurt?"

The burro pawed at the shed.

"Well shit, Motley, I didn't know you were going to be back. I don't have any more hay." She quickly went over in her mind what she had in the trailer. There had to be something he could eat. "Tell you what. I'll get you some water and see what I can find."

Turning to head back to the trailer, she found Trace right behind her in all his naked glory. And it was glorious. "Shit, you're going to get stung by a scorpion walking around barefoot."

He looked at her feet. "And you're not?"

"Yeah, I know. I just have to get him some water and find him something to eat." She walked by Trace and headed inside for her old boots. After slipping them on, she came back outside and grabbed a bucket from under the trailer and filled it with water from the outside spigot.

As she lugged it toward the burro, she noticed Trace smoothing his hand over the animal's side. "Careful. He's wild."

Trace looked up. "He's also pregnant."

She dropped the bucket down and stared. "Well strip me naked and throw me in a lava pit. I never even checked. Why would I?"

He grinned, his white-toothed smile visible even in the starlight. He should do one of those toothpaste commercials.

"She must need some food."

Trace shook his head. "Not necessarily. My guess is she is going to foal soon and considers this a safe spot."

Whisper liked that. Just the thought of having a baby burro around was enough to make her happy. Happy? She was downright excited. "If she's pregnant then she probably does need food. But there's a palo verde right there, so why scrape at the shed door?"

Trace left the burro and moved toward her. "My guess is you already figured it out. Look at her drink."

They stood side by side watching the burro get her fill of water. Trace put his arm around her and pulled her against his side. "This has to be the best New Year's I've ever had."

She silently agreed.

~~*~~

Trace glanced over at Whisper sitting right next to him. She met his gaze for a moment and gave him a smirk. He returned his attention to the road. He was happy this morning as they drove back to Last Chance Ranch to get Joey.

After the burro incident, he and Whisper had made love again, but despite his intention to do so all night, they fell asleep in each other's arms. For the first time since he'd been served divorce papers, he was honestly happy. What was better, was he saw no reason for why he'd stop being happy for a long time to come.

He drove up to the house and parked his truck. The only vehicles in the yard were Logan's, his grandparents and Lacey's. Cole and Lacey had stayed in a casita at Poker Flat for a weekend honeymoon until Cole could get off work for a week.

Getting out, he didn't make it to the other side in time. "Whisper, you're supposed to allow me to open your door."

She brushed him off. "Really? That's fine when I'm in a skirt, but I'm perfectly able to get out of a truck on my own."

"Plus you're very excited to see Joey, aren't you?"

"Yeah, I —"

A ruckus in the barn interrupted Whisper and they both looked at each other. A loud neigh was followed by more banging. It sounded like a horse was breaking apart the barn.

He turned and ran, Whisper right behind him.

Logan stood across from a stall where a beautiful black horse reared then came down, pounding at the stall door.

"What's going on!" He had to shout over the noise.

Logan ran to them. "Stay away, that horse is mad."

"Where'd he come from?" Trace could see even from the doorway that the horse was showing the whites of his eyes.

"He's another rescue. They dropped him off, all drugged up. We barely got him into the stall because he was so drugged and didn't want to go. I went out with the guy to sign the paperwork and as soon as he left I heard this banging. I don't know what the story is on this one, but he's going to hurt himself if we don't calm him down. Can you stay here while I get far enough away to make a call to Jenna? This boy needs more sedation."

Trace nodded and watched his brother stride away. When he turned around, Whisper stood opposite the stall and his heart lurched up into his throat. "Whisper!"

She ignored him, instead moving closer to the wild horse.

He started for her when she opened the stall door and the horse charged out. He slammed himself up against the wall as it ran by. "Fuck, Whisper, you can't just let out a wild horse." He grabbed her by the arms. "Are you okay?"

She shrugged him off. "Of course I am." She headed for the barn door and he grabbed her arm again. "Wait. You could have been killed. What were you thinking?"

She finally took her focus from the horse and onto him. When she did, her attitude softened, at least as much as Whisper could soften. "You were afraid for me. I didn't mean to scare you. The horse needed to get out."

"What the hell? " Logan's voice outside had Trace fearing for his brother's life now and he ran to the barn door.

The horse stood still next to one of the training corrals, its breathing heavy, its nostrils still flaring, its body shaking, but its ears were back up and it eyes no longer rolling back in its head. Logan stood frozen halfway to the house.

Whisper walked by and approached the horse. She called to Logan. "What's his name?"

Logan looked at her like she was crazy. "Black Jack."

Trace followed her. "Whisper, not every animal will respond to people. Be careful."

She remained focused on the horse as she approached his head. "Black Jack. You're okay now. It's all right." She held out her hand as if she were going to shake hands with the horse then turned her palm toward the ground.

Trace stayed right behind her, ready to push her out of harm's way at the least sign from the horse.

Whisper lowered her arm.

The horse responded by lowering its head.

Trace had never seen anything like that. Still, as Whisper stepped closer, he stayed vigilant.

"Black Jack. You're okay now. No one will put you away again. I promise." She stepped even closer and raised her hand to pet his nose. Black Jack's ears were forward, listening to Whisper, but when she touched him, he nudged her shoulder.

"Good boy. You're okay now." She moved to his side and stroked his neck.

Trace watched in fascination as the horse's breathing evened out and he stopped shaking.

Logan came up behind him. "I wouldn't have believed it if I hadn't seen it with my own eyes, but I gotta tell you, I'm glad she was able to calm him down. He's a real beauty. I'd hate to see him hurt himself."

Trace had to agree. The black quarter horse had a long mane and tail and a perfect white star on its forehead. "Did you get a hold of Dr. Jenna?"

Logan shook his head. "No. She's at another ranch treating a sick cow, but her office said they'd get word to her."

Trace never stopped watching Whisper and Black Jack, ready to step in if he had to. "Whisper, is he okay?"

She looked at him. "He is now. You can pet him."

Logan stepped past him before he could move. "What was wrong with him and why is he better now?"

She looked Logan in the eyes sternly. "He was panicked. He's claustrophobic. You can never put him in the barn again."

Logan's eyes widened. "It's not too cold here in the winter, but he'll need shelter from the rain. I can't just leave him out here."

She shrugged. "Try a carport then. He can't go in a stall. This isn't just a small issue. This horse is terrified of being closed in."

Logan crossed his arms over his chest. "And you know this how?"

"I just do."

The two glowered at each other, not looking away, and Trace finally stepped between them. He faced Logan. "What's Black Jack's story?"

"I don't know. I didn't even have a chance to look at the paperwork before he started banging down the stall door."

"Maybe we should find out." Trace raised his brows at his brother.

"Fine." Logan went up to the porch and opened a folder on the table there.

Trace turned around to find Whisper watching him.

"I'm right."

He grinned. "I know you are."

Her stance relaxed. "Thank you for that. Most people just think me crazy. Black Jack just doesn't like closed-in spaces."

Trace gave the horse a stroke along its withers before remembering it wouldn't mind being touched on its face. Lightyear had him well-trained.

Logan came back and stared at Whisper before addressing Trace. "She's scary."

"No, she isn't." He frowned at his brother. "She's gifted."

Logan looked at Whisper. "Black Jack was discovered in an old copper mine. Some teenagers heard the horse making a racket and not knowing it was a horse, called in rescue crews."

"It says that the owner had been in the mine with the horse when it started to cave in. He ran out but the horse didn't make it, so he thought Black Jack had been buried alive. When the horse was returned to him days later and he tried to put him back in his old stall, the horse went wild, so animal welfare brought him here on drugs. They think the horse was in that mine for three days."

Trace thought the light made Whisper's eyes look silver, but as she turned toward the horse, he could see the water in her eyes. He hadn't seen her cry before and it bothered him. She was so in tune with animals, it was as if anything they experienced had happened to her.

She stroked the horse along his nose. "You poor boy. You're safe now, Black Jack. They will take good care of you here." She faced Logan with a stern look, all trace of tears gone. "Right?"

His brother stepped up to the horse and gave it a stroke along its neck. "I will personally insure he is well taken care of." The horse nudged Logan's shoulder. Logan switched his gaze to the horse. "Okay, Black Jack. Let's see if the corral is more to your liking." Logan picked up the halter he'd left on the corral fence and methodically put it on.

Whisper stepped away and let him work. Trace couldn't resist her another moment. He was damn proud of her and yet pissed that she'd put herself in danger. Wrapping his arms about her waist from behind, he rested his chin on her shoulder. "I don't think you could ever stop surprising me."

She relaxed against him. "That's only because I'm different." She turned around in his embrace and looped her arms around his neck. "I'm so glad Cole has this place and that you help him. I wish every unwanted and abused horse could come live here."

"I'm afraid that would put Cole in the poor house too quickly and then all the horses here would lose their home. It's better that he finds loving homes for them after they are rehabilitated."

She raised her brow. "You mean like Lightyear?"

He grinned. "Okay, so I've grown a bit attached to him. I may have to buy him from Cole so I can keep him."

"I think that's a great idea. Now can we go get Joey? I'm sure all the activity has made him tired."

Trace didn't want to let her go, but she was right. It was almost noon on New Year's Day and Joey had been in a much busier and louder environment than he was used to. "You're right." He released her, but wasn't happy about it.

They'd made it to the porch when a car pulled into the yard. Trace turned around and groaned. "Now what is she doing here? I thought she would be well on her way to Orson to wallow in her disappointment over Cole."

Whisper butted his shoulder with hers. "Be prepared to be blown away."

He chuckled as his aunt Beverly exited her vehicle and walked toward them in her high heels, white slacks and flowered blouse. "Trace, Whisper, I'm so glad I caught you."

Damn, she actually wanted to talk to them. He'd been hoping she was here to see her mother. "Hello, Aunt Beverly."

She pulled off her sunglasses as she walked up the three steps to the porch. "You were holding out on us, Trace."

"I was?" As was common, he had no clue where his aunt was coming from.

"Yes, about Whisper." She turned toward Whisper, who at least hadn't started to frown yet.

"What about her?" He wrapped his arm around Whisper's waist to be sure his aunt understood exactly what she meant to him. Whisper seemed perfectly happy that he did so, leaning against him.

His aunt took one of Whisper's hands and he cringed. Not a good move.

"That your Whisper Adams is the daughter of Annabelle Adams, the heiress who died in a plane crash twenty-two years ago. I would have never connected the dots if Hailey hadn't finally remembered where she'd seen Whisper's face before." His aunt turned her gaze on him even as he felt Whisper become stiff in his arms.

"It wasn't that she'd actually seen Whisper, but Hailey is in flight school and she studied up on Arizona small plane crashes and saw a photograph of Anabelle Adams. Whisper, or rather Melisandre, looks just like her mother. Imagine my surprise to learn you were actually dating an heiress."

Chapter Nine

Trace looked at Whisper, expecting her to deny it, but she didn't. In fact, her face revealed that she was this heiress. He stepped away, not quite ready to accept the full impact of her betrayal. "Why are you living in a trailer if you have money?"

She looked at him. "I've been in hiding. I have two cousins who won't stop looking for me. They want the money, so I had to go off the grid."

"See." His aunt continued as she clapped her hands together. "I knew it. Oh, I must tell your grandmother. Excuse me."

His aunt walked between them and into the house as if she hadn't just destroyed dreams he hadn't even admitted he had.

He stared at Whisper, who seemed preoccupied. "Were you going to tell me?"

She shook her head.

"Why not?" The pain in his heart built as the reality sank in. She was rich and he had nothing.

"It didn't matter. Like I said, I've been hiding. I didn't want anyone to know."

In other words, she didn't want him to know. "Why? Because I'm broke?"

"No, the money is a curse. It hounds me, making my life difficult, forcing me off the grid and away from civilization. It always had…until I came here."

He thought of the trailer. It was state of the art inside. It had to cost as much as his grandparents' house. He was so blind. "So all along you could have been paying Cole rent to be on the land where your trailer is."

She frowned. "That's his land?"

Trace snorted. "Yes, and he wanted you off because he was afraid you would gain squatter's rights. Little did we know you could afford to pay rent, eliminating the whole issue."

"I didn't know that was an issue. I didn't know it was anyone's land up there." Her puzzled expression fueled his anger.

"No, you didn't because I was protecting you." He took another step back. "Hah. Stupid me. I even had Lacey working on getting Cole to change his mind."

"Trace, I don't understand why you're so upset. The fact that people know who I am, especially your aunt, is a lot worse than the fact that I have money."

He stared at her, not even trying to comprehend her logic. "Was it because I might lose everything? Did you pity me? Is that why you hid that little fact about having tons of money?"

She stared at him as if he'd morphed into a horse. "Why would it matter if you're broke? I don't understand why this is an issue."

"Because I love you, dammit! Because I thought we might

have a future together. What an idiot I was." The confused look in Whisper's eyes was the last straw. She just didn't get it. Maybe she didn't get human emotions at all, only animal ones.

He turned on his heel and bounded down the steps of the porch, striding to the barn to saddle Lightyear.

"Come on, buddy, I need to run off some steam and you are just the one to do it." Kicking the horse into a gallop, he headed toward Cole and Lacey's unfinished house.

His heart was tearing in half. Not only had she hidden her money from him, but she didn't grasp that he loved her. It was as if she'd never considered such a thing.

It was his own fault. He'd told himself he wouldn't get involved with a down-on-her-luck woman again and he did, only to discover it was worse than he thought. She had more money than he'd know what to do with.

Compared to what his wife had done, Whisper was by far the crueler of the two. His wife took everything he owned and left him with nothing. Whisper ripped out the only thing he had left to give, his heart.

Whisper stared after Trace as he disappeared. He loved her? She searched her heart for a responding feeling, but she had no idea what it would feel like. She liked how she felt around him, except it hurt inside that Trace was upset, just like she hurt when an animal was in pain.

The ache persisted. She'd talk it over with Uncle Joey when they got home. He could help her figure this out, and they needed to go home now. She didn't like that Trace's aunt knew who she was. That woman would tell everyone, if she hadn't already.

Shit, Trace was supposed to take her and Joey home. Now

what was she going to do? Her gaze fell on Logan, who was watching Black Jack in the corral. He would have to do.

In no time, she and Joey were on the road with Logan. She was surprised how quickly he'd agreed to help them and by how gentle he was with Joey. Maybe he wasn't all bad, even if he still had that anger boiling right beneath the surface.

Logan slowed down as the speed limit dropped, signaling the town line. "We need to stop at Dr. Jenna's and let her or her staff know we don't need her help."

"Okay." She liked Jenna because she helped animals and always did what was best for them.

Logan pulled up outside the vet's office. "Would you mind running in and letting them know?"

She frowned. "Why don't you do it? I'm in the middle here."

Logan looked uncomfortable. "I'd rather you did."

"You don't like Dr. Jenna, do you?"

Logan's hands loosened on the steering wheel then gripped it again. "It's not that I do or don't like her. We just don't see eye-to-eye when it comes to horses. If I go in there and she's there, we'll just get into an argument. If you don't mind waiting for that to be over, I can do it."

Really? Why was she suddenly reminded of those teenagers she had nothing in common with?

She looked at Joey. He rolled his eyes before jerking his head, yes.

"Let me out."

Since she sat in the middle, Logan had to exit for her to leave the vehicle. She ran up to the porch of the vet's office and opened the door. She proceeded to the desk. "I have a message for Dr. Jenna. Tell her Last Chance doesn't need her to come out."

The older woman with gray hair smiled. "Actually, she just got back." The woman rose. "Let me get her for you."

"No, that's okay, just…" She gave up, the woman having walked away already.

She turned around to see who else was there. Two people waited and one dog. She met the big pit bull's eyes and smirked. He was pretty happy to be there. That made one of them.

She turned back toward the desk at the sound of a door closing. Dr. Jenna hurried toward her. Instead of stopping at the desk, she came around and grabbed her arm. "Come."

Whisper frowned but let herself be pulled into a nearby exam room. As soon as Jenna closed the door, Whisper pulled away. "What is it? I just came to—"

"Those men came back."

Whisper's heart froze then kicked back in double-time. "Keith and Timmy?"

Jenna nodded. "They were waiting for me in the parking lot when I got back from a ranch call. They said they saw on the internet that you were at a party on Last Chance Ranch. They wanted to know if I'd ever seen you there."

Fear coursed through her veins. They knew she lived on that land. "What did you say?"

"I told them I hadn't seen you at all and asked them why they were looking for you again. They told me you were mentally unstable and if I saw you to call the police because you were dangerous."

Damn them. Once she was in police custody, they'd have her, her word against theirs.

Jenna grabbed her arm. "I pulled up in your truck. Luckily,

they didn't investigate it, so as soon as they left, I brought it home and put it in the garage."

"Shit. I'm going to have to move again. Joey and I really liked it here."

"Maybe you shouldn't. Maybe it's time you stood up to them."

Whisper's gut started to burn with hurt at the prospect of disappearing again even as she shook her head. She needed to leave as soon as it was dark, so no one would see her pull the trailer onto the highway outside of town. She had a lot to do before then, including emptying the shed and digging up the money. "I can't chance it. Can you bring my truck to the trailer at sundown? You can have the ATV."

"I can, but are you sure you don't want to fight them? I can stand up for you as a witness to your sanity."

The offer was tempting, but she couldn't involve Jenna in her troubles. Keith and Timmy were dangerous. "No. We have to go. Thank you for warning me. I just hope I can leave in time."

Jenna finally nodded and gave her a hug.

Thanks to Lacey, Whisper had become used to hugs and embraced Jenna. She hadn't even realized it, but she had two friends she'd have to leave. Just another reason not to make friends.

When they parted, Jenna had tears in her eyes. "I'll be there at sunset."

"Thank you." Whisper left the exam room and walked into the waiting area. She glanced at the happy pit bull. What would happen to Faust and Viola and Sebastian? She wouldn't be around to see Motley's baby either. She swallowed hard as she moved to the window.

She scanned the road to see if Keith and Timmy were in

sight, but it had been two years since they'd last caught up with her and she had no idea what vehicle they could be driving. Another disadvantage to being off the grid, she couldn't search public records for the car. Then again, they could easily rent a car.

Taking a deep breath, she walked out onto the porch. Her plan, if they saw her and headed for her, was to run.

All the way to the truck, she watched her surroundings, her heart pounding, expecting a hand to clamp on her shoulder at any moment.

Logan stepped out of the truck and she scooted in. Once he started driving again, she checked behind them, but no one followed.

"What are you looking for?"

She turned back around. "I was checking to see if anyone followed us."

Logan's brows lowered. "Why? What did Jenna say? She knows not to come to the ranch, right?"

"Damn, I forgot to tell her."

"What? You were in there a long time. What were you talking about? Horses? We better go back."

Whisper grabbed his arm. "No!"

"Whisper, you better tell me what's going on."

She looked over at Joey and he looked up. He wanted to know, too. He could probably feel her agitation.

"You need to get us home so I can pack up the trailer and leave. My two cousins know I'm living on Last Chance land and they will go over every square foot of it until they find me. My only chance is to get out of town tonight."

Logan didn't slow down, but he did scowl. "Why do you have to run away from your cousins?"

As briefly as she could, she explained the situation starting with the attempted kidnapping and finishing with the last attempt to have her committed. "If I'm committed or dead, they can legally inherit the money."

Logan turned onto the dirt path to the trailer. "Holy shit, Whisper. Does Trace know?"

Trace. She wouldn't get to say goodbye to him. Her heart constricted, tightening in her chest just like it had when Joey told her that her parents had died. Oh, damn. She must love him. She didn't want to leave him and it hurt. She shook her head at Logan's question, her throat too tight to allow her to speak.

Joey grunted and she looked at him, unable to hide her tears. Joey moved his eyes from side to side telling her no, not to leave. But she couldn't allow them to hurt him. She had to think about more than just herself.

"You need to tell Trace. I don't think he'd want you to leave."

She swallowed hard. "I don't think he cares anymore. Remember when you told me you'd find me if I broke his heart. I already did that."

Logan parked in front of the trailer but made no move to get out. "Then you need to un-break it."

"I don't think that's possible, especially not now. Now let me and Joey out."

Logan didn't budge. "Listen, Cole has a friend in the police department."

"I know. I met detective Anderson. He interrogated me at the New Year's Eve party last night. I don't think he's on my side since I admitted to wanting to kill that animal abuser who hurt Lacey's horse."

The one hand Logan had on the steering wheel loosened and gripped it again. "You just said what we were all thinking. Let us at least talk to Sean."

That wasn't going to get her anywhere and she knew it, but Logan wasn't going to let her out and time was ticking. She had Sal in her jeans, but there was no way she could shoot Trace's brother. "I'm leaving as soon as it's completely dark. If you can work some kind of magic with the detective let me know before then, otherwise, tomorrow morning we'll be long gone.

She sensed Joey's relief next to her. She'd have to make sure he didn't get his hopes up.

Logan let go of the steering wheel, climbed out of the truck and held the door open for her.

A shot rang out and he went down. "Logan!"

Whisper leaned over to see Trace's brother lying still, facedown on the desert floor. "Shit, shit, shit." She stayed low, beneath the dash, and unbelted Joey. Laying him down on the seat, she lowered herself to the cab floor and met her uncle's worried gaze.

"I'm going to get you out of this safe and sound, old man. No need for concern."

Joey grunted.

"Yeah, we're all going to get through this." She glanced at the now vacant driver seat, worry making her stomach feel like she swallowed a bees' nest. She met Joey's gaze again. "You saw it. They made the first shot."

He jerked his head.

She needed to figure out where her cousins were shooting from and draw them away from Logan. She opened the passenger side door fast.

Another shot was fired near it. She crawled to the edge

of the truck and studied the ground. There. There was a hole where the bullet hit the dirt. Thanks to the dry earth, it was easy to see the angle.

She closed her eyes, picturing where they had parked in relation to where the shot was fired from. Her cousins had to be standing in the bed of a pickup truck in the Joshua Tree forest because there was nothing high enough and nothing to hide behind in that direction. Keith may be smart at hacking accounts, but he knew very little about guns. It meant Timmy was shooting. Unfortunately, he was an excellent shot.

Making a guess as to where they might be, she stayed on the floor and put her gun's barrel in the crease in the door where it wouldn't be obvious. She dared not stick her head out to aim, but she angled her hand the best she could and fired.

"Fucking Christ, that bitch almost shot me." Keith's voice was loud and clear and not that far away.

Timmy yelled out, "Millie! Come out and leave your weapon in the truck and we won't hurt anyone else. All we need is you."

That wasn't going to happen. Instead she focused on where the voices came from and angled the gun again and shot.

"Shit!"

Silence followed her last shot. She itched to look above the dashboard. If she stayed below it, she was a sitting duck. One of them could keep firing while the other sneaked up to the truck. Plus, she only had a few more rounds. She looked above the seat to see a rifle hanging there. Thank you, Logan.

She crawled back to the other side to check on him. He lay in the same position, but blood seeped out from under his leg and a stain was growing on his calve. If his shin was shattered, he was in trouble.

She could sense the pain he was in, but the low-grade anger he carried around with him was much stronger, like a full-blown rage. It shook her and she crawled back to where Joey was. She had to take a chance to peek. Instead of looking over the dashboard, she shot again and immediately pulled the gun away and looked through the opening.

She couldn't see anything. Damn it. There was no return shot. She needed to draw their fire. Taking off her boot, she raised it in front of the passenger seat.

A shot shattered the front window of the truck, but the tempered glass kept it all intact in a spider web fashion, sparing Joey any glass shards. The bullet buried itself in the seat cushion two feet above his body and gave her the exact location of the shooter. Unfortunately, he was on foot and too close.

~~*~~

Trace let Lightyear run, the rhythm of the horse a soothing balm to his tattered heart. Maybe he'd expected too much from Whisper. After all, he was technically still married, plus her experience with men was limited. Hell, her experience with people was minimal compared to most Arizonans.

Still, he thought he at least had a special place in her life, especially after their night together. Shit, he could make up every excuse in the world, but the fact was, she fascinated him. And she held his heart.

The money was an issue. He was hurt because she didn't trust him to tell him, but his pride smarted to know he couldn't provide for her, not yet anyway, and she didn't even need him to. It was the complete opposite scenario from the wife who was leaving him.

Everything about Whisper was different. That's why he

was so attracted to her. The idea that she might not love him in return hurt too much.

The echo of a shot caught his attention. He slowed Lightyear, trying to figure out where it came from. It could be hunters. Hell, his own grandfather was out hunting today, but he'd gone north. Not hearing anything else, he turned Lightyear around to head back. He'd told Whisper he'd bring her and Joey to her trailer and had left her at the ranch house. Someone else might have driven her back, but he should—

Another shot rang out and he held Lightyear back. Two more followed.

That wasn't hunting.

Whisper's words on the porch, which he didn't pay attention to then, chilled him now. I've been in hiding. I have two cousins who won't stop looking for me. They want the money, so I had to go off the grid.

Fuck. If Whisper was home, she was in danger. He turned Lightyear toward the canyon wall. And if she wasn't? That meant she was safe and he had to get his head on straight and figure out how to make her love him just as soon as he investigated what was going on in the middle of the desert. The echoes made it hard to know where the shots were coming from. For all he knew, they were in town and he was a fool.

But once Lightyear made it over the rim and another shot was fired, his gut tightened with fear. He had to slow the horse to get through the Joshua trees, and he flinched as three additional shots rang out. How many people? How many guns?

When he got close enough to see the trailer, he quietly pulled out his rifle and slipped off Lightyear. At the sight of Logan's truck and the window with a bullet hole through it, his muscles tensed. Two of the most important people in his life were in danger.

Another shot was fired from the truck's passenger door. That meant at least one person was alive. The question was, which one? If Logan brought Whisper home, then Joey was around too. Was he in the truck or already in the trailer? Fuck.

Frustrated at not being able to see anyone, he worked his way around the long way, toward what he hoped were the shooters. The Joshua trees offered little cover, but he had to do something. Even now someone could be dying. He couldn't even contemplate having someone already beyond his help.

As he passed two Joshua trees next to each other, he caught sight of one of the shooters walking toward the truck with no cover. Trace dropped to the ground. Luckily, the thin man with the long goatee was too focused on the truck and getting close to it.

From this angle, Trace could see someone lying on the ground. His heart stopped. It was the driver side. Logan? Even as his heart insisted on pumping the pain of loss through his veins, the person moved beneath the truck.

He released the breath he held. Logan and Whisper were both alive. A surge of adrenaline ricocheted through him. There were two shooters. If he could distract them, then Whisper or Logan, whoever was in the vehicle, could take down one while he took down the other. The problem was, from where he crouched he could only see the man with the goatee.

And that man was getting too close to the truck. Trace had to move now or the person inside was dead. He jumped up and ran through the trees quietly, watching the goatee man. As he stepped into the clearing, he yelled, "Stop right there!"

It all happened fast. The other shooter shouted and Trace

turned, shooting a large bald man in the shoulder. At the same time a shot was fired behind Trace. He spun to see the man with the goatee fall to the ground, clutching his knee even as blood dripped from his forearm. Trace ran to the vehicle and stared.

Whisper was on the floor, Joey lay on his side on the seat and Logan looked up at him from beneath his truck. Relief threatened to buckle his knees, but once ascertaining they were all alive, he ignored the crying of the shooter with the goatee and grabbed up the man's gun.

Whisper jumped from the truck and threw herself at him. "Trace! I love you." She didn't give him time to respond. Her lips planted firmly on his.

He wrapped his arms around her and squeezed her hard as their tongues locked, his heart beating faster than a rattler's rattle.

"Ahem, do you think someone could give a wounded man a hand up?"

At Logan's voice, Whisper spun out of his arms. "You're alive!" She was so pleased Trace had to chuckle, knowing how the two didn't get along very well.

"Whisper, get the gun from that bald man while I help Logan."

"Right." She ran over to the man he'd shot in the shoulder while he bent and helped his brother to stand on one leg.

"That looks like it hurts. Let's get you to the tailgate." He helped Logan to the back of the pickup and opened the gate. "Now stay there."

Logan held up one hand. "Hell, you don't have to tell me twice."

Trace started for the bald man when a grunt from the cab

reminded him there was someone else who was happy to be alive. He leaned in and brought Joey up to a sitting position. "Hey, Joey. Good to see you alive and well."

Joey rolled his eyes and Trace gave another chuckle of relief.

Whisper came back with the bald man's gun. She handed it to him with one hand while she pointed back with the other. "The one you shot is Timmy and the sneaky one here that Logan and I hit is Keith. They're my cousins. They've never gone this far before."

Trace glowered at the Keith. "And now they've sealed their fate. They shot my brother and the truck is excellent evidence they wanted to shoot you as well. They aren't going to bother you again where they're headed."

She smiled, that heart-stopping smile that he'd only seen once before. "I meant what I said. I love you. I didn't realize it until I thought I would have to disappear again. The thought of leaving you cut into my heart. I get it now."

For a passionate declaration of love, it lacked subtly, but from Whisper, it was music to his ears. He pulled her against him. "Hell, woman, I love you too."

"Good. Now kiss me."

He laughed before lowering his lips and giving her everything she demanded…and more.

He grasped Whisper's hand as they sat in the kitchen of the ranch house and laughed at Lacey, who had her hands covering her ears as she explained the noise level in the house the day before.

Cole made a big show of pulling Lacey's hands away from her head. "No need for that this afternoon…sweet pea."

Whisper squeezed his hand but didn't look at him.

Lacey growled. "I can't believe my father told you about my old nickname. I outgrew it ages ago."

"I like it." Whisper's voice was quieter than usual, a subtlety he was becoming more adept at catching.

"Why?" He was learning to ask about everything, otherwise his amazing woman wouldn't think to share.

She looked at him. "My dad used to call me that."

As much as he wanted to take her in his arms, he'd also learned she didn't like that when she felt vulnerable. Instead, he gave her a self-deprecating smirk. "I get that. My dad used to call me piglet because he said as a baby I ate more food then he could afford." He smiled sadly at the memory. "Luckily, he dropped it by time I was five, or I may have tried to prove him right." He winked.

Cole looked at his wife, the newlywed glow still obvious. "Then I guess I should just call her by my nickname for her."

"Cole Hatcher, don't you dare." Lacey lifted her hand to cover his mouth as if she had any chance of stopping him.

Trace couldn't resist. "You have to tell us now."

Getting up from her chair, Lacey doubled her efforts to stop her husband as he opened his mouth.

Finally, Cole laughed. "She's my Racy Lacey."

Lacey smacked him on the arm. "I can't believe you told them."

Cole pulled his wife onto his lap. "They won't tell, right, Trace?"

He chuckled. "No, your secret is safe with me."

Whisper's brow furrowed. "Why is she racy?"

Cole opened his mouth, but Lacey spoke before he could say a word. "I like to wear sexy lingerie under my clothes." She looked back at Cole. "He really likes it."

Trace could tell Whisper's mind was working a mile a minute just from her concentration. When she turned to him, he found himself anxious to find out what she would say.

"Would you like that?"

His cock started to harden just at the suggestion. "I would, but just once in a while. Surprise me."

Whisper nodded. "Good." She looked at Lacey. "You can help me pick some out."

Lacey laughed. "You bet. I'll show you my favorite stores. We can go next weekend."

His cock was now rock hard, but then he grinned at Lacey. He could just imagine Whisper asking Lacey about each and every product in that type of store. "That should be interesting."

Lacey waved him away. "Trust me, Trace, I'm not easily embarrassed."

He raised his brow even as the image of Whisper holding up an anal toy appeared in his head. Shit, now his jeans were stretched to their limit. He needed a change in topic. "So you were saying how thrilled you were that it was quiet today. Is everyone gone?"

Cole nodded. "No idea how that happened. We didn't even arrange it. Besides our chores, the only thing we had planned was you two coming over for lunch."

"And it was a great lunch, Lacey. Thank you." Trace looked at Whisper. "We wanted to talk to you about paying rent for the property we have the two trailers on. Now that the divorce is final, my ranch should sell soon and I'll receive half the profit, so I'm happy to make monthly payments. I know that's important to you." He kept his eyes on Cole.

Cole snorted. "First, you're family, so I'm not worried. Second, you two have done enough as it is. And third, I asked detective Anderson about the squatter laws and it's far more complicated than I realized. You two are fine up there. Besides, you gave old Billy a new purpose in life."

"What? How?" Trace looked from Cole to Lacey.

Lacey grinned. "He was fine being Grandpa's helper whether it was carting his hunting gear around or being his caddy on the golf course, but I guess those two pursuits don't allow for much talking."

Trace laughed. "Oh yes, that old man loves to talk. Hell, he even does it in his sleep." He looked at Whisper. "Remember how I told you I'd slept on the couch before?"

She nodded.

"That was because I roomed with old Billy and between him talking in his sleep and his snoring, I was getting less shut-eye than Logan. I figured two grumps in the house was one too many, so I would sneak down and stretch out on the couch."

He turned his attention back to Cole. "So why does Billy feel visiting Uncle Joey is his new calling?"

Whisper smirked. "Because Billy can talk all day and Joey doesn't interrupt. Joey is loving it. Billy is even reading the paper to him. I should have thought of that."

Lacey jumped in before Trace could say anything. "You had a few too many other things to think about. Speaking of, now that your cousins are in jail, I'm thinking we need to do something for Sean. The poor guy lost both Christmas and New Year's days to trouble on Last Chance ranch."

Cole grinned. "At least this time it was Trace's trouble and not ours. We've used up all our credits with that man."

Whisper's eyes lit. "We should give him a week at Poker Flat Nudist Resort."

Cole coughed and Trace chuckled, even as Lacey shook her head. "I'm pretty sure Sean's wife wouldn't go for that. Besides, as a detective, he can't accept anything too expensive."

Whisper's shoulders slumped. "There goes my other idea."

Ever since Whisper was free to put her money in a bank and other financial institutions, she was more than ready to spend it. The new trailer she bought for them with three slide outs instead of two, and the trust she set up for Last Chance horses with the help of Lacey was proof of that. He squeezed her hand to get her attention. "Maybe it needs to be something that can't be bought."

"Like what?" Her gaze filled with curiosity.

"How about public recognition. We could each write a letter to the Police Chief recognizing Sean for his good deeds."

Cole pointed at him. "I like that."

"Me, too." Lacey smiled and looked to Whisper who gave a nod.

"Then it's settled. We'll do that." Trace was very grateful for Sean's help. The detective even said they could spare Joey having to be a witness, but Whisper wanted her uncle to testify, to bring home exactly what kind of people her cousins were.

Whisper stood up. "We'll leave now."

He looked at her then at Cole and Lacey before he shrugged and stood also. "I guess we have to go."

Whisper nodded. "Yes. They want to have sex and there is no one else around, so we should leave."

Lacey turned two shades of red and Cole hid his embarrassment by setting Lacey on her feet and standing as well.

Trace grinned. "Hmm, that's not a bad idea." He pulled Whisper against his side.

She looked at him, her eyes darkening with the idea. "That was my thought."

Cole laughed as he walked around the table to shake hands. "I'm glad you two are our neighbors."

Trace shook then grabbed up his hat and headed for the door. "Better that than living with you, cousin." Opening the door for Whisper, he stepped aside and she walked through. "I hope for your sakes the house is finished soon." He jogged to catch up with Whisper.

Cole and Lacey stood on the porch as he raced down the steps to open the truck door for his woman. She just shook her head at him and climbed in.

He closed her door and tipped his hat at the newlyweds. Walking around the truck to his door, he smirked at the carport standing next to the barn. Black Jack stood in its shade, taking a light nap. How had they all managed to function before Whisper?

Jumping into his truck, he waved one more time and drove toward home. The trip was a quiet one. Another change in his life he'd adjusted to.

As he turned onto the dirt road that would bring them back to Whisper's old trailer and the new one parked within sight of it, she spoke for the first time since getting into the truck. "Why did they say Keith and Timmy were your trouble? They were after me, not you."

He smiled. "Because you are my responsibility now, so it all fell squarely on my shoulders."

"That's not true. My cousins were my problem."

He slowed, bringing the truck to a stop halfway down the three-mile dirt road. "That may be true, but it's my job to take care of you."

She glowered at him and opened her mouth, but he pressed his finger against her lips.

"And it's your job to take care of me."

Her face changed and he knew he'd guessed right. He loved trying to stay one step ahead of her.

When she licked his finger, he started. Now that he hadn't expected.

She grabbed his wrist and sucked his finger into her mouth.

His cock immediately started to swell. "If you keep that up, I'm going to strip you right here."

She paused and that special gleam came into her eyes. "Great idea."

Before he could respond, she'd whipped her shirt over her head and her breasts caught and held his attention. He quickly unzipped his pants. Whisper was never one to slowly take off clothes. She said she liked touching skin to skin. Hell, so did he.

When she was naked, she opened the door and stepped out of the truck.

Shit, what was she doing now?

He laid his hat on the dashboard and pulled his t-shirt off over his head. When his face cleared the neckline, Whisper slammed her seat back. In her arms was the emergency blanket he kept in the truck. She stepped away and closed the door.

Toeing off his boots, he pulled down his jeans and jumped out stark naked to find her. He didn't have far to look.

In the bed of the truck was Whisper, completely naked and sitting on the blanket. She looked like a wild woman, her black hair loose and messy about her bare shoulders and a predatory look on her face.

He sat on the tailgate and swiveled around to face her.

"I want to make love out here where it's free." She opened her arms wide, as if she could feel nature itself.

"I'm happy to make love to you anywhere you want." He crawled toward her, letting her determine what they would do. He loved it when she wanted to experiment. He definitely needed to make reservations at Poker Flat for his wild woman.

He'd thought about introducing her to sex toys on Valentine's Day, but with Lacey taking her out next week, she could choose what she wanted to try first. One thing he didn't have to worry about with Whisper, was wondering what she thought of something.

When he knelt in front of her, she surprised him by

turning her back, pulling her hair forward over one shoulder and kneeling. "Touch me."

He grinned. Placing his hands on her shoulders, he ran them down her back, smoothing them over her skin and rounding over her ass to her thighs. He purposefully didn't go near her favorite spots to build her anticipation.

Again he ran his hands over her back, but this time brushed her sides as well, barely touching the edges of her breasts. When he got to her ass, he squeezed each cheek, separating them from each other a bit before running his hands to the insides of her thighs and down, still avoiding what she wanted most.

"You're teasing me, aren't you?" Her voice was even more husky with her libido revved up.

"Yup." This time he knelt a little closer and brought his hands down her arms, under them, along her sides, and around the fronts of her thighs, careful not to touch her with his body.

"Trace. I'm wet for you."

His cock moved at her statement. "Really?" He moved his body up against hers, his erection nestled on her ass, his chest against her back. "Do you want me to feel you?"

She nodded, her breath coming out short now. He started at her shoulders and smoothed his hands over her breasts, under them and down her waist before grabbing her thighs and pulling her hips tight against him.

"Oh."

Finally, he moved both hands toward her pussy. She was more than wet. With his left hand, he slipped a finger inside her opening. With his right, he spread her moisture over her clit and proceeded to rub it gently.

As her head fell back on his shoulder, he wondered at the

circumstances that had brought them together like this. Body to body, beneath the warm Arizona sun in the back of his pickup where he would take her, body and soul to nirvana and back. They'd come a long way from her holding him at gun point to him holding her in his arms.

Her head came off his shoulder. "I want you inside now."

So did he. Slipping his fingers from her, he turned her slightly so she faced the side of the truck. "Hold on."

She bent forward and braced herself.

Spreading her legs father apart, he pressed his cock against her opening. "Ready?"

She took a deep breath. "Yes."

He grasped her hips, knowing full well she couldn't wait. He kneaded her skin. Upping her need like a race car driver revving an engine.

"Trace, please."

He rubbed his thumbs back and forth across her hips, making her wait. He could barely hold on himself, so he pressed forward just a bit, just enough to push her opening wider, but he held on, daring himself not to plunge.

Whisper moaned in frustration and wiggled her hips, trying to push back.

"Shh, wait for it. Let it build."

She moaned again, but he kept her hips where he wanted them as her wetness seeped out and over his cock. He gritted his teeth, focusing on the feel of her entrance. She loved it when he surprised her. If he could just hold on another few seconds.

He couldn't. He pulled his hips back then slammed forward.

"Yesss!"

His orgasm rose up. No, not yet. He moved his hands from her hips to her breasts and squeezed them lightly before finding her hard nipples and pinching them. Her hips pulled forward and banged back against him, pushing his finale too close to the edge.

He couldn't stop. She pulled back and thrust her hips toward him. He let go of her breasts and grasped the side of the truck on either side of her. Rhythmically, he pumped hard, the feel of her body against his chest spurring him on, making it difficult to hold back.

But when her sheath tightened around him, he let loose his own pleasure and pounded into the woman he loved, his world complete…perfect.

Whisper's screams of ecstasy were lost in the vastness of the upper desert, and he held her to her orgasm as long as he could. When her body quieted, he knelt back, taking her with him, keeping them connected as she sat on his lap.

She flipped her hair back, most of it landing on his back and the soft feel of it sent a trill of excitement to his cock, making it jump inside her.

She reached down between her legs and touched him. "You're still hard."

"No, I'm getting hard again."

"Hmmm." She wriggled against him. "I like that."

He chuckled. "You are insatiable, but I know exactly what to do."

"What?" He could hear the excitement in her voice.

"This." He reached one hand down and flicked at her clit. "Are you ready to come for me again?"

"Always."

He grinned against her hair before he leaned his head to

the side of her neck and kissed her at the same time his fingers twirled around her hard nub and her breathing escalated.

"Always" sounded good to him.

The End

Fletcher's
FLAME

BY

LEXI POST

Fletcher's Flame: Last Chance Series, Book 3

By Lexi Post

Can he get her to see her own worth before they both go up in flames…literally?

Dana Wilson has one mission in life – to save animals. Thanks to her life's calling, she's developed a distrust of men in authority. So when Bo Fletcher, a cowboy firefighter, decides to appoint himself her bodyguard, her hackles rise.

Bo's physical attraction to Dana Wilson has him digging deeper into her personality, a need to understand her burning in his gut. Unfortunately, that's not the only thing burning. An arsonist appears to be nipping at Dana's heels and Bo is determined to protect her.

As sparks fly between them, the fires come closer and closer to claiming Dana. Can Bo protect her or will his own words be her demise?

Author's Note

Fletcher's Flame was inspired by Bret Harte's short story, Mliss, published in 1869. Mliss is the daughter of the drunk founding father of a small western town. She is odd according to her peers. Even the school teacher, who she tells she wants "learning," isn't sure what to make of her, but he lets her attend the one room school house anyway. It turns out she is quite bright, and despite her father's suicide, she begins to gain respect for her intelligence, if not for her ladylike comportment. She doesn't try to be like the other girls and knows what she wants out of life.

Eventually, the teacher decides to take a new job in a new town and Mliss finds out before he can tell her. She feels betrayed and plans to leave town with a traveling band of actors. The teacher is outraged that she would risk her life by leaving with the actors and saves her from her fate.

But what if she equates all authority figures with her father and won't accept the protection she needs? What would it take to get through to her that she is worth so much more than she realizes even after being betrayed again?

Chapter One

Dana Wilson moaned as the smoke alarm blared from her ceiling. Really? She'd just put new batteries in that stupid thing. Pulling the pillow over her head, she tried to keep out the sound.

"Ugh." Lifting up one side, she peeked at the clock. 3:17 a.m. She had to get up in two more hours. Frustrated, she took a deep breath.

She sniffed. Was that smoke? Crapola on a bun, it is!

What an idiot! Whipping off the covers, she swung her feet down and into her slippers, her long t-shirt twisting up to bare her ass. A shout came from below.

High pitched whining followed by someone running down the hall upstairs made it clear her apartment building was on fire. The three story building was at least a hundred years old, one of the reasons she moved into it, but it would go up like a tinder box.

Stay calm. Nothing ever came of panicking. It's no different than the time you were on that cliff with the baby deer.

She turned on her lamp before running through her bedroom. As she rounded the corner into her tiny vestibule, she hit her bare thigh on the small table against the wall. Stupid thing. Rubbing her leg, she finally reached her apartment door. She unlocked both locks and pulled it open.

Smoke billowed in, smothering all her senses before she slammed the door shut, coughing as the foreign matter filled her lungs. Not good.

Quickly, she ran into the kitchen, grabbed the hand towel and soaked it with water. She brought it to her face and hurried back to her door.

Here goes nothing.

As she opened the door, smoke streamed in and she dropped into a crouch. Stay low. Remember the barn fire in Maryland. Smoke rises. After the initial billow, she found she could stand without too much smoke. Looking up, she froze.

Hell. I'm in hell. Black smoke covered the hallway ceiling, billowing like an upside down wave, slowly lowering. Yellow flickers lit it sporadically like heat lightning in the clouds on a summer evening.

"Get out of my way." Randal who lived in 204 pushed by her, his Chihuahua in his arms as he headed for the stairs.

"Excuse me." She yelled as she turned to follow him.

She glanced across the hallway making out the numbers 202 through the thickening haze. Surely Tanya had made it out. Unable to leave without checking, she stepped across the small hallway and banged on the door. "Tanya, wake up!" She tried the door but it was locked.

Her neighbor must have left already. Or she could be at her latest boyfriend's house.

"Help! Help us!" At the sound of yelling coming from

behind her, her blood ran cold. Holy moly, the Sheridans were still in their apartment!

She looked longingly at the stairs not twenty feet away, but turned her back on them. The smoke hung lower and she bent over to avoid the worst of it.

Now she truly walked toward the gates of hell. At the end of the hall, where an old couch sat was the inferno. Flames reached up the wall and toward the ceiling, licking their way closer to her neighbors' door.

"Somebody help us!" The high pitched yell had to be Mrs. Sheridan.

Dana wiped at her eyes with her wet towel, or rather damp towel. Then she took a breath into it and removed it from her mouth. "Mrs. Sheridan! Unlock your door!"

"We're in here!" The high pitched voice came closer. "We're in here!"

She moved along the wall between her apartment and the Sheridans'. The old three story building had never been renovated, so despite the blaring smoke alarms, there were no automatic sprinklers to slow down the fire.

The flames moved closer to the opposite side of the Sheridans' door from her. If she was actually going to help, she had to do it now. She banged on the door. "Hurry! Open the door!"

The sound of fire engine sirens drowned out her words.

"Please help us!"

Her pulse raced so fast, she was surprised she remained conscious. The heat from the fire was worse than a Dallas sidewalk in August and it seemed to billow towards her. It's now or never. She grabbed the doorknob.

The sirens stopped. They must be here. She could let

them do their job. But even as the thought crossed her mind, she turned the knob.

As the door swung open, Mrs. Sheridan screamed.

Just like with her own apartment, black smoke poured in and she ran in after it. "Come on, you have to leave now." She pointed back behind her.

Mr. Sheridan rose from his recliner, the chair creaking as he lifted his bulk from it. He coughed as he reached his height, breathing in the black smoke. "Is that what the firefighters said?"

He never believed she knew anything even when she was proven right, so she lied. "Yes, they said we were to leave immediately."

The man raised one brow in doubt.

Really? His front door was on fire and he expected the firefighters to say stay inside?

"I told you, sweetie." Mrs. Sheridan coughed daintily. "Please can we go now?" The elderly woman was as thin and petite as her husband was heavy and large. She never did anything without his approval, and he rarely gave his approval.

"You want to go through that?" He pointed toward the open door.

One side of the door jamb was lit with small flames. How did firefighters get through to people like this? "Yes, because if you wait any longer, the whole door will be filled with fire and you'll be stuck in here and eventually the floor will give way and you'll burn to death."

Mrs. Sheridan gasped then proceeded to choke on the contaminated air.

Maybe she'd laid it on a little thick, but at least she got her point across. Mr. Sheridan actually moved, right past his wife, bumping into her as he lumbered toward the exit.

Dana squelched her instinctive retort and instead grasped Mrs. Sheridan by the arm and guided her out, pulling her lower to avoid the descending smoke. As they entered the hall, a figure appeared at the top of the stairs. The bulky outline told her a fire firefighter had arrived.

A surge of relief ran through her until another man appeared behind him. She tried to swallow, but her throat was raw from the smoke and her dry dishtowel was technically worthless.

The second firefighter had to be almost seven feet tall and his shoulders looked four feet wide. He carried a huge ax making him appear even more impressive. She squinched her eyes in a fruitless effort to stop them from watering. Holy moly, the man was a giant! It's just a firefighter like the one who helped you get out of the barn with Wind Dancer last year—

Hell and damnation. "Mrs. Sheridan, where's Misty?"

The older woman shook her head, her focus on the approaching giant. The other firefighter had already begun to guide Mr. Sheridan down the stairs.

There was no way she would leave the cat behind. As the giant reached them, she pushed Mrs. Sheridan at him. "Here, take her." She doubted he could hear her, her voice raspy in her own ears, but it didn't matter.

She turned quickly.

"Stop! Come back!"

The command in his voice had her halting instinctively, but she forced herself to run away from him and the safety he represented. She couldn't count on them to save Misty.

She thought he swore, but she couldn't be sure as she made it to the Sheridans' doorway. The entire door was now on fire, flames starting to lick the walls inside.

She still held the towel over her nose and mouth, even

though it did little to keep the smoke from scratching at her throat like a frightened cat. Misty had to be scared to death.

Where would I hide if I was a cat? She ran to the Sheridans' bedroom, the smoke not quite as heavy, and flipped the switch. The overhead light came on, but flickered. Dropping to her knees, she looked under the bed.

Glowing eyes met her gaze and her heart cried. The white Persian was petrified. It lay near the head of the bed, its whole body scrunched against the wall.

"It's okay, Misty. I'm going to get you out of here. Can you help me do that?" She'd never had a frightened cat help her save it. Never. So she didn't wait for that.

Instead, she stood and threw her useless towel on the bed. Grasping the headboard, she pushed with all her might and it moved away from the wall.

Luckily, the cat remained where she was, but Dana still couldn't reach her.

Walking to the other side of the bed, she heaved again. That proved successful, but she had to stop as a coughing fit took her. Stupid smoke.

After she stopped choking, she wiped her eyes. When she could finally see again, the cat was gone.

Really? I don't expect a rescue to go smoothly, but it would be nice if one thing went right.

Dropping to the floor again, she looked under the bed.

Misty looked back at her without blinking.

How did cats do that, especially in all this smoke? She didn't hesitate. This was a familiar scenario. Looking around the room for anything long, she found a cane and grabbed it. Getting on the exit side of the bed, she swept the cane under it toward Misty, forcing the kitty toward her.

Misty walked from beneath the bed slowly, and as soon as she wasn't pushed anymore, promptly lay down again.

Smart cat. The heavy smoke was almost as low as the top of the bed. Luckily, on the floor, breathing was a tad easier.

Dana moved slowly, keeping the cane where it was so the cat couldn't scoot back under the bed while she kept her body between it and the door to the living room. As her right hand grasped the back of the cat's neck, the light went out.

That couldn't be good. Pulling the struggling cat into her arms, she took a minute to assess her position.

It wasn't the first time she'd rescued an animal in a dangerous situation, nor was it her first fire. She tried not to think of her few belongings going up in smoke. She'd become used to living with very few personal items since she was a child, so she wasn't attached to most of her things. Life was much more precious, especially that in her arms.

She kissed the top of the cat's head then wiped her mouth on her sleeve—the cat's fur was covered in dust. Crawling on all fours wouldn't be easy with Misty, but it was their best chance for getting out of the building.

Scooting over to a dresser near the doorway, she opened the bottom drawer and pulled out what looked like a summer housecoat. Carefully, she wrapped it around her and tied it in front of her to hold the cat. Unfortunately, it probably left her backside bare since all she had on was her extra-large t-shirt and slippers, but her dress wasn't her priority.

With the cat secured, she crawled into the living room and stopped as she stared at the door to the hall. It was now completely engulfed in flames.

Crap. Crap. Crap.

She coughed as the smoke filled her lungs again and Misty squirmed in her cocoon.

Sorry sweetie, but you need to stay with me.

Water. Water put out fire. She had to get water. Oh, a wet blanket!

Moving into the bedroom again, she pulled the summer blanket off the bed and crawled with it to the bathroom. Turning the shower on she managed to get the blanket into it and pulled it over herself.

She crawled back to the living room, her progress slow as fits of coughing made her stop. She checked on Misty and the cat appeared sluggish. No more squirming.

Come on Misty, don't give up yet.

She drew closer to the door, wishing the paper thin wall between her apartment and the Sheridans' really was paper thin, but it wasn't. The old building may be worn, but it was well built.

She stopped before the flaming doorway. She thought she'd seen hell earlier, but this looked seriously demonic. Could she crawl through and then…and then, what would she do then?

Did it matter? Hell was waiting for her. She moved one knee forward but coughing stopped her. She had to get out. She had to save Misty.

When her coughing stopped, she checked Misty, rubbing the cat's head. There was no response. Her eyes welled with tears. Please Misty. You have to make it.

She wiped her face with the wet blanket then tried breathing in it. It was too thick, so she pulled it away. Maybe the firefighters would put the fire out. Then she and Misty would be all right.

You're losing it.

She lifted her head and stared at the flames. Maybe she could make a run for it. She coughed even as she took a breath. Her muscles weakened as she tried to fill her lungs with oxygen. She couldn't stay on her hands and knees anymore.

She rolled to her side and cradled Misty. We're going to get out of this, sweetie. I promise.

Another coughing fit caught her up and she tried desperately to breathe, but it was no use. Everything went from gray to black.

Bo guided the older woman outside, keeping his grip gentle even though every muscle in his body was tense.

Tenants from the building gathered on the opposite side of the street, but they weren't all out yet. He'd never lost a person in a burning building and even though he was only on loan to the station for a month, he wasn't about to start now.

He walked the frail lady toward the paramedics. "Why did that woman run back into your apartment?"

The lady looked confused at first, her gaze on her husband who was being helped onto a gurney by Rick. Finally, she focused on him. "Oh, she went back for Misty."

Misty? There was another woman in the building? Bo pressed his radio button. "Rick, there's two more."

The firefighter he'd been partnered with jogged over to him, and without a word, they both ran back into the building.

A one-and-a-half-inch hose was being pulled up the stairs, even as he and Rick ran up behind them. "Misty!" He hoped to hear some kind of response. He should have asked the frail lady which apartment the two women might be in.

The water started and smoke obliterated all sight. He pressed his radio. "I'll take the apartment on the left."

"I've got the one across the hall." Rick's voice reassured him they had the apartments closest to the fire first.

Feeling his way along the wall, he found a flaming doorway. "Need water over here!"

The men on the hose moved the stream of water to the door, effectively squelching the flames. The smoke billowed out again as they moved back to the base of the fire along the back wall.

Bo didn't wait for the smoke to clear away. "Misty! Misty!"

When there was no response, his stomach tightened. She had to be here somewhere. He moved forward blindly, the fresh smoke making it impossible to see…and breathe if anyone was in the apartment.

His heart started to race even as his foot hit something soft on the floor. He dropped to a crouch and found a body. No! No bodies on his watch! Dropping his ax, he felt for a face.

The smoke rose, giving him a visual. A blanket practically smothered the person on the floor, and he whipped it aside. Long dark hair fell on one side of the woman in a fetal position. Her arms were wrapped around the bulge of her stomach.

Pregnant. Great. So much for an over-the-shoulder carry. He should grab her under her arms and drag her out, but one look at her bare legs and ass had him nixing that idea. He pressed his radio button. "I've got a pregnant woman. Coming out."

He sat her up to move one arm behind her back. He wriggled one arm beneath her knees and rose. She wasn't the heaviest thing he'd lifted, but with fifty-four pounds of fire gear on, she definitely challenged him.

He quickly headed out, carefully maneuvering them both through the smoking doorway and into the hall.

Rick met him there and spoke without the radio. "I searched all three apartments, there was no one else. Are you sure there were two?"

He shook his head. "No. I only saw one, but was told she'd gone in for another. I found this one in the first room. There might be another further in."

Rick nodded. "I'll check."

"I need to get her out."

"Go ahead. We've got it under control now. I'll make them stay until I come out." Rick patted him on the back and headed into the apartment.

Bo started down the stairs, hoping there was no one back there. He hated the idea of anyone not making it.

He exited the building and made a beeline for the ambulance. Two paramedics steadied a gurney as he gently laid the woman on it. One of them was his cousin Lexi, who'd transferred to Station 58 not long ago. Quickly, she threw a blanket over the woman's bare, soot covered legs and covered her mouth with oxygen.

He should go back and help Rick search for Misty, but he needed to know this victim would make it.

Lexi cut the flowered clothing from around her patient and a white ball of fur slid off. His cousin caught it and turned to him with a smirk. "We've got her, Bo, but you might want to take care of this." She deposited the limp figure in his hand.

Chapter Two

A cat? She wasn't pregnant? Damn. Bo strode to Engine 82 and pulled an infant oxygen mask from a compartment before he held it over the cat's face. He massaged the animal's dirty tummy with one of his fingers.

Irritation at the woman brewed. She could have been killed. For a cat.

Rick's voice came over the radio. "No one else on the second floor."

Relieved but puzzled, he focused on bringing the cat to consciousness. In the back of his practical mind was the unrealistic belief that if he could bring the cat back, his cousin could bring the woman back. She must have loved this cat to have risked her life to save it. He didn't want to be the one to tell her it didn't make it.

He continued to work on the ball of dirty white fur, pressing its little chest in quick rhythm. "Come on, kitty. Your mom needs you."

Bo looked at Trent and Lexi, who still surrounded the woman he'd pulled out. Then they rolled the gurney to the ambulance and hoisted it in. She was bound to have lung damage. Shit.

Rick approached, pulling his SCBA off. He stared at the small bundle in his arms. "What you got?"

He grimaced. "Cat."

Rick shook his head as if he thought the animal was a lost cause.

Bo didn't consider himself overly obsessed with animals, but this time he needed this cat to live. Ignoring Rick's obvious prognosis, he continued to tend to the kitty.

The cat's paws started to twitch and relief surged through him. As superstitious as the next firefighter, he read the cat's movement as a sign the woman would live.

He lifted the mask away for a moment to see if the kitty had its eyes open. It didn't. Moving his hand to cover the cat's face again with the oxygen, his gaze caught a small shiny tag on the animal's collar. He flicked it with his finger.

"Misty."

More relief came as he replaced the oxygen mask over Misty's face. Now at least he knew for sure there was no one else on the second floor of the old building. All four apartments were clear. He should probably get the animal to a vet soon.

How could she risk her life for her cat? He had to be thankful she hadn't endangered anyone else besides herself. Still, the thought that she might not make it because she loved her animal so much, twisted his gut.

"Misty!" The frail woman he'd helped out of the building earlier came toward him, her hands clasped together in front of her. "I thought I'd never see her again."

He frowned at the woman. "This is your cat?"

She nodded, tears in her eyes. "My husband told me to

leave it. Thank you so much for saving her. When Dana went back for her, I thought I'd never see her again."

Bo's anger over the woman named Dana risking her life for someone else's animal made him even more uncomfortable than taking credit for something he didn't do. "I just gave it oxygen. Your neighbor found your cat." If he called the cat by its name, it just might put him over the edge. Of all the stupid, asinine things to do while a fire was eating away at—

"She'll be alright, won't she?" The frail woman looked at him with fear. "I couldn't lose her."

He had to switch his focus from the woman on her way to the hospital even now to the cat in his arms. Didn't anyone in that building understand that human life took priority?

He looked down at the furball in the crook of his arm and took away the mask. The cat's light-blue eyes stared back at him like a deer in headlights. "I think she'll be okay." He lowered the mask again. "But you'll need to bring your cat to a vet."

The woman looked toward the ambulance that housed her husband.

That it hadn't left the scene like the other one told him the man's injuries weren't serious. He pushed aside his brewing anger at the uncertain look in the fragile woman's eyes. "Ma'am, would you like an officer to bring you and your cat to an emergency vet clinic?"

The woman tore her gaze from the ambulance. "I'm not sure. My husband—"

"Will be fine." In fact, he wouldn't be surprised to hear the man had exaggerated his condition. Any man that leaves a burning building before his wife is a loser. He took the mask away from the cat and it opened its mouth, but no sound came out. "Here. Take your kitty, and I'll have someone take you to a vet."

The woman cradled her cat in her arms where the animal actually appeared to relax.

He guided her to a female officer and explained the situation. Luckily, the officer was very sympathetic and ushered the frail woman to her cruiser. He opened the door and helped her in, cat and all. He kept the door open and leaned down. "Can you tell me Dana's last name?"

The woman smiled. "Of course. That's Dana Wilson. She's an angel. I'm going to make her a big pan of lasagna just as soon as I get back home." The woman's gaze shifted to the now smoldering building. "If I still have one."

He gave her a sympathetic grin. "That you and your loved ones got out alive is most important."

She nodded and smiled at her cat. "Thank you again for saving Misty. If it weren't for you and Dana, I know I would have lost her." She looked up at him with tears making their way down her face. "If there is ever anything I can do for you, just let me know. I'm Mrs. Sheridan."

He swallowed. It was like watching a mother with her baby. "Take care of yourself." He closed the door quickly and stepped back as the cruiser pulled away from the curb.

Dana Wilson and he had a very important conversation coming about not running back into burning buildings. He took a shaky breath. If she still lived.

His gut clenched. It was more than simply his record of not losing a single person. It was about human life. He hated that fire could take it in such an agonizing way.

Even as the image of his best friend writhing in agony began to fill his head, he shut it down and strode toward the fire engine.

As Bo reached it, Cole Hatcher pulled up in his truck. He and Cole used to run into each other on the rodeo circuit when they were younger, when they thought they could master any bull.

Then a particular bull named Hades sent them both to the hospital for a week, where they shared the same room, and they'd become friends. He liked to believe he'd given Cole the idea to become a firefighter since it had been his plan since he was eight.

He grabbed a water bottle and chugged half of it down before Cole reached him. He'd liked Cole from the start. Easy going, played by the rules, and as big as he was. Cole was the only person he felt normal next to, as opposed to being the giant in the room. His friend owned a horse rescue ranch in Arizona but was in town for arson school. They'd reconnected over a few beers and a Rangers game a couple nights earlier.

"Hey Fletch. Guess you've got a possible arson here."

"We do?" He hadn't paid much attention to the fire's behavior. His sole purpose was to rescue anyone inside.

"Yeah, your captain called it in and my trainer sent me to shadow the fire investigator. All part of arson school."

"Well, I hope they have better luck with this one. The last arson case, they couldn't prove the guy had burned his building down for the insurance money. They could prove it was arson, but they couldn't determine whether it was him or his biggest competitor."

Cole nodded. "They couldn't convict based on doubt, right?"

He nodded. "Luckily with that one, it was a business and no one was in the building at the time."

His friend moved his gaze to the apartment house and then to the remaining ambulance. "I take it there were people in this one?"

"People, animals, prized possessions, everything."

"Damn, that sucks."

"Yeah." He and Cole stood in silence for a moment watching the men pull the one-and-a-half-inch hose out of the building. "What's weird is the fire started on the second floor. Why not the first floor?"

Cole chuckled. "You sure you don't want to become an arson investigator, too?"

He took another swallow of water. "No, thank you. I'd rather save lives and douse fires than pour over details after the fact."

"I get that. But where I'm from, the towns are so small we need someone to be trained in this." Cole shrugged. "It doesn't hurt that it comes with a pay raise and I'll still be fighting fires."

"Not here." Bo nodded toward the street. "We have a huge crew in the Dallas Fire and Rescue department. Everyone has a specialty. Mine is saving people."

"Did you save anyone tonight?"

He nodded. "One went to the hospital though. I'm not sure yet if she's going to make it." His gut tensed at the thought of Dana Wilson dying. She didn't seem that old, maybe a little younger than himself.

"I've been lucky. Haven't had any deaths yet, but I feel like I'm waiting for the other shoe to drop. Know what I mean?"

Bo rubbed the back of his neck and his hand came away sweaty. "Yeah, I do. Instead of feeling confidant in my ability to save everyone, I feel like I'm waiting for my first fatality. Captain Stewart says you remember every one. I don't want to remember any."

"I hear you." Cole turned his head as a Dallas Fire Department SUV rolled up. "That must be my boss for the remainder of the night and probably morning." He grimaced.

At least he could be thankful his shift ended soon. "Hey, so have they taught you yet why someone would want to start a fire on the second floor of a three story building?"

Cole turned toward him. "Yes, and it isn't good."

He furrowed his brow. "I didn't expect it would be with arson."

"Right. Sorry, still waking up. They had us in class until nine last night and we had homework."

Bo opened his mouth to ask about that, but Cole shook his head and responded. "The reason the fire in this building was started on the second floor was because someone in that building was the target. Someone on the second floor."

Bo's blood stilled at Cole's statement. Burning a building for insurance money was one thing. Burning it to kill someone was a different matter altogether.

"I've got to go. We're still on for Johnny's Sports Pub tomorrow night, right?"

He nodded before his friend turned and headed for the fire investigator just now exiting his vehicle.

Who was the target of the arsonist? He scanned the buildings' residents, particularly those who resided on the second floor. There was a man about his age with a Chihuahua in his arms, the Sheridans and their cat Misty and Dana Wilson. But there had been four apartments. Was it one of the three here or the mysterious fourth occupant? Was it Dana Wilson?

A chill ran up his back. Had the arsonist succeeded?

~~*~~

Dana opened her eyes, but quickly closed them again. Crap. The lowlighting and tan room could only mean one thing. She was in the hospital…again.

She covered her eyes with her hand and slowly opened them. There was a window and the sun streamed into the room. That was nice. She hoped she had a roommate because individual rooms were murder on her budget.

She turned her head and something on her face moved with her. Oxygen mask. Uh-oh, that wasn't a good sign. She raised her hand to remove the mask, but before she could, someone grabbed her wrist.

"Hey, you're awake."

She looked toward the feminine voice and found Laura Owens, the owner of Rainbow Acres Refuge. Dana opened her mouth to ask how long she'd been there, but as she tried to speak, her throat constricted and pain worse than the strep she had three years ago, filled her throat. She swallowed in response then wished she hadn't and grabbed at her neck as if that would help.

"Oh honey, don't do that. Don't speak." Laura's worried tone had her loosening her hold.

She looked at Laura, the tears of pain in her eyes making her friend blurry, but she could tell Laura had her pale brown hair pulled back in the usual ponytail. She pointed to the plastic bubble on her face and at the room.

"You were in a fire at your apartment building. They brought you here to the hospital. You inhaled way too much smoke, so you're on oxygen. They gave you other medicine, too. They called me when they found your phone in your apartment."

Memories of the fire flooded her. Misty! Oh God. Was Misty okay? More tears welled in her eyes, but as her throat closed, the pain returned.

Okay, okay I get it. No crying. But she had to know about Misty. She made the motion of writing with a pen.

Laura's blue gaze lit with understanding. "You want to write something? Okay, hold on." She stood then strode out the door, the unbuttoned long-sleeved shirt she wore over her tank top, the last part of her to disappear.

Please, let Misty be okay. She remembered having Misty tied to her and planned to crawl through the burning doorway, but she lost consciousness. Misty was only a fraction of her size. Poor kitty.

Tears threatened again. No. Stop. What are you, a masochist? There's no crying after smoke inhalation. Fine, she'd just think about something else until she could write to Laura. So who rescued her?

It had to be the firefighters. She owed them a big thank you. Maybe they would like a pet from Laura's place.

"Here we are." Laura breezed back in and a nurse followed her. "She has to see how you're doing then I can give you this." She held up a pad and pen.

With her eyes on the writing instrument, Dana kept herself still as the nurse checked the machines and asked her a couple questions that she nodded or shook her head to.

As soon as the nurse left, she held her hand out for the writing materials.

"Wow, this must be important." Laura handed over the pad and pen.

IS MISTY OKAY? THE SHERIDANS' CAT?

Laura read the message. "Oh, I don't know."

She wrote underneath it. CAN YOU FIND OUT? PLEASE?

Laura's face softened in sympathy. "Of course. The Sheridans are your neighbors, right?"

She nodded.

"They haven't come by to visit, but the other woman on your floor, Tanya, I think her name was, stopped by. She's a little strange. She seemed relieved that you were asleep."

Dana nodded. That made sense. She always had the feeling that Tanya really didn't like her, but since she dog-sat for Tanya, her neighbor was civil. Tanya probably came by to be sure her dog sitter was still alive.

"Oh, and a man." Laura frowned for a moment then she smiled. "Jim, that was his name. He stopped in too. He said he was your neighbor."

Jim Lawrence lived on the first floor. She only knew him because they both had a similar schedule and ran into each other often at the mailboxes. He was a nice guy, but a lot older than she was. He was some kind of legal researcher for a big law office.

She was glad Tanya hadn't been home. She must have had her dog with her because a person couldn't walk down the hall without her Maltese barking. With the smoke detectors going off, the dog would have been non-stop and she'd heard no barking.

She refocused on her pad and wrote down the Sheridans' phone number, the word MISTY, then ripped the paper from the pad and handed it to Laura.

Her boss and only friend in Dallas understood. "I'll be right back. You okay if I leave you alone for a few minutes?"

She nodded again.

Once Laura left, she tried not to think of Misty. She rubbed her eyes to keep from crying and focused on what she was supposed to do at the ranch. It wasn't really a ranch. It was more of a house with three additions built on, a couple of kennels and a barn that could hold about two horses. Laura didn't turn any animal away, no matter its condition.

Luckily, the woman was really good at raising money. Dana was supposed to take care of the animals for her as well as meet the volunteer transporters who traveled from neighboring towns to bring them any animal on the list to be put down.

Right now they had a deaf Corgi, a German Shepard with an abscessed foot, a new litter of kittens, three blind ducks, a pig with worms and a dozen baby chicks that needed her attention. The rest of the menagerie Laura could handle as they only needed feeding and watering. The cage cleaning could wait until the weekend.

She stared at her hospital room door. What was taking so long? Probably Mr. Sheridan giving Laura a hard time.

She glanced at her monitors. How bad was it this time? When she was in a barn fire, she'd only had to stay overnight for observation, but that time she'd walked out on her own two feet after guiding the pregnant mare to safety. This time she hadn't done such a great job. I definitely need to thank the firefighters.

The door to her room opened and Laura strode in with a smile. "Misty is on the mend. She's on oxygen and resting comfortably at the vet's."

Dana sighed with relief into the oxygen mask. Limbs she didn't know were tense suddenly felt like oatmeal. She'd never come this close to failing a rescue. She wrote on her pad. YAY!

Laura patted her hand. "You did good, kid. Now you need to get well for the others who are counting on you."

She nodded and crossed her chest with her finger.

"You cross your heart you'll do as you're told to get better?"

Dana nodded again and smiled, not that Laura could really see it. She loved that her boss could read her so well, especially when talking was out of the question.

She'd only worked for Laura a few months, after she had overstayed her welcome in Greenbriar, New Jersey. Shutting down a dog fighting ring had made it too dangerous to stay there. She took risks but she wasn't stupid.

"Good." Laura placed her hand on Dana's wrist. "I need to get back to the refuge and take care of our TLC cases."

She put the pen to paper and wrote. TAMMY NEEDS HER MEDICINE TWICE A DAY.

"Got it."

She turned the pad back and wrote again. DARLING'S BANDAGE SHOULD BE CHANGED AFTER HER DINNER, OTHERWISE SHE GETS IT FULL OF FOOD.

"Okay, I'll do it then." Laura smiled kindly.

She wrote again. BE SURE TO PLACE RANDAL AND—

Laura's hand covered her own, effectively stopping her from writing. "We've got this. You just concentrate on getting better."

She looked up at Laura's smiling face and nodded.

"Good. Now get some rest. I don't need to worry about my star employee with all the animals we have in TLC. When you're better, call me." Her boss walked out the door with that, leaving her alone.

Star employee? I'm your only employee. Dana sighed and let her body relax.

Maybe a few more hours of rest wouldn't kill her. Certainly not like a burning building would. Did they save the building? Did she even have a home left to go to?

~~*~~

Bo moved his large hand up silky long legs that ended in the nicest ass he'd ever touched. His cock hardened. The woman in his arms was sexy and fit him perfectly. Her overly large t-shirt had hiked-up about her waist and he could feel the strands of her long hair where his fingers rested on the small of her back.

Black. Her hair was black.

He racked his brain trying to remember who she was. By the feel of her through her shirt, she was tall and toned, her pert breasts pressed flat against his chest. Had he met her in the gym?

Why couldn't he remember her? There was no way he'd have sex with her if he couldn't remember her name, or where they'd met, or—

She let out a small moan, the sound a pleasant tone.

He had to see her face. Gently, he rolled them over, so she was beneath him. In the darkness of his room he peered at her, but her long hair covered her features. "Hey, are you awake?"

He balanced himself on one arm and pulled her hair away to reveal her face. Her eyes were closed, the long lashes resting against her tanned cheeks. Her nose was slim with a slight upturn at the end and her lips were a deep rose hue, naturally red with no lipstick. As he stared at her, he noticed she wore no makeup at all. He liked that.

Her hair had fallen on his pillow and he could see she had ears that were a bit large for someone with such a narrow face, but they were elegantly shaped as was her neck. Her features jogged his memory but he still couldn't remember her name or where he'd met her. Was it so long ago that it didn't come quickly to mind?

She moaned again or was it a groan and moved beneath him, her skin sliding against his and causing him to grow even harder. He wanted more than anything to wake her up with a kiss, but he couldn't bring himself to do it without a name.

He glanced down at her perfectly shaped breasts, her nipples the color of her lips, but not erect in her sleep. Who was she?

Something soft brushed against his leg and he looked over his shoulder. A furry white cat rubbed its head against his calf, its purr loud in his silent room. At the sight, his brain tripped into gear and he knew who his lover was.

"Fuck."

Bo opened his eyes in shock, relieved to find his black cat Buca sprawled over his feet. It was a dream.

Why had he dreamed about sex with that woman? He swung his legs over the side of his bed and sat staring at the clock. It was just past one in the afternoon. That gave a new meaning to the phrase catnap. He'd only been asleep a couple hours.

Running his hands over his face, he blinked a few times as Buca jumped down and rubbed against his calves, the feeling eerily echoed the one in his dream.

He'd never fantasized about someone he'd rescued before, never mind having them in his bed. It was just weird. When Lexi called and told him they had stabilized the woman and she'd probably be treated and released, he'd finally felt successful.

What Dana Wilson did was irresponsible. She could have been killed. Maybe he dreamed about her because he wanted to let her know the danger she'd put herself in.

Right. So why was he ready to have sex with her while she slept? A dream interpreter would probably say it was him exerting power over her or some stupid nonsense. The fact was, when he'd found her, she was naked from the waist down and despite focusing on getting her out alive, he'd noticed her state of undress. It didn't mean anything more than that, except maybe he was long overdue for a date.

He stood, wide awake now, and stepped around his cat. He'd go back to the apartment building and talk to the Dana woman to avoid any more strange dreams.

They'd let everyone back into the building once it had been inspected for structural stability, except for the two apartments closest to the fire. Those were probably not available, but he doubted there was much left in them anyway.

Since he was off now for a couple of days and had a night out with Cole planned later, he might as well visit Miss Wilson and put a little fear of fire into her.

Chapter Three

Having showered, Bo dressed in a pair of jeans, blue t-shirt and cowboy boots. Checking Buca's food dish, he topped it off with a teaspoon of banana ice cream, the cat's favorite monthly treat. "See you tonight, buddy."

Grabbing up his black Stetson, he stepped out onto the porch of his house. He smirked at the cat as he locked the door. Sometimes it was as if he had a dog. Buca sat perched on the back of the couch, watching him from the bay window. He waved and jogged down the three steps to the walkway. He'd left his pick-up outside the garage since he planned to use it later anyway.

The historic section of Dallas with the preserved homes wasn't that far from where he lived. Dana's apartment building was on the outskirts of that. He didn't mind old buildings, but his ten-year-old home was much more to his liking. It was made of the newest fire resistant materials and had hardwired smoke alarms.

Jumping into his truck, he started it up then backed out onto the quiet suburban street. He didn't need his truck for hauling trailers any more, but once a cowboy, always a cowboy.

It took less than fifteen minutes, traveling the back roads, to get to the site of the fire. To look at the front of the building, the average person wouldn't know there had been a fire.

But he'd helped Tory and Jax break up the couch and throw it out the back hallway window after the Fire Investigator had taken what he needed from it. There were floor boards and wooden slats from the wall on the back lawn as well.

He was surprised to see both the Fire Investigator's and Cole's vehicles were still there. It's not like he was on official fire department business, but it wouldn't be the first time he'd stopped back to see if the people he'd saved were okay.

The stairs were a lot easier to climb without fifty-four pounds of gear on. Before he reached the top, he heard voices. When he stepped into the second floor hallway, he found the Fire Investigator talking to another man while Cole looked on. The back half of the hallway was roped off, a testament to the crime that had been committed.

Cole saw him and walked over. "What are you doing back here already? I thought you'd be asleep, which is where I'd like to be right now."

He looked past his friend at the burnt walls. "Everything okay here?"

Cole shrugged. "Yes and no. The landlord is being very cooperative. It was easy to determine the accelerant used was gasoline and it was poured over that couch your company threw out as well as the walls and floor."

"That sounds promising."

"But we can't tell who the target was. On first glance it

would seem to be the couple at that end of the hall or the man who lived across from them."

He nodded. That made sense.

Cole nodded toward apartment 202. "But we can't rule out the single women in each of these apartments because it could simply be that the fire was started at the back because there was something flammable to light. Here by the stairs, there's no furniture, not even a rug."

"I see your point." Bo looked around the landing. There wasn't anything that would feed a fire for any length of time. "But wouldn't the arsonist trail gas toward the apartment he wanted to ignite?"

"Maybe. If the arsonist was a firefighter he would know that these other apartments wouldn't catch before a crew arrived, but if he isn't a firefighter, we can't depend on the criminal having any working knowledge of fires and suppression."

Bo frowned. "But I thought an arsonist is someone fascinated by fire. Wouldn't he know what it did?"

"Normally, I'd say yes, based on what I've learned so far in the classroom, but thanks to this shadowing, I'm getting a crash course on what can trigger an arsonist."

Something in Cole's face had Bo wary. "Why do I get the feeling this is worse than a typical arsonist?"

"Because it is."

Great. Here he was on loan to Station 58 for a month and that's when a killer-arsonist decides to show up. Unless the Fire Investigator could catch this guy right away, the chances of him losing a person to a fire just rose about a hundred percent.

His gut tensed as an image forced its way to the front of his mind of Deacon flailing in the living room of his family's house while fire engulfed his body. Bo shook his head to clear it. "Has the Fire Investigator explained why this is worse than a typical arsonist?"

Cole looked back at the charred floor and doorways for a moment then sighed. "Yes."

The conversation broke up between the Fire Investigator and landlord and both walked toward them. The Fire Investigator jerked his head toward the stairs. "Let's go."

Cole started to follow, but Bo grabbed his arm. He wanted to know what they would be dealing with. "Why is this worse?"

"Because this arsonist has just started to experiment."

Bo let go of Cole as dread spread from his gut to every part of his body. He watched his friend descend the stairs. When Cole disappeared from view, he turned and walked to the rope that cut off the back two apartments and stared at the charred mess. *Who do you want? And if you kill him or her, will it be enough?*

His entire body chilled at the prospect of the weeks ahead. He'd become a firefighter so he'd never again have to stand helplessly by while another person burned to death. Knowing the chances of that happening again were high, brought back the anger and frustration from his past.

He clenched his fists. *Not on his watch. Never again. If he had to—*

The closing of a door behind him had him spinning around. He'd forgotten they had allowed the residents back inside since the structure was deemed safe.

"Oh. Who are you?" An attractive black woman in her late twenties with a tiny dog in her arms stared hard at him.

He smiled to put her at ease. "I'm one of the firefighters who worked on the scene this morning."

She looked him over skeptically. "So what are you doing here now?"

His purpose for returning to the building came back with a vengeance. "I'm here to talk to Dana Wilson."

The woman stiffened. "Why?"

"Because…" Actually, it was none of her business. "Because I have information for her about the cat she saved." The lie tripped off his tongue easily.

The woman shook her head. "That cat landed her in the hospital. In fact, that's where you'll find her."

At first he thought the woman was being protective, but now he wasn't so sure. "If your puppy was in your apartment at the time of a fire and you weren't home, would you have wanted her to save him?"

She scowled. "First of all, my dog is full grown, and second of all, she is a female. Her name is Tiara." She stroked the white dog in her arms as it lapped her face. She smiled at her pooch before glaring at him. "Lastly, I would never leave Tiara alone at home. She either comes with me or goes to a pet sitter's." The woman glanced at the door across the hall.

Since she'd come out of 202, that meant Dana Wilson lived in 201. That was good to know.

It was clear the woman didn't like him. Not that it mattered. She'd told him what he needed to know. Dana Wilson was still at the hospital.

"Do you have any other business here?" The woman looked pointedly at him. Obviously, he'd overstayed his non-existent welcome. "No, Ma'am." He tipped his hat to her. "Thank you for your help."

As he strode by her, the small dog in her arms looked at him with its mouth open and its tail wagging. Not exactly a protective breed. After opening the front door, he heard her light tread on the steps above him, along with the baby talk she used to communicate with her pet.

He headed for his truck. He'd never talk to Buca like he was a baby. He had a little more respect for his cat than to do that. Once in his truck, he called Lexi to find out which hospital Dana Wilson had been taken to.

In no time he was being ushered into Dana's room. As the door closed behind him, he stared. She slept, her face toward the door and every detail above the oxygen mask was exactly as he'd envisioned it in his dream. His body reacted in a completely inappropriate way, and he gripped the brim of his cowboy hat.

Shit.

Dana opened her eyes to find the man of her dreams staring at her, not that she had a man of her dreams, but if she did, it would definitely be this big, hunky cowboy. She must have done something right in her life to have him in her hospital room.

The man exuded male from his broad, muscular shoulders which were well defined by the tight tee, to his huge biceps, to his square jaw. She'd bet he spent his Sundays playing full tackle football instead of watching it on television.

His brown hair was cut short, but his green eyes were intense, like there was a lot more going on in his brain besides rodeos and beer. His nose and cheek bones softened his look, keeping him from being too hard. But cripes, his body was hard, hard as a Jersey barricade.

She gave him a small smile, not that he could see it. Was he even real? Grabbing her pad that had fallen by her right hip, she quickly wrote. HI.

His brow furrowed. "Hi."

The deep voice with that one word stimulated parts of her body she hadn't had stimulated by another person in years. Who was he? Holy moly, let him be in the right room.

He turned his cowboy hat in his hands. "How are you feeling?"

Crappy. NOT BAD. She showed him the pad.

He looked at it then locked his gaze on her. "It could have been a lot worse."

Huh. How did he know what happened to her? WHO ARE YOU?

"You probably don't remember me. I tried to get you to come out of your burning apartment building, but you ignored me and ran back toward the fire."

Oh, shootin' sheep herders, it was the giant firefighter! If she'd known he was that hot, she would have listened to him.

Hah, who was she kidding? He could have been Prince Charming and she still would have gone back for Misty. She wrote on her pad. SORRY. I HAD TO GET THE CAT.

He shook his head, his frown deepening. "Miss, that wasn't a very smart thing to do. You could have died in there. You need to trust the firefighters to do their job."

Really? He was here to lecture her like she was twelve years old? She was a thirty-year-old woman who was all too aware of what damage fire could do. She pointed to her pad and tapped her pen on the words, I HAD TO GET THE CAT.

"No, you didn't. What you had to do is get yourself out of the burning building. What if we couldn't contain the fire? You would have died."

She wrote faster. WOULD YOU HAVE GONE IN FOR THE CAT IF I WASN'T STILL IN THERE?

His frown disappeared and his eyes widened. "No, my job is to save people."

Heat rose in her cheeks as her anger surfaced. AND MY JOB IS TO SAVE ANIMALS!

He stared at her pad, puzzlement clear on his face. "Miss Wilson, I don't think you're trained in saving animals from burning buildings. If you were, you—

She wrote furiously as he talked. I AM TRAINED TO RESCUE ANIMALS. I WORK FOR RAINBOW ACRES REFUGE FOR ANIMALS. She spun the pad around, surprised when he stopped talking to read it. Wow, I'm pretty good if I can interrupt with a pad of paper. Either that or he's too polite to keep talking.

He looked from the pad to her and back. "If you were trained to rescue animals from a fire, you wouldn't have gone back in."

Was there a training she could take for that? She'd trained in numerous ways from rock climbing, after her scare on the cliff, to safely handling loose electrical wires after her telephone pole episode with the parrot. Now, her curiosity was piqued. She had to ask. WHAT SHOULD I HAVE DONE INSTEAD?

He lost his frown, finally, and she liked him a lot better that way. She was so used to people frowning at her that she had a short fuse with it. Now, he looked like a nice guy. Maybe he could even help her.

"What you should have done was come outside with me and then told me about the cat." He gave her a polite smile.

THEN YOU WOULD HAVE GONE IN?

He moved the cowboy hat in a circle in his hands—his very large hands. "If there was time and I knew about the cat, I would have gone in."

That wasn't what she wanted to know. She wanted to know what she could have done differently given the situation. WHAT IF THERE WASN'T TIME?

He stared at her pad a lot longer than it took to read her words. Finally, he looked at her. "Miss Wilson, you have to understand that I'm trained to save people. Wouldn't you agree that people are more important than animals?"

Of course! She wasn't stupid. That's why she helped the Sheridans. She so wished she had her voice so she could be as condescending as he was. How could she get that across on paper? She swallowed to check her throat and winced.

"I apologize." The cowboy's green eyes softened. "You're still recovering. I will let you rest. Time and rest is what you need. I'm just glad you weren't burned or worse."

He sat his hat on his head and turned away toward her door.

Wait, our conversation isn't over! She scribbled on her pad. WHAT IS YOUR—

He opened the door and looked back at her. "Don't go back into any more burning buildings, please."

"Wai—ack." She grabbed her throat as the door closed. Tears stung her eyes at the pain, but she pushed them back. That would just make it worse. Cowboy, we are not done here. I'm going to find out who you are and set you straight.

So much for the man of her dreams. He was like every other man in authority she'd ever encountered. It might be said that a woman had to kiss a lot of frogs before she found her prince, but as far as she was concerned, she'd rather have a frog.

~~*~~

Dana strode out of the Baylord Pet Shelter with a lighter heart. After three days, she was back to work fulltime, doing what she loved. Two dogs and a senior cat would all be going to Rainbow Acres Refuge by this evening. She stopped in every Sunday to discover which animals would be put down on Monday, then came back in the evening right after closing and picked them up.

Luckily, there were very few kill shelters in the city of Dallas. Not like in some of the other places she'd worked. She'd even heard of county commissioners in some states trying to pass legislation regarding how long a pet could stay in a shelter before being euthanized. One nut suggested any dog over six be put down upon entry. Really?

Yup, she was liking the Dallas area more and more. It seemed to have a good heart for animals. Unlocking her light brown SUV, she jumped in and started it up, setting the air conditioner on high. The temperature had gone far beyond eighty, "a hot one for May" the shelter owner told her, and she'd parked on the street in full sun.

She grabbed up the note she'd thrown on her passenger seat and plugged in the address for Fire Station 58 into her GPS. So many men had talked down to her throughout her career that it was like water off a duck's back by now. But for some reason, hunky cowboy/giant firefighter pissed her off. Maybe because he never finished the conversation with her when she was in the hospital.

Or maybe because he went out of his way to start the conversation in the first place. That was probably it.

Pulling out of her parking space, she spent the next twenty minutes navigating the traffic and planning her argument. She could kill two birds with one stone on this visit. She could discover if there was some kind of "putting out fires and rescue" training she could take as a citizen, and set the record straight with Prince Not So Charming.

When she arrived, she parked on a side street and walked up to the open garage door. She could see a couple of men washing one of the engines in the driveway. One had no shirt on and the other's t-shirt was plastered to his body. A definite distraction.

A few men stood off to the side just inside the open bay. Two wore uniforms and the other was dressed in shorts and a t-shirt. The casually dressed man yelled over to the men at the engine. "Rick, you missed a spot."

"Better watch it, Tory, or the minute you step away from the Captain, you're going to get wet."

The casually dressed man, Tory she presumed, grinned. "Maybe, maybe not."

She wasn't dressed up either but she still didn't want to risk getting sprayed, so she made her way closer to the uniformed men. "Excuse me. Could you help me?"

She spoke to the official looking men, but Tory turned around to look at her.

"Oh, better watch out, Tory. Turning your back on us, isn't so smart."

The man called Tory gave the men the finger.

"Don't mind them, Miss. How can we help you?" The distinguished, slightly gray-haired man with a name plate that read Stewart on his breast smiled at her.

"I'm looking for one of your firefighters. He's very tall and broad and wears a cowboy hat."

The other man in uniform with a name badge that read Boone answered. "That's got to be Jax."

"Or Fletch," the Captain added.

"That's right." Boone looked at her. "We have two on this shift, at least for this month."

"Oh." She hadn't counted on that.

Boone continued. "I think Jax is upstairs, but Fletch is washing the truck." He looked past her and yelled. "Hey, Fletch!"

She turned around to see the man of her dreams walk around the back of the engine in nothing but a pair of shorts and sneakers, a soapy sponge in his hand. Suds and water dripped down his chest and onto his shorts. He wore no hat and he squinted as he looked over, but there was no mistaking that body.

"Yeah, Lieutenant?"

"Is that the man you're looking for, Miss?"

She swallowed hard at her suddenly dry mouth and answered. "Yes. It is."

"Come over here, Fletch. You have a visitor."

She whipped back around to address the Lieutenant. "I didn't realize he was busy. I can come back another time."

The older man frowned at her, but the Lieutenant, grinned. "I'm sure he doesn't mind taking a break. Right Fletch?"

She turned around to find "Fletch" just three feet away.

"Dana Wilson?" His eyes rounded and he took a step back. Then he addressed Boone and Stewart. "Captain, Lieutenant, this is Dana Wilson, one of the people we rescued from the apartment building early Thursday morning."

She turned away from the hard abs and muscle-bound shoulders that made up Prince Charming and smiled politely at the uniformed men.

Stewart nodded. "It's very nice of you to show your appreciation, but it's all part of their job."

She kept the smile pasted on her face, not willing to disabuse him of his assumption. But she was happy he reminded her of why she was here. She finally faced her rescuer. Now, she just needed to get "Fletch" to put on a shirt so she could concentrate.

"I didn't expect to see you." His tone made it sound like he was happy she stopped by.

She needed to keep looking at his emerald green eyes and not at what was below them. "I have a few questions for you."

He looked around her. "Mind if I take her inside?"

At the approval of the uniformed men, he ushered her into the shade of the large bay. He stopped by a chair that had a pile of towels on it and quickly dried himself off.

She thought he would take her inside the building but instead, he guided her behind more emergency vehicles to a corner that looked like a mechanic's shop.

Bo still reeled from seeing Dana. Her face was breathtaking and she stood with a bearing that had him intrigued, in a good way. He'd noticed her intelligent hazel eyes at the hospital, but her straight nose and wide mouth with the deepest color lips he'd ever encountered had his body more than paying attention.

Couple that with her extra height and long, wavy black hair, and he was more than mildly interested. He was captivated.

He stopped behind the ambulance his cousin rode in and faced Dana. "You're taller than I expected."

Her eyebrows lowered in puzzlement. "Maybe because I was lying down both times you met me."

The sound of her voice made him think of a day spent in bed making love. "Your voice is husky. Is that normal or is that the residual effects of the smoke?"

She met his gaze, hers having turned almost blue. She cleared her throat. "This is my normal voice."

"I like it." He liked a lot about her. She had an energy that seemed to radiate from her as if standing still for too long would make her bolt. He didn't want her to bolt.

Her gaze wandered over his face and down toward his chest.

He didn't know her at all, but he wanted to. "I'm Bo Fletcher, by the way." He paused. "You really are beautiful."

Taking a deep breath, he stepped closer. He had to kiss her. There were a hundred and one reasons why he shouldn't, but he wanted to more than any of them. Tilting her chin slightly upward, he waited, giving her the opportunity to pull away.

She didn't. Her eyes closed and he lowered his mouth to hers. Her lips were soft and pliant beneath his, just as he expected.

Her hands came up against his chest, sending hot fire from her touch straight to his crotch. He wasn't sure if her intention was to push him away or to feel him.

"Ahem. Fletcher, you have another visitor."

He pulled away fast at the sound of Captain Stewart's voice.

"And when you're done here, I want to see you in my office." The Captain gave him a hard look before stepping to the side to reveal the blonde woman who had accompanied him to the corner of the bay.

Shit. It was Mandy, the woman he met Tuesday night when he'd gone out with Cole. What was she doing here? Had he told her where he worked?

"I was just leaving." Dana spun on her heel and stalked around the front of the ambulance.

Chapter Four

Bo looked at Mandy. "I'll be right back." Racing around the vehicle, he caught up with Dana before she walked into view of the other men. He grasped her arm, gently. "Wait."

She stopped and looked at him in surprise, a hint of embarrassment in her eyes. "What?"

"That, what I did, I mean…you came here looking for me. Did you want something?" He hoped she'd come for his phone number.

She looked confused before she shook her head. "It wasn't important."

She turned away and he stepped in front of her. "It must have been for you to come down here. I'd be happy to help in any way."

She refused to look at him and instead moved around him.

"Wait, how can I find you?" He forced himself not to grab her arm.

She didn't look at him, but spoke over her shoulder. "You know where I live."

He watched her leave the bay. She didn't sashay or strut. Her stride was hard, confident, as if she were comfortable in her own skin. He found that very attractive.

"Bo, is there something you want to tell me?" Mandy slipped her arm in his as she moved in front of him to catch his attention, but her height didn't impede his view of Dana, nor did she soothe his tension when he noticed a couple of the guys watching Dana leave.

The woman in front of him placed her hand on his chest, but hers didn't heat him up like Dana's. He lowered his gaze to her. She was definitely pretty in a cheerleader sort of way. He'd bought her a drink after she initiated a conversation, but he hadn't expected to see her again. "How did you find me?"

She cocked her head to the side. "That was easy. You told me you worked at Station 58. It wasn't hard to look that up and get directions."

He disengaged his arm from hers and took a step back. "I think you heard my Captain wants to see me. Was there something you needed?"

She shrugged. "Just to see you again." Her gaze raked over his naked chest, and he suddenly wished he had his shirt on. "I'm really glad I stopped by."

Bo made himself smile politely. "I'm sorry I have to go, but it was nice to see you again."

She laughed. It was a high pitched sound that made him think of diamonds. That alone had him backing up. "I better get going."

He was open to finding the right woman to share his home with someday, but he wasn't looking for an "in debt ever after" woman, and from Mandy's painted nails, to her designer suit to her artfully arranged hair, a very different look than when he saw her in the sports pub, expensive was written all over her. He'd prefer to steer clear of that.

"What about your number?" She pulled out her cell phone from inside a large purse. "I can punch it in."

He kept backing up. "Sorry, I really have to go." As soon as he was around the ambulance, he strode along the backside of the garage and into the building. He usually wasn't such a coward, but Dana had him completely off balance.

Taking the stairs to the Captain's office two at a time, Bo kept seeing Dana's startled look when the Captain caught them kissing. She hadn't expected the strong physical attraction between them.

He grinned as he thought of their last conversation and opened the door to Captain Stewart's office. Nope, there was nothing in his interaction with Dana at the hospital that would have forewarned him either.

"What are you smiling at, Fletcher?"

He closed the door and moved toward the large desk that had a computer on one side and various piles of paper on the other. "Just a memory, Captain."

His superior frowned. "I don't know what you do down at Station House 23, but I don't approve of my men dating two women at the same time, nor am I happy when my men date people they rescue from burning buildings. You do know that it could simply be some hero worship going on and not real feelings, right?"

Bo opened his mouth to assure the Captain that nothing like that was happening, but the man held up his hand.

"Yes, I know Jax saved Skye from the hotel fire, but that was different. They grew up together. I'm assuming you have never met this Dana Wilson before the fire at her apartment building, correct?"

"Yes, sir, but—"

"As I expected. That means that whatever she feels for you, after only three days, may not last." The Captain walked over to him and put a hand on his shoulder. "I'm just giving you fair warning, son. You're probably better off with the blonde. Now get back down there and put away the gear. The boys finished washing the truck while you were otherwise occupied."

Bo wanted to tell the Captain he was way off base, but he was only scheduled at Station 58 for three and a half more weeks and then he'd be back with his own crew. Better not to rock the boat.

He let the Captain walk him to the door. "Yes, sir."

"Good man."

Bo stood outside the Captain's office. He'd never even think of dating two women at once, but for it to be assumed he did, rankled. He finally walked away, reaffirming his decision not to make a big deal of it.

As he strode into the bay, the three other men he'd been washing the engine with started giving him a hard time.

"Quite the juggler, huh, Fletch?

"Which one is your real flame? Hey, she's Fletcher's flame."

"Is one for day and one for night?"

"Nah, he has them both at the same time."

He smirked despite himself. He didn't mind ribbing from the guys. He wiggled his brows. "If you need lessons, just ask."

The wet sponge hit him square in the chest. He caught it before it could slide off and onto the ground.

Tory laughed. "Just trying to clean you up a bit."

Bo whipped the sponge at Tory's crotch and the man doubled over.

Grasping the sponge, Tory stood straight again and lifted it away from his khakis. "Shit, I look like I just peed my pants."

Bo shrugged. "Better that than the bed."

The guys behind Tory ooohed, their smiles proving they were loving it. Tory grabbed a bucket of soapy water nearby.

Bo dove for the sprayer and the water fight was on.

~~*~~

Dana finished brushing Cyclone and stepped off the stool. "You're a good looking horse, handsome." She patted his side, letting him know she was done. But you're not the only one who's handsome. That firefighter has me all hot and bothered now.

She needed to remember Bo Fletcher's condescending lecture in the hospital and not his muscular chest and commanding lips. How could she have let him kiss her? I would have had to be made of stone not to let him.

"Now we just need to find you a new home and a pretty filly. What do you think about that?"

The horse stomped his foot, and she laughed. "I'm glad you agree." Maybe that's what I need, a date, but not with a man who thinks I'm stupid but pretty enough to kiss. To be fair, he did like her voice and her height didn't bother him at all. She shook her head. Nope. Not going there.

Putting the curry comb away in the cabinet built into the wall of the tiny barn, she shook her head at the horse. "I can't believe no one has adopted you yet. But don't worry, it will happen someday."

Cyclone stomped his foot again and shuffled backward.

"Oh, come on. Sharing your space with a sheep isn't that uncomfortable." She looked over the half wall that divided the structure in two. "Molly's a great roommate. You're going to miss her when she leaves next week."

Cyclone didn't react, having found his dinner.

Just as well. She needed to get back into the city and pick up their new visitors. She secured his stall with a crowbar between two iron loops. Cyclone would kick the door open if she didn't. Clydesdales were strong.

Closing the barn doors behind her, she headed for the second kennel, waving to the three dogs in the other one who barked excitedly as she strode by. "You guys are all fed and watered. Tomorrow morning Sadie and Betty will be here to play with you."

When she arrived at the second kennel, she took the dog bone she had in her pocket and placed it on the clean doggy bed, all ready for the Collie mix she'd be bringing back. Then she continued into Laura's sprawling house.

Each room was designated by animal and need. The senior cat would stay in Laura's room her first night, but the other dog would be added to the small dog room, if he was friendly.

She grabbed a bone from the cabinet in that room and placed it on the bed in a roomy cage then she closed the door. "No, Putsy, you've had plenty to eat already today."

The Schnauzer mix in the next cage cocked his head as if completely baffled by what she said. She chuckled before giving him a quick pat on his nose. "I'm not falling for that, silly pup."

Straightening, she walked into the storage room and retrieved a new knitted blanket. There were still three left, but she'd let Laura know they were running low.

Laura had a wonderful group of volunteers, and some of them made lap throws for the cats. She placed the blanket in a heap at the end of Laura's bed. She hoped the twelve-year-old kitty she brought back would last longer than the last senior cat she saved.

Henry had been fifteen and didn't last more than six months, thanks to cancer, but he had a comfortable and loving final life with Laura.

With everything ready for the new arrivals, Dana stepped into Laura's office. Her boss was on the phone, so she mouthed that she was leaving and grabbed up her keys.

I love my job.

She had that thought at least twenty times a day. She could probably make more money as a teacher now that she had her online Bachelor's degree in education, but it just wouldn't be as fulfilling as what she did now.

As she headed into the city, the traffic slowed to a crawl. Once she and the rest of the thousand cars squeezed around the accident in one lane, she glanced at the clock. Crapola, I'm late. Mr. Shaunessy better still be there. If not, I'm camping out overnight and I'll wait for him to show in the morning. No way would she let any animal be put down.

As she pulled onto Renard Drive, red lights reflected off the buildings. The flickering reminded her of her entrance into hell at her own apartment. Another fire? She made the turn onto Pleasant Lane and pulled over.

No! No!

The animal shelter, tucked between a warehouse and a thrift store, was covered in flames. Water from two firehoses sent smoke billowing into the air.

The animals! She ran toward the building, her destination

the back door, when something caught her around the waist, knocking the wind from her. When she discovered it was a man's arm, she struggled wildly. "Let me go! There's over twenty animals in there!"

"We know. They're going to be alright."

The familiar voice in her ear caught her by surprise. Turning, she found the man that had kissed her for the first time that very afternoon. "Bo, we have to save them."

"We are."

"How can you say that? Look at that fire and smoke." She tried to peel his arm from around her waist, but it was like the lock-down bar on a rollercoaster.

"Dana, listen to me." He squeezed her a little harder, and she lifted her face to look at him again.

"We have the fire under control. See those yellow flames?"

She looked at the building, the gray smoke smothering it but still a yellow flame would burst through. She nodded, swallowing at the smell and remembering the feel of that smoke in her throat.

"Those yellow flames are weak. It's almost out."

"But what about the smoke? The animals? Misty barely made it and I had her low to the floor."

"Look." He pointed to the alleyway between the shelter and the warehouse. "They're bringing them out."

Even as she focused on the firefighters carrying cages, she heard a couple barks. What would happen to them? What about the ones she'd come to save? "What will they do with them?" She hated the fear creeping into her voice, but she could easily imagine city officials putting them all down because they had no place to house them.

"They're going to Little Critters who will farm them out

to the various no-kill shelters in the greater Dallas area because no one shelter can handle them all."

She turned and looked at him. "I should have been here on time. I was supposed to take two dogs and a cat to Rainbow Acres. They were scheduled to be euthanized tomorrow. Do I need to find them or will they also be given to no-kill shelters?"

Bo frowned. "Is that why you're here? Not because you saw the smoke but because you were supposed to be here earlier?"

"Despite what you think, I'm not a fire engine chaser. I was supposed to be here at seven to pick up three animals."

He pulled his phone out and looked at it, then looked at her. "We need to talk to Lieutenant Boone."

She didn't like the hardness of his voice, but as she watched more animal crates being loaded onto a truck, she worried. Maybe seeing the Lieutenant and asking him directly where the animals were going would tell her if it was true or not.

She didn't trust officials when it came to animals. After she'd convinced the police in Greenbriar to shut down the dog fighting ring, they told her all the pit bulls would be adopted out. It was two weeks later when she accidently discovered that eleven of the fourteen dogs had been put down.

"Okay, let's go talk to Lieutenant Boone." She expected him to let her go, but he didn't. Instead, he continued to hold her waist and guided her around the firetruck where the Lieutenant stood back from the fire, speaking into his radio.

"Lieutenant Boone?" They waited as the man in question barked another command over the radio.

Finally, he looked at them and scowled. "What is it, Fletcher?"

"I think you need to hear this." Bo turned toward her. "Tell him why you're here."

She moved her gaze from intense green eyes to hazel ones. "I was supposed to be here by seven to pick up three animals that were going to be euthanized, but I understand all the animals are going to no-kill shelters. Is that true?"

The man's scowl deepened. "Of course. That's what we always do in situations like this. It's protocol." He turned toward Fletcher. "Why is this important? I'm trying to get this fire doused."

She looked at Bo as well, not sure what the big deal was.

"Sir, this is Dana Wilson. One of the women who lived in the apartment building we rode to on Thursday. The arson fire?"

"Oh."

"What?" She ignored the Lieutenant's surprise to confront Bo. "What do you mean arson? Someone set our apartment building on fire on purpose?"

Bo rubbed the back of his neck as Dana turned her scared gaze on him, but before he could reassure her, his superior spoke.

"Miss Wilson, would you mind staying here for a while? We'll need you to talk to our Fire Investigator."

She looked about to argue, so Bo squeezed her waist and her gaze flew to him. He nodded at her.

She turned back to Boone. "I don't have to return to Rainbow Acres now, if I'm sure all the animals are going to be safe."

Boone nodded, his face relaxing, which made him a lot less intimidating. "I assure you, Miss Wilson, that every single critter will arrive safely at a no-kill shelter after being thoroughly examined by a vet."

She stared hard at the Lieutenant then sighed. "Okay, I'll stay."

Boone moved his gaze to him. "Fletcher, watch out for Miss Wilson while we finish dousing this fire."

"Yes, sir." He guided Dana from the command spot to a relatively quiet area away from the rescue crew and the gawkers that had come out to watch a building burn.

Cole had regaled him the other night with his story about putting out a fire on a nudist resort where his wife worked. He said naked people had driven over in golf carts to watch the fire. Bo couldn't imagine that. He'd bet Cole had exaggerated.

What his friend hadn't exaggerated was that arsonists like to watch the fires they start.

Bo scanned the onlookers. A blonde with a face he remembered caught his attention, but when he looked back, he couldn't find her. What would Mandy be doing at an animal shelter fire? It was probably just someone who looked like her.

He continued to study the crowd. One of the people with their backs to him could be here to see if Dana had died in the fire.

A chill stole through him at that thought, and he walked Dana past the area he'd planned to stop at and took them around the corner where they couldn't see the burning building but he would see the Fire Investigator pull up.

The minute they'd arrived on scene, they'd known it was arson.

"What are you doing, walking me home? I thought your boss wanted me to stay." Dana pulled away from him.

He stopped at her question. "I just want to keep you at a safe distance."

She rolled her eyes. "I think a half mile back that way would be safe. I can't even see the building from here or the animals. Or is that what you wanted me to forget about, the animals?"

He grabbed her by the shoulders to face him, needing to get her to understand the serious danger she was in. "Listen, sometimes it's about more than the animals."

Her eyes widened. "Of course there's more to it, but you, your boss, the Fire Inspector and even the neighbors are going to be concerned with keeping people safe and stopping the fire from spreading."

His muscles relaxed at her words. He'd been afraid she was one of the militant animal rights people, but she was obviously simply very concerned.

"That's why I have to be focused on the animals. They are a second thought to everyone else, so they need to be my first thought. They can't speak up for themselves. That's my job."

He tensed, his relief short-lived. "Dana, this isn't about the animals. This is about arson."

He felt her body freeze beneath his hands, her shoulders stiff. "What do you mean? Wait, you said that someone set my apartment building on fire."

Even in the growing darkness, he could see the fear in her eyes. He wanted to assure her she was safe, but he needed her to understand her own danger. "Yes, the Fire Investigator discovered accelerant had been used on the couch in your hallway before it was torched."

She frowned. "And here?"

He squeezed her shoulders gently, wanting to comfort

her, but holding himself back. "We found a deliberate pattern to the fire. It was started intentionally."

She looked away, obviously processing the information.

"I'm not an expert, but in talking to a friend of mine who is being certified as an arson investigator, this arsonist is just getting started."

Her gaze flew back to him and her eyes widened. "I was at both places. Is he targeting me?" Her throat worked as she swallowed hard, but her voice still came out barely above a whisper. "Does he want me dead?"

Chapter Five

Bo couldn't resist any longer, his protective instincts rising up hard. He pulled her against him and wrapped his arms around her. "Don't worry. We aren't going to let that happen."

Her head rested against his shoulder, but her arms remained limp at her sides. She wasn't shaking or crying, two reactions he expected from a woman who had just been told an arsonist was out to kill her.

Curious, he gently pushed her back.

Her brow wrinkled in confusion and her dark lips were pursed together tightly on one side. Finally, she met his gaze. "Do you know who it is?"

He shook his head. "No. So far the only two arson fires we've had this week were your apartment building and this shelter." The rest were accidental or people just being stupid."

He frowned as he remembered the drug addict mom who caught her apartment on fire lighting up crack. If not for her ten-year-old, she and her two kids would have been toast by the time his crew arrived. It had been their first call of his shift.

"I think I know who it might be." Dana's shoulders straightened beneath his hands and her chin came up a notch.

This woman's courage had his heart taking notice, but he kept his mind focused on the problem at hand. "You do? Who?"

"I think it might be one of the men who owned pit bulls in the dog fighting operation I got shut down in Greenbriar, New Jersey. I moved to Dallas after my life was threatened. I thought they wouldn't follow me. I guess I was wrong."

Shit! He wasn't sure if it was bravery or a lack of common sense, but he definitely admired her. "How exactly did you shut down a dog fighting operation?"

She pulled away from him, putting at least twelve feet between them. His gut reacted and he scanned the immediate area, more sure than ever that Dana was the target. The Fire Investigator's car took the turn onto the road with the shelter, but she didn't notice.

"I witnessed the fighting and followed every member to his home, taking pictures of where they lived. I tried to get police to shut it down then, but they said they needed more than just my word and pictures of houses and apartment buildings. So I went back and took videos." She clenched her fists. "It was the hardest thing I've ever done. They pitted the dogs against each other until one was dead."

She stood there, fists clenched with the streetlight reflecting in her tear-filled eyes.

It took all his willpower to stay where he was. "Does that mean you didn't have to testify? Did you take the stand?"

She nodded, but didn't say a word.

Fuck. She was lucky she hadn't been shot. Even the thought of her taking videos secretly had his heart dropping.

They needed to tell Boone. Damn, he needed to protect her until they found the bastard that was setting the fires.

It all made sense. Cole said it wasn't a pyro, but a newbie, and what better way to kill Dana and not trace it back to the scum in Greenbriar.

Her mission in life may be to save animals, but now his was to save her. He scanned the area again to make sure no one watched them, but it was empty.

He strode toward her. "Let's go back. The Fire Investigator is going to want to know what you just told me."

"Of course." She didn't look at him. Instead, she turned away and headed back toward the animal shelter.

He didn't let more than a foot separate them as he followed her, watching the onlookers slowly dispersing now that the excitement was over and the smoke had diminished. When they arrived at the command spot, Boone wasn't there, but Cole was.

"Hey, Bo. Looks like you've got another, huh?"

"Yes. Do you know where the Fire Investigator is? Boone wants Dana to talk to him."

Cole's green gaze shifted to Dana. "Are you Dana Wilson?"

"I am."

"Then you are the last person I need to talk to." Cole smiled warmly.

"You?" Bo kicked himself at the sudden spurt of irritation when Dana returned Cole's smile. Cole was a happily married man. He did nothing but sing the praises of his wife, Lacey.

Cole gave him a quizzical look. "Yes, me. The Fire Investigator has me interviewing the witnesses while he goes over the evidence."

Dana spoke up. "Did you say witnesses? Someone saw

something?" She gave Bo a worried glance before returning her attention to his friend.

Cole looked down at the pad of paper he held, its small size looked awkward in his large hand. "Yes. There was a Mr. Shaunessy and—"

"That's the owner of the shelter." Dana looked at Cole. "Is he alright?"

"Yes. He just had a little smoke inhalation."

Bo nodded. That made sense. He'd pulled the man out before they even had water on the fire, but unlike Dana, he hadn't been on the floor, instead he stood in his back room coughing. "Who else?"

Cole looked down again. "A Miss Tanya Robinson."

"Tanya?" Dana looked at Bo then back at Cole. "She lives across the hall from me. I dog-sit for her on occasion. What was she doing here?"

"According to my interview with her, she was looking to adopt a pet for her niece, but Mr. Shaunessy wouldn't let her because he was closed. He closed the blinds on her and she pounded on the door yelling for him to open up. I guess she yelled for quite a while with no luck and was about to leave when she smelled the smoke. She walked down the alley toward the back and saw flames, so she called 911."

"That's weird." Dana's frown told him it was more than just Tanya's behavior.

"Why is it weird?"

She looked him in the eye. "Tanya doesn't have a niece."

Cole raised an eyebrow at that information. "She's obviously hiding something. She's also another link between the two fires."

Bo voiced what he'd bet they were all thinking. "She could

be the arsonist or the one the arsonist was after and he just didn't know that she wasn't home Thursday night."

"Which brings me to Miss Wilson." Cole focused on Dana again. "Why am I supposed to talk to you? Were you here when the fire started?"

She shook her head and took a step closer to him. Bo put his arm around her shoulders, an action Cole noticed if his look was any indication. "Go ahead, Dana. Tell him about why you were supposed to be here."

While she filled Cole in on her animal pick-up and the dog-fighting ring, Bo watched her carefully. If he hadn't noticed her running toward the building and caught her, she would be considered a suspect.

She was driven beyond common sense. Ordinary people didn't run into burning buildings to save pets, which meant she was extra-ordinary. At first he'd been angry she'd risked her life and made his job harder when he had to rescue her from her apartment building.

Then he'd written her off as simply too kind-hearted for her own good when he'd seen her lying in the hospital bed.

It wasn't until she'd walked into Station House 58 that he'd seen her as a beautiful, confident woman, except for perhaps in his dream, but now, after seeing her race toward yet another burning building, he wanted to know what made her tick.

He also wanted to keep her safe.

"So can I leave now?"

Dana's question sent his adrenaline racing. Not by herself she couldn't. "Let me just tell the Lieutenant and I'll escort you home."

Dana's surprised look was mirrored by Cole.

"What?" He addressed Cole. "We just figured out that

Dana might be the target of an arsonist. I think someone needs to be sure she makes it home safe."

"I'm perfectly capable of getting in my car and driving myself home if that's where I want to go. As a matter of fact, I need to grab dinner first." Dana crossed her arms as if that settled everything.

There was no way he would let her drive across town by herself when the possibility existed that—

"Miss Wilson, I have to agree with Bo."

He snapped his gaze to Cole's. He hadn't expected support from that quarter.

"If the Lieutenant will allow it, I suggest that Bo go with you."

Dana opened her mouth to speak, but Cole held up his hand. "Please. I do feel your life is in danger and if not Bo then I will have to suggest police protection."

Bo started to shake his head, but at Cole's look, he caught on. They both knew the Dallas PD wouldn't assign an officer to Dana. In Texas it was Rangers who provided protection, but for some reason, Cole was helping him out, and he wasn't about to look a gift horse in the mouth. "Listen, Dana. I promise to simply shadow you. I won't interfere at all."

She scowled, obviously not happy with her choices.

He held out his arms. "Come on, I'm not that bad, am I?"

Her lips quirked just a bit. "Will you teach me how to handle myself in a fire? That's why I came to the fire station today. I want to be trained in fire suppression or whatever it is you train in."

Huh? There was no such training unless a person became a firefighter, but she'd get pissed if he told her that. Shit. "I can definitely teach you a few things that could aid you in a fire, if you are ever in another one." Now that he'd said it, it made a lot of sense to make sure she knew the basics with an arsonist on her heels.

She stared hard at him in the flickering lights of the emergency vehicles. If he didn't know better, she was trying to decide if he told her the truth. Now that rankled.

She held out her hand. "Okay, you have a deal."

She wanted to shake on it? If it wasn't such a serious situation, he'd laugh with disbelief, but she was completely serious. He shook her hand, surprised how cool it was. The sun may have gone down, but it was still well over eighty degrees even without the remaining heat radiating off the building.

"I'll call Laura." Dana held up her phone. "She's expecting three more animals that won't be coming. Then I'm ready to get out of here."

"I'll talk to the Lieutenant and meet you at your car."

She nodded even as she walked a few yards away to make her call.

Bo turned back to Cole. "Thanks."

"If it was just your interest in her as a date, I wouldn't have said that. But my instructor is confident that this arsonist is going to escalate and if either she or her neighbor is the target, there's a good chance he will succeed unless we catch him first."

"Keep me updated even if it's 'unofficial' information. I want to be one step ahead of this bastard." Bo unzipped his turnout gear, ready to leave the scene as quickly as possible.

Cole stopped him by grabbing his arm. "Hey, what is it with you and this woman?"

He lifted his hand to rub the back of his neck, and Cole let go. "I don't know. She's interesting, in a good way. For now,

I just want her to live. That would go a long way in helping me get to know her."

"Okay. Just be careful. I'd hate to see you get burned both figuratively and literally."

Bo chuckled and stepped out of his bunker gear. "Don't worry, I've been through my share of relationships and fires, and I'd say the first is a lot more dangerous."

Cole laughed then headed back toward the street where the Fire Inspector stood next to his SUV, talking on the phone.

~~*~~

Dana finished her second slice of pizza and broke their silent dinner. "You can have the rest."

Bo's large hand stilled on its way to the pizza box. "The rest? You can't be full yet."

She waved him off. "I'm a grazer. I eat a little all day. Go ahead." At his doubtful expression, she nodded emphatically. "If you don't finish it, I'll just bring it to Darling."

He finally picked up another slice which he dropped on his paper plate. "Darling who?" He took a bite of his pizza.

She frowned at him. "Darling the pig at Rainbow Acres. She loves scraps."

At his self-deprecating chuckle, she smiled. "You're not jealous of a pig, are you?"

He finished chewing before he answered. "That depends on if you're talking about an animal or a police officer."

She laughed, which made her feel a little more at ease. Having a man in her new apartment was a first, but having such a large man in it made it feel small, like they were forced to be closer than they needed to be. "I'll take an animal over a cop any day."

"Why?" He looked at her quizzically. "I noticed you don't really care for authority."

She shrugged as she rose and threw out her dirty plate. "Let's just say they've let me down too many times." She leaned her hip against the kitchen counter. She preferred being a little taller than him and it could only happen with him sitting down and her standing.

They'd stopped at the fire station so he could stow his gear and put on his cowboy boots and hat. He'd taken the hat off as soon as they entered the apartment and set it on her vestibule table. At least that table was good for something.

They'd also picked up a pizza on the way, which she could tell he was enjoying immensely. "What about you? Did you always want to be a fireman when you were growing up, or had you planned to be a rodeo champion and didn't quite make it?"

A fleeting glimpse of pain in his eyes was the only sign that her question had struck a nerve, but he smirked, easily covering it up. If he was that practiced about it, it had to be an old agony.

"Like any tyke, I started out dreaming of the big rodeo buckles, but when I was a teenager I saw a fire and decided I wanted to be less self-involved and help people. Even though I did do the rodeo circuit for a little while during high school. Yes, I won a buckle. But after both Cole and I got busted up riding Hades, I stopped. As soon as I graduated, I went to college for a Fire Science degree and directly into training. I've never looked back. Never lost a person either."

He took another bite of his pizza, which consisted of half the slice, giving her time to digest all that. They weren't really that different when it came down to it. They were both rescuers.

"By the way, it's 'firefighter' not 'fireman.' A fireman is the man that shovels coal into steam engines."

The way he stated it, she could tell he'd done so thousands of times. "I'll remember that." He would be a good one for talking to kids in the classroom. His friendly smile, polite manners and overall large presence would have both boys and girls worshipping him as their hero.

She crossed her arms over her chest. In reality, he was her hero. He saved her from her own burning building. She was also impressed with his size and the muscles beneath his t-shirt and pants. So why couldn't she relax around him?

Because he's one of those male authorities I can't trust. Just like dad, pretending to be important, when he was passed over for promotion. Telling her mom he had to work late and then coming home smelling like pot roast. Not that he'd let her mom spend money on a roast.

"Your turn. How did you get into rescuing animals? Last I heard, there was no school you can go to in order to be trained in that." Though Bo smiled as he asked, her defenses went up.

"Actually, those who work in animal welfare in certain cities get extensive training, and there is wildlife management training as well. I did take a few of those, but for the most part, it's all on-the-job training. Sometimes off the job, too."

He picked up the last piece of pizza. "What type of job?"

She shrugged, starting to relax. "I've only worked for nonprofits that save animals. It's the best way for me to help because there is never enough staff so as an employee, I get to do everything eventually." Usually she'd stop her explanation with that, but Bo didn't appear bored. He focused all his attention on her, even missing the fact he had a bit of tomato sauce on the side of his mouth.

"I've always worked for rescues and shelters that don't put down animals. If I'm going to put my life in danger to save an animal, I certainly don't want it killed just because it hasn't been adopted in a certain amount of time."

"That makes a lot of sense."

"I also focus on domesticated animals, not wildlife, though I have rescued a few of those when they have been endangered by humans."

At his look of curiosity, she dropped her arms and explained. "For example, I was driving on the Kancamagus Highway in New Hampshire when the pick-up truck in front of me hit a white-tailed deer. The driver stopped and called the wildlife department to let them know and waited for them to arrive. What he didn't realize was that when he hit the adult, her body slammed into her baby, who fell over the side of the road. So I went down and rescued it."

Bo put down his half eaten piece of pizza. "Rescued it from what?"

"Down the side of the road was a bit of a cliff and the fawn had tumbled down to a shelf. It bleated for its mother, but otherwise was unhurt. It tried to scamper back up, but fell again, and I could see it could easily go over the edge, so I climbed down to make sure that didn't happen."

"And you climbed up with the fawn?" Bo's doubt was obvious.

"Of course not. It was a cliff. I kept the fawn on the ledge until the wildlife management rescued us. After that, I took a few lessons in rock climbing, in case I found myself in a similar situation."

Bo nodded. "Which is why you want to learn about being safe in escaping a fire."

"Yes." That he understood had her pulse racing. "The more I learn, the better prepared I am and the less danger the animal and I will be in next time."

Bo finally took his gaze off her and brought the last part of the pizza to his mouth.

She watched as he folded up his paper plate and with a stretch of his arm, dropped it in her trash basket. That arm bulged with muscle, causing his department t-shirt sleeve to stretch to the maximum. No wonder he rescued people. He had the sheer strength to do it.

He stood, causing her to switch her gaze to the rest of him. She was tall for a woman at six feet one inch, but he had to be at least six six. For an authority type, he actually seemed like a decent man. She had been enjoying his company and now he'd have to leave. Her disappointment surprised her.

It must be the cowboy side of him she related to. He, at least, understood animals. Reaching behind her, she picked up her keys. "You left your vehicle at the fire station, right?" She could ponder her interest in him after he was gone.

Bo didn't move toward her vestibule to pick up his hat. Instead, he crossed his arms and shook his head. It was an intimidating look. She hated that look.

"Dana, I'm not going anywhere."

Chapter Six

A tiny slice of panic started in Dana's belly. "What? You have to. You have to go home and go to work."

"I don't think you understand. You have an arsonist on your tail, and I'm here to protect you. I don't work again for two more days, so I'm sticking close. Tomorrow when you have time in your schedule, we can stop at my place so I can pick up a change of clothes. My guess is you don't have anything here that I could wear." He winked, which spoiled his intimidation look, but sent another whole vibe through her body.

She swallowed hard. This wasn't what she'd expected when she'd agreed to let him come home with her. "I thought…"

Bo moved around the table to stand in front of her. "I know this is hard, but it's only for a short time. Just until they can find this maniac."

Her stomach felt like it was in her throat. "What if they never find him?"

"Then I guess I'll have to stay with you forever." He grinned.

Her face must have reflected her panic because he raised

his hands in surrender. "No, I'm kidding. They'll find him. Don't worry."

She slid her hips along the counter until she could walk out from behind the table and into her living room. "I think you're making more out of this than there is. It could be Tanya that is the target or it could simply be coincidence."

His eyes reflected hurt before he scowled at her. "If not me, then the police."

"No!" She'd never trust an officer again. Her father had lied to her and her mother too many times to count, finally shacking up with her mom's cousin and blaming her mom for that, too. "I mean, if that's my only choice, then I'd rather have you as my watch dog."

"Why do I get the feeling you're choosing the lesser of two evils?"

"It's not personal. I just don't know you."

Bo rolled his eyes and repeated. "I saved you from a burning building while you were unconscious and half naked. I think you can trust me."

Her pulse slowed at that. He made a good point. Maybe she could trust him not to take advantage of her, but could she trust herself not to take advantage of him? The kiss in the fire station brought her body back to life and she wasn't immune to the memory of him holding her at the fire tonight.

He was hard, strong, easy to rely on. That in itself scared her. She didn't rely on people like him. She pointed to the couch. "I don't have another bedroom. All I have is this couch and it's not even a pull out."

"Not a problem." He strode over and sat on it as if testing it. He leaned back, stretching out his long legs and crossing them at the ankle. "Perfect."

She had to smile. "Really? That thing has to be two feet too short for you."

"Hey, beggars can't be choosers."

Should she offer him her bed? She really didn't want him to stay, so if he insisted then he could suffer with it. But he's staying to protect me.

She pushed her thought away. "Let me see what I have for extra sheets and blankets." Walking into her bedroom, she let out a breath.

There hadn't been a man in her house since she was eight years old. She'd had a few relationships, but had always managed to go to her "boyfriend's" house. Of course, none of them lasted. They all wanted too much of her time and didn't understand the risks she took for animals.

She moved to the closet and pulled her extra set of sheets for her bed from the top shelf. At least they were king sized, though she wondered if he would even fit on a bed that big. She didn't have any extra blankets, but there was an afghan on the chair he could use.

She glanced at her bed and paused. She really should offer it to him. He'd probably say no, since he was raised that way, but the chip on her heart just wouldn't budge, and she finally gave up.

He would need a pillow because she didn't have the fancy couch pillows other people had. She grabbed one from her bed and headed back toward the living room.

When she entered, she found him holding the picture of her receiving the Citizen of the Year award in Gasten, Mississippi.

"I see you were honored."

She shrugged, a little embarrassed he'd seen it. "Here's

a set of sheets and a pillow." She stripped the pillow of its case. "And if you need a little warmth, there's this afghan." She dumped the pile on the easy chair.

He held up the photo. "Citizen of the Year?"

He wasn't going to let it go, was he? "You want to know why I got it, don't you?"

Bo grinned, his green eyes lighting up like a young boy who'd just been told he could have ice cream for dinner.

She sighed. "I just did my job. I saved some animals when the town flooded. It's a small town and most of the people there were very attached to their pets."

She moved into the kitchen to grab a bottle of water for her bedside. "A lot of people lost their homes and the shelters wouldn't take pets, of course. Those places are chaos with humans, never mind throwing pets into the mix. So I opened my house for all the animals and took care of them with volunteers until people could take their pets back."

She closed the fridge and looked at him. "Do you know that every single owner came to visit their pet once a day, except those who were hospitalized. I was able to recruit volunteers to bring those people their animals a couple times a week."

"That's impressive." He put the picture down. "I'm guessing you went into the flood waters to retrieve the animals."

Crap. Now he's going to lecture me on letting rescue crews do their jobs.

He opened his mouth, but she didn't let him speak. "Luckily, I was able to obtain a canoe. All the other boats, and there weren't many, were being used by emergency personnel. I got to one dog just in time. He was on a chain bolted to the cement patio trying to keep his head above the rising water. I took his collar off and dragged him into the canoe. He was so tired he just lay there shivering. I covered him with my coat until I could get him to dry land and my crew of volunteers."

He didn't respond, but he did close his mouth.

"Anyway, I have to get up at five tomorrow. Do you plan to go everywhere I do?"

He nodded but still didn't say anything.

"Okay, well, goodnight." She turned toward her bedroom but hadn't taken one step before his voice stopped her.

"Why animals?" His tone was gently curious.

However, his question caused a maelstrom of emotions to swirl within her. Images of her childhood stray cat, her father, the argument, the pain. She choked down the lump in her throat and blinked at the tears. I am not going there. Without turning around, she threw her answer over her shoulder. "Why not?" Her voice, far raspier than usual, wasn't very loud.

When his step sounded on the wood floor behind her, she jumped into motion, quickly striding out of the room to her bedroom where she closed the door.

Crapola, there's no lock. Not one of the modern conveniences the landlord had thought to add to a one-bedroom apartment in a hundred-year-old building.

She leaned her back against the door and listened for his footsteps. She heard them, but they didn't come any closer. He was probably making his bed. Finally pushing away, she placed the water bottle on her nightstand and changed into her extra-large t-shirt. The water was a new habit she'd started after the fire. She woke up a few nights with a sore throat and the water helped.

Ready to brush her teeth, her hand was on her doorknob when she stopped. She hadn't told him where the bathroom was.

Listening through the old six panel door, she heard nothing. Stealthily, she opened it an inch and peered across the way to see her bathroom door shut. Yup, he found it. She closed the door and sat on the bed, listening for him to leave.

Maybe she should put a chair or something under her doorknob. Better yet, jingle bells so she would wake if he came in. Jingle bells? Really? He saved my life. I don't have to worry with him. He's a firefighter, not a cop. He's just a cowboy doing whatever it is they do.

She'd only met a couple cowboys since she rarely rescued horses, but the few she'd met had been very polite, but distant.

At the sound of her bathroom door opening, she stood. This one wasn't distant. He was very close. He also seemed very personal.

His focused attention on her, what she said and felt, unnerved her. And just gazing at him anywhere below the neck was distracting. There was way too much strength in the man's body for her to be completely immune to the physical attraction sizzling between them.

Plus, she wasn't used to sharing her space with another person. On one hand, she didn't want him in her apartment, but on the other hand, she was grateful and wanted him to feel comfortable.

Wait a minute. Do I still have that robe I bought when I went on the weekend cruise to Cancun?

She walked to her closet and dug through it. "Hah." Grasping the typical white robe with the cruise line name embroidered on it, she pulled it out. It was a "one size fits all" type of thing, so it might just work, though she couldn't imagine the company that made the robe had men the size of Bo in mind.

Pleased she might be able to make him a little more comfortable, she left her room and walked into the living area. She stopped short at the sight of Bo, butt naked, placing the pillow at the end of the couch.

He stood, and she stopped breathing.

Every inch of the man was solid muscle from his ripped abdominals to his corded thighs to his bulging calves. She didn't miss the large cock nestled against dark pubic hair either before he covered it with the pillow he grabbed up.

Her whole body heated at being caught staring. "I'm sorry. I didn't know you were, ah, I just thought you might, um— here." She thrust the robe toward him.

He moved forward, the sliver of a smile on his lips. "Thanks, I obviously need it."

Her cheeks heated more at what he must have perceived as an insult. "No, not at all. You have an amazing body. I didn't know you would walk around naked, that's all. I thought you'd be stuck in your jeans so I wanted you to have that." Her voice trailed off as his grin grew wider.

"Thank you."

He didn't move to put it on. He just stood there smiling at her.

She found herself wishing he would drop the pillow and the robe. Holy moly, what had gotten into her?

"So you think I have an amazing body?" His smile had changed, his whole look turning seductive.

Uh-oh, now you're in for it. "Are you fishing for a compliment?"

He took a step forward. "Maybe."

Two could play this game. "If you want one, you'll have to show me everything." She smirked, confident, based on how quickly he'd covered himself, that he would back down.

To her horror and delight, he threw the pillow on the couch and spread his arms. She sucked in a breath as her gaze roamed over every inch of tautness, his cock now hard and protruding outward. When her eyes reached his, he cocked an eyebrow.

Her body revved like an engine ready for the starting gun. Though she should feel embarrassed, she didn't. Powerful was more the feeling, though from the man before her, she should feel weaker than a day-old kitten. She lifted her hand and made a circle with her finger. "Turn around. I need to see everything if I'm going to pass judgement."

She saw more than heard his silent chuckle as he turned his back on her.

Shootin' sheepherders! He was just as hot and tight in the ass as he was in the front. His back muscles rippled as he looked over his shoulder.

"Well?"

She swallowed hard, her belly doing flip-flops over the view of him. "You'll do."

He turned back around and closed the distance in one stride. "I'll do?"

She forced her gaze up to meet his. "Yes." She tried to grin, to lighten the mood, but the electrical attraction she felt wasn't going anywhere.

"I'll do for what?" He eyed her seriously, all traces of humor gone.

Good question. She didn't have the answer. She couldn't think with him so close, except about how much she wanted to touch his hard chest.

"I don't know. I better go to bed." She started to turn but his hand came down on her shoulder.

It wasn't hurtful, just detaining, holding her there. "Dana." His tone softened and her heart squeezed, a long buried need to be cared for rising up, yelling at her that this man could do it.

She stared at him, her hope fighting with her doubt. Why would he want to care for her? Her own parents fought over who would get custody, neither wanting her. Just because he was strong and caring didn't mean he'd want her either.

His other hand cupped her cheek. "I like you. I find you fascinating, in a good way. Let me kiss you again."

It was no more than a physical want, but at that moment, with all that was happening to her, she'd take it. She gave him the slightest nod possible, but she could sense his tension ease, even as he lowered his head and his lips touched hers.

Like at the fire station earlier, he was gentle, as if she were the most precious person in the world. Her cynical self crumbled as his tongue breeched her lips and explored her mouth. He tasted of mint, and he smelled so masculine, a combination of smoke and musk.

She leaned toward him and placed her hands on his chest. The second she felt his warmth, her nipples hardened. Unable to resist, she smoothed her palms over the mounds of his pectorals, even as she sucked his tongue into her mouth.

His hands left her face and shoulder to pull her tight against him, his strength exciting her, telling her she was safe, cared for, and very much wanted. His mouth became more demanding as his tongue swept over hers and learned every inch of her.

She moaned, pressing her hips against his thighs, her

sheath moistening with need. *I want this. Just for tonight. Just to pretend.*

As if he sensed her capitulation, his hand moved to her thigh, stroking upward to her ass where he squeezed one cheek. His own hips pressed his hard cock into her abdomen, setting aflame the tindered ash of her desire. Her sheath contracted.

Bo's hand continued its ascent up her back until he broke their kiss to pull her t-shirt over her head.

As the coolness of the air conditioner touched her skin, her brain started to focus. *What am I doing?*

Before she could react, he was kissing her neck, bending her backwards, trailing nips along her skin until he reached her nipple. His tongue swirled the hard nub then his lips closed over her areola and he sucked.

The tension between her thighs grew, and moisture dampened her outer lips. She wanted him inside her. As his tongue traced a path to her other nipple, she moaned again, finally rasping out what she could. "I need…"

His mouth sucking her nipple hard made her gasp as fire shot from there straight to her core. Then his other hand found her thigh and moved toward her mons.

Oh yes, please. She spread her legs, barely aware he held her whole weight on one arm.

A knock at her door halted everything. "Hey Dana, are you awake?"

Tanya's strident voice impinged on her euphoria, breaking whatever connection she'd let herself make.

Bo must have felt it too. His mouth left her breast as he pulled his hand away and he raised her straight.

She opened her mouth to answer her neighbor, but Bo's shaking head stopped her.

"Dana? Shit. Come on Tiara. I guess you'll have to come with me tonight." Tanya's high-heeled footsteps sounded loud in the uncomfortable silence. *Crap, how did I not hear those?*

Bo still held her, but she stepped out of his embrace and grabbed her t-shirt. Throwing it over her head, she struggled to get her arms in her sleeves, but finally did. She looked at Bo, who watched her, no expression on his face.

"I… I…" What could she say? That is was a mistake? That she wanted him to be her Prince Charming, but that was just a fantasy? She finally gave up saying anything and walked out of the room, her body urging her to go back, her heart begging her to return and her mind telling her to stay as far away from the man as possible.

Bo watched as a myriad of emotions crossed Dana's face, everything from disappointment to hope to fear. But he knew she wouldn't stay. Something in her actions and words over the day told him she wouldn't find fulfillment in his arms after they were interrupted.

He rubbed the back of his neck and sat on the couch, pulling the pillow out from behind him. His body was more than ready for her, but he forced himself to think of something other than her body, Dana as a person instead.

She had more depth than most of the women he'd dated. She had enough layers to keep him digging for years. He'd learned a lot about her in just one day, more from what she didn't say than what she said.

Even as he'd thought of ignoring the uncomfortable moment when she found him naked, there had been such hopeful yearning in her eyes that he'd couldn't resist. It was the same at the station house. She not only attracted him, but she intrigued him.

Lying back, his legs hitting the arm of the couch at his knees, he stared at the ceiling. There was a smoky smell to the furniture thanks to the fire, but not too strong. It actually made him feel at home.

His gut told him the key to unlocking Dana was in her mission to help animals. If he could discover that, he had a feeling everything would fall into place. The problem was, he was as interested in unlocking her body as her mind and that was a heady distraction.

He put his hands beneath his head. Tomorrow would be enlightening, a day in the life of Dana Wilson. Maybe it would shed some light on what made her tick…and hopefully Cole could shed light on the arsonist.

Bo closed his eyes. Between the short couch and his hard on, he doubted he'd sleep much, but he had no doubt his dreams would be filled with Dana. A very naked Dana. He grinned.

~~*~~

Bo found Dana's life a lot more interesting than his own. He hadn't realized how much time he spent with his firehouse friends. Dana, on the other hand, was around all kinds of people…and animals.

Their first stop that morning had been Rainbow Acres, where she decided he might as well help her with the morning feeding and crap dumping. While comfortable with the cats, dogs, pig, sheep and horse, feeding the bearded dragon, the parrot and the corn snake was a new experience.

Then they were off to the community center where she

gave an orientation to prospective volunteers for Rainbow Acres. Their next stop had been a meeting with a woman who gave the term "Cat Lady" a whole new meaning.

Dana hadn't said a word about what almost happened between them last night and he wouldn't bring it up. He'd been ready to continue what they'd started, and his dreams had confirmed that, but he held back. She wasn't ready.

Now they were headed to his house, and while he'd learned a lot about her, he still didn't know what he wanted to know.

He directed her around the last corner onto his street and they pulled into his driveway.

"You live here?"

"Yes. Why? Were you expecting a mansion?" Did she originally come from money? Was that why she didn't trust him?

She snapped her head around to look at him. "No, of course not. I was expecting a ranch."

With his ego soothed, he was able to smile. "I'd love a ranch, but it's a long drive into the city. I know of a few firefighters who own ranches, but they have help. Firefighting and ranching are both full time jobs."

"Then why do you wear cowboy boots and a hat?"

He raised his eyebrows. "You haven't lived in Texas long, have you?"

She shook her head.

"I grew up on a ranch, even participated in the rodeo circuit for a while like I told you last night, but I was meant to be a firefighter. That doesn't exclude me from being a cowboy though. A cowboy is more than just riding horses and roping cattle. It's a life choice, but it's also a way of life, a way to live life." He took a deep breath. "I'm probably not explaining it right."

Her hand on his thigh surprised him.

"No, you explained it perfectly. I get it now."

Her smile was kind. It was the same one she used when talking to the animals. In a way he was insulted, but considering what high esteem she had for animals, he took it as a compliment.

"Come on in." He opened his door and jumped out.

Dana followed him up the small brick path.

A weird excitement built inside him, curious to know what she'd think of his home. After unlocking the door, he pushed it open and stepped back. "Here we are."

Curiosity made her eyes light as she stepped into the small but tall vestibule. Buca waited for them and rubbed against her ankles.

"You have a cat?"

Her surprised tone of voice coupled with the fact that she immediately crouched down to pet Buca had his pride in his home deflating quickly.

Buca, the traitor, was practically in her lap. No, make that now in her arms as she rose with his cat butting its head against her chin.

He closed the front door with a thud. "Yes, I have a cat. His name is Buca."

"Hey, Buca. Did you miss your daddy? He's been gone a long time, hasn't he?" She gave him a scowl before returning her attention to his cat.

He should have known. Throwing his keys down on the side table beneath an antique framed mirror, he faced her. "Buca is used to my schedule. Twenty-four hours on, forty-eight off. As you can see, it's not as if he missed me. He's a rather independent cat."

She cuddled the traitor, scratching behind the cat's ears, causing a purr so loud it almost echoed. "Where did the name Buca come from?"

He headed for the kitchen. "He's black like licorice but I didn't want to call him that." He heard her footsteps following him as her sneakers squeaked against the title. "So I named him after the licorice flavored liquor Sambuca, but as you can see, he's a small cat."

"So you shortened his name." She kicked out a chair in his breakfast nook and sat, the cat still loving all over her.

Damn, to be that cat right now. "It was better than calling him Bananas. He has a freakish love for that fruit." He shook his head.

"I had a black cat once." The soft tone of her voice caught his attention.

"When you were young?" He leaned his butt against the center island in his kitchen and watched her carefully.

She didn't look at him, just nodded, keeping her focus on his cat.

"What happened to him?"

She continued to stroke Buca, who settled down on her lap and lifted his head to receive each new pet.

Just when he thought she would ignore his question, she spoke. "He was poisoned on Halloween. Probably some teenagers did it. You know, all that superstition about black cats. When he came by my house, I wanted to get him to a vet, but I was only eight and my mom didn't want to spend money on a stray."

She paused and he held his breath, not wanting to interrupt, but anxious to learn more.

"Zorro may have started out a stray, but I fed him regularly and hid a cleaned out cottage cheese container full of water behind our shed. He was my cat and he loved me. He was my best friend." The lost expression on her face had him aching for her.

She shook her head. "I threw a temper tantrum, demanding that Mom take him to the vet. By time my dad got home, she was ready to get Zorro help just to shut me up."

His gut twisted. Instinct told him this didn't end well. His own voice was barely above a whisper. "The vet couldn't save him?"

She stopped petting Buca. "He never made it to the vet. My father was pissed at my mom for wanting to spend money on the cat and even angrier at me for being a 'wimp.' He said he'd take care of the cat."

Dana finally looked at him and the agonized grief in her eyes made him tense. He wanted to know what happened, but her face told him he didn't.

"My dad went out back where Zorro was lying on an old t-shirt of mine, too weak to move and trying to breathe. Dad took his nine millimeter out of his holster and shot him."

Chapter Seven

Stunned, Bo's gut felt like he'd been punched, hard. His heart ached for Dana, an image of her as a child standing in her backyard, tears streaming down her face froze him in place.

She returned her attention to Buca. "Zorro was short-haired like your kitty. Did you know that female all-black cats are very, very rare, but males are common?"

He blinked at her statement. She acted as if she didn't just knock the air out of him with her story. He couldn't stay away from her a moment longer.

It might be an old grief, but he wanted to comfort her. Somehow saying "I'm sorry about your cat" just wasn't enough.

He walked toward her, not sure what he could do, but wanting to offer comfort. Before he reached her, Buca jumped off her lap and rubbed himself across his shins. He lost his balance, and not wanting to step on his cat, he swung his arms wide to catch himself as he hopped over Buca.

He ended up on his knees in the middle of his kitchen floor.

Dana knelt in front of him in a heartbeat. "Are you okay?" Concern mixed with laughter in her eyes.

He smirked, happy to see the sadness gone from her face. "Yes. It's not the first time he's done that."

She smiled that warm smile that wasn't meant for an animal. "I'm sure he has, and yet you and he have both lived to talk about it."

A quip was on the tip of his tongue about how Buca talked enough as it was, but her expression was so unguarded for a change, he couldn't resist. He pulled her to him and kissed her.

Her arms wrapped around his neck and his whole body relaxed with her acceptance. As their tongues entwined, a new need grew, not between his legs, but in his heart.

Dana moaned as she pressed herself against him, her soft curves accommodating his hard body.

He moved his hand to the back of her head and tilted it so he could better taste her even as he breathed in the scent he remembered from the night before, a light lemony scent that made him think of summer days gone by.

He left her deeply colored lips for her enticing neck and shoulder.

Her hand grasped his ass hard and his groin responded. He pressed his erection against her belly. "Dana." He spoke against her skin, his hunger for her growing.

She let go of his neck and pushed away from him, sitting on her butt on the floor. Her breaths were quick, her hazel eyes dark, but she shook her head. "I'm not sure this is a good idea."

"Why?" He wasn't sure if it was a bruised ego on his part or her skittishness that irritated him, but this time he would get an explanation.

She didn't look at him. Instead, she pulled her legs

underneath her. "Because once the arsonist is caught, you'll move on, and I don't want to get involved with someone who isn't going to hang around." She lifted her head and looked at him. "Been there, done that."

He'd never had that experience, but he could understand her hesitation better. Still, his ego wasn't assuaged. "Why do you think I'll leave after the arsonist is caught?"

She shrugged. "Because you're doing your job. When your job is over, then you'll protect someone else or go back to whatever it is you do on your two days off."

He wanted to tell her it wasn't his job to protect her, but he was sure she'd tell him to get lost and that she could take care of herself. Plus, his gut was absolutely sure she'd be pissed to learn she didn't have to have him for protection…legally anyway. "I'm not kissing you because it's my job. I'm kissing you because I'm attracted to you and you are to me."

She nodded, at least giving him that.

"Then there's no reason we can't enjoy each other's company like any other consenting adults."

She looked away, a sure sign she hid something else. Something that kept her from connecting with him, but was it him or a past experience that held her back?

He didn't understand this need he had to get to the core of who she was. Pushing her didn't work so well. She kept pulling back. Maybe he needed her to come to him.

Buca took that moment to rub against him. He scratched the cat behind his ear before stroking its silky back up to its tail. He watched as Buca then sauntered to Dana, rubbing against her so she would pet him as well. Hmm, maybe that's what he needed to do. Let her know he wanted her, but let her make the moves.

Pleased with his new plan of action, he rose and reached out his hand to help her stand. She didn't ignore him. He had to keep himself from pulling her against him. "I guess I should feed this feline and pack up some clothes. Would you like something to drink? I'm pretty sure I have beer and ice tea. Maybe even some cola."

She shook her head. "No, I'm good." She left the kitchen as he dished out wet food for Buca, then he filled the bowls with cat chow and fresh water.

When he walked into the living room, he found her looking at a picture of him and his family. "It was taken last year when everyone descended on my aunt and uncle's homestead in San Marcos for Christmas. We make quite a crowd."

She pointed to Lexi. "She looks like the paramedic I saw when I woke up in the ambulance."

"She is." He liked having family in town. "That's Lexi, one of my younger cousins."

"I thought two family members couldn't work in the same department." She finally looked at him. "To avoid fighting or collusion."

Collusion? He only heard that term used in the police department. "I'm only assigned to Station House 58 for a month. They had some people out on medical leave and needed help. So I'm on loan, and yes, I did volunteer. My aunt wanted me to see if my cousin's relationship with Dane Chandler was as wonderful as she made it out to be. Turns out it is." He smiled to reassure her because she looked very concerned.

She turned back to the picture. "I was an only child."

He didn't need to see her face because the tone of her voice told him she wasn't simply an only child but a lonely child.

That made the death of her cat that much more devastating. He took a step toward her and stopped. "Being the oldest of four added a lot of pressure."

She looked over her shoulder at him. "Pressure?"

"Yes. I was expected to be the role model for everyone and my parents were much stricter with me." He folded his arms. "The rodeo circuit was the one way I could escape that, at least for a little while."

Her look was pensive. "I can see that. I guess I was lucky. No one was looking up to me." Her smile was short and she continued to peruse the pictures he had scattered about the room.

She picked up one of his old horse, Flint. She smiled at it, probably because there was more horse than him in that one. He was only nine. She didn't ask any questions, just put it back down.

He should go upstairs and grab a few items for staying at—he had a better idea. "Maybe you should stay here tonight."

Her gaze snapped to his. "Why would I do that?"

He shrugged, pretending it wasn't as important as it was. "I have two beds here. The one upstairs in my bedroom and the fold out one in this couch. You could take my bed and I could stay down here. That way anyone after you would have to go through me first."

"Oh." She glanced at the couch and back at him. "Okay."

Okay? Now he was completely confused. He expected a number of arguments, but he wasn't going to look a gift horse in the mouth. "Great."

~~*~~

Dana grabbed up clothes for the next day and a t-shirt to

sleep in and threw them in a canvas bag while Bo waited in her vehicle outside.

She'd been surprised Bo owned a cat. Buca wasn't only well cared for, but well-loved as evidenced from Bo's patience with him, especially when the cat climbed up his jeans to get his attention. She grinned, her heartwarming as she recollected how gently Bo had pried the cat's claws from his pants and apologized for the cat's bad behavior.

It had been a wonderful afternoon. Bo had her practicing with a fire extinguisher, discovering where they were located in the buildings she was in regularly, and buying one for her apartment since hers had expired. She'd even bought two for Rainbow Acres, one for each exit as he'd taught her.

He even explained how sprinkler systems worked in buildings, what to do if she or an animal was on fire and had answered at least a hundred of her questions.

That he took her seriously and understood she wasn't some crazy woman, knocked down her trust barriers. The fact was, she trusted Bo with her life. She'd lucked out that he volunteered to protect her. Having a police officer hanging around her apartment would have been awkward at best. Bo was nothing like her father or the other police, fire and city officials who lied to her.

How many years had her father promised to take her to Sandy's bakery to pick out the biggest birthday cake they had and never did? How many times had he told her mother he had to work late and then came home smelling of scotch? The worst was when he apologized for shooting her cat and told her he'd get her two more. It was the worst because she knew he was lying, even at eight years old.

He kept them poor while he spent his salary, saying he'd

earned it risking his life and he'd spend it as he saw fit. Of course, he was just the first to lie to her.

She shook her head and shoulders in an attempt to dispel the negative squalor of her childhood. She was an adult and she made her own money and her own choices now. Bo Fletcher was a good choice as a protector.

Still, she should have her head examined for going to Bo's house for the night, but after all he'd done for her, she just couldn't make him sleep on her couch again.

Picking up the bag, she paused. She could have him sleep with her in her bed. There was no doubt they both would enjoy that, but she wasn't a casual sex kind of person. The thought of being with him and then him leaving her life when the arsonist was caught already had her heart aching.

She left her room and headed out the door. They would stop by the station so he could retrieve his truck then she'd follow him to his house. Running down the stairs, she dug out her keys to open her mailbox.

"Hey, you look like you're going out, not coming in." Jim surprised her as he stepped out of his first floor apartment.

"Are you home early?" She unlocked her box and pulled the mail out.

He joined her at the mailboxes, his forehead, which was rather high due to a receding hairline, sweaty. She'd seen him push his hair back a number of times as if his receding hairline made it so much easier to do.

He reached into his own box. "Hmm, junk, junk, junk, oh a bill. Now there's something." He snorted quietly, which was so like him. He closed his box. "How's your apartment upstairs? You need anything? A rug cleaner? I have one if you want to borrow it."

She shook her head. "No. There's a lingering smoke smell, but I threw out the rugs. I'm thinking I'm going to need to wash the walls and floors and everything else before it will be completely gone."

"I'm sorry. Is the woman across the hall from you with the yappy dog in the same situation? I haven't seen her since the fire."

She glanced up the stairs. "No, I haven't seen Tanya." Though I certainly heard her.

"I stopped by the hospital to see if you were okay, but you were sleeping." He looked hopeful, like he might gain brownie points from a teacher for his thoughtfulness.

"I heard." She smiled kindly. "Laura told me. That was very nice of you."

He blushed and held up his mail. "Guess I better go read my junk."

She nodded before he shuffled back to his apartment. Then she stuffed her own "junk" in her bag before heading out to her vehicle.

"Everything okay?" Bo's scowl seemed out of place as she sat behind the steering wheel.

"Sure, why?"

"That gentleman wasn't giving you any problems, was he?"

Ah, he saw Jim through the tall glass windows on each side of the door to the building. She chuckled. "Hardly. That's Jim Lawrence. He was one of my visitors while I was at the hospital." She pulled out onto the quiet street just a block off a major thoroughfare.

"He did? Hmm. What does he do for work?"

"What are you thinking? That he's the arsonist? I'll have

you know that despite being in town for only three months I had two other visitors, Tanya and Laura. If you investigate Jim, then you'll have to investigate them, too."

"And me."

She glanced at him as she stopped at a red light. "And you what?"

"I visited you at the hospital too." He gave her a sly grin.

She watched the road as she drove to the fire station. "Yes, but you weren't there to see if I was okay. You were there to lecture me because I ran back for Misty." She tensed, expecting him to continue that lecture.

He surprised her. "Did the cat recover okay?"

"Yes. In fact, I'm going to see her and the Sheridans tomorrow. They are staying at Mrs. Sheridan's sister's house outside Dallas and it sounds like Mr. Sheridan is not happy." She pulled into the fire station parking lot and stopped her SUV. "I guess Mrs. Sheridan's brother-in-law expects Mr. Sheridan to pull his own weight." She grinned. "I so want to see that."

He looked at her, his green gaze alight with amusement. "You have a mean streak in you, don't you?"

She shrugged. "Maybe."

He jumped out of the vehicle and strode to his truck. She sighed. *That man has the nicest ass. And boy would I like a piece of it.*

She gripped the steering wheel. *What about not wanting to get hurt? Crapola, it was far too late for that.*

She started to fall for him the minute he kissed her in the station. When she saw he owned a cat and then he took her seriously, she fell way in over her head.

Bo pulled out and she followed him.

He's going to leave as soon as they find the arsonist. He's just doing his job. Don't be an idiot.

~~*~~

Bo glanced at Dana as he loaded the dishwasher. She sat at the kitchen island where they had eaten, now slowly peeling the paper off her water bottle. He could sense her nervousness over staying with him. She'd been fine during dinner, actually opening up a little about her past.

He'd learned her parents had divorced shortly after the cat episode and her mom had wanted her to quit school at sixteen, but she'd finished, working after school instead to help pay for food. After landing her first job, she'd gone to college online, finally graduating with a degree after eight years.

Dana had a way of making him look at things differently. He liked that about her. What he didn't like was that she was uncomfortable now… with him.

Part of him wanted to reassure her while the other part felt guilty she was with him under false pretenses. But he was one hundred percent positive she'd leave if she thought she wasn't required to have protection, and he was one hundred percent positive she needed it.

With the last dish loaded, he closed the machine and wiped his hands on a towel. He leaned back against the sink. "Did you like my meatloaf?"

"Huh?" She looked up at him startled. "Oh yes. It's better than I can make. Is it true firefighters are good cooks?"

He nodded. "For the most part, but it's not a hard and fast rule. I think they should add a cooking course to our degree program, even if it's an elective. We need one easy A."

Her lips quirked at that.

"Would you like to go for a swim? I don't have the hot tub running anymore, but the pool is fairly warm."

She turned her head to look out the sliding door off the kitchen. "No, I didn't bring a bathing suit."

He wished he could say she didn't need one, but that would just add to her unease. "Then why don't we bring our drinks outside and enjoy the sunset."

She raised her bottle. "I think I would like something a little stronger than this."

He nodded. Turning, he opened the refrigerator. "I have beer, wine and…well, beer and wine. Unless you consider milk stronger than water." He looked at her and winked.

It worked. Her shoulders relaxed an inch or two. "I'll have a beer."

He opened it for her, and they headed outside beneath the awning. He waited, watching the sky as it started to glow. It was still a little warm in the shade, but a light breeze blew. He took a swig of beer, hoping she'd eventually speak.

"Why did you become a firefighter?" She didn't look at him when she asked, her gaze on the horizon.

That wasn't exactly the topic he'd hoped she'd bring up. "I wanted to save people from being burned to death. I'm usually on the ladder truck, or the engine if the ladder isn't needed because my specialty is rescue."

She finally looked at him, her hazel eyes an even mix of colors in the fading light. "No, I mean why? What made you decide you wanted to risk your own life to save strangers?"

Shit, he should have known she'd want to dig deeper. If he'd been dating Mandy from the bar, he'd bet they'd be talking about the latest movie or the next band coming to town. Actually, if Mandy was here, they probably wouldn't be talking at all. He'd rather be talking to Dana than in bed with Mandy.

Despite having come to terms with it, it still scratched at the wound in his heart to relive it. He took a deep breath. "I was a teenager. Like most boys that age, I had lots of buddies, but one particular guy, Deacon, got me. We both loved riding and wanted to be bull riders."

The image that had haunted him for years rose up again, the memory refusing to fade with time. "I wasn't old enough to drive yet, so my dad took me over to Deacon's. We'd planned to go hunting for the weekend."

He forced his mouth to form the words. "We arrived at his ranch after the fire trucks."

Chapter Eight

Bo stared, seeing the entire scene, feeling the heat from the blaze. "The fire department only had the water in the engine, the tanker still on its way. Back then it wasn't automatic to send a tanker as some ranches had ponds or dry hydrants. Deacon's didn't."

Dana laid her hand on his forearm and he looked down at it, not really seeing it, but definitely feeling the comfort it offered. "The house was an inferno. I guess the old wood was a treat to the fire. It just gorged itself. Between that and the breeze, like the one right now, the fire was happy to devour everything in that house."

"Including Deacon?"

At her question, he looked at her. "Yes. He tried to get out of the house. I saw him in the bay window. He was on fire. It smothered him like a swarm of bees. No matter how he moved, it covered him. I started to run forward to help, but one of the firefighters grabbed me and wouldn't let me go. They'd seen him and turned the hoses his way, but it was too late. He didn't survive."

The rosy hue of the sunset bathed her face in pink, but her eyes had turned a smoky gray with her sympathy. "I'm sorry."

He grimaced. "They taught us to stop, drop, and roll back then, but we hadn't paid much attention. We didn't even have fire extinguishers in our house. My parents were very patient with me when I made them buy five for our own home and two more for the barn."

Her lips quirked up. "You wanted to make sure you wouldn't lose anyone else you loved."

"Yes." Her understanding caught him off guard. "Everyone else just thought I'd been too influenced by the firefighters that day, but actually I resented them for the longest time. I really thought I could have saved Deacon. I know better now. They did the right thing."

"I'm glad they kept you from being hurt, but I imagine you face that every day."

He grinned before taking another swig of beer. "Not every day. Only on the days I work."

She rolled her eyes and removed her hand from his arm.

"I'm glad I was working the day your apartment caught on fire. Or I would have never met you."

She stopped smiling. "You only met me because I went back into the Sheridans' apartment to get Misty and that pissed you off, so you had to lecture me at the hospital. I was so pissed I couldn't talk and set you straight."

"You're right." He chuckled. "I didn't know you spent your life rescuing animals, though what you did still wasn't the right thing to do."

Her eyes grew crafty. "So if this place was on fire and you weren't here, you wouldn't want me to find Buca before leaving the house?"

Damn, she was good. He loved that feline like it was his own child, but as he looked at her, he imagined her finding Buca hiding under his dresser. She'd try to move the heavy thing and pull Buca out even if fire nipped at her heels. He looked straight at her. "No. I would want you to be safe first."

She blinked, her eyes widening. When she opened her mouth to voice her next argument, he cut her off, not wanting to debate the issue.

"Then I'd run in and find the blasted cat."

She closed her mouth and grinned before taking a sip of beer.

"I meant what I said about being glad I met you." He wanted to say more, tell her he thought there could be a real relationship with her, but he swallowed his words. He needed to let her make the moves. She was like a feral cat he'd once rescued from a manhole.

"I'm glad I met you, too." Her smile remained.

That was progress. They sat in companionable silence as the pale pinks in the sky turned brighter only to be covered with dark purples and grays as the clouds blocked out the last rays of light.

When the sun disappeared, he asked her about Rainbow Acres Refuge and she talked for an hour. It also provided some interesting insights into who she was. She donated half her salary back to the ranch, didn't trust any man in authority what-so-ever, and was selfless to a fault when it came to animals.

She also revealed something that concerned him even more than the arsonist targeting her. Dana didn't worry about herself at all. To her, the only reason she existed was to rescue animals. They were her only purpose in life. She didn't even have any dreams of settling down with a man, having children and then taking in stray animals. She lived only in the present.

As a man who rescued people for a living, he understood how precious the present was, but life was supposed to be full of dreams and goals.

"So are you hoping to be Fire Chief some day?" They had moved back into the kitchen and her question caught him off guard.

He held up both hands. "Oh no. That is far more responsibility than I ever want. I would have to live with the fear of losing one of my men every day. I much prefer being one of the men." He paused.

She had opened the door on the topic of the future, so he might as well step through. "I want to have a family. That may not seem like much of a goal, but finding a woman who understands and can live with the risk I take every time I go to work will be difficult."

"I understand completely. Then again, that might be because I do similar work. I don't expect a man to ever accept what I do." She shrugged like it didn't matter.

He moved in front of her, not quite pinning her against the counter she leaned on. "I understand what you do. It's similar to my job. I now see that you do value human life and you are simply filling a gap that most people don't think twice about."

Her eyes lit, turning almost blue in her excitement. "Yes. That's it exactly."

He had promised himself to let her come to him, but she was like a flickering flame that could ignite or blow out. He might just need to pick her up and show her some love. He nixed the picking up part. His instinct said she'd resent him taking that much control, but he could show her some love.

He smiled, letting his admiration for her show. "You are an amazing person." He raised his finger to stroke her right cheek.

She blushed and shrugged again, but she didn't look away. "Not really. Like you said, I just fill in a gap."

He shook his head slowly as he lowered his face until he felt her quick breaths on his lips. "No. You're special. Precious."

Her lips opened to protest but he captured them with his own and kissed her, forcing his hand to no more than cup her cheek while his other remained at his side.

Her tongue met his, and he let her have her way as she explored his mouth.

Her scent of tart lemon filled his nostrils reminding him of the last time they'd kissed, and he had to stifle a groan. She grasped his waist and pulled him closer to her.

This is what he'd been waiting for. Deepening the kiss further, he ran his hand up her side and leaned his chest away to access her breast. He cupped the soft mound, rubbing his thumb across her nipple, feeling it harden through her tank top and bra.

She ran her hands to his back and pulled his shirt from his jeans. At the feel of her palms against his back, his cock reacted.

Pulling his lips from hers to allow himself deeper breaths and access to her neck, he trailed light kisses along her skin, keeping his desire in check.

Dana's hands ran up his back, kneading at his muscles, making him want to shuck his shirt, but this was about her. He lifted his hand to her shoulder and pulled the strap of her tank down then moved his finger lightly along the top of her breast.

Her pulse raced beneath his lips, so he dipped one finger between her bra and skin and stroked her nipple. She moaned and her hands burrowed beneath his jeans, grabbing at his ass.

Bo's balls tightened. He wanted this woman in so many ways he couldn't even fathom them at the moment. Bending her farther back, he used his hand to pull her bra cup down and latched on to her nipple with his mouth, sucking.

"Holy moly that feels good." At her husky words, he smiled, keeping her hard nub between his teeth before rolling it back and forth. His cock was harder than his ax and it strained against his tight jeans.

Dana suddenly pulled her hands from his butt and squirmed to get away.

Shit.

He let her go, holding her up as she grasped his arms. "What is it?"

"I need your clothes off." Her look was so intense, his need rose hard in his groin.

He took a steadying breath. "I want yours off too, but not here. You deserve better than the kitchen counter."

Her brow knit in puzzlement.

His stomach twisted. She didn't recognize her own worth. He set her back and took her hand. "Come."

Without a word, she followed him upstairs to his room. When he opened the door, she finally spoke. "This is nice." Her surprise bothered him.

He scanned the pale gray walls with white trim. The silver and gray quilt on the bed was thick and rarely used. "What did you expect?"

She shrugged. "I don't know. A mess I guess."

He grinned, pleased that she wasn't disappointed in the décor. "Part of our firefighter training is putting everything in its proper place. It's a habit."

She stood in front of him, but as she finished scanning his room, including his California king bed, she backed up a step.

He put his hands on her shoulders. "I think there is a place for you as well."

She turned to face him, her hazel eyes bright with uncertainty, and he let his hands drop.

Before she could say a word and put her concerns verbally between them, he kissed her with everything he felt—caring, protectiveness, desire. She tasted of beer and her own sweetness, which he craved.

She responded to his kiss, finally letting her passion gain control. Her arms slipped around him.

He broke the kiss and gazed at her closed eyes. She was everything he didn't know he needed. He wanted her in his life…always. The realization didn't scare him. Instead, a peace filled in the empty spots in his soul. He felt complete.

Her eyelids fluttered open and she looked back at him. She was strong, courageous, beautiful and intelligent. He couldn't ask for more. "Let me make love to you." His voice came out a low whisper.

She shivered slightly in his arms and licked her lips. Then she nodded once.

He grinned and swept her up into his arms.

"Ack, Bo! I'm too big."

He gently laid her down on his bed, still smiling like a fool. "How do you think I carried you out of your burning building?"

Her eyes widened. "All the way down those stairs?"

He nodded as he pulled his t-shirt over his head.

She moved her gaze from his face to his chest, his abdominals, his shoulders and arms. It reminded him of the night before when she caught him naked in her living room. There was appreciation and desire in her eyes.

She finally brought her gaze up to his. "More."

Need shot from his chest to his cock at her single word. Without hesitation, he toed off his boots, stripped his jeans and underwear before removing his socks. When he stood straight again, her gaze was sweeping over him once more.

He wanted her to want this as much as he did, so he turned around like he had the night before and looked over his shoulder, pleased to see he kept her interest. When he turned back, he set one knee on the bed beside her. "Your turn. I want to see every beautiful inch of you."

She blushed. "I'm not as perfect as you."

Her gaze fell and he tilted her chin up. "You are. You are amazing inside and out. You can't imagine how much I want you."

She glanced down at his cock, missing the true depth of his words, then she smirked. "I might have an idea."

She didn't though. He'd fallen hard and fast and he was determined to take her with him. Leaning over, he kissed her shoulder, her neck, her chest above her tank top.

Her hands ran through his short hair nudging him on.

He pulled her to a sitting position then grasped the bottom of her tank and drew it over her head. Without letting her finish taking her breath, he wrapped his arms around her and unhooked her bra, tugging it from her body as she lay back again.

Desire and uncertainty fought for supremacy in her eyes, and he silently cursed her parents for failing to love her. Despite his need to have her entire naked body against his, he stopped undressing her to pay attention to her breasts. Not that it was a hardship.

He gently caressed them, loving their light weight in his palms as he stroked her nipple with his thumb. Her nipples were large and hard, as dark as her lips and they begged for his attention.

Her hands rested on his arms as if she might stop him at any moment.

Lowering his head, he took one rosy tip into his mouth, loving the texture as he swirled his tongue around it before lightly biting with his teeth. When Dana's hands grasped the back of his head, he sucked the large nub gently at first then harder until she moaned.

He left that breast to perform the same ministrations to the other, first licking then biting and finally sucking the nipple hard enough to make her arch into him while her hands pulled his head toward her.

Licking the hard nub one last time, he moved lower, placing light kisses under her breasts, on her ribs then exploring her belly button with his tongue. He wanted her to know that every inch of her was precious. He needed her to understand that her being alive was important.

As he licked his way down to her jeans, the heady scent of her desire mixed with her citrusy fragrance, sending need rifling through him. Lifting his head away from her belly, despite her pull on him, he took a steadying breath.

He focused his attention on unbuttoning and unzipping her jeans, and her hands fell away. "Lift."

She did, pushing her hips up so he could move the pants over her hips and down her legs. Her sneakers were already off on the bed, so he pushed them onto the floor and let her jeans follow. He stood at the end of the bed and looked at her long body. "Beautiful."

"Not exactly." She pointed to a scar on her thigh. "That was a dog bite in Kentucky." She moved her hand to her left arm. "That was a barn fire in Maryland. This was a snake bite from Arizona." She'd pointed to her left ankle.

"And these." She covered her breasts. "Were just born small. You'd think with such large tips, there'd be more beneath."

He forced himself not to frown, but anger that she would think so little of herself cooled his need. "First, I love your breasts so I would prefer you don't insult them. As for your scars, they mean you've lived, had experiences, and in your case, were brave when others weren't. If you want to compare scars, I would be happy to show you every one of mine, but then we wouldn't make love for the next two hours."

Her lips quirked at that. "Point taken."

Relieved that she acceded the point, he quickly knelt on the bed and pulled her striped panties down. At his first glance of her moist folds, his desire returned full force. He knelt between her legs, fully intending to continue his trail of kisses, but her hands pulled on his arms.

"I want you." Her eyes showed that mix of uncertainty and need again, as if he would stop.

He wouldn't stop for anything, except a fire because the one burning inside him was about to explode. He would simply have to show her how much he enjoyed every inch of her after he satisfied her. "I want you more."

"I don't think that's possible."

Her husky voice and serious tone had every part of his body tensing, readying itself. "Do we need protection?"

Her brow crinkled in confusion before it relaxed. "No. I have an implant so I won't get pregnant. Are you, um…"

He smirked. "I've been tested and passed with flying colors. You?"

"Me too."

"Good because I want to feel every inch of your pussy as I slide in."

Her eyes widened at his words before they turned dark, almost gray. "And I want to enjoy every inch of that hard cock that's brushing against my thigh."

If her words hadn't affected him so much, he'd chuckle, but they did and he couldn't wait. He wanted to make her his.

He lowered himself to his elbows and kissed her as he positioned his cock between her legs.

Dana was wet with wanting but uncomfortable at being so worshiped. She pushed the strange feeling away and focused on the mass of muscle against her. She ran her hands over Bo's biceps, loving the bulges that proved his strength. Crap, the second he'd picked her up, she'd melted.

At the nudge of his cock, she spread her legs, anxious to feel him, if he could even fit. Like the rest of him, that piece of his anatomy was large, and she wasn't immune to the anticipation of having it inside her.

She gazed into his eyes, his green gaze almost the color of an evergreen forest now. She felt his stomach muscles tense against her as he moved his hips higher to better find her opening. She lifted her own, anxious to have him.

He lowered his head, and she closed her eyes for his kiss. His tongue breached her lips at the same time his cock inched into her. As he spread her, gliding along her wet sheath, his tongue tangled with her own.

She opened her legs wider, silently inviting him home.

Bo pushed farther into her until he was totally buried inside.

She broke their kiss so she could focus on the feelings rising inside her. She'd never been so completely full. He stretched her where she didn't dare move, yet every inch of him sent tingling sensations flowing from her core to the tips of her fingers.

Taken. Wanted. Loved.

She opened her eyes to find him staring at her with so much caring that she had to blink to keep her eyes from watering.

"Are you okay?" His deep voice filled all the chips in her soul.

It was beyond intimate. "More than okay. I think I'm in heaven."

"Good, because right now we are headed for paradise."

She didn't have a chance to respond because he pulled his hips back only to slide right back in, causing tingles of pleasure to sparkle through. She grasped his head and pulled him down for a kiss, filling a strange need to be even closer.

Bo acquiesced and drove his tongue between her lips as he pushed his cock into her again. He continued to do so, his hips moving faster, beginning the friction in her sheath that stoked a fire of need.

She moaned into his mouth as she arched her breasts against his chest then pushed her own hips upward, comfortable with his largeness and wanting more.

She was greedy. She grasped his back and wrapped her legs over his waist, tilting her hips. His cock hit her cervix lightly, and she dug her fingers into his hard muscles. She broke their kiss. "Yes. More."

Her instinct that he'd been holding back was correct. As soon as she asked, his thrusts grew stronger.

She reveled in the motion of her body as it moved on the bed, back and forth, her clit against his skin as she met each of his thrusts with a tilt of her hips.

"God woman." His voice, a whole octave deeper, sent her to her peak.

"Bo!" She screamed his name as her orgasm exploded like a bomb, shards of joy slicing through her. Her whole body shook with spasms of ecstasy. He continued to pump into her, causing the fire to consume her. She held on to him with all her strength, the only solid thing in her abstract vision.

Bo shouted and warmth flooded her sheath, prolonging her orgasm as he shuddered against her.

His rhythm slowed sporadically, and she grasped him tighter, tears threatening, her emotions a mess. He was so much more than anything she'd imagined. He made her feel something she never had.

Loved.

Bo lifted his head and brushed her hair back from her face. "Hey."

She smiled tentatively. "Hey."

"Sorry that was so fast."

She raised her brow. "If that was fast, I'm not sure I could survive slow."

His grin was pure male pride. He wiggled his brow. "Just give me a minute and we'll find out for sure."

Her heart stopped at the look in his eye. *Crap, I'm falling for him and I don't give a rat's ass. I should have my head examined.* She raised her head and gave him a quick kiss on his chest, the only place she could reach. He lowered his face and captured her lips with his own.

The kiss, unlike earlier ones, was sweet and gentle, and tears threatened again. *Holy moly what's wrong with me?* Nervous at the strange feelings coursing through her, she broke away. "If you like, I'd be happy to get things started." She winked, hoping to break the serious moment.

He raised an eyebrow. "I didn't know you liked to ride."

She opened her mouth to disabuse him of his assumption that she knew how to ride a horse, when he rolled them both over, keeping them well attached at the hips. The surprise made her tense and his cock was still hard inside her.

Now she lay on top of all that strength. *Ah, he wants me to ride him. Now that I'm more than willing to try.* Carefully, she moved her legs and bent her knees. His cock in this position, even not completely hard, filled her to the end of her sheath.

He took one of her hands and kissed her palm. "Now you're in control."

He didn't smile, his implied meaning not lost on her. Again, his seriousness scared her, so she lightened the mood again. "Aren't I always?"

He nodded. "Yes, you are." He winked at her. "Now, let's see what you do with all that control."

Just as he said the words, he lifted his hips, causing his cock to hit her cervix, and she arched back.

"Whoa, hold on there." He tweaked her nipples with his fingers, and she bowed forward again. "Haven't you ever ridden a bronco?"

Her heart raced at the sensations in her body and she laughed at his sly expression. She may not know how to feel about the man, but she knew how she felt about his body. Tonight was going to be amazing.

Chapter Nine

Dana opened her eyes to the daylight streaming into the room. The giant black stallion painting on the wall reminded her of where she was and how she ended up in Bo's bed. She grinned before turning to find him gone.

Though disappointed, she didn't mind being alone to luxuriate in her memories. Crap, that man was strong. It was his strength, and his unrealistic view of her as precious, that completely suckered her in.

She stretched and found herself happily sore between her legs. It was well worth it after the heights he'd taken her to. Finally, she sat up, reluctant to get out of bed just yet, almost as if were she to start her day, everything would disappear like a dream.

"Hope you're hungry." Bo walked into the room, a loose pair of sweats dipping nicely to show off his abdominals all the way to his pubic hair. She finally focused on what he held in his hand. "What's this?"

"Breakfast, what else?" He put the tray on his dresser then added his pillow to hers and set them behind her back. "There you go." He placed the breakfast tray in front of her.

"Oh wow. Are those blueberry pancakes?" She took a deep breath to smell them even as she reached for the coffee.

"I wasn't sure if you wanted cream and sugar. I can go get some." He stood watching her.

"I'm good with black. This looks fantastic. I've never been served breakfast in bed before." She winked at him. "Better be careful, I might get used to it."

He smiled, his bright teeth gleaming as his eyes lit up. At least he didn't scare away easily.

"I can't wait to taste these." Digging the fork into the stack, she quickly cut off a bite and popped it into her mouth. "Hmmm." She closed her eyes. Holy crap, I'm going orgasm over his food, too.

As the mattress dipped beneath his weight, she opened her eyes.

"That's what you sounded like when I pumped into you the first time. If you keep making that noise, I'm going to have to ravish you again." His eyes gleamed with laughter, but his desire was evident in the ridge beneath his sweats.

She swallowed the luscious pancakes. "And if you keep looking at me like that, I won't be able to eat another bite."

"Like what?" He widened his eyes in innocence for a second before the devilish gleam was back in his gaze. "Maybe I should just get under the sheets in case you need any help with those moans."

"Don't you dare." She rolled her eyes at him. "I have to go to the Sheridans this morning and—"

"We have to go to the Sheridans this morning." He lost his smile.

She really did like his smile. "Yes, we have to go check on Misty, then we have to clean out the barn, pick up supplies, take two dogs to the vet, visit the ladies who make blankets for the animals, and stop in at Precious Pets this evening to pack up when my volunteers are done."

She took another bite, stifling a moan to avoid being late.

When she looked back at him, his gaze was so full of caring that she quickly turned away.

He rose from the bed and walked around to her side. "I have to admit, I've never been so busy on my days off."

"I'm sorry. As soon as the arsonist is caught, you can have your days back. Will you receive any extra days off for protecting me?"

He strode into the bathroom. "No. But that's okay. I find your work interesting."

She swallowed another mouthful of pancake as she heard the shower start. "I think yours is too."

He came out of the bathroom. "I know." He stood next to the bed on her side. "Are you done?"

She looked down at the tray. She'd eaten almost all of the pancake stack. As much as she loved them, she couldn't fit anymore into her stomach. Taking a forkful, she raised it toward him. "I can't eat another bite. Can you help?"

Bo opened his mouth and she fed him the last two pieces, the experience much more sensual than she expected.

"You have some syrup right here." She wiped at the drop on the side of his mouth with her finger until he opened his lips and sucked it in.

"Oh." The feel of his tongue circling her finger in his warm mouth had her body revving up again.

He let go suddenly and pulled the tray from her lap. "Your shower awaits." He bowed like a butler, but he was more Prince Charming to her.

She rose naked, blushing as he watched her walk to the bathroom. Once inside, she peeked her head around the corner. "Coming?"

He dropped the tray on his dresser and strode toward her. "Not yet, but you can take care of that in the shower."

She laughed then jumped into the warm spray, floating on a cloud. When Bo's large hands encircled her waist and pulled her against him, she melted into him. She'd never been so happy in her entire life. *I feel like I've just saved every pet in all of Dallas county.*

Bo's hard cock pressing against the top of her ass had her focusing on the man behind her. She wiggled her hips and his hands left her waist.

"Keep that up and this won't last long." His deep voice in her ear sent shivers of excitement straight to her sheath.

After his slow lovemaking last night, she'd love a quick, hard one. She wiggled her hips again.

Bo's reaction was fast. In an instant, he spun them around so she faced the wall of his walk-in shower and pushed her against it. The cool tile sensitized her nipples as she let her head fall back against his shoulder.

His mouth sucked at the side of her neck while his right hand worked its way between her and the tile to explore her folds. His broad finger slipped into her opening then out to circle her clit.

She pressed against his hand, lifting her leg to give him better access, but instead of his finger, she felt him slide down her back a few inches until his cock was between her legs. His fingers moved back to her labia and spread her as he glided into her in one long stroke.

His breathing was rough in her ear. "I'm going to come inside you in about five seconds."

At his words, her sheath tightened and she tilted her hips back.

He growled and his fingers came up to her clit again as he pressed her from behind into his hand.

Pinned as she was against the tile wall, she could do nothing but enjoy, and she did.

Bo pumped into her hard, sliding her up the wall with the force of his thrusts, rubbing her breasts against the small tiles. She squeaked as her orgasm started, the multiple sensations converging in her core. He thrust twice more, rocking into her from behind, holding her in place as she splintered around him.

His shout filled her ears and brought her bliss to an apex, satisfaction filling her in the profound way it had last night, as if she finally belonged somewhere—in the arms of Bo Fletcher.

"What you make me feel." His guttural voice sent joy tingling through her like the remnants of a firework.

She squeezed her sheath, eliciting a quick inhale on his part. "I feel you. All over."

He pulled them away from the wall, but still held her pelvis to his. "Kiss me."

She turned her head and showed him with her mouth how wonderful it felt to be with him. When she released his lips, his gaze was far too serious for her.

"I think I like quickies." She wiggled her eyebrows since wiggling her hips at the moment was out of the question. The man's hold was tight.

"They do have their advantages, but only after a slow burn." He punctuated his statement by thrusting against her before pulling out.

She leaned against the wall again, too limp to wash up quite yet.

"Oh no, you have a cat to visit." Bo pulled her against him and this time took the soap and proceeded to wash her all over. His ministrations had her moistening again, but he didn't stop to explore, which was just as well. The man was large and her body needed some time to recover.

When he was done with her, he wrapped her in a towel before jumping back in to clean up himself.

Finally feeling more like herself, she stepped into his bedroom and found her bag of clothes. Dressing quickly, she brushed out her damp hair. At least May in Dallas was warm. Her hair should be pretty dry by time they arrived at the Sheridans.

She'd just put her brush away when Bo came out of the bathroom stark naked and smelling like the musky soap he used. She smelled like it too, like him. That fact warmed her heart.

He grinned. "I'll be ready in two secs."

Oh, I don't mind. Take your time. She gazed at his muscular butt as he turned toward his dresser and took out clothes, his thigh muscles contracting with his movements. When he turned around, she let out a purely feminine sigh. I can't believe that's all mine.

Her heart cooled. No one said he belonged to her. But I want him to. I want to belong to him. What if he doesn't feel the same?

"I'm ready. Am I dressed okay to meet Misty?" Bo's innocent look, had her pushing her wishes aside.

"I think you'll do just fine." For Misty…and for me.

~~*~~

Bo walked hand and hand through the mall with Dana. She'd slipped her hand in his while they'd been looking at a pair of cowboy boots in a store window that he told her would look great on her.

There was a significant change in her since the day before. She'd started to relax around him then, but today had been a pleasure to spend with her. Once again he learned more about her, the most surprising fact that she had a fun sense of humor.

He actually looked forward to this pet shop visit, now that he had a feeling of how things worked. Dana wasn't just good with animals. She was good with the volunteers and owners of pets. It was only the official type people, like himself, that she was on guard around.

Lucky for him, he'd toppled that distrust, or he hoped he had.

"Hey, Dana." A man in a pair of khakis and a sport shirt hailed her.

She didn't tense, but he did, not because he was jealous of the man with the receding hairline, but because he didn't want her attention diverted from him. His shift was looming and he wanted to enjoy every minute with her.

"Oh, hi." She smiled her animal smile and he grinned inside. The animal smile was heartfelt with the critters, but when turned on people it was secretly lukewarm. "What are you doing here? I didn't think you came out this far."

The older man lifted his forearm. "I had to get a new battery for my watch. The kiosk next to the candle shop is the only one I've found who can replace it without scratching up the back cover."

"Oh. I see."

"I'll bet you're here for the pet adoption set-up. Do you ever stop working?" The man shook his head, the message clear that she shouldn't work so late.

Dana smiled a genuine smile. "I love my job, so it's not a chore."

"Wish I could say the same." He looked at his watch then back at her. "I better get going if I'm going to catch the bus home…unless you're heading that way shortly?"

"I'm afraid not. This will take a while."

The man nodded. "Okay. See you later."

"Who was that?" He had an idea, but wanted to be sure.

"That's my neighbor. Oh, I'm sorry. I should have introduced you."

"I got the feeling he'd prefer I didn't exist."

She looked up at him. "I was thinking the same thing. That's odd."

It was, but since he'd never met Jim before, he couldn't imagine why, unless the man had a crush on Dana. "So where is this pet store? I have to admit I haven't been there. And how did you get them to agree to offer Rainbow Acres pets once a week when they have their own pets to sell?"

They started walking again and she became animated. "Oh, that was all Laura. She set this up long before she hired me. It's a mom and pop chain and they decided that the products they could sell were enough to help out unwanted animals. Besides, our pets aren't always pretty, or young, or perfect, so people still buy animals from the store. We like this small chain because they are very particular about where they get their pets."

He noticed other men admiring Dana as they walked, which just made him feel luckier than ever. Looking ahead, he saw Mandy headed their way. Quickly, he pulled Dana toward a store front.

"Bo, what are you looking at?"

He focused on the display window and grinned. The red and black corset with the thong beneath would look great on Dana. "Do you like it?"

She flushed. "Those are too expensive. I'd rather spend my money on dog food for the refuge."

He met her gaze. "I mean if you received it as a gift?"

She looked at it again, tilting her head. "I don't think I'd know how to put it on."

He chuckled. Now he was definitely going to buy one for her. Glancing over his shoulder, he relaxed to see Mandy had passed. "That's okay. I like you in nothing better."

She rolled her eyes. "Come on. Enough window shopping."

As they turned the corner, he heard the short, high-pitched barks of excited critters. The front of the store had a number of large cages where dogs of all sizes barked at the people walking by…or attempting to walk by. Nine out of ten had to stop and talk to the puppies.

"Dana? Where have you been?" Dana's neighbor from across the hall stopped them in their tracks, her little dog's eyes zeroing in on him. "Are you okay?"

"Of course I am." Dana tried to release his hand, but he held her tight, earning him a look of irritation. "I was in bed the other night."

Tanya finally looked at him. "Hello. Did we meet?"

He nodded, but didn't say anything.

Dana finally relaxed her hand. "I'm here to check on the pet adoptions at Precious Pets."

"Oh, I was just in there and they do have some cuties. I really like the little Schnauzer, but Tiara didn't care for him." Tanya looked disappointed. What had Dana said? Tanya didn't have a niece?

"Are you looking for another dog?" He watched her closely and was satisfied when she grew uncomfortable.

"Oh, I just like to look, you know." She shrugged and turned back to Dana. "Will you be home later? I was thinking of going out. There's a new group playing at The Cave and I would like to check them out."

He squeezed her hand. He wanted her with him again tonight.

She caught on to his silent message. "I'm sorry. I won't be home tonight. I have other plans."

Tanya glanced at him again. "Well, I guess I can go to the club another night. I wouldn't leave my Tiara alone." She gave the dog a kiss and returned her gaze to Dana. "Let me know when you can dog-sit again."

"I will." Dana watched Tanya saunter off.

As she took a step toward the shop, he held her back. "She's hiding something."

"Like what?"

"I don't know, but I bet it has to do with her being at both the shelter you were at the other night and this pet store."

Dana's eyes revealed her mind's thoughts. "I'm not exactly quiet about the places I go. Tanya knows I save the animals at the shelter and she also knows about my pet adoption nights because I can't take care of her dog on those evenings."

He lowered his head and whispered in her ear. "But if she doesn't have a niece, why is she going to places that sell animals?"

She snapped her head toward him, her eyes wide.

He took advantage of her surprise to kiss her right there in the middle of the mall.

She blushed and pulled away. "Bo."

"Yes?" He winked at her.

She squeezed his hand. "Behave. I'm on the clock."

He sighed dramatically. "Then let's get back to work."

"Right." She looked confused for a moment then blinked. "This way."

They were three steps away from the store when an explosion sounded in the back of it. He let go of Dana's hand and ran inside. People screamed, running by him. He caught an employee on the way out. "Call 911!"

The woman nodded and pulled out her phone as she exited. He moved forward, checking all the aisles to be sure people got out. One older woman had fallen and was panicking as she tried to right herself. He helped her up and escorted her into the mall.

As soon as she was out, he ran back in. As he passed the first glassed-in area that held dogs, he noticed one wasn't barking. Instead, the little white poodle puppy stood there shaking, its rounded-eyes following him. Shaking off the puppy's unspoken plea, he moved past the glass area with the cats. Many meowed and a few scratched at their cages to get out. One furry black and white cat was curled up and sound asleep.

Smoke billowed from the back room, and he quickly closed the door, denying the fire one of its feeding elements.

His gaze fell on the fire extinguisher usually mounted next to the door. It was on the floor, spent.

Movement in the last glass room directly to his left caught his attention.

Dana! His heart stilled for a split second.

She stepped through the open door of the room with

four cages. "I put the fire out here, but the back wall is hot. We need to empty that room."

Pride in her fast thinking warred with anger that she would put herself in danger. "Go, I'll get the rest."

"You will?" Her surprise tilted his emotional balance in favor of anger. "Yes. Now go!"

She did, and he ran into the room. There had to be fifteen more cages in it, mostly smaller critters. He picked up three rabbit cages and three guinea pig cages and ran to the front of the store where she took them from him.

He sprinted back. The sound of sirens coming closer spurred him on as he grabbed up six more cages. When he made it to the front, he had to skirt around the volunteers removing the animals that belonged to Rainbow Acres.

Once again he handed cages to Dana, who worked with practiced efficiency. As he turned to get the last of the animals, a hand clamped down on his arm.

"We've got this." A firefighter from another shift of Station 58 held him back.

Bo nodded. "Everyone's out. I closed the door to the back room, but the animals closest to that wall are at risk."

The man's eyes dawned with recognition. "Okay, got it." He let go and strode through the store, his partner close behind.

Dana came to stand next to him.

"They'll get the rest out." He looked at her.

She kept her gaze focused on the men. "They better."

Her attitude irritated him. "They will." He wanted to yell at her and hold her close all at once.

Suddenly, the ramifications of the explosion fully materialized. The fire was at the store Dana always came to on Tuesday evenings. A chill swept through him. If they didn't find a legitimate reason for the explosion… "Do you ever go in that back room?"

Dana continued to watch for the firefighters, her body clearly on alert. Not until they brought the last of the cages out and set them down in front of her did she finally address his question. "Yes."

Then she looked at him. "It's where they let us store our supplies, including our signs. I break down our display and keep it there for the next week." Her voice was flat but her eyes were wide. "I could have been back there."

He finally gave into instinct and pulled her to him, wishing he could take away her fear, wanting to protect her and for the first time, wondering if he could.

She stayed there a minute before pulling out of his arms. "I'm going to send the animals back to Rainbow Acres with the volunteers. I don't think there will be anymore adoptions tonight."

It was obvious she didn't want to think about the possibility that the pet store had been targeted because she would be there.

He let her go, but watched her as she directed the loading of the animals into vehicles. She had just started breaking down the display when the Fire Investigator and Cole arrived. The minute Cole saw Dana, he stopped.

Bo walked over to him. "She's the target. She always comes here on Tuesday nights and goes into that back room. The explosion was meant to kill her."

"Shit." Cole shook his head. "We'll figure it out. Don't worry." For the second time that night, a fellow firefighter put his arm on him.

Bo shook it off. "Yeah, but will you figure it out in time?"

Chapter Ten

Dana parked her car on the side road to the fire station. She hated to admit it, but she missed Bo helping her all day. After another night at his house and in his bed, she had to squash the need to be with him. He'd grown on her so fast, but had been true to his word, an aberration in the sea of officials in her past experience.

When he asked her to promise to stop by, she'd wanted to blurt out yes like he'd asked her to marry him. Somehow, she just smiled and said she would. But the joy of being around him was addictive.

Excited to see him, she strode up the driveway past the ladder truck he worked. The engine was out there, too. Maybe they needed to be washed after last night's fire.

No one was around. She walked to a door she'd noticed last time she was there and hesitated. It opened suddenly and she stepped back.

"Oh, you surprised me. Can I help you?" The firefighter with dark blond hair and friendly hazel eyes smiled.

He reminded her of Bo with his build. "Yes, I'm looking for Bo Fletcher."

"Oh, you must be Dana. Nice to meet you, I'm Tory. Bo's in the shower. We just came in from a two alarm fire."

Her heart tightened. "Is Bo alright?" He seemed so capable that she hadn't really considered he could get hurt.

Tory waved it off. "He's fine. It was a storage facility of combustibles, so no one to run in and save." He grinned. "We had to work the hoses instead."

Her shoulders relaxed at the relief that surged through her body, her heart able to slow again. *Crap, I must like him a whole lot more than I thought. If this didn't feel so amazing, I'd walk away right now.*

"He should be down soon." Tory continued. "He's got truck washing duty. One of the perks of being on loan."

Obviously, the man was happy he didn't have to do it. She didn't like that. "I would think with him protecting me from the arsonist, instead of the police, the Captain would cut him a little slack."

Tory's brow furrowed. "Protection from an arsonist? No one is entitled to protection from an arsonist. Even if they were, they'd be protected by Texas Rangers, not the police. I guess you haven't lived in Dallas very long."

Her whole body froze. *Bo lied to me?*

Her heart, so open and filled with joy seconds ago, closed down hard, stopping her breath and causing her stomach to tighten unbearably.

"Hey, you okay?" Tory moved toward her.

She stepped back, throwing her arms up. *I'm an idiot! I knew better and I fell for it.*

Footsteps on the stairs behind the door sounded like nails hammered into her heart.

"Here he is." Tory turned his head and called out. "Bo, I think your girlfriend needs some help."

Girlfriend? She shook her head as Bo came out the door.

"Dana, what is it?" He moved toward her, concern in his green gaze.

She backed away, crossing her arms over her chest. "Don't. Just don't!"

He stopped. "What? What is it? Are you hurt?"

"Hah." More than you will ever know. "I'm done with your lies."

He looked back at Tory, who shrugged his shoulders.

Bo's voice softened. "Dana, tell me what you think I lied about."

Think? Think? Rage covered the hurt in her chest and allowed her to speak. "You told me I would need police protection if you didn't stay with me."

His gaze left hers and his whole big body seemed to deflate in defeat. It was all the proof she needed. "Don't you come near me ever again." She turned.

"Wait, Dana. I only let you believe that because I wanted to keep you safe."

She looked over her shoulder and glared. "You didn't even know me. If you wanted a quick lay, I'm sure the blonde you had sniffing at your heels would have been happy to accommodate you." Furious, she stalked out of the station.

"Wait! That's not it!" Bo's yell did nothing but make her move faster.

Tears welled in her eyes. He'd seemed so real and honest. That's what hurt the most. She knew better than to trust an official.

Her father, Detective Wilson, had been so good at that. Lying to her, his wife, his boss. When statements were made with absolute confidence and authority, he could get anyone to do anything.

She sat in her SUV and turned the key. She had to go somewhere, but she couldn't remember where. She kept seeing Bo's guilt, the image replaying in her mind, and the burn in her heart grew.

I wanted to believe him. I wanted it to be real.

The pain was too much, keeping her from any reasonable thought, so she headed for Rainbow Acres. Talking to Molly the sheep or hugging Cyclone might sooth her ache and help her grow a stronger shell.

Why do I have to live with a shell? I'm not a turtle.

Bo's gut hurt as he watched Dana walk away over Tory's shoulder. The man had stepped in front of him and he was about to deck him, when Dane grabbed him from behind. If Dane had been anyone but his cousin's fiancé, he would have been on the ground by now.

"Let her go. Even if you can fix this, it won't happen if you try right now. She's pissed. Wait until she has time to cool down. Your chances will be better."

He growled at Dane. "You know this from experience?"

The man backed away. "Hey, just some friendly advice for my future in-law is all." He motioned to Tory. "Leave him. He has to figure this out for himself. Let's get some chow. I'm starving."

Bo rubbed the back of his neck. Fuck. Now she thought everything they had was a lie. He had to get her back and in the meantime keep her safe.

He had planned to tell her about the Fire Investigator's

findings. The explosion at the pet shop was definitely arson. If it was the same arsonist, he'd learned a thing or two since the first fires.

He couldn't lose her. He loved her. If he'd had any doubt about that, it disappeared the second she walked away with his heart. He needed them both back.

"Shit." He couldn't even think straight. Pulling his phone from his waist, he dialed Cole. "Hey, can you stop by?"

"Already on my way. I have a theory on who the arsonist is. See you in ten."

Bo hung up and walked out into the sunlight of the warm May day. People strode down the sidewalks, anxious to get wherever they were headed. Cars jockeyed for position on the busy street. Even the pigeons fluttered on rooftops waiting for a stray potato chip or bread crumb from a patron of the sandwich shop across the street. They all acted as if today was like any other day.

But it wasn't.

He felt like he was at his own point of origin and his entire body was about to burst into flame. He'd finally found the woman he wanted in his life and because he wanted to keep her safe, he'd lost her.

No fucking way. He would get her back. First, he had to keep her safe whether she wanted him to or not.

Cole's truck pulled into the parking lot.

Bo strode toward him, determination burning through him. "What do you have?"

"I'm good. How about you?" Cole's raised eyebrows made him feel like an ass, but he didn't care.

"I'm in hell right now and I'm hoping you can pull me out."

"What happened?"

Bo kept his explanation short and to the point.

"Shit. Sorry about that. I forgot I was in Texas when I told her she'd needed police protection."

"It's not your fault." Bo sighed. "I wanted to keep her safe."

"I got that and I agreed with you. We were both right."

Bo tensed. "Is it the dog fighting ring she shut down?"

Cole shook his head. "No. I looked into that angle and those men are currently serving time."

"Really? For dog fighting?" He didn't think the police looked at that kind of crime so seriously.

"No. After they lost their dogs, they thought it would be entertaining to pit teenage boys against each other. They offered a cash prize and the kids beat the hell out of each other. When they ended up at the hospital a few too many times, the police caught on."

Sometimes it was hard to keep his faith in humanity, especially with scum like that around. No wonder Dana preferred animals and had little faith in officials. After all she'd seen with the animals she'd rescued—

"I have it narrowed down to two people." Cole continued. "Amanda Switzer and Jim Lawrence."

Amanda? Oh, Mandy. "Why those two?"

"First, that chance meeting at Johnny's Sport's Pub was not chance at all. It turns out you have a stalker."

"What?" He thought back to his meeting with Mandy. "If you mean because she came to the station the day Dana was here then I wouldn't call that stalking."

"It's a lot more than that. She's been posting on social media about her firefighter boyfriend and she has photos of you at Dana's apartment fire, the shelter fire and the pet store fire."

"Fuck. But I thought women aren't arsonists."

Cole's look turned smug. "Usually, but seventeen percent of arson fires are set by women. Part of what I've learned in this arson course."

Great, so he had a stalker who might be endangering Dana. If that was the case, he needed to stay away from her. "Wait, what about Tanya then? She lied about getting a dog for her niece as a reason for being at the shelter. Could she be part of the seventeen percent?"

"No." Cole chuckled. "I found out why she lied and it wasn't hard. She's not a quiet woman and when I went to question her, she was on her phone and signaled me to wait. Turns out, she wants to get another dog for her Tiara, but the landlord only allows one pet. She told her mother if she ever got caught with it, she'd just claim it was Dana's."

"Damn. So once again, Dana is on the short end of that proposition. So what about Jim Lawrence?"

Cole wiped his brow and started to walk toward the garage. "He's been at all the fire scenes, but I can't find a motive. He seems to like Dana."

Bo's protective instincts went into overdrive at the mention of another man liking his woman. "I knew I didn't like him. Since he's a man, isn't he your prime suspect?" They'd reached the shade of the garage and Bo led Cole toward the back.

"He would be if he had a car."

Bo opened the door to a small fridge the guys kept in the garage for water and handed Cole one. "But you said he was at every fire scene. I saw him at the mall and it was his apartment building that burned, but what about the shelter? He was there?"

Cole took a swallow than capped the water. "He was, but he didn't arrive until the fire was contained. An arsonist likes to see his work."

"But how did he know it had happened? For that matter, how did Mandy know to come to the fires I worked? Or has she gone to all of them?"

"We think she has a scanner. Either that or a friend in dispatch."

That sounded more like the woman. "Is there anything I can do to get her off my case?"

"Not really." Cole frowned. "Until she threatens you, you really can't get a restraining order. If she's really unbalanced, then your relationship with Dana could be what is setting her off. She may want Dana dead whether you know she exists or not. If she's just desperate, then she may not be setting the fires and we're back to Jim."

Damn, he hated that he might be endangering Dana, but the need to be near her to protect her wouldn't go away. "So if I stay away from Dana, it might keep Mandy from setting more fires, but if it's Jim then I'm leaving her wide open."

Cole pointed at him with the water bottle. "You'd be better off sticking close no matter what. We are working with the police, but since nothing important has burned like a bank or a government building, it's not a top priority."

Bo rubbed the back of his neck. "She's really angry. It won't be easy to stay nearby. I'll basically have to stalk her."

"Then do it. Either that or get her to forgive you. That explosion at the mall was well planned, but the arsonist had to set it off. Next time, he or she might have figured out how to detonate remotely."

"Shit."

"Tell her it was my fault. I forgot which state I was in, which is the truth."

He shook his head. "No. I'm not blaming you on this one. I made my own mess. I'll clean it up."

"Good luck. In the meantime, I'll see if I can't find something to point toward who our culprit is."

Bo walked Cole back to his vehicle. "Thanks for coming by. How much longer will you be in town?"

"Not much. I leave the end of the week, but don't worry. This is my top priority. This and passing the final exam." Cole grimaced. "I could really use Lacey to help me with that, but she's working, so I'm on my own."

"I appreciate all you're doing. I know the Fire Investigator wouldn't be nearly as concerned." He never thought when he and Cole Hatcher landed in the same hospital room over ten years ago that he'd need his help to save the woman he loved. "If you want help studying, just let me know and I'll do whatever I can."

"Thanks. I may just take you up on that." Cole strode to his truck.

Bo watched as his friend drove away. As soon as he got off shift, he had a woman to find and convince that he only wanted to protect her because he loved her.

~~*~~

Dana ignored the buzz on her phone as she lugged the bag of feed to the barn for Molly. Bo kept leaving messages. It had been two days and she'd ignored them for a whole day, but this morning she listened to them.

Every single one.

Now she ignored his calls because she was afraid she'd cave in and forgive him. Maybe she wanted to too much. Her feelings for him were stronger than she'd thought. It wasn't until he broke her trust that she understood exactly how far she'd fallen.

But she swore she'd never be like her mother, living in a dream world only to be tossed aside when something better came along. She had her eyes wide open.

Yeah, even with them open and knowing how officials lie, I still tripped head over heels into love with Prince Charming.

As she opened the barn door, both animals lifted their heads. Molly greeted her with a "baah" hello and Cyclone came up to the stall door to see her. She dropped the feed and gave Molly a rub on her head before moving down toward the back where Cyclone nodded at her.

"Yes, I have an apple for you. Just don't tell Laura I gave it to you. She'd have my head. I think you deserve a treat once in a while."

Cyclone nudged her shoulder and lifted his head, refusing to be stroked until he had the sweet he smelled in her shirt pocket. Pulling it out, she handed it to him. "Sure. I know how important I am to you. If I didn't bring you food, then you wouldn't know I existed."

She stilled. She hadn't given Bo anything, but he'd known she existed. She'd like to say he only wanted sex, but that was a lie. She'd kept him at arms-length as much as possible. Yet he'd listened to her and opened his mind to her passion. Crap. Was her own past barricading her way?

She shook her head as she opened the sheep's food bag and scooped it out for her. The fact was, he still lied. He may have had good intentions…she dropped the scoop in the bag. Her father never had good intentions.

He treated her and her mother like criminals, always trying to trip them up, always lying to make himself seem even more important. Telling them how he'd caught a murderer because he was a bad ass then they'd see the officer on the news who had actually made the arrest, her father nowhere in sight.

Bo had never done that, never pretended to be something he wasn't. He never promised something he didn't give. She pulled her phone out of her pocket.

One message.

She couldn't resist listening.

"Dana, I'm sorry. I'll say that for the rest of my life if I have to just to have you forgive me. I thought I was keeping you safe, but I understand that was your choice. I'm weak when it comes to you. I don't want anything to happen to you. I'm concerned. It's been two days without a fire. Cole says that means the next one will be big. Please. Call me."

Shootin' sheepherders, how am I supposed to resist that? She looked at Molly. "Do you think I should forgive him?"

The sheep continued to chow down, completely ignoring her. "I know. It's my problem and I need to solve it. As soon as I finish the feedings, I'll call him. Can't hurt to talk. Maybe then I can figure out what to do."

Cyclone whinnied.

"So you agree with my plan, big man?" She closed up Molly's feed bag, but as she tied it off, the horse whinnied again and his hooves hit the stall door, rattling the crowbar. "What is it, Cyclone?"

She left the feed bag and walked toward him. He backed up for another run at the door. "Whoa, wait. It's okay. What's the problem?" She looked in his stall to see if there was a bee or something, but had to stand back as he pawed at the door again. Luckily, it held…but barely.

She lowered her voice. "It's okay, sweetie." She searched for the cause of his agitation, but couldn't figure out what the problem was.

She took a deep breath, ready to try and sooth the horse again when she smelled it.

Gasoline!

The next moment the doors to the barn exploded and she went flying.

~~*~~

Bo heard the explosion from the other side of the rambling home known as Rainbow Acres. Dialing 911 as he left his truck, he ran to the house. From his side, he didn't see any fire or smoke, but Dana had gone in there and he had to get her out.

His heart beat twice as fast as he yanked open the front door. He'd followed her for the last two days, afraid something like this would happen. Racing through the home filled with agitated animals, he yelled. "Dana!"

He could barely hear himself among the noise of barks, meows and bleats. She wasn't there, nor was the fire. It had to be at one of the outbuildings. Running back outside, he rounded the corner and saw the blaze. No!

Movement in his peripheral vision caught his attention. He turned to find Jim throwing down an empty gas can and lighting a pipe bomb. In a split second, his mind registered the smell of gasoline as he'd left the house. The man had poured it from the front door to halfway around the side, intending to burn the animals alive to get to Dana.

Without another thought, Bo ran at the surprised man and tackled him to the ground. The lit pipe bomb rolled against the house. Fuck.

"Get off me! I'm not hurting anyone!"

"You fucking bastard! Dana's in there!" He punched the surprised man in the face, knocking him out. Then he jumped off.

The gasoline had lit immediately and flames lapped at the two walls. He let it burn. He had no idea what fire station had this district, but he hoped they arrived soon.

He had to save Dana.

Dana landed on the bales of hay at the back of the barn. Tiny flames flickered near her. Jumping up, she turned. She thought the fire at her apartment was hell. This one was far worse. The doors of the barn were gone, leaving an opening surrounded in fire.

Cyclone screeched and pounded at his stall door. She ran to him. Fire covered his side.

"No." Spying a horse blanket that had been blown to the floor, she grabbed it up. She only had one chance at this. Before she lost her nerve, she pulled the crowbar from the stall door and stood to the side.

Cyclone battered the door and as it opened, she threw the blanket over him. He galloped straight outside, the blanket already starting to fall off.

She stepped forward to follow him when a piece of the roof fell, catching her on the back and throwing her down. Fire scorched her and she screamed.

Pushing the board off, she rolled onto her back like Bo had taught her. It hurt like hell but the burning stopped spreading.

Rolling back over on to her hands and knees, she took short steadying breaths, not willing to breathe too deeply. She started for the opening, wishing Laura had thought to put a back door on the barn.

She kept low as Bo had reiterated. If she could just see him again. She'd tell him she loved him. He'd been right. She had needed protection and she had been too stubborn to accept it graciously. Oh God, she wanted to see him, hold him, make love again.

Tears clouded her vision as she crawled around burning hay, her back sending jolts of pain with every movement. As the heat built, her need to escape spurred her on. For the first time in her life while she was in danger, she thought of herself. She wanted to live. She wanted to see Bo.

Another piece of roof landed on her burned back and she screamed again, fighting the blackness of unconsciousness as the pain took her breath away.

But the darkness was so enticing.

Bo sprinted past the dog kennels, their barking making it hard to think. Luckily, he only had one thought on his mind. Save Dana. As he came closer to the completely engulfed barn, the roof collapsed.

A scream split the air over the roar of the fire.

"Dana!" He ran into the yawning opening engulfed in flames. In front of him was the burning wood of the roof. Heedless of the fire, he threw back one board after another. Six feet into the mess, he grasped her.

"Bo?" Her voice was weak.

He let his training take over, carefully extracting her from the burning roof. He hauled her over his shoulder and crouched low as he made his way out of the barn. He dropped to his knees a safe distance away and lowered her to the ground.

She screamed as he laid her on the grass and he quickly rolled her over.

"Holy shit." Her shirt was gone and her back was a puckered mess. "Dana, you're going to be okay." His heart lodged in his throat. Please let her be okay.

"Bo?" She lifted her head to see him.

"I'm right here." He felt the sting of tears. He could lose her. Where was the damn fire engine?

Her pain-filled gaze moved past him and her eyes widened. She coughed as she tried to speak. "The house." She coughed again. "The animals." Tears flowed from her eyes and he looked back to see the walls burning high.

"Please." She grabbed his forearm, her grip hard. "Save them. Caged. Helpless."

"I can't leave you."

Her fingers bit into his skin. "Must. Love you, but will hate you."

She loved him? Elation warred with fear, but he had no time to understand exactly what he felt. Her nails scratched him hard.

"Go." She scowled at him, her eyes filled with fear, not for herself, but for the tiny creatures in the home.

He wished Lexi were here to take care of Dana. "I'll go, but you have to promise to stay awake until I come back."

She smiled weakly. "I will."

He'd seen the number of animals in those rooms and there was no way he'd be able to move them all to safety. His only option was to put out the fire.

Leaving her killed him, but if the animals in the house died, it would kill her.

He ran back to the house, calling 911 again to request an ambulance. Racing through the front door, he grabbed the fire extinguisher he'd noticed on his way in. He noticed it because it was new and not mounted yet. One of the purchases they had made for Rainbow Acres.

He ran back outside and sprayed the base of the fire on one wall as far as the extinguisher held out. Even if he could just slow the fire down until the engine arrived that would be enough. Shit, they weren't exactly in a neighborhood and laying down a line wouldn't be an option. He hoped they brought a tanker.

Running to the other side of the house, he stopped to roll Jim farther away from the flames. The man remained unconscious which meant Bo didn't need to waste time tying him up.

He unraveled the garden hose and put it on full blast. Spraying a gas fire of this size with a garden hose wouldn't put it out, but it could slow it down. He focused on the other wall, making the fire work for every inch of fuel it wanted to consume.

Finally, sirens sounded in the distance and relief barreled through him. As soon as the fire trucks were in sight, he dropped the hose and sprinted back to Dana.

Her eyes were closed.

His gut tightened as he fell to his knees in front of her. He swallowed down the lump in his throat, his chest so tight he could barely get the words past his lips. "You promised."

Her eyelids didn't even flicker. "I'm awake. My eyes hurt. Did you save them?" Her words, barely audible, enabled him to breathe again.

He glanced back at the flickering flames. The fire station had brought a tanker and would finish the job he started. "Yes. The rest of the fire is being doused now." He took her hand in his, unable to keep from touching her one more minute.

"I love you, Dana. You have to get better so I can show you how much I love you."

Her mouth quirked up just a bit. "You already did."

Dana sat on the stool at Bo's kitchen counter in a halter top, her go-to clothing these days because it was the easiest to wear with no back. This one was particularly nice because Bo had bought it for her and the material was extra light and soft.

Her very own Prince Charming came in from showing Cole the pool. "So they found enough evidence to convict him?"

Cole closed the door behind them. "Yes. Jim Lawrence will be going away for a long time. A lot had to do with your testimony. I knew he was involved, but I hadn't thought he'd rent a car just to set a fire. The man doesn't even have a real license."

"I didn't like him from the start, but that's never enough to convict someone." Bo came by and kissed her on the cheek before moving to the fridge to take out a beer with his left hand, his right still healing from his own burns. He handed the bottle to Cole then looked at her. "Would you like another?"

She held up her half-finished beer and shook her head. "Did Jim ever explain why he was so intent on killing animals? Or more specifically, the animals I helped?"

Cole pulled up a stool. "I think it was your neighbor's dog. His apartment is right beneath hers and in addition to the barking, I guess the dog ran around all night. The guy was probably sleep deprived and couldn't think straight. He knew you worked with animals, so by following you and knowing your routine, he was guaranteed to find places that had a lot of them."

Bo stood near her but only took her hand, always sensitive to her burns. "He didn't do a very good job if he was trying to rid Dallas of pets. He failed at every attempt."

"Except one." She looked at Cole. "Molly was killed by the explosion. Actually, two. Though Cyclone is alive, his scars are going to make it impossible to find him a good home. As if his penchant for kicking wasn't bad enough, he now looks awful on one side. Laura is worried about how she can keep him."

"I'll take him." Cole's offer surprised her.

"In Arizona?"

He glanced at Bo. "You didn't tell her?"

"Tell me what?" She frowned at Bo.

He gave her hand a reassuring squeeze. "Cole is not only a firefighter, but he owns a horse rescue ranch. He takes in all kinds of horses. When and if they're ready, he sells them to good homes."

She sighed in relief, the problem of what to do with Cyclone had weighed heavily on her mind since the barn fire. "That's perfect. He's not ready to travel yet, but the vet we have is very good. Maybe by next month. How can we get him to you?"

Cole raised his bottle and gestured toward the driveway. "I'll just come back with my trailer. It will give me a chance to visit Dallas again."

She smiled. "I'd love that. You did so much, keeping Bo in the loop. If he hadn't been at Rainbow Acres…"

Bo kissed her temple. "But I was."

She swallowed back the fear that still plagued her at night and gazed at him, his green gaze comforting. "And you saved all the animals." She looked at Cole. "Would it be possible for us to visit Cyclone at your ranch?"

"Of course. Lacey and I would be happy to have you. And you would get along great with my cousin's girlfriend, Whisper."

"Whisper? That's an odd name."

"I know, but it fits her. She's an animal whisperer. She's already helped us out with a few horses and one stubborn coyote."

Dana liked the woman already. "That sounds intriguing. I look forward to meeting her."

Bo put down his beer. "Now I just need to take care of my stalker."

Cole laughed. "Actually, you don't."

Oh yes, he does. She wasn't having some woman salivating after her man. "Why not?"

"She's moved on." He kept grinning. "It appears that with Bo out on medical leave, something Captain Stewart is not happy about, by the way, Mandy needed someone else for her social media boyfriend."

Before she could ask, Bo did. "Who?"

"Rick."

Bo laughed.

She loved that sound. "Why is that funny?"

Cole lifted his beer in salute. "Rick is a lady's man. Mandy is going to have to work hard to get a photo of him without another woman on his arm."

"Oh. I guess that is fitting in an ironic way."

Bo clinked beers with Cole. "In a good way. Maybe they will teach each other a lesson."

Cole took a sip and put his bottle down as he lost his smile. "I need to apologize to you, Dana."

"You do?" She'd hardly been around him long enough in the last couple weeks for him to have done something to apologize for.

"I do. I was the one who told you that you would need police protection from the arsonist. I wasn't being a jerk. I truly felt we needed to keep you safe." He looked at Bo.

She tilted her head so she could gaze at the man who loved her enough to risk himself to save her. "There's nothing to forgive. If you hadn't, I'm absolutely sure I would have died in the shelter fire or the mall fire."

Bo's relief was obvious in his gaze and this time she squeezed his hand.

Cole cleared his throat. "Well, I should probably hit the road. I've got a long drive and Lacey said she had a surprise for me."

From the man's secret smile, she had a feeling it might involve the bedroom. He bent down and kissed her on the cheek. "Take care of yourself and him." He pointed to Bo.

"I'll do my best."

Bo left to walk Cole out, but she wasn't alone. Buca jumped down from the bay window seat and rubbed against her legs. "Oh sweetie, I can't pick you up."

"I'll get her for you." Bo strode in and lifted the sleek black cat onto her lap. She scratched him behind his ears, which caused him to purr.

Bo stroked the cat as well. "Why don't you own an animal. With your interest in their welfare, I'm surprised you don't have one."

She took her gaze from Buca and met his. The image of Zorro lying motionless in her backyard flashed through her mind. "I didn't want my heart ripped out again."

Bo stopped stroking Buca and lifted his good hand to her cheek. "What your father did was wrong in every sense. But you're right. Our animals don't live as long as us, but I think they deserve to be well cared for while they are here and you would definitely do that." He watched her for something, but she had no idea what.

If he expected to talk her into adopting a pet, he would be disappointed. "I agree, which is another reason I've never owned a pet because I didn't have enough time to give an animal the attention it deserved."

He grinned, raising one eyebrow. "Well, you do now, so you better get used to it."

She frowned not sure what he meant until he dropped his gaze to her hand, which rested on Buca's back, the cat already asleep on her lap. "But he's your cat."

"Not anymore. Now he's our cat. You're going to have to share in cleaning his litter box, learn when he can have his banana ice cream, and let him sleep on your lap while you watch a movie. You have no choice. You will have to move in with me and help me take care of him."

Joy burst through her chest, causing her eyes to water. "Really?"

His face turned serious. "Dana, I love you. I want you with me night and day. And when I can't have that I want to come home to you or meet you at the mall to take down adoption signs or help you transport baby rabbits or—"

She put her finger over his lips. It was as if her whole life had led up to this very moment, a moment she wouldn't trade for anything. Holy crapola. I really did find my Prince Charming! She spoke softly, unable to believe this was for real. "I'd be honored to be Buca's mom."

Bo's smile warmed her heart and as his lips descended on hers, he lit a flame that would consume them both…in a good way.

The End

Read on for an excerpt from Logan's Luck (Last Chance #4)

Chapter One

"What the hell is she doing here?" Logan Williams looked up from where he knelt on the barn floor to scowl at the local vet.

His brother stepped up next to her. "Dr. Jenna's here to help."

He glared at Trace. "I don't remember asking for any help."

"You never do. Maybe if you did, life would go a little smoother for you." He grinned. "Now, no fighting while I'm gone." Trace winked then turned on his heel and strode out of the barn whistling.

Damn troublemaker. It was just his luck that when he moved to the Last Chance horse rescue ranch, his extended family had retained the services of Dr. Jenna Atkins, local vet and former one-night-stand. She was the only woman he'd fought the urge to call for a month before their night together was finally put to rest where it belonged. "Well, since you're here, you might as well make yourself useful. Go to the house and get me a couple bottled waters. This is going to be a while."

The five-foot four-inch woman in a white button down collared shirt and snug blue jeans crossed her arms over her bountiful chest. Her blue-green eyes sent need spiraling up his spine, despite the anger in them. "Let's reverse that, shall we? Since I'm the medically trained vet," she lifted her large leather bag of medicines and equipment, "I suggest you go get *us* some waters and I'll take mama's vitals. What's her name?"

He ground his teeth at her logic, trying to find a way around it. He couldn't. "Her name is Macy."

Jenna opened the stall door and walked in crooning to the horse, who, damn her, nickered at the vet. Jenna stood right next to him and set her bag on the concrete floor. "You're in my way."

Swallowing a completely inappropriate response, he rose to his feet, purposefully towering over her. "I'll be right back." His words came out like a threat, but he didn't care. Brushing by her, he exited the stall and stalked out of the barn.

Thoroughly pissed off, he swore if he ran in to Trace he would lay him out cold. Ignoring the final reds and purples in the darkening sky, he took the three steps to the porch and threw open the front door. The screen banged against the doorframe as he stalked down the hall to the kitchen.

When he stepped into the room, he halted at his grandmother's scowl. "Don't you go slamming my doors. How old are you? Thirteen?"

It wasn't his grandmother's scolding that calmed him so much as it was his sleeping fifteen-month old daughter in his grandmother's arms. "She's getting too big for that, Gram. Here, let me put her in our room."

She looked down at his daughter and her scowl faded. Charlotte had that effect on everyone who helped out at the ranch. Despite how rambunctious she was while awake, everyone doted on her.

When she slept, you'd think she was the Queen of Sheba the way they all tiptoed around the ranch house. The thing was, Charlotte was as likely to sleep at mid-afternoon as at night, her schedule like that of a puppy, which unfortunately, gave him little sleep. Luckily, the night sleeping had improved.

"She'll never be too big for my arms." His grandmother practically crooned her words.

"Come on, Gram. I bet your left arm is completely numb now. Let me take her up."

His grandmother nodded, and he lifted his daughter into his arms. As he turned away to head upstairs, he caught his grandmother in his peripheral vision, shaking out her arm.

He didn't say anything as he turned the corner and climbed the stairs. Everyone in the house, which luckily was just his grandparents and himself now, doted on his daughter.

When he'd first arrived, a new single dad without a home, the place was bursting at the seams with Cole and old Billy, not to mention Cole's now wife Lacey. Since his cousin, Cole, jointly owned the horse rescue ranch with their grandparents, Logan really couldn't say anything. Then his brother Trace had shown up during his divorce and getting sleep had been more a wish than a reality.

At the top of the stairs, he turned left and brought Charlotte into his room with the two twin beds. Next to one of them was Charlotte's crib. There was an empty room across the hall, now that everyone had moved out, but he wasn't quite ready to have his daughter that far away from him. The small bedroom at the end of the hall his grandfather was renovating, so it was unusable.

Gently, he laid Charlotte down, her little hand still holding her teddy with the cowboy hat. His grandmother had insisted that she have a horse as soon as she could crawl, even if it was a stuffed one, but that animal remained in the crib all day while the teddy went everywhere.

He gazed down at his daughter, still amazed that she was really his. Despite all his precautions, all his maneuverers to avoid any kind of entanglement with a woman beyond a quick night of sex, something had failed. At first, he thought it was just more of his perpetual bad luck, but having Charlotte in his life had changed everything…except his luck.

He brushed her thick brown hair, kept short after she started chewing on it. He'd had to cut his own hair short after she pulled it one too many times, leaving sticky syrup in it that would have taken days to wash out.

He still didn't know anything about being a dad. All he had to go on was what he remembered with his own father, who he admired most of his life…until the end just before he passed. That's when his bad luck had really started.

Thanks to his grandparents though, he was learning a lot more about being a parent and especially about being a parent of a little girl. Hopefully, she'd have better luck and be more successful than he ever was.

Turning away, he gazed at her from the doorway then turned off the light. A little pony nightlight illuminated the floor so he could find his way to his bed once it was dark. He chuckled silently as he descended the stairs. He would have been mortified if his mother had put a nightlight of any kind in his bedroom when he was a boy. He'd been tough, but Charlotte was soft and sweet.

Entering the kitchen, he found his grandmother had moved to another room, so he opened the fridge, grabbed four bottled waters and headed back outside. He wasn't about to tell Jenna, but he was worried about Macy.

When he approached the stall, he heard Macy whine. Damn, he was right, it wasn't going well. He set the water bottles on a beam and leaned over the stall door, in no hurry to get into such a confined space with Jenna. "What's wrong?"

She didn't look at him. "The foal's legs are both coming out at the same time. That won't work. We need to get her up and walking or you could lose both of them."

"Fuck." He pulled open the stall door, his aversion to Jenna forgotten in his concern for Macy.

"Help me get her up."

"Up? She's trying to give birth." He looked at the small legs sticking out the vulva. "If we get her up, the foal might fall back in."

Jenna finally gave him her undivided attention. "That's what I'm hoping."

"What?"

"Listen, if we don't get her up and walking around, you're going to have one dead foal and one sick mama. Darn it, I wish I had Whisper here. At least she'd help instead of question everything I say."

He'd been about to argue, but at her last comment he shut his mouth and moved toward the horse. His brother's girlfriend, Whisper, was amazing with animals, but she was a bit odd. That Jenna would prefer her over himself irritated him, motivating him to show he could help.

With a few coaxing words and a push in the right direction, they got Macy up on her feet again. As he expected, the foal's feet disappeared into Macy.

"Now we need to walk her." Jenna issued orders like she was born to it, which rankled. He was the one who had run a ranch before. *Yeah, and what a mess that was.*

Swallowing his pride, he grabbed a halter. He hoped she knew what she was doing. He'd only had one mare in his lifetime have a difficult birth and they had lost the baby. At the time, it was all they could do to save the mother. Now, he couldn't imagine losing the foal. Must have something to do with being a parent himself.

Jenna walked Macy down to the opening of the barn and back a few times, then she handed him the leads. "Hold those for a moment."

He did as instructed, determined not to say a word. If he did, it wouldn't be helpful, of that he was sure. His gut felt like a bulldozer ran through it.

Jenna moved her hands over Macy's enlarged abdomen then she looked up at him. "Lead her into the stall. I think the foal has moved and Macy is not going to wait much longer. I just hope it has moved enough."

He led Macy inside to the fresh hay he'd put down when he'd noticed her condition. Quickly, he removed the halter. "Okay, Macy. It's up to you now, girl. Don't let me down."

Macy stood still as they backed away, then slowly lowered herself to the floor of the stall again and rolled on to her side. She started to breathe heavy and then the contractions began.

"Here we go. Cross your fingers, pray, or just hope that the foal exits correctly this time, or I will have to perform a cesarean in not so sterile conditions."

"Can't you do something to increase the odds in her favor?" She was a vet after all. "Like drugs or something?"

She frowned at him but turned her attention back to Macy when the horse whined. She spoke quietly. "Do me a favor and stay out of the way."

He ground his teeth to hold in his response. For Macy's sake, he'd step back, but after this, the woman would be getting an earful of opinion from him whether she wanted it or not.

The first hoof appeared enveloped in the white birthing sac. That was a good sign. Another couple heaves on Macy's part and another foot appeared slightly behind the first. *Yes! Come on, Macy!* The next part was critical. *Come on girl. Let's see the head.*

Logan gripped the top of the stall door, his heart beating as if he'd just galloped across the valley and back. He must be getting too old for this because he'd never been this tense with a birth when growing up on his family's ranch.

The mare chuffed and whined as two more contractions hit her. They were very rhythmic so that was good, but he glanced at Jenna and the concern on her face made him want to yell.

Another two heaves of the mare's sides and more of the white sac slid out onto the new hay. He stepped forward only to find his way blocked by a stiff arm.

"Stay out of my way." Jenna moved past him and with practiced precision, slit the white sac to reveal the foal's head. She delicately cleared the animal's orifices before she stepped away again. At the smile on her face, his entire insides relaxed.

Macy gave another whine and the foal spilled out, except for its hind feet. Jenna glanced over at him and nodded, her lips still curved in the joy of a new birth.

At that moment, in the dimly lit barn, she looked like an angel. Her thick brown hair pulled back away from her face, emphasized the flush of her cheeks and the soft curve of her neck. In her happiness, her blue-green eyes almost sparkled.

It took everything he had inside him to stay where he was and not pull her into his arms and kiss her. She made it worse by walking over to him, keeping herself far from Macy and the new foal, who was not yet completely out of its mom's body but would be soon.

"She should be fine, but I'll check them both in about twenty minutes." She kept her voice low, like she had when they were in bed. "It'd be best if we left them alone right now."

He stared at her. He should open the stall door for her, but if he moved his arm, it would wrap around her of its own accord. He couldn't allow that, but he wanted it so much he couldn't think straight. "Jenna."

His voice was husky with his own need.

Her brows knit together in puzzlement. "What? Do you have something you want to say?"

Yes! I want to tell you I want you so much I'd take you right here in the next stall. Instead, he swallowed hard against his own weakness. "I can take it from here."

She frowned as she pulled the stall door open just far enough to slip out before holding it for him. "We can discuss that once you get out of there."

There was nothing to discuss. He'd lived on a ranch his whole life. He could take care of a new born foal, dammit. *Yeah, but you also lost the ranch, so what does that say about your expertise, smart ass?* He stalked through the opening then spun around to confront her.

She quietly latched the stall door. Without turning to look at him, she strode toward the barn exit.

Oh no, she wasn't getting away that easy. He caught up to her just before she reached the open barn doors and grabbed her arm. "There is nothing to discuss. I'll take care of the foal and Macy."

At her surprised look, he lowered his tone. "I didn't call you."

She pulled her arm away. "No, you didn't. You're not very good at that, are you? Returning calls isn't one of your talents, is it?"

It didn't take a brain surgeon to figure out she was talking about the days after their night together when she called him and he didn't return her calls. When he lived near Catalina, he thought someone like her from out of town would be easier to keep away. Joke was on him. He cracked two of his knuckles against his thigh. "Listen, it's just that—"

"Oh, spare me the excuses. We both know I was just some easy lay for you." She stepped closer to him, staring him down even though she was at least ten inches shorter than him. "For your information, I don't do one-night-stands. There was nothing easy about it for me."

Her blue-green eyes sparked with anger, but that very energy called to him as it had that night. Damn. He grabbed her by the shoulders to push her away, but instead, pulled her toward him, his mouth descending.

"I heard Macy was foaling. How's it going in—" Cole's voice stopped him cold.

What the hell was he doing? He dropped his hands from Jenna and stepped to the side, ignoring the surprise in her face. "It started out sticky, but Dr. Jenna got the mare back on track. They're bonding now."

Cole, still in his fire department t-shirt, looked at him then at Jenna then back again. He must have just come home from his latest shift. What timing.

Logan's cousin frowned before retuning his gaze to Jenna. "Were you leaving? I'd like it if you could check on them in a bit. Could you come inside for a cup of coffee?"

She faced Cole. "I would be happy to if you could switch

out that coffee for a beer. It was a little nerve-wracking there for a while."

"Of course, whatever you want." Cole opened his arm toward the ranch house, but after Jenna walked by, he shook his head at Logan before following.

Logan could hear him as they walked away. "I hope Logan didn't get in the way. He can be hardheaded at times and that foal is important…"

He fisted his hands to keep from running after them, mainly because he didn't know if he could keep himself from punching Cole or kissing Jenna. Either action would cause a hell of a lot more clean-up than he was willing to commit to, so instead, he strode outside and around to the side of the barn where Black Jack was housed beneath a roof, but with just a steel pipe fence to keep him in.

The horse snorted and moved toward him.

He felt a certain sympathy for the claustrophobic horse. He certainly understood wanting to remain free. "What do you say we go for a quick ride? Then I'll come back and see how the new foal is doing."

Black Jack lifted his nose over the fence.

Logan shook his head, but stroked the horse on its nose, the white star in the middle impossible to ignore. "If you let me in, we can head out."

The horse nudged him, looking for a treat.

"You have a one-track mind, my friend." Stepping away, he moved to the small shed he'd built against the outside of the barn, next to Black Jack's cover. He hefted the saddle from the bench and grabbed the horse's bridle.

In no time, he had the Quarter Horse ready to ride and jumped up on his back. Though Black Jack wanted to head for the valley, he turned him toward the long dirt road that connected the ranch to civilization. The valley terrain was too rough to risk at night. Black Jack had enough trauma for one lifetime.

He had thought he had too.

Jenna followed Cole to the house. She'd made it appear that she needed a drink after helping Macy, but it was Logan's almost-kiss that had her wanting a beer. He'd rattled her far more than the new foal's malposition had. Animals she understood. People she understood. Logan, she didn't.

As she walked up the steps to the porch, she was thankful he'd disappeared. She didn't want to lose the Benson-Hatcher business, but every time she arrived, if Logan was around, he argued with everything she said. If she didn't know better, she'd think he was afraid of her knowledge, though his concern for the horses was real.

She refused to be intimidated. The horse rescue ranch needed her more than any other client she had and they were quick to pay, especially since Whisper had set-up a trust for the care of the horses. She just had to forget she and Logan had one amazing day and night together.

The house was a bit warmer than the cool September evening. At least the heat of the days dropped below triple digits on occasion now, always a welcome reprieve for native Arizonans like herself.

"I'm sure everyone is anxious to hear the good news." Cole looked back at her as they headed for the kitchen. "We haven't had a baby born here since I turned it into a horse rescue ranch."

She smiled, happy to have another topic to focus on.

"The foal shouldn't have any long-term complications from the difficult birth. I'll make sure in a few minutes. I don't want to infringe on the bonding period." And hopefully, Logan wouldn't either.

They turned the corner into the large kitchen. The matriarch of the family, Annette Benson, grandmother to Logan and Trace, and their cousins, Cole and Dillon, greeted her first.

"You must tell us. Do we have a new baby to welcome?" The fit, older woman with pristine white hair pulled back in a ponytail, stood, reaching out her hands in welcome.

Jenna grinned as she took them in her own. "You sure do."

Annette squeezed her hands. "This is wonderful news. Cole, get the lady a drink."

Cole, already at the refrigerator, smirked. "On it."

"Come sit down and relax a bit." Annette pointed at Trace who sat on the other side of the empty high chair. "Give your seat to Jenna. She's worked twice as hard as you today."

Trace laughed as he rose. "Gram, I don't doubt it."

Jenna rolled her eyes at Trace, who since falling for her odd friend, Whisper, seemed to be in a perpetually good mood. "Thank you."

He bowed before moving around the table to sit opposite her.

Cole handed her a cold beer after first twisting off the cap.

She took a very unladylike gulp then raised it toward him. "Thanks. I needed that."

Annette frowned, resuming her seat. "Was it that difficult?"

Trace answered before she could open her mouth. "Macy wasn't the problem. She had to deal with Logan."

His words hit far too close to home for her to come up with a suitable response. Luckily, she didn't have to.

"That boy." Annette shook her head. "He needs a good kick in the pants."

Surprisingly, Trace came to his brother's defense. "Now, Gram, I think he's probably had a few too many of those already."

"Well, he obviously needs one more."

Not sure what Trace referred to and uncomfortable with the subject, Jenna changed it by addressing Cole. "Where's Lacey?"

Cole's face softened from firefighter/ranch owner to totally smitten husband in a split second. "She's on her way. She and Whisper just got back from Poker Flat."

Jenna swallowed the beer she'd just sipped and raised her eyebrows. "Poker Flat? Lacey took Whisper to the nudist resort?"

Cole grinned and nodded toward his cousin.

She turned her head to find Trace frowning. "Yeah. Supposedly, there was a wild burrow there who wouldn't leave one of the guests alone. Followed him everywhere. Lacey said she needed Whisper's help to find out what was wrong with the animal."

Cole laughed. "He thinks it was all a ruse to get Whisper to the resort. My fine cousin here is jealous."

She grinned before taking another swig of her beer. To discover easy-going Trace wasn't happy made her feel appropriately avenged since he enjoyed it just a little too much that she rubbed Logan the wrong way.

Trace grumbled. "Wait until one of the women decide to take Charlotte to Poker Flat, then see who gets pissed."

Annette shook her head. "Being around Lacey and Whisper would be good for her. Maybe she'll discover an interest in music or dance. It's bad enough she's growing up among so many men folk."

Jenna doubted very much that Charlotte would be anything but a tomboy, especially with Logan for a father. She might have a chance at girly hobbies with Lacey, but Whisper was more likely to teach her how to suck the moisture from a cactus than discuss the latest boy band. Whisper probably didn't even know what a boy band was.

Jenna examined the high chair next to her where Charlotte usually sat. When she was younger, she'd had a plan. Go to school, meet the man of her dreams, then on to veterinary school, buy a house, set up practice, and have a baby then two years later have another.

Her entire plan went off track when the man of her dreams turned out to be an avid hunter and her loans from graduate school made it more than difficult to make ends meet.

If it hadn't been for Whisper keeping her truck at Jenna's place and letting her use it when she needed it, she wouldn't have been able to take on the additional ranches she had. Her little sedan couldn't reach some of the ranches thanks to the rough terrain and Monsoon washes.

Lacey and Whisper walked into the kitchen. Cole was already out of his chair to give his wife a kiss and a hug, and Trace wasn't far behind.

The love of the Benson-Hatcher-Williams family just accentuated her own loneliness. Even when she was growing up, it had only been the three of them.

"Jenna? Why are you here? Were there problems with the

birth? Is Macy okay?" Whisper's usual bluntness didn't bother her in the least.

"There were, but nothing I couldn't handle. Would you like to—"

Heavy footsteps striding down the hallway announced the newest arrival just before Logan's body filled the doorway, a scowl on his face as he scanned them all until he settled on her. "You better check on them now. It's getting late."

She purposefully looked at her watch before taking another sip of beer. She set the empty bottle down before responding. "I was planning to." She moved her gaze to Cole. "I appreciate the beer, but you're still getting a bill."

He chuckled. "Of course. I just hope you don't charge me extra for having to deal with him." He hooked his thumb toward his glowering cousin in the doorway.

She smirked. "Have I yet?"

Cole laughed, and she rose from her chair.

"Thank you for the hospitality, Annette."

The older woman nodded regally. "You're welcome any time. Thank you for helping the latest addition to our family arrive safely."

She smiled before heading for the door.

Logan stepped aside and followed her out. She kept her walk to a stroll despite her growing irritation with the man behind her.

"It's been well over a half hour. I expected you to have checked on them and left by now."

That was it. She spun around and he halted, stepping back as his eyes widened in surprise.

"What the hell do you have against me?" She pointed at him, poking her finger into his hard chest, then wishing she hadn't when the image of his naked pectoral rose inside her brain.

She pulled her hand back as if burned and squinted at him. "Do you think the veterinary school I attended wasn't accredited? Do you question the validity of the degree hanging on my wall? Or is it that I simply wasn't a good enough lay for you?" Ah, damn, she didn't mean to say that part out loud.

Mortified, she ignored his stunned expression and turned, marching across the yard as if she could pound out the humiliation of having revealed her insecurity. When she reached the barn, she softened her steps until she arrived at the stall.

Glancing in at the new baby suckling its mother's teat helped calm her. Silently, but speedily, she ducked into the stall and stepped behind the two. The placenta had still not been expelled. She certainly wasn't going to wait for it, not with Logan around.

Reassured the two horses were bonding, she stepped back into the dimly lit barn to find Logan waiting for her at the entrance. Ignoring him, she packed up her bag and hefted it over her shoulder then strode toward him. Her plan was to brush by him without a word, but his hand shot out and grabbed her arm.

She tried to pull away, but he didn't let go.

"Dammit, Jenna." His voice was husky, like it had been that fateful night when she'd thrown caution to the wind and had fallen for the charming, considerate, cowboy—who turned in to the man before her.

"What?" She tilted her head back to look him in the eye. He was too darn tall and too good-looking.

"I—ah, hell."

His mouth came down on hers so fast, she froze. But as warm tingles trickled across her skin and her muscles weakened, she pushed away, shaking her head at him. "No." It came out choked, almost like a cry and she cleared her throat. "No, I'm not going there again. You burned that bridge, buddy."

He stared at her, but there was no scowl on his face. There was no expression either, or another word.

Ugh, the man was impossible. Hefting her bag from the ground where it had fallen, she stalked away. She tried to get her heartrate to slow, but her breath was still coming too quickly. When she reached her car, she threw her bag in the back and jumped inside, locking the doors to keep him out and her in.

As soon as the car revved to life, she backed out only to see Logan still standing there watching her. Darn, she forgot to tell him to call her if the mare had trouble with the placenta. Screw it. She'd call Cole when she got home. Hopefully, Logan also knew about the umbilical cord, but she'd remind Cole anyway. He might not live in the main house anymore, but he could pass the word on to Logan.

Hitting the gas, she drove down the long dirt driveway, watching for animals in her headlights, refusing to look in the rearview mirror again until a second curve made it absolutely impossible to see him.

Once she turned onto the paved two-lane highway headed toward Wickenburg, she finally gave in to the turmoil inside her heart, angrily wiping away the tears in her eyes.

She didn't cry for what could have been with the man who kept their relationship to a one-night-stand. That was her fault for falling in love with him after no more than a day at the fair and a night of amazing lovemaking.

Nope, she cried for herself because as long as he kept a

piece of her heart with him, she would never find someone else, and she was sick and tired of being alone.

Dillon's Dare
(Last Chance Series: Book 5)
Riley's Rescue
(Last Chance Series: Book 6) *Coming Soon*

Aloha Cowboy
(Island Cowboy Series: Book 1)

Military Romance

When Love Chimes
(Broken Valor Series: Book 1)
Poisoned Honor
(Broken Honor Series: Book 2)

Paranormal Romance

Masque
Passion's Poison
Passion of Sleepy Hollow
Heart of Frankenstein

Pleasures of Christmas Past
(A Christmas Carol Series: Book 1)
Desires of Christmas Present
(A Christmas Carol Series: Book 2)
Temptations of Christmas Future
(A Christmas Carol Series: Books 3)
One of A Kind Christmas
(A Christmas Carol Series: Book 4)

About Lexi Post

Lexi Post is a New York Times and USA Today best-selling author of romance inspired by the classics. She spent years in higher education taking and teaching courses about the classical literature she loved. From Edgar Allan Poe's short story "The Masque of the Red Death" to Tolstoy's War and Peace, she's read, studied, and taught wonderful classics.

But Lexi's first love is romance novels. In an effort to marry her two first loves, she started writing romance inspired by the classics and found she loved it. From hot paranormals to sizzling cowboys to hunks from out of this world, Lexi provides a sensuous experience with a "whole lotta story."

Lexi is living her own happily ever after with her husband and her cat in Florida. She makes her own ice cream every weekend, loves bright colors, and you will never see her without a hat.

www.lexipostbooks.com

www.ingramcontent.com/pod-product-compliance
Lightning Source LLC
Chambersburg PA
CBHW071429190726
48292CB00001B/170